THE WAR BENEATH

S. R. HUGHES

PERMUTED
PRESS

A PERMUTED PRESS BOOK
ISBN: 978-1-68261-859-2
ISBN (eBook): 978-1-68261-860-8

The War Beneath

Cover art by Cody Corcoran

PERMUTED
PRESS

Permuted Press, LLC
New York • Nashville
permutedpress.com

Published in the United States of America

because there are too many victims

"We're all going to die, all of us, what a circus! That alone should make us love each other but it doesn't. We are terrorized and flattened by trivialities, we are eaten up by nothing."

—Charles Bukowski

PROLOGUE

Two and a Half Years Earlier...
(when what has happened cannot be changed)

"It wasn't always like this, you know," Virgil said.

Rain slurred Oceanrest into a surreal grayscape against the windshield. Paul dragged his gaze from the slouched suburbia outside but made no response to the older man's statement. A voice both distant and inside his head rasped (*please help, they fed me to the shrieking steel and I can't hear myself think*) and Paul struggled to ignore it.

"I'm not saying nothing bad ever happened," Virgil continued, steering the silent-sirened cop car through once-prosperous Denton, "but not like what this guy did."

Through the blur of rainwater, Paul saw the ghost reach to-ward them.

(*please, I can't stop hearing it*)

He knew the feeling.

He darted his eyes away from the specter, focusing on Virgil. "People have been doing shit like this since there's been other people to do it to."

Virgil turned his seafoam eyes on Paul's hazels, tightened old-man knuckles along the steering wheel. "Not here, they haven't. Not like this. Not some guy from Denton."

Denton had once been beautiful, allegedly. The still-wealthiest suburb of economically withered Oceanrest, the paint of its white fences now peeled back to rot and splinter. Among the off-white collars of the drowsy burb, a blade had sharpened itself into a killing tool. The Static Killer, the *Chronicle* called him. He'd claimed four lives. At each crime scene, he'd left a DVD, and every DVD showed the same thing: static snow, loud roar, muttered sermons back-masked beneath. The Static Killer considered himself a prophet of some esoteric deity, an all-consuming "Hollow One."

"More'n twenty years on the force and I'll never understand what makes a man do something like that."

"You're not supposed to," Paul said.

"You do."

"I just write the profiles. I've only been right about half the time."

Paul hadn't worked on a case since his days in New York, hadn't so much as seen a crime scene photo since moving to Oceanrest. But once the PD had uncovered the third body, Virgil called in a favor. About a year back, Virgil had buried a DUI charge for Paul Somers, and the forensic work served as Paul's penance.

"You ever think of going back?" Virgil asked.

"No."

"You're a better profiler than you are a professor."

"So my students tell me. The dean too, but he's an asshole."

A stoplight glowed bloody through rainwater, glistening the windshield into a crime scene.

"You ever notice it's the things you want to change that never do?" Virgil asked. "And all the shit you want to keep always ends up changing?"

Paul hadn't always seen ghosts.

"I don't know if too much ever really changes," he said.

Virgil snorted, let off the brake.

Paul shifted in his seat, avoiding the sight of another gruesome specter desperate for attention.

(*you too, soon…*)

They were sad things, the dead—creatures of fractured memory and fraying humanity, shambling unseen through the material world, raging against their losses. Some of them became quite powerful, the literal forebear of the mythological poltergeist. All of them, eventually, went mad.

Paul usually drowned his sixth sense in booze, marijuana, and psychic downers, but the Static Killer case warranted extreme measures. After grudgingly agreeing to become a civilian asset, Paul went sober. He opened up his sixth sense and reached out to see if he could reach the spirits of the victims, to see if they'd know how to track down their murderer.

He'd found none of them. And none of them had found him.

That was why he'd requested the drive-along. He needed to know how the killer had dissipated even the lingering spirits of his victims, to look him in the eyes and see what lived behind them. See what kind of man could wield such absolute power over existence and non-existence. Then he'd light up the joint of psychic depressants in his pocket, empty the flask in his jacket, and dull his sixth sense into quiet oblivion. He'd smother his preternatural impulse before another broken ghost could find him. Before his daughter could find him. Before he had to see the thing she'd become.

"There it is." Virgil shifted the car into park and inclined his head toward the most ordinary-looking house Paul had ever seen.

Paint peeled back from wood rot, a once-white fence.

Virgil pulled his hat down over graying hair. "You ought to stay in the car."

"I want to see him." Paul adjusted his own ratty knit cap and popped open the passenger door.

"Keep your distance then. Officially speaking, you're still a civilian."

A dozen officers approached the house. Three were posted around the garage, four in the backyard, and two groups of two stationed at either side. Virgil went for the front door, flanked by two uniforms with guns already drawn. Paul followed at a distance.

Virgil knocked and announced the warrant.

The warrant had come about as byproduct of a dirty deal. After the suspect list narrowed enough, a pair of Québécois thugs had gone on a spree of burglaries, including break-ins at every suspect's home. One of the burglars came up with evidence: the murder weapon and the suspect's stolen driver's license. The thief agreed to testify to his findings in court, made a statement to a judge, and somehow a breaking-and-entering charge never landed on the guy.

Quelle surprise.

Virgil stepped back from the front door and drew a non-standard-issued sidearm—a large-mouthed weapon of history. A hand-me-down from an officer in one of those wars that were supposed to end all those other wars. For a few long seconds, Paul heard only rain.

Then came the breach.

On cue, multiple doors burst open, and police poured into the house. Crashing and shouting echoed inside, the clamor of arrest-in-progress turning the quiet suburb into thunderous news. Paul sprinted toward the action, his sneakers squicking across slick grass, wet soaking into his socks. One of his legs slipped out from under him as he ran, but he managed to rebalance himself in time to tear through the house's open-lipped threshold.

A uniformed cop turned toward him as he rushed in but made no move to stop him.

At the center of the noise, the killer sat as a mote of frigid calm. Dressed in full business attire, kneeling genuflective on the kitchen linoleum, hands already behind his head, he smiled. "It told me you were coming."

"On the floor! Now!"

"You're all blind to the truth of things. Didn't you listen to the background radiation? The era of man is over. Look around you, look at the slouch of the world."

"You have the right to remain silent…" an officer began, hinging the compliant killer to the floor.

"There is a sinkhole under civilization and It starves for us!"

Virgil white-knuckled his pistol. "Somebody shut him up."

"…have the right to an attorney…"

"Do you think The Hollow One is the only of its kind? That I'm the only of mine?" The killer snickered, lips carved wide over tombstone teeth. "There's a war going on behind our world, *beneath* it! We are on the fulcrum of apocalypse!"

"I said shut the hell up," Virgil snarled. "Somebody get the basement open."

"Do you see my altar? The window? Did you not hear its hunger in the static prophecy? You can't—"

Virgil moved with speed and strength a man his age shouldn't have had, pushed aside the arresting officer, interrupted the Miranda speech, and hauled the killer to his feet. Before anyone could stop him, Virgil had thrown the man into the kitchen table, furniture and body both crashing to the ground. Virgil dove gun-first, cracking the butt of his pistol into the killer's face, and again, and again. "You think you're smart?" Virgil growled, grabbing at the killer's collar. "Think you'll get an insanity plea out of us? You're going to rot, you piece of shit."

Paul joined one of the uniforms in grappling Virgil, prying the older man free of his quarry.

"Get off me!" Virgil yelled.

"Get a hold of yourself!"

After a couple seconds' struggle, Virgil came loose. The older man staggered backward, breathless, as if waking from a nightmare.

"What the hell was that?" the arresting officer asked.

Virgil glanced around as if only then remembering where he was. "I, uh, I just…" He straightened himself out and holstered his weapon. "It wasn't right, what I did, but I think we all saw it. The man was resisting arrest. He went right for the door. Somebody had to stop him."

The killer giggled through grue-specked lips. "They yearn for what they fear for. There'll be more."

Paul backed away from the composing chaos, from the babbling killer and the conspiring cops. He turned to head back outside, giving up his earlier ideas, but froze when he saw the pantry.

The pantry doors hung open, painted black. The inside, painted black. The shelves had all been removed and an altar stood in their place, black. The base structure could have been stolen from an abandoned church, more than a few of which dotted Oceanrest's farther outskirts, but the additions were what caught Paul's gaze. Long, ebon-painted branches arced up from the lectern to create broken, concentric circles. The top of each arch was missing, a path of notched nothing carved through the spiral and leading into a rough-hewn hole in the back wall, just above the altar top.

Without being told, Paul knew with certainty that the hole looked in on a black-painted, windowless room. He knew with certainty that the parts of the victims that hadn't been found at the scenes would be inside.

Faint static crackled from the other side of the hole (from the back of his head) and the world quieted around it. Paul took a step forward. The blackness beyond the busted portal seemed to undulate, to squirm. The static rush crescendoed. Was something back there, waiting? Another victim? Something worse? Paul stepped forward. Were there spirits trapped in that windowless room? Was there something hungry pulsing in that dark?

His vision began to blur.

"Paul!"

Virgil's voice snapped him back to the kitchen.

"Huh? What?"

"Don't get too close to that," Virgil warned, coming up behind him. "Crime scene guys are on the way and they'll want a look at it."

Paul realized he'd come within a foot of the altar, his arm outstretched, his fingers reaching. "Sorry. I haven't seen anything quite this *elaborate* before."

"Me neither." Virgil took his arm, gentle but insistent, and got him away from the painted pantry. "Look, Paul, I know I lost control for a second, there, but…what that man did to those people, the way he cut them up…

the smirk on his face…" Virgil took a deep breath. "If there are questions later about what happened here—"

"He tried to run," Paul said. "You stopped him."

"Great. Thanks. Listen, we've got about a mile of paperwork to start on here. How about I take you home?"

"I think I'll walk, actually. Get some air. I'll see you tonight?"

"Sure," Virgil said. "Tonight. The bar."

"Right."

Paul glanced back at the strange altar and the lightless gape above it. It was just a serial killer's sculpture project. The hole was just a hole in a wall. There were bits of yellow-brown wood jutting out like teeth, unpainted. There was no static, there were no whispers. There were no ghosts trying to escape a windowless prison.

Right?

As he exited, the murderer said again: "They yearn for what they fear for," and Paul shivered at the words.

Once he got away from the unspooling police tape and the scene of the arrest, he took the joint out of his pocket and lit it with a cheap plastic lighter. Supernatural drugs, psychic downers meant to bury his sixth sense coma-deep, filled his lungs. By the time he got to the bus stop, he'd inhaled the whole joint. He knew no more than he'd known that morning. Sitting on the bus, the behemoth vehicle heading toward the university across town, he was uncertain if he really wanted to know more. Some days he didn't want to know anything at all. And yet…

Flecks of the murderer's blood dotted the bottom of his pants. Using the wetness of his cap, he swiped them away.

He needed a drink.

CHAPTER ONE

The Present...
(when all is yet unfinished)

Deirdre winced at the slug of kleren and pulled the bottle from her lips. She swallowed, turned in a circle, candle first, muttered the ritual words, spun another circle. She didn't usually drink, but the ritual required it. She took another draught of kleren and knelt to the floor. With the candle flame, she lit the curled tobacco leaves in the offering bowl. In the overgrowth of her backyard, a red rooster sprawled its wings wide, throat open, beak pointed south.

She dug into the reservoir of her will and formed the spell again. A simple cantrip, an activation of part of a larger whole. She finished the whispered prayer at the offering bowl and put her hands on the glyphs carved into the cement basement floor. She braced herself for the force of the magic. Hydroponics burbled and hissed. Warm mist coiled around her.

The glyphs lit up amber-gold and hot under her palms. A singed ozone stench wafted the air. The cantrip jolted through her, electric heat gnawing her bones. More sweat slicked her back and forehead, frizzed her hair. Her tank top suctioned to her flesh. She shuddered. The air hummed.

Deirdre had been born a witch. Mysticism resonated in her blood.

Although that didn't make magic easy, it made it easier. For someone born without the natural aptitude, a ritual like this might take days. For her, it only took nine hours. Nine long, sweat-soaked, repetitive hours, during either the Full or New moon, using simple cantrips and complicated spellcraft to ensure a strong harvest of her esoteric flora.

The glyphs pulsed golden light. Pulse, flicker, pulse.

The synchronicity had started after the third hour. Birds flocked to the tree line and watched her house in sunset. Small animals scritched and roved around the overgrowth of her squat's backyard. None of them touched the rooster's corpse. Now the bottle of kleren sat half-empty, the candle burnt low, and the offering bowl glowed with embers. She leaned back from the ebb and flow of the sigils' glimmer and clasped her hands. Prayer, they called it in some circles. The truth was more complicated. Words and meaning, context and history, all arranged in rhythm, in certain order. Magic took many forms.

She prayed that the pulsing light would stabilize.

Otherwise, another hour…

The light faded and grew, faded and grew. She muttered the last words of the last spell in the ritual, craned forward again, and pressed her palms to the symbols carved in the floor. She reached into herself for will, for energy, for intent. She focused her existence into a flare, a bright burn.

The spell kicked through her again and she groaned with exertion.

The glyphs lit up brilliant bright—not just the two she touched, but the whole twenty carved into the basement floor. For a few seconds, the basement erupted into blinding gold. The air crackled. Burnt ozone filled her nostrils. She spasmed in the intensity of it all, braced on her knees, back arching.

She blacked out.

She awoke again not long after. The whole room bristled with mysticism. Her skin prickled into gooseflesh and all the hair on her arms stood on end. She knew the spell had worked because she'd gone through the ritual hundreds of times. She knew the signs. The shivering dreamer fruit ready to bloom, the unfurled leaves from the lotus plant, the rising bloom of sirentouch.

She wiped sweat from her brow and put on the finishing touches. While the ritual ensured the growth of climate-disparate and esoteric flora, specific plants required specific rituals. Her pockets hung heavy with small plastic baggies. From one, she fingered loose a lock of her own hair, honey-coated. Digging a small hole in the wisp-bulb's planter, she dropped the hair inside. Pale stalks of prehensile root reached out, wrapped up her offering, and pulled it out of sight.

She patted the planter back down and tended to the other plants in order. Sirentouch needed its leaves stroked every week, or it would shrivel and die. Dreamroot needed whispered stories told over its roots. Deirdre knew every intricacy, every detail. She'd been an apothecary for fourteen years, after all.

The work done, she clambered upstairs to her den, toward her slouched, second-hand couch and her library of books. Toward a night of petting her cat, drinking tea, and reading something a little mindless. Something relaxing. Something to take the edge off of a day spent attuning her sixth sense, of a day spent engaged in ritual magic.

A detective story, maybe.

She'd bolted the basement door's frame locks into the floor, snapped the deadbolt shut, and keyed the other half-dozen locks before an insistent knock dashed her hopes of a tranquil night. She sighed, pocketed the keys, and walked down the main, candlelit thoroughfare of her squat toward the foyer. The knock seemed unthreatening, but she kept her palm atop the polished grain grip of her hipslung .357 just in case.

A series of candelabra led to her front door, where all the overhead bulbs had gone out one by one over time. She'd never replaced the electric lights, except in the kitchen. Something about candleglow seemed more natural, more alive.

Peering through the front door's peephole, she saw Razz scuffing a hightop against her porch.

A runaway, like herself, Razz had been her houseguest for the better part of three years, breaking away seven months earlier. Nineteen years old and tree-branch scrawny, his time as a squatter and vagrant had started showing, waning the crescent of his smile, hollowing the joy of his cheeks. Razz thinned emblematic of their dying city.

She unlatched the door and opened it. "Awful late for a social call."

He scuffed his shoe against her porch again. "Sup, Dee?"

"Deirdre," she corrected.

"'s a white-ass name," he smirked.

"White people don't own names."

Her skin shone the same shade of darkness as deep, rich soil.

"Own every other goddamn thing."

"*Shhh*, they might hear you."

"It is literally a Celtic name, though."

"And from what root language came 'Razz?'"

"Just something they used to call me back…" and the patter slowed, lost some of its humor. A hesitated word evaporated. He chuckled, shook his head. "So, *Deirdre*, what's up?"

New names cost. They'd sacrificed things in their transfigurations. Tyrell Meeks. Imani Greene. Razz. Deirdre. They'd carved open their histories and offered up their guts.

She peered past him at the nighttime sky, moonless and overclouded. Moonless nights unsettled her. Under lightless skies, dark things flourished. "Come on in," she said, gesturing his entry. "Tell me wherefore the late-night social call."

He shouldered past her and made for her den. "Not totally social…I got some orders to fill out in Denton. Some big dumb party."

She shut the door, latched it. "I don't work on the New Moon."

"C'mon, ma, a kid's gotta eat, right?"

She sighed, looked him over. "I'm 'auntie,' tops." She flapped a hand toward the couch and cat. "Keep Samedi company and I'll see what I can grab for you."

He smiled, a crescent moon fading. "Thanks."

Razz went for the den, for the library and the cat and the mug of cooling tea she'd made an hour earlier. Deirdre followed the candelabra back down the main hall of her squat and into the electric-lighted kitchen. The stock cabinets were full that night, but most were already claimed. Randall's dreamer and psychic stimulants, Rehani's order of the same, three whole crates of various samples for the Winters siblings, psychic depressants for Paul, and a small stash of stimulants and depressants for her own personal use—nothing she'd pass on to Razz. Picking through the back of an over-stove cabinet, she dug up a baggie of MDMA infused with a mild love potion derived from siren-touch. Nothing too serious, and purer than what most peddlers pumped into the streets.

In the den, she found Razz settled into the couch, Samedi stretched over his lap.

Abruptly, Samedi leapt up, a blur of sable fur. He went to the plywood-boarded window and gazed outside, one golden eye, one blind white one. His half-length of tail flicked side to side.

"What's up with Sammy?" Razz asked, gesturing to the apprehensive feline.

Deirdre shrugged. "I dunno. Samedi's been acting weird all night. Maybe it's the new moon."

Or the ritual spellcraft.

"Hey. You put that white dude up to pressing me again?"

"Who?"

"That teacher dude. I ran into him the other day and he braced me on the GED thing."

"Huh. Imagine that." She tossed the plastic bag on the long table between them, on top of the GED study guide Razz had left behind during his move-out. "Though, if I remember right, you did promise to take it. You were scheduled for a test two months ago, never showed up."

"I got sick."

"What a coincidence. Take that book with you when you leave."

Razz's exit seven months before had come as both a sharp pain and a breath of relief. She'd never told him about magic being real, or about the specific properties of her goods. She'd told herself she was protecting him from dangerous knowledge, from a dangerous, clandestine world, but that hadn't been true. Not really. She'd kept her secret hidden out of fear. Because of how he might react if he didn't believe her. Or worse, because of how he might react if he did.

How that might've broken her.

Or maybe she'd been half-right in her justification. Maybe there was a part of her that just wanted him to have a normal life. No magic, no monsters.

He'd started to ask about the basement. In response, she'd redoubled her stern, disciplinarian attention to his study habits. She created harsh rules, demanded things she'd known she'd had no right to demand. The center, as was so often the case, did not hold.

Razz pulled a handful of crumpled bills from his pockets. "What I owe you?"

"Take the damn GED."

"Come on."

She waved the money away. "Keep it. A kid's gotta eat, right?"

"Thanks. I owe you one."

"Just one?"

He showed her his middle finger.

Still smiling, she narrowed her eyes. "Put that shit away before I snap it off."

Razz chuckled dryly, complying with theatrical remorse. "Well, thanks. For real."

"You don't need to thank me, just take the study guide with you when you leave. And don't get sick on the next test day."

At the window, Samedi mewled.

Razz stood from the couch, crumpling bills back into his pockets, taking the Ziploc and the study guide both. "I'm gonna go check out this party. Suburban teen girls, you know. Target demographic."

She made room for him to brush past. "Have fun, kid. And be careful. The suburbs aren't kind just because they're quiet."

"No shit." Razz unlatched the deadbolt and pushed the door open. Hesitated.

"Something wrong?" she asked, coming up behind him.

"Nah," he said, a second too late to mean it. "Just thinking."

"About what?"

He shrugged, a sharp gesture of narrow shoulders, and stepped outside. "Nothin'. Catch you in a couple days."

In half a second, Razz was off the porch, sneakers scuffing broken asphalt back south. Deirdre pressed her lips together and watched him vanish into darkness. The sound of sneaker-scrape receded, the echoes leaving something heavy between her lungs.

No single week seemed so different from any other week, and yet the years did.

She tried to imagine Razz going to UM Oceanrest, getting a job at Winters-Armitage or Malleus Industries. Wearing a suit, owning a car, waking up to a bleating alarm, driving to work at one of the tall new buildings downtown. The fantasy was no different than it had ever been, except that it seemed more and more like a fantasy.

A car turned the corner in the distance, headlights slicing the night, and she snapped back from the reverie. It was probably Paul, judging from the slight swerve of the vehicle, but she let her hand drape over her pistol grip just in case. Samedi wove between her legs, purring. Overhead, clouds shrouded the stars, and no moon shone.

■■■

Paul parked the car on the side of the street and tried to wipe the ghost's afterimage from his eyes.

(a woman at the foot of his bed, orbless sockets drooling blood)

(a Pollack spatter of grue on a white tunic)

He took a swig from his flask. She'd woken him from a dream, and he'd mistaken her for Cassandra before noticing the wounds.

(her tongue missing yet her voice pressing into his thoughts: help me I don't know what to do. you're the only one who sees.*)*

He popped open the car door, tossed the flask on the passenger seat, and climbed out into shin-high overgrowth.

"The garage door works, you know."

Deirdre's voice surprised him. So did his brief, weak smile upon hearing it.

"Yeah, well, this way I can make a quick getaway."

She hoisted a lantern over her head, more for his benefit than hers, and gestured him to the porch. He crossed the overgrown lawn to the steps and made his way up. Orange-yellow lantern glow flickered her cheekbones, glimmered along the angles of her face, a halfway-smirk frail on her lips.

"Does nobody remember that I don't work on new moon nights?" Deirdre asked.

"Apparently not. If it makes you feel better, it's kind of an emergency."

She huffed, shook her head, and gestured him inside. "Come on in then."

Paul sniffed, bracing for the cat dander as Deirdre pointed him into the den. His eyes itched already.

(the woman's face, sockets like gaping mouths)

"How much you looking to pick up?" she asked at the den threshold.

He got his wallet from his pants and grimaced at its contents—a crush of white receipts drowning a few skinny greenbacks. "Forty bucks? Fifty?"

"Make yourself comfortable, I'll be back in a second."

Deirdre vanished into candle glow and he moved to the couch.

Sans cat dander, the den would be a comfortable place. A big, beaten-up couch, three worn leather armchairs, one big table and two little ones, surrounded on all sides by bookshelves. One window looked out into front yard and tree line, the glass crisscrossed by boards of plywood.

Samedi hopped up on his lap and began kneading his thighs. Paul's nose tingled with the threat of a sneeze. He stared down at the cat and the cat stared back, challenging.

"You're a real prick, you know that?" he said.

Samedi purred, curling up on his legs.

"He likes you." Deirdre came from the shadowed hallway through the threshold, a plastic bag full of oily-seaweed looking leaves in her hand.

"He knows I'm allergic. He's taunting me."

"They make pills for that. And I've been working on something more herbal."

"Sure. If it works."

She dropped the baggie on the tabletop and sat in the armchair across from him. "You need papers?"

"I've got plenty. If I run out I'll just use textbook pages. Or receipts." He offered a joking smirk as he emptied his wallet of its remaining green. She took the money gingerly, folded it, and pocketed it in her athletic pants. Samedi didn't move a muscle for the duration of the handoff, forcing Paul to maneuver around him.

"You mind if I ask what you saw?"

"I didn't see anything."

"Mr. Kind-of-an-Emergency didn't see anything?"

He hesitated, choked back a half-sneeze. "One of them showed up in my room. It wasn't the worst I've seen, but..." his hand absently went to Samedi's ebon fur. He'd get a rash, he knew. Still, any comfort was comfort. "She was burning memory just to reach out."

"Plan to do anything about it?"

"Like what? Lead Virgil on another wild goose chase, waste time, get another call from Dean Bayer about professionalism?" He sagged into the couch, ignoring the prickling of the skin on his fingers. "I'm one strike away from a forced resignation."

"It's the middle of summer."

"Still. I've led the cops down enough dead-end paths to kill any favor I ever had with them. I'm out of favors to spare."

They settled into silence for a few seconds.

Paul finally sneezed and broke it.

Deirdre chuckled.

"I don't know why I'm petting the fucker," Paul said. "My fingers are going to itch for hours."

"It's instinct. Man sees a cat, man pets a cat."

Paul didn't make the obvious joke. Which might've been a mistake, because the brief lull in conversation led to a change of subject.

"How's your other habit?" Deirdre asked.

"Still a habit." He shrugged, stopped petting. Deirdre stared at him for a long time, her dark eyes speckled gold like vast reaches of space pockmarked by stars. He didn't stare back, averting his gaze to the cat curled in his lap, Samedi's heterochromia. "How's everything with you?"

"I can't complain."

"I'm sure you could."

"Yeah, well, complaining is a hex."

He chuckled. Samedi roused from his lap and leapt over the arm of the sofa. The animal rushed to the boarded window and began to hiss, his half-length tail angled floorwards. Paul watched, amusement creasing into bewilderment across his brow. "What's that about?"

"He's been acting out all night. Must be something in the air…"

Samedi curved into a pouncing pose and hissed, hissed, hissed.

Deirdre rose from the chair, hand resting on the polished grip of her gun. She cocked her head toward the board-slatted window. Paul turned that way too, and barely heard it—the rumble of a distant engine dying out. The faint squeak of a car door opening, closing again.

"Paul," Deirdre said, "in the kitchen, under the sink, there's a baseball bat. I need you to get it. Make sure the back door's bolted, get the bat, and wait."

"What? Why?"

"Go."

Paul pushed himself to his feet and maneuvered past her to the main hall of the house. He turned left and went for the kitchen, casting a single glance over his shoulder to see Deirdre shooing Samedi upstairs on her way to the peephole. He strode past the steel-reinforced frame bolts of the basement door, crossed from hardwood to tile, and hitched a breath.

Paul found the Louisville Slugger where Deirdre told him it would be. The age-worn wood felt smooth in his hands. He gave it a practice swing, found it lighter than expected. Powerful enough to stop a modicum of trouble, but how much were they expecting? He turned back to the hallway to ask and saw Deirdre bathed in candlelight, a finger pressed against her lips. He nodded, and she turned back to the door.

Paul retreated from the threshold, pressing himself against the wall by the table and chairs of the eat-in kitchen. Cold adrenaline pulsed in his veins, his heartbeat growing louder by the second. For all the locks on her doors and the vacant, boarded-up decay of Squatter City, he'd never thought of Deirdre's place as particularly dangerous. Until now. A clatter of claw scraped hardwood; the cat running up and down the stairs.

"Scram," Deirdre whispered.

Samedi gave a plaintive mewl.

"Scram!"

Paul braced himself against the plaster.

The cat went through the kitchen, paused at the cat-flap on the back door to glance back at Deirdre, and then exited.

Paul swallowed, tightening his grip. He heard the scrape of metal against leather as Deirdre drew her revolver from its holster. His senses sharpened around cat-dander itchiness and the absence of all other stimuli.

"Shit!" Deirdre yelped.

The sound of shoes scraping hardwood, Deirdre in retreat.

Something crashed into the door, splintering wood. The hammer on Deirdre's gun cranked back. Paul closed his itchy eyes, trying to be quiet and breathe steady in growing panic. Another groan of breaking wood, the front doorway threatening failure. A gunshot filled the hall, loud enough to make Paul jump.

"You're fucking with the wrong house!" Deirdre shouted.

A third crash against the door followed.

"Deirdre!" a voice called from outside. "Don't make this harder'n it has to be."

Paul couldn't place the man's accent—Quebec by way of Georgia, all the vowels falling wrong.

"Randall?" Deirdre asked. "Are you fucking kidding me?"

"'Fraid not."

A basso blast echoed from outside and wood shrapneled down the hall. The door banged open.

Deirdre's gun barked twice. Paul winced at the sound again, too loud in the tight, empty house and the silent, lightless night.

Another shot boomed from a larger gun outside. Wood and plaster splintered to pulp under buckshot. Paul sucked air through his nose, trying to slow his runaway heart. Sweat slicked his palms around the grip of the bat. Seconds ticked by in silence.

"Look, Deirdre, I hate to do this to you, I really do," Randall called from outside, "but the stars are right and the fog's brewing up and there's not much more need for the niceties. Now, I bet that's your six-gun you're holding onto, and there's still four of us unwounded, so if I were you, I'd do the smart thing and set it down."

After a moment's hesitation, Deirdre yelled back, "How do I know you won't chop me when you get in here?"

Randall's laugh echoed deep and loud. "We known each other for years, Deirdre. You know I don't wanna hurt you. You're one'a the good ones. Besides, if I was gonna do ya, I would'a done it already. Got four shotguns out here and enough shot to turn your house to Swiss cheese."

"Get off my property."

"What, you gonna call the cops? Maybe after they get you for squatting they can take a sniff around your basement, eh? Come on, now, let's not waste any more time with this. Look, Zeke ain't even mad you shot him."

Someone outside groaned a disagreement.

"Oh, come on, Zeke. You'll live."

"You don't get more after this, Randall," Deirdre said, her voice calm and icy. "I'm the only one in the goddamned state who makes this shit. You fuck with me and you'll never see another bag of it."

"Don't think we'll need much more, in earnest. Now, you planning to put down the gun, or are we gonna have to start off enough fireworks to bring every cop this side of the border down on your little homestead?"

Something boiled over the ice in Paul's arteries. It tingled in his veins. His knuckles seared white around the Slugger's handle. An urge tunneled through his musculature, an impulse to swing the bat into the face of whoever waited outside, to bring it down on someone's skull and feel bone rupture beneath the wood. For the first time in years he wished he had a gun.

But he didn't, and they did. Four of them, allegedly.

"Last warning, Deirdre," Randall said. "You either put the gun down or put Zeke outta his misery. Either way, the rest of us are gonna storm in there and finish the job."

Paul heard Deirdre set her pistol on the floor. Hardwood creaked as she shifted her weight, put her foot against it, and slid it back toward him. Its small, snub-nosed body stopped at the kitchen threshold, just outside his reach.

"You're going to pay for this!" Deirdre shouted.

"Honey, we're *all* gonna pay for it. Isaiah, why don't you head on in there?"

Paul's eyes flicked from the bat to the gun. If he lunged for it, he could grab it. He could get his hand around the wood grain grip and turn its steel mouth toward the New England redneck rejects and see if it would eat them. But there were four of them, only three bullets left, and he hadn't fired a gun in half a decade.

"There we go," Randall's voice was closer, now. Inside. Paul could hear other people too, the sound of weight crossing old Victorian floors. Someone heavy enough to sag the floorboards stepped into the den.

"Randall, ah, what are we gonna do about that car out there?" this one was definitely a down-east accent, a stereotype of the *heah* unreachable from *theah*.

"So who's the houseguest, Deirdre? That kid'a yours? One of your other lowlife friends?"

"Go to hell."

"You hear me in there?" Randall raised his voice to the whole house, filling the halls. "We got plenty'a firepower down here, whoever you are, and we ain't afraid to use it. If you haven't done the smart thing and run away by now, I advise you put down whatever heat you're carrying and act wise."

Paul's heart punished his chest.

Floorboards creaked as someone moved toward the kitchen. Paul struggled for quiet, his breath coming sharp through his nose. A footstep creaked his way. Another. How many steps between the kitchen and the door? What were the chances he could get the gun before someone brought bullets thundering down on him?

"You want the shit or what?" Deirdre asked.

"Sure, sure. Why don't you just unlock that basement door and my boys will handle the rest of the house?"

Metal squealed as Deirdre yanked on the deadbolts built into the basement door's frame. Keys jangled. Steps creaked closer to the kitchen. Paul stopped blinking, dry eyes glued to the threshold. One man in the den, another wounded outside, and three in the hallway—that was his count. But the hallway was too narrow to fit more than two abreast, right?

The barrel of a shotgun caught candlelight, sticking through the threshold.

Paul brought the Slugger down.

The kid with the shotgun yelped and the weapon clattered to the kitchen tile. Paul pivoted from the wall and saw the boy's face, all cheeks and patches of pubescent facial hair. A backwoods cub scout. A kid barely old enough to drink with a satchel full of bright red shotgun shells and a tunic the color of fresh asphalt.

Paul thrust the head of the baseball bat into the boy's sternum and sent him to the floor.

The shotgun was in his hands a second later, rifle stock pressed against his shoulder. He turned the sights down the candlelit hall.

Randall had the barrel of his own shotgun leveled at Deirdre. The other kid, Isaiah maybe, pointed a deadly looking rifle at Paul.

Randall's grin glinted in candle glow. "Should'a just laid down, buddy. Now we gotta hurt you."

Deirdre glared. "Don't touch him."

"Don't worry, hon, it won't be anything permanent."

"Get away from her," the words left Paul's mouth without consent and hung in the air.

A chuckle flared joy across Randall's face. "Geeze, gods! You hear that shit, Deirdre? You sure know how to pick 'em." Randall's eyes were the color of a shallow, rock-filled lake that looked deeper in the sun. He turned them, amused and confident, toward Paul. "I don't know who you are, dear infidel, but if you got half as much brains as you got balls, you won't be dumb enough to pull the trigger on that monster."

Isaiah squeezed past Deirdre and moved toward Paul.

"Alright, get that basement open," Randall went on. "Mr. Hero over there's gonna take a lickin' but I promise he'll still be standing tomorrow. Let's make the rest of this clean and we can all part ways as amicable enemies."

Paul's finger tightened on the trigger but didn't squeeze.

Deirdre undid the last latch on the basement door and yanked it open. Scents of black earth and raw magic rose up from below. "Paul," she said, not looking at him, "just put the gun down, okay?"

"That'a girl." Randall grinned.

Paul hesitated, cold-hot sweat rolling down his skin, pulse battering his skull. His fingers itched. But Deirdre was right. It was a losing fight. He swallowed thick mucus down his drug-dry throat and set the shotgun back on the floor. The kid he'd taken it from wheezed air through a bruised sternum.

Isaiah closed the rest of the gap to Paul.

"It's nothing personal, sir," the boy said, polite enough to mean it.

Then he spun the butt of his gun into Paul's head.

Paul went down in a tangle of limbs and an animal yelp. He grabbed the side of his skull but couldn't tell if he was bleeding or not through all the pain. The back of his squinted-shut eyes flashed kaleidoscopic.

"I'd stay down if I were you," Isaiah advised.

Paul stayed down.

CHAPTER TWO

Deirdre strained against the ropes twining her arms.

"Now, now, don't be mad," Randall said, leaned up casually against the threshold of her den while his boys hauled crates out to the truck. "It's nothing personal."

Semi-conscious, Paul sagged in another chair across the room, also bound.

"What the fuck is it then?" Deirdre growled.

A slice of teeth gapped Randall's lips as he pushed away from the threshold. "Just something's gotta get done," he cooed patriarchal as he crossed toward her. "Something bigger than you and me."

She spat at him, jerking her weight forward, shins and forearms straining against rope.

He glanced down at where the saliva landed on his shirt and turned his knife of a grin back on. He stepped toward her on heavy brown boots. Reached out. His palm hovered by her cheekbone, the heat of it prickling her skin. She tried to maneuver away from his touch, straining her neck. He chuckled, put his hand on her cheek, and stroked. "You know, you're kind'a a handsome one. Pretty, even."

"Don't touch me."

"You like being tied up."

"Fuck off."

"Didn't put up much of a fight."

Deirdre wrenched her face away, but his hand caught up in half a second, her chin between his thumb and forefinger. He tilted her face toward his, and she spat again. This time the saliva caught his cheek, half an inch from the upper corner of his grin. "Get out of here," she said, trying to snarl but too scared to get the tone right.

Upstairs, something crashed to the floor. Violent looting banged through the halls.

"We'll be gone soon as the boys're done searching." He didn't even take his hand away to wipe her spit off his face. He smiled wider. Traced her features up along the side of her face to her hairline. "See, Deirdre, this could all be a lot uglier for you. I'm being downright gentle, so far as these things go…" he took a pinch of her hair, ground it between his fingers. "Huh."

She jerked her head sideways, wincing when a few coiled strands plucked from her scalp. Her breath came hot and dry through her nose.

Randall chuckled again and backed away. Wiped her spit off his face and then wiped his hand on his jeans. He stared purposely, noticeably, at her legs. At where her legs met her hips. He pulled his bottom lip into his mouth, poised his teeth over it. Raised his eyebrows. The glimmer in his eyes warmed from wolf to puppy. The warmth vanished instantly. The lip returned to its place. He'd made his point. "You gotta know when to fold 'em, Deirdre," he advised, his tone fatherly again. "You push too far, you might not be able to go back."

She fought for composure against the cool chill of adrenaline, fought to mask the bodywide relief she felt when he turned his back on her.

"Alright, boys!" he called out. "Let's get a move on!"

Overshoulder, as he left the room, he winked at her.

■■■

Deirdre wrangled her right hand free about an hour later, during the violet darkness just before dawn. She freed her left arm a minute after that and got to work on the ropes binding her legs. Out of the corner of her eye, most of the way across the room, Paul's head lolled sidelong on a limp neck. She jerked in her chair and banged its legs against the floor. "Wake up!"

Paul bolted awake in his own struggles, dazedly working to loosen the ropes coiling his arms. "Sorry."

She threw the ropes away from her legs and crossed the room to Paul. Yanked the blindfold from his face and tilted his head to examine the wound. Blood matted his hair. The gash hadn't cracked the skull as far as she could see, but it rent three inches across the side of his head.

"I'm fine."

"It needs to be cleaned," she replied. "And you'll need a salve."

"I'm sorry I—"

"Don't. Nothing you could've done."

Paul got back to work on the ropes twining his arms. She helped him get his right arm loose. Flexing his hand, he peered woozily up at her. "Thanks."

She offered a thin smile in response.

She went for the kitchen first, storming past the basement door. Cupboards and drawers hung open, even her cauldron rested empty on its side. The Winters-Armitage shipment was gone, the back stock was gone, Razz's share, the unsorted product—everything. *Almost* everything. They hadn't cleaned the plants out of the basement and she hadn't seen what they'd done upstairs yet. Her revolver winked candlelight at her from the threshold. She scooped it from the floor and holstered it before heading upstairs.

They'd gutted the upstairs storage room, leaving behind only empty crates. They'd trashed Samedi's room, too, dismantling the cat castle and upturning the litter box all over the floor. They'd had a run of the bathroom, scattering toothbrushes, toothpaste, shampoos, and conditioners all over the tile. They'd broken open her jar of coconut oil and emptied it into the tub. Scoops of shea butter had been hurled like baseballs at the walls and someone had taken a shit in her toilet. She followed the mess of secondhand towels across the hall into the bedroom, where they tangled into secondhand clothes.

They'd torn through her bedroom like the speed freaks she suspected they were. They'd stripped the sheets from her sweat-stained mattress, upturned her box-spring, and demolished her bedframe. Her antique sewing machine, destroyed. Safety pins, needles, and unspooled thread strew the floor. Her desk sat gutted in front of the unboarded window, its drawers wrenched out and scattered. Notebooks, letters, and miscellaneous papers lay crumpled everywhere. Had they stolen all her pens? They'd certainly had a run of her closet. Athletic gear, Goodwill salvages, leather jackets, jeans, all the clothes she'd labored over at her now-demolished Singer cluttered the hardwood like garbage washed up on an Atlantic beach.

Burning in rage, she rushed to her bedroom closet and ran her hand along the smooth wallpaper at the back. Pressing a fingernail against the spot where she'd covered up a mouse hole before Samedi moved in, she smirked. The wallpaper caved, brittle and thin. She tore a sheet of it off to reveal a small square of storage space, just enough hollowed wall to fit a locked box, a first aid kit, and two boxes of .357 FMJ-BT ammo, 50 count. She tossed the lockbox into the wreckage of her bedframe and left the ammo behind.

First aid kit in hand, she rushed back downstairs to Paul. He'd worked both hands free and was trying to untie his feet when she came in. The blood from his head wound had matted down more of his thinning hair. She threw the kit on the floor next to him and took out a bottle of disinfectant alcohol.

"This will sting," she warned, tipping the bottle over and pouring more of its contents than was necessary down the side of his head. He sucked air through clenched teeth but didn't complain. Parting the hair around the wound with her fingers, she leaned in to examine it. It was going to bruise and leave a long, narrow scar, but he'd live. A concussion, she thought. Nothing too serious. Setting the disinfectant aside, she fished out one of her pre-made salves.

"Is that going to sting too?" Paul asked.

Without answering, she smeared the herbal mysticism against one of her alcohol-soaked fingers and spread it across the wound. The salves weren't miracles, but they worked. They enhanced the body's natural healing capabilities for better, faster recovery and smaller scars. And when combined with a healing cantrip...

She put her hand to the side of Paul's head and closed her eyes, digging magic up from inside her for a healing spell. It sapped energy from her, but it would stop any internal bleeding and it would help the salve do its work. The cantrip went off as a pulse of energy down her arm and up into his skull. The damage was worse than expected. She focused the spell on the internal damage, trusting the salve to work on the laceration itself.

"Thanks," Paul muttered, getting back to work on the ropes around his legs.

"It doesn't look bad. It should be just be a little scar in two, three days."

"Better than the alternative." Paul stood up and wobbled on unbalanced legs. Deirdre rushed forward, caught him before he fell over. The two of them staggered for a second, each half-beat and using the other for support. Once steadied, he turned toward her. "Who were those people?"

"Randall?" She realized her arms were still around him and let go. "Just a client. Once or twice a month, good money."

"What kind of client?"

"Sixth-sense stuff. A lot of it."

"How much?" Paul cradled the side of his head in one hand, the other arm still looped across her shoulders.

"A lot. Mostly psychic uppers, some dreamer."

Paul's weight shifted onto her, his body still off-balance from his injury. After he settled, he asked, "Why? What for?"

"I didn't ask him a lot of questions. He paid on time."

He moved away from her, his arm falling from her shoulders, and tested out his legs. "They took everything?"

"Almost."

"The downers?"

"Yeah."

Deirdre followed him around the room, waiting for him to lose his balance, again, but he didn't. He stopped walking in front of the couch and massaged his face with his hands. "Jesus Christ."

"What?"

"Are *you* okay?"

She pursed her lips, thought about brushing it off. Couldn't. "No," she whispered. "No, I'm not."

One of his hands touched her, gently, on the shoulder. "What do you need? I have a little set aside in my savings, stuff I held over from New York. It's not much, but maybe—"

"That's not it."

"What can I do?" he asked.

"I don't know." She pulled away from him, pushing past the threshold to the long hall and moving for the kitchen. "It's not a money thing."

Paul lagged behind. "So what is it?"

The truth was that it was a lot; a crushing weight of nebulous things, a bogeyman, a history. The truth was too many things and most couldn't be fixed by the two of them. But the pressing part, the necessary part, the part repeating itself in looping whispers inside her head—there was something they could do about that.

"My clients. Some of them aren't…" she bit back even the full explanation of this, not having the time or patience to go into the details. The situation was too complicated to unravel in one conversation. "I don't need money, I need *product*. I need to make deliveries, most of them in the next day or two. I don't need cash, I need my shit back."

"How?" Paul asked, hazel eyes tired and wet as he waited for her answer.

The house settled around them.

Paul broke the silence. "Alright. Where do we start?"

■■■

Dawn painted the horizon in impressionist streaks of yellow and purple.

"It's not much of a plan," Paul said, jingling his keys in his hands.

"It's what we've got," Deirdre answered.

Paul nodded. "I'll call you later then."

"Yeah. If they left any downers, I'll let you know."

She crossed through reaching grass to her porch and glanced back to watch Paul pull away. In the receding wake of the engine, night faded into day. Birds twittered in the growing forest. All around her, a sprawl of rotting ex-suburbs roused its wheezing way into sunlight. Vines clung to abandoned houses like lover's limbs as if saying *come back to the earth with us. come back to the earth and sleep.*

The train that had brought her to Oceanrest fourteen years earlier had dropped her off at the north end of town, a neighborhood that the rail company had paid to level after it had been empty for over a year. She'd headed south on foot. It was that first night she'd realized Oceanrest wasn't a normal town. Not at all. She could feel it coming from the woods, something uncanny, something *wrong*. Something anyone blessed with a sixth sense of any kind would pick up on immediately.

That first night, she'd stumbled across an abandoned cemetery in the forest. It wasn't like the sprawling graveyard south of Denton or the fenced-in burial grounds behind the east-side churches—it was ancient. Forgotten. Tombstones jutted up from the dirt like remnants of lost cities, the names worn from their antique faces. She'd heard animal grunts coming up from the gravesites and she thought she'd seen a creature digging in the earth, its body caught in a haze of moonlit mist. She remembered long arms, spindly and clawed, and a squat body with no neck, eyes jaundiced yellow as it turned itself around. She'd been out of breath by the time she'd stopped running.

She'd heard other stories from her clients. From the transient sixth-sensers who wandered through on their way elsewhere and from the squatters who took up scavenged residence along Oceanrest's withering extremities. From old fishermen and hunters and sleepless cops who refused to work the north end of town. Secrets and superstition defined the northern and eastern swaths of the city, too many tales to guess which were true and which weren't. Too many stories to bother separating fact from fiction.

But there was more magic in Oceanrest than just witchcraft. That much she knew for sure.

come back to the earth and sleep, nature flirted, pulling civilization into ruin.

Strangeness composed the constant background thrum of Oceanrest.

"Hamlet was right…" she whispered.

The summer breeze blew the leaves around in response. The forest snickered.

Samedi padded his way through the over-tall grass and onto the porch. The cat butted his head against her shin before turning to join her in staring at the vast, encroaching wilderness. Averting her gaze from the deciduous and coniferous, she bowed to scratch Samedi behind the ears.

"Litter box is out of order," she said. Samedi licked the space between her thumb and pointer finger. She scratched around his ears for a few more seconds and straightened up. Pulling the phone from her pocket, she punched in Shoshanna Winters' phone number. The line trilled in her ear and Samedi pawed his way into the house.

The call connected. A drowsy voice, sleep-dumb, mumbled, *"Hello?"*

"Shosh, it's Deirdre."

"Oh, oh, hey," the voice said, rousing, clumsy-mouthed at dawn. *"How are you?"*

"Not great."

"What's the matter?"

"I won't be able to make delivery today. Or tomorrow."

Waking up, Shoshanna replied, *"Don't worry, I'll just tell David it's a slight delay. When can we expect—"*

"It'll be a while. Not this week, maybe not next. There was an accident. I lost the crates."

A long silence on the other end of the line. Shuffling.

Deirdre coughed. "I can have more in a couple weeks, maybe sooner."

"I, um, I understand." Shoshanna seemed pretty awake now. *"But David, well, you know how he is."*

"He's your bother. Just talk to him for me."

"It's—it's not that easy. You know it's not that easy."

"I just need some extra time."

"I'll try, but I can't promise anything."

"Yeah, I know. I get it."

"Deirdre, I'm sorry, I am, but my hands are tied on this. It's his name on all the bills, it's his name on the property deed."

Dierdre's fingers tightened around the phone. "If he shuts me down, I can't make *more*. If he cuts the electricity—"

"He wants you in our labs."

"I'm not an employee." She struggled to restrain the heat in her voice. "I work alone. Out here. Where I live."

"Maybe it's not such a bad idea? You could make a real living then. Our facilities are—"

"Shosh. Please."

Shoshanna sighed, practiced. *"I understand you don't want to work under him, but we could negotiate a contract where you would only answer to me and—"*

"Shosh," she repeated, harder.

Another sigh. *"Okay. You value your freedom, I understand that. I'll try to get him to understand it too."*

"Thanks. I mean it." She hung up and slipped the phone back into its cradle. She rubbed her face with both hands and screwed up the tall coif of hair she'd kept on the crown of her head. David Winters was just slightly less of a prick son of a bitch than Randall, but David paid the water, gas, electricity, and property bills on her squat. Technically, she wasn't even a squatter—she was a guest. In exchange for said arrangement, she provided the company bi-weekly deliveries.

Except Randall had swiped the whole shipment, all of her back stock, all of her unsorted stock, and all of her harvests.

Now David Winters had leverage, and his sister was Deirdre's only backup if she couldn't get the product back.

"Goddammit," she muttered.

Another breeze blew through the forest and set the leaves to laughing.

CHAPTER THREE

Paul parked his car outside Atlantic Claire's, a streamline moderne diner that sat at the rear of a parking lot like an on-ramp to a fantasy of the 50s. Even at 6:00 AM he could see some of the older early-bird types slouching in red leather booths. He swung the door of the car open with a rusted squeal, stepped out, and crossed the lot to the restaurant.

Sarah smiled at him from behind the coffee bar. She'd taken his 300-level forensic course the semester before, a third-generation legacy student who knew her way around campus better than he did. She had blonde hair coiled in post-War Victory Curls and blue eyes that could have sold anything to anyone, but for one reason or another, she'd opted to study forensic psychology. He offered her a smile. She glanced up at the bandage wrapping his head, then politely looked away.

"Looking for Virgil?" she asked.

"Yeah."

"He's not in yet. His booth is in the back."

"Thanks."

Virgil's usual booth sat at the rear of the diner by a street-facing panoramic window. Paul slipped into the leather seats and collapsed back with an exhausted sigh. He ordered eggs, toast, and bottomless coffee. He ate slowly, scratched the faint rash on his fingers, and stared at passing cars until Virgil sauntered in at 6:20.

Early morning sun glinted off Virgil's badge, an old-fashioned gold emblem tagged to an old-fashioned blue parka, the word "police" faded on the back. Walking in, Virgil shook Sarah's hand. They spoke for a few seconds before Sarah pointed toward Paul, and Virgil's smile vanished. He gave Sarah a polite nod and ambled over. "Surprised to see you up and about so early."

"I, ah…I need your help, actually."

Virgil snorted, sliding into the booth across from Paul. "Figured that from the head wound. What's the story?"

"I need to ask a few questions. Off the record."

"Uh-huh. What kind of questions?"

Paul turned the story over in his head, trying to figure out how to tell the tale. "Well, I was up by Lafayette last night—"

"That's your problem, right there," Virgil interrupted. "We call it 'Squatter City' for a reason, Paul. Nobody up there except vagrants, squatters, and criminals. Addicts. It's not the kind of place a man like you should want to go, especially not after dark."

"I was up there, in any case, visiting a friend."

"A friend?"

"Yeah."

"You happen to owe this friend any money?"

"No."

"I understand you have certain *needs*, and considering what all you went through back in New York, I can't blame you. All I'm saying is—"

"Listen you—" Paul leaned forward, muscles coiled. Froze. He took a breath, steadying himself, and slumped back in his seat. "Look, I was up there visiting a friend, and some crew of lunatics busted into the place and robbed us."

Virgil leaned back and whistled. "Je-sus, Paul. That's something else. You got descriptions on these guys?"

"Yeah. I've got a name on one of them too."

They fell into a brief pause as Sarah came over to take Virgil's order: western omelet, grapefruit, bottomless coffee. She smiled and gave each of them a nod before leaving.

Virgil cleared his throat. "You know, Paul, the reason cops don't go up to Lafayette isn't 'cause we don't care about people. We scare them. Everyone up there's got ten different reasons to be scared of cops and not one to talk to us. Before I had run of the show, PD used to run raids up there every other week. Now we let them rest, we let them set down roots. We don't ruffle feathers unless we have to."

"You don't do much to protect them, either."

The policing practices of the OPD along the northern and eastern fringes of town were a popular source of op-eds and protests. To the north, cop cars rarely patrolled, but when they did, hell followed with them. To the east, around the Section 8 houses especially, a constant police presence created harassment. Violence trademarked police involvement in both places.

Paul had heard Virgil's justifications half a dozen times.

Virgil clenched his jaw and took a long, dry breath before replying. "Half the people up there are trainhoppers and bums. Plenty of 'em aren't even in the system. You know what booking's like for that? Hell, forget booking, how do you even find a perp up there? They'll just hop another train in a couple'a days, hole up in another squat, wander off into the damned woods. It's not like their names are on the deeds."

"Guess not," Paul conceded, not wanting to delve into it again.

"Ten, eleven years ago, before we started easing off the pressure up there, a guy like you would've been more likely to end up dead up there than mugged, tell you that."

Paul held up his hands in surrender. "Alright, alright, I get it. But this guy's not like the other squatters."

"Oh, yeah? What makes him so different?"

"I'd bet money that this guy's got a record. Randall Hill. Sounded like he was from somewhere down south, maybe Alabama or Georgia or—"

"Or some other Confederate-type state?"

"He was older, maybe older than me."

"Off the record, what is it exactly you want me to do?"

Paul hesitated. Sarah sashayed her way back to the table with Virgil's coffee and a refill for his own. Paul stared at the steam coiling up from the mug and waited for the waitress to leave before answering. "I want to check his records. Frankly, I think he's a sociopath, and not particularly high-functioning. If you let him run around long enough, he'll kill someone."

Virgil put two packets of Sweet'N Low and a small creamer in his coffee, stirred. "That's a big favor."

"Look, I'm not asking you to put guys on it. I know you don't like your men getting involved up there unless they have to. But this could preempt a real investigation…and you have to admit, busting someone who scares the other squatters would help your image. If I can find something you can bring him in on, I've got you on speed-dial."

Virgil considered his coffee. Nodded. "Alright, I'll make you a deal. I'll check this guy out, run his name through the system, whatever suits your fancy, but I need something from you too. A few days ago, some hunters found a body out in the woods, northwest of town. Now, it's not breakfast conversation, but this wasn't our killer's first vic, and the FBI sent someone up here to help look into it…except the kid is about as green as fine Denton grass."

Like an icicle shot through his spine. Paul pretended not to shiver. "You want me to lend a hand."

"That's right."

(*eyeless sockets, tongueless jaw*)

Paul swallowed. "That hasn't always worked so well in the past."

"But sometimes it has, and two heads are better than one."

Silence overtook them. Sarah delivered the food, not bothering with niceties this time, perhaps sensing the tension brooding around the table. When she left, the two men stared at each other for several seconds.

"That's the best I can do, Paul."

Paul nodded. Forced his jaw to move. "Alright then."

■■■

Deirdre sighed. She'd exhausted her phone of its contacts and discovered nothing new about Randall Hill. The idea had seemed so simple, at first—find Randall, steal her stash back, set things right with David Winters; but nobody she knew had intel to offer her. At least, nobody she knew who owned a phone.

She pocketed the cell and went out to knock on a few doors.

She froze on her porch, ice fear and prickly heat commingling in her veins.

David Winter's car idled on the roadside, pulled up right to the overgrowth of her lawn. As soon as she left the house, David Winters exited the vehicle, shadowed by two bodyguards. David Winters had inherited the paler genes of his Polish-Iranian ancestry, skin the shade of his button-up; so white he blazed like a flare in the summer sun. His face was shadowed in all angles, sharp cheeks, sharp nose, sharp jawline—some of it crafted less by genetics and more by scalpel.

"I heard bad news," he said, approaching her.

His twin shadows smirked threats and adjusted their jackets around poorly concealed firearms.

"I'm working on it," Deirdre replied, not moving from her doorway.

"Shipment's due today."

"I got robbed."

"Robbed, burgled, raided—do I care?"

Deirdre shifted slightly, putting the door between her and the approaching trio of men. "I'm handling it, okay? I just need the motherfucker's address and I'll have the shit back ASAP."

"That so?" David walked up the porch steps and slipped one hand into a pocket. His bodyguards folded their own arms across bulging chests, still smirking, eyes glowing with the promise of violence. With his free hand, David gestured at the front of the squat. "Mind if I take a look inside? I do own the place."

"We had a deal."

"Yes, and you've broken it. So either step aside so I can evaluate my property, or I'll call the police."

"You wouldn't."

"No? Why not?"

"If I get carted off, you'll never see another sample."

David nodded. "Hm. Suppose you're right. But what about this—a squatter disappears from Squatter City, the police ask if I knew someone was living here, and I say 'no.'"

"You wouldn't—"

David held up a hand to silence her. "You wake up in a sub-basement with no idea where you are, maybe Oceanrest, maybe Chicago or Detroit, and—"

"—You motherfucker—"

She moved, and his bodyguards moved in mirror. She shoved the door and reached for him, and the bodyguards grabbed one arm each and threw her hard into the side of her house. The blow banged up her spine, along her bones, but she braced against it. In the electric tension afterwards, she stayed pressed against the linoleum, panting, while the bodyguards grinned down at her.

David cleared his throat. "Your existence out here, your continued *unmolested* lifestyle, is due entirely to my beneficence."

Deirdre dammed her teeth against a flood of expletives.

"You provide samples, we provide a legal veil for your criminal enterprise; we ensure that electricity, heat, and water keep pumping into your little…" he waved with practiced distaste at her home, "…well, whatever you call this. Ramshackle little life." He peered over at her as if daring her to try something else. When she didn't, he smiled. "But you've lost the samples."

"I said—"

"I don't care what you said. I don't care about you."

"I'm the only one—"

"In New England, yes, you're the only active and skilled apothecary we know. But there's a fifth-generation druid we've found outside of Detroit and we've also recently gotten news of a paranormative botanist working out of Philadelphia. Don't think you're somehow irreplaceable." He turned to face her, his smile dissolving into a flat, emotionless mask. "So either find the shipment or come up with more."

Deirdre scowled back. Her nostrils twitched uncontrollably, every muscle of her body working to hide the reflexive sneer trying to coil its way across her lips.

"Good," David said. "Now. Did these alleged looters take *everything*, or just most of it? Is there anything left in that basement of yours?"

Another car screamed around the intersection, a duplicate of David's own black sedan. The only difference between the two vehicles showed in the license plate—David's car labeled WA-LAB1, and the approaching clone, WA-LAB2. The bodyguards stepped away from Deirdre as the thing swerved, braking hard, and stopped halfway on the lawn.

"David!" Shoshanna shouted, clambering half-assembled out of the back seat. "What the fuck are you doing?"

David and the bodyguards sank back from Deirdre, their smirks vanishing instantly.

"I'm pursuing the issue you called me about—"

"Fuck you are!" Shoshanna replied, still yelling even as she crossed the shin-high grass merely ten feet away. "We had an agreement!"

"She broke—"

"Not that. *We* had an agreement as in *you and I* had one."

Shoshanna climbed the steps to the porch all but heaving steam from her lungs.

David blinked at his sister a couple times and drew a long, deep breath. "Promises were made."

Shoshanna's bodyguard lumbered out of the driver's seat of the sedan. A man of the approximate dimension and density of a brick wall, he stood a foot taller than either of David's guardians, and likely as broad as both combined. Gray-faced and eternally expressionless, Shoshanna's bodyguard always gave Deirdre gooseflesh. Something about him hummed with occulted secrecy, something about him tied into the secret parts of the world. Deirdre felt it in her sixth sense, and her sixth sense wasn't very strong.

Shoshanna herself wore a matching white button-up to David's, but with sleeves rolled halfway up her forearms, her skin the terra-cotta of sun-boiled desert. Her hair usually tumbled down in curls to her shoulders, but Deirdre guessed she'd dressed in a rush, as currently it bristled messy and tangled in something trying, and failing, to be a simple bun.

"David."

David maintained a long stare with his sister, but his shoulders slumped. "We need the shipment, Shosh."

"Ten days."

Deirdre stepped away from the linoleum, "I don't know if I can—"

"Ten days," Shoshanna interrupted, flicking a warning look at Deirdre over David's shoulder. "That's all she'll need."

Deirdre frowned.

"She shouldn't be left alone all the way out here," David said. "This could happen again."

"If she wants a bodyguard, she'll ask for one."

"That's not the point."

"It is."

"We need the shipments—it doesn't matter what she wants."

"It matters to me," Shoshanna muttered, the heat of her voice sabotaged by her disarray. "And since it matters to your sister, it matters to you, too."

David took a step back, peered at Shoshanna's wall of bodyguard, then back at Shoshanna. "I think it might be time to renegotiate terms."

"Then we'll renegotiate them in ten days, when everyone is calm."

David sighed and nodded. "Fine." He paused for a few more seconds, as if to press the issue, then turned abruptly away and started down the porch steps. Shoshanna's bodyguard moved aside to let him pass. Halfway across the lawn, David turned back. "Ten days. That's all. Ten days."

Deirdre and Shoshanna waited while David and his bodyguards climbed back into their sedan and turned around. Waited until they'd reached the corner at Lafayette and vanished back through Squatter City toward Ocean-rest proper.

Shoshanna broke the silence. "I'm sorry about David."

"Yeah, well…" Shoshanna reached out for Deirdre's shoulder, but Deirdre shrugged it off. "You handle your brother," she said. "I've got missing goods to find."

"Do you have enough raw material to make a new batch?"

"No." Deirdre shut the front door, moved to lock it, and saw the lock twisted and useless, mutated by buckshot. "Especially not with a ten-day deadline."

"It's the best I could do."

Deirdre tried to extinguish the blaze-heat smoldering in her chest, but couldn't. She coughed and pretended instead. "Thanks, Shosh. I appreciate it. Now if you'll excuse me, I got things."

"Right. I'll talk to David. And," Shoshanna turned to follow David's path back to the street, "we should talk."

"Later." The word sharpened between her teeth, turned to a dagger by the time it left her lips.

Shoshanna caught the message. "Right. Later."

Shoshanna and her mountainous bodyguard returned to their car, and Deirdre watched the plume of exhaust tailing David back into town.

She followed not long after, down the sinewy, patchy path of Black Watch Hill to the wider avenue of Lafayette.

Ten days. She had ten days to find Randall Hill's place and steal her shipments back. Or.

Or what?

Or Shoshanna would be the only shield between her and David's wrath.

Shit.

CHAPTER FOUR

Virgil's office was on the third floor of the precinct, tucked away in the back with exterior windows overlooking the remnants of Oceanrest's industrial district. Even in the light of the coming summer morning, it all looked gray. Malleus Industries had bought two buildings—an old warehouse, an old factory—and a stretch of dock space, but most of it sat shuttered. Beyond the slouch and decay, sun blazed against sea.

"This your guy?"

Paul crossed from the window to the old CRT computer monitor, leaning forward to look over Virgil's shoulder.

Randall Tyler Hill, born 1974 in Prattville, Alabama. A few years Paul's senior, after all.

"That's him. What's the story?"

Virgil shrugged, leaned back in his office chair. "Nothing special. His family came up here sometime late-seventies, back when things weren't quite so grim. Sometime in the eighties, Randall fell in with a gang of ARA types, Aryan Nation, and he spent most of the nineties in lock-up for aggravated assault."

"You knew him?"

"Arrested him once, maybe ten, twelve years ago. Surprised to hear he's still around."

"Why?"

"Well, Randall and the rest of the white power crew mostly disappeared after the riots."

"Riots?"

"Back in ninety-seven. Terrible, what happened."

"What was that, exactly?"

Virgil folded his arms over his chest. "That depends on who you ask."

"I'm asking you."

Virgil chewed his response for a while before speaking. "It wasn't just one thing, I'll say that. It was a long, hot summer and a long, bad year. Unemployment was on the rise, crime on the rise…there was a big strike, all the union boys picketing along the docks, and there was the civil rights folks protesting Butler's radio show, and Butler was on his pulpit and on the airwaves talking about all sorts of nonsense."

"Butler?"

"Howland Butler. Some crazy revivalist. He showed up in the early eighties with a bunch of tents, a small traveling congregation. Fast forward a few years, and the guy had a regional radio show, a website, and a big, pay-to-pray church. He got tied into some bad crowds, Aryans, Québécois…"

"What happened to him?"

"Church burnt down in the riots. Understand, these riots were some of the most violent days Oceanrest ever saw. The whole thing lasted three days and by the time it was over, Butler's church was burnt down, a trailer park caught fire, and half the state was pouring water on the forest. I'd never seen anything like it. Still haven't, twenty years later. Anyway, Butler took off after he got his insurance settlement. Most of the Aryan crew vanished soon after."

"Rivalry with the Québécois?"

Virgil ignored the question, leaning toward the screen. "Says here we brought him in back in 2002 for pandering, but the charge didn't stick. I got him in '03 for drunk and disorderly. After that, nothing. His last known residence was up on Waverly back in '02, but that's Squatter City now."

"You have any info on any other known Aryan gangsters? Or anyone affiliated with Butler's old church?"

Virgil snorted. "I'm not giving you that kind of info. The guy you're looking for, he's a criminal, he's got a history, but I'm not telling you what church people went to twenty years ago. Whatever they were involved in back then, however it ended, it's over, now."

"Maybe it's not."

"Then find proof. I'm not telling you who went to which church or who believes in what god. We did the whole 'Satanic panic' nonsense when I was still a rookie. What I can do is see if there are any other active Aryan Nationalists with criminal records running around town, CSA or Loyal White Knights or some other bullshit, but anything more than that, you'll have to work the beat yourself." He paused, unfolding his arms to rub his face and sigh. "You know, not everyone in the congregation was a bad sort."

"Sure."

"I'll put some feelers out for this Randall Hill fellow, see if I can't dig up anything else. In the meantime, you'll be meeting with that Fed, a'yeah?"

"Yeah. Give him my address, tell him to drop by sometime today."

"You won't wait fifteen minutes to see him here?"

"You know how I feel about the precinct." Paul went for the door back to the station proper. "Don't like to be here too long. Brings back bad memories."

Virgil's eyes sharped. "Don't be a bigger asshole than you have to be, Paul."

"I'll do my best."

He pushed Virgil's office door open and froze.

Virgil laughed.

In front of him, a suited man, late-twenties or early-thirties, stood mid-stride, a thick manila folder under one arm. Sand-blond hair, ice blue eyes. Too-white teeth, too much jawline. "Doctor Somers?" the suit asked. "Thanks for coming by so early. I'm Simon Perdue, I'm with the Bureau." He held out a hand.

Paul masked a grimace and shook it. "A pleasure."

"I'm glad you're here. This case needs immediate attention. Come with me?"

Virgil's laughter faded to a wheezy chuckle.

Paul pretended a smile. "Sure. Lead the way."

■■■

Nobody talked. Two hours after David Winters' visit to her homestead, Deirdre didn't know anything she hadn't known that morning. Perhaps she'd uncovered one new tidbit of intel: Randall scared people. Scared their tongues straight out of their heads.

But at the bottom of the Squatter City barrel, one man owed her more than all the others.

She'd saved Frank's life three times. Once from a crew from the Section 8 houses, once from an overdose, and most recently from the Québécois. She'd cashed out a lot of that debt when she'd asked Frank to give Razz a place to sleep after Razz moved out of her squat, but she hoped that life-saving debt accrued enough interest to keep paying out.

Yet at the end of so many fruitless hours, she wasn't terribly surprised when he shrugged at her question and said, "I ain't heard much about the guy."

Deirdre sighed into a miasma of dust and drug-stink. "No shit."

Frank sprawled in the corner his room clad in a sleeping bag and a sweat-stained beater, pale shoulders covered in black hair. His right hand rested on the floorboards, inches from a sawed-off baseball bat. His left hand was a knobbed mess of arthritic bones, stitched back all wrong after a series of bad moves he'd made before trainhopping his way to Oceanrest. He scratched at his wiry beard with the ruined hand and shrugged again. "Randall don't come 'round my way much. Different, uh, classes."

"You know anything about him?"

"I know he's in with some of the Quebecs. I know he's got a stable of girls hid out somewhere."

"Girls?"

"Real expensive types. Outta my price range."

"People make appointments with these girls?"

A third shrug. More scratching. "I guess? I mean, gotta be some way he does biz with 'em."

"Can't think of any specifics?"

"I heard some rumors." Frank smiled plaque.

Deirdre wrangled a crumpled tenner from her pocket and passed the bill off to him. "What kind of rumors?

Still grinning, Frank buried the cash somewhere within the sleeping bag. "He uses that Frenchie bed-and-breakfast for some of the appointments. Quebecs get a cut, I think, and he pays 'em off for something else too, but I don't know what. Any case, he's in pretty good with 'em, and nobody wants trouble with those froggy fucks."

She unfurled another rumpled tenner and passed it off. "You hear anything else, you run to the payphone. Sound good?"

The second bill disappeared as the first. "Peachy."

Deirdre turned toward the door. Paused. Turned back. "You still have a place to shower?"

"Yeah. Some lady friends just got out of the squats, moved to a real house. They let me use theirs."

"Lady friends?"

"Just friends, but they're ladies." A wheezy snicker cracked his lips. "I'd'a liked to get romantic with 'em, but they bat the other team. Lezzies."

"Keep your ears open. Call if you hear something."

"Will do, Sheriff."

"Deirdre," she corrected.

"Will do, Deirdre."

"Talk soon, Frank."

Out of his room and down the hall, she walked down a flight of creaking, moldering steps to the front door. Five squatters shared the place, but only two had been there when she'd arrived. The other one, a gold-faced Hispanic girl named Olly, had made a similar report to Frank's, no useful leads and no idea where to start. Deirdre hopped down from the half-collapsed porch into the bracken and bramble of the lawn. Already the sun descended west from its zenith, and Randall Hill had slipped her grasp.

She stood on the cracked sidewalk in front of Frank's squat and stared off in thought. Randall had been her steady client for over six years, an enormous part of her regular income. He bought enough sixth-sense boosters and dreamer every month to keep twenty full-grown men high around the clock, enough smokable magic to turn their lungs black. What did he do with it all? Sell it? To whom? It wasn't as if there was some hidden enclave of witches and psychics hiding out in rural Maine.

She started down the street back toward Black Watch Hill, but paused when a breeze blew cold through her jacket. She turned, staring into the nascent forest carving its way southward. Vines clung to aging facades. Grass and weeds reached up through splintered concrete.

(*come back to the earth and sleep*, nature crooned)

She shivered and turned her back on the reaching trees. Across the street, a line of battered cars sat on an uneven shoulder. In Squatter City, most of them were abandoned. Some served as transient housing. Several were drop points for Québécois criminals. But one of them looked new, a scratched-up blue-painted Ford with a shattered driver's side window. She frowned at the toothy glass and jogged toward the car.

In the backseat of the truck, curled in scavenged blankets, Razz slept.

One side of her face twitched. She cast a glance back at Frank's squat, the place Razz was *supposed* to sleep.

Except…

She reached one hand in through the broken driver's side window and unlocked the car. Razz stirred briefly, stretching and shifting beneath the blanket, but he didn't wake up. At least, he didn't wake up until she flung the rear door open and grabbed his leg.

A yelp burst from Razz's lips and he spun onto his back, kicking out with his free leg and missing Deirdre's arm by an inch. She wrenched on his body and pulled him halfway out of the car. "What the hell do you think you're doing?"

Razz scrambled to push himself up, eyes shock-wide, body blanket-tangled and clumsy. "Dee—"

She put one hand in the center of his chest and pushed him back into the vehicle. "Why aren't you at Frank's?"

"Whoa, whoa, Dee, hey—"

"Why are you in this car? Do you *own* this car?" She grabbed his shoulders and held him down, her upper body craning into the vehicle.

"Frank kicked me out."

Hot blue lightning crackled through her skull. "Excuse me?"

"Fucking cracker hit me with a goddamned bat, man. Chased me right out. Olly tried to stop him but—"

"Wait here," she interrupted. A coiled dragon roused between her lungs. She pushed herself off of Razz and turned back to Frank's squat. Razz shifted in the seat. Without looking back at him she snapped, "I said *wait*."

She burned across the street like ball lightning, crashed through the front door of Frank's squat, and hammered across the floor toward the stairwell. Olly eyed her from a camping tent pitched in the living room. The young woman started to crawl out, but Deirdre spun toward her. "Stay there."

"You—you saw Razz?"

Deirdre took the steps in three bounds and rushed down the hall to Frank's door. She put her foot to it and busted the lock from its frame.

Frank yanked his good hand out of his sleeping bag mid-masturbation and scuttled backward. He held his bum hand up to shield his face and fumbled at the floor for his bat.

Deirdre loosed her revolver and cranked back the hammer. "Who the fuck do you think you are?"

"Whoa, whoa, hey!" Frank stopped going for the bat and held both hands up against the gun barrel. "Deirdre, hey, what's going on? I told you I don't know nothing, I promise. I said—"

"You kicked Razz out?"

"No, no, listen, that one's not on me."

"It isn't? We had a deal."

"I know, I know, just—the kid, he's running with a bad crowd."

"I don't give a shit. You owe me. The deal was I get you out of your fuck-up with the Québécois and you give Razz a place to sleep. Do you not remember the deal?"

"Hear me out, man, I swear it's not the way you think."

"So what way is it then? Spill, Frank, before I lose my temper."

"The kid's running with those Section 8 ni—guys, those kids always getting into shit with the Quebecs. He brought the motherfuckers to my house, man. To my *house*. What if my dealer was in? He's a frog. I can't have that kinda risk here." Frank panted through the explanation, panicked.

Deirdre stared. "He got in with a crew?"

"Past couple months, yeah. I mean, it was bound to happen, sooner or—"

"Don't you dare."

Frank stopped talking.

She lowered her gun to her side, safety still off. "You listen close, Frank. We've known each other a long time, maybe not what you'd call 'friends,' but…something. The thing is, Razz is *mine*. So if you fuck with him, you fuck with me, get it? And I don't care how long you've been squatting here, if you hurt him, I'll fucking kill you. You think the cops will go out of their way to look for a train-hopping heroin junkie if he goes missing?"

"Come on, man, I can't have that kinda shit around here, you know that. Why don't the kid just move back in with you?"

"That wasn't the deal."

"The deal didn't involve some saggy-pantsed n—*kids*—getting drunk in my squat."

"The deal involved saving your life. There aren't any subsection clauses to that. I saved your life. And if you hurt that kid, I'll take it back."

Frank's lips flapped, making sounds but not words.

Deirdre didn't wait for him to figure out how to speak again. She slammed the broken door behind her and tore down the stairs. Olly had gotten out of her tent and stood near the front door, high cheeks and jutting jaw accentuated by curled ink. "What did you…?"

Deirdre didn't answer. She blew past Olly, out the front door, over the lawn, back into the street.

Razz leaned against the bed of the truck, eyes downcast.

Deirdre disengaged the hammer and switched the safety on, holstering her gun.

Razz glanced up, saw her, and stared back down. "Look, Dee—"

"You were sick the day of the test, huh?"

"Dee—"

"You're running with a crew? You're on your own for less than a year and you're already working for a crew? Who?"

"I just didn't wanna be alone out here, man."

"You *are* alone out here," Deirdre barely restrained the urge to yell, aching with the memories of so many other arguments they'd had before he'd left her house. "Everyone's alone out here. Maybe, *maybe* you find one or two people who have your back, who want to help you, but that's it. Hooking up with some bullshit gang doesn't change that, it just makes you feel safe when you aren't."

Razz stared at a patch of yellowed grass fighting its way up from the concrete.

Deirdre sighed pure heat. "You promised, Razz. You promised. You'd take the GED, get a decent gig—"

"There's no gigs out there, Dee."

"That's not my name."

"There aren't any goddamned jobs!" Razz finally brought his eyes to hers. "You been paying attention out here? Some of these squatters been on a waiting list for Section 8 for years. You think they're homeless on purpose?"

"So, what, you sell drugs for the rest of your life? You know how that turns out?"

"Just until something else opens up. And now I got people who have my back, help me out."

"These people don't care about you. They don't. If they did, you wouldn't be sleeping in a truck, right now. And if it comes down to it, they'll flip you. Why do you think the eastside gangs stay so small? Think about it. The Québécois have been running Oceanrest for decades. The cops work *with* them half the time. And when people complain about drug dealers, drug violence, whatever else, who do you think the cops come down on? *Who?*"

Razz opened his mouth, dropped his gaze back groundwards, closed it.

"Yeah. And when someone gets big enough to be a real threat, when someone gets big enough to make the Québécois nervous, they just go missing. You think the cops go out of their way to investigate that shit? How hard do you think homicide would work if *your* body showed up on the side-walk? Or didn't show up at all? How hard?"

"So what do I do? Take the GED? You know how many squatters got a GED? Shit, Frank's got a goddamned college degree."

"Frank's a heroin addict."

"I'm just trying to do okay out here, you know?"

"Nobody does okay out here. Look around you. Trainhoppers, junkies, mental hospital drop-outs…no one in Squatter City does okay."

"You do."

She stepped back, losing heat. "I don't want what other people want."

"I don't get it, though. How'm I supposed to make money all alone out here? And what am I gonna do with a degree when half the money in town is dirty as shit?"

"There's plenty of clean money in Oceanrest."

"Where? The Winters suits? Malleus? You think those people would hire *me*?" he asked, his hand on his chest, fingers splayed.

"I do."

Razz let out a peal of fraying laughter. "Bullshit."

She took a step toward him, reached out. She wanted to pull him into a hug but somehow couldn't. She put a hand on his shoulder and squeezed instead. "I don't want to hear one day that you got hurt, okay? You can move back in with me or tough it out with Frank or…or find some old bag out in Denton or Deer's Head renting out a place over her garage. But I need you to work with me, because there's nothing good waiting at the end of what you're doing now."

He shrugged off her hand and moved as if to walk away. Didn't.

"I'll come back to talk in a few days," she said, moving to stay in his vision. "I better hear some good news."

Still averting eye contact, Razz shrugged.

"Look at me. I'm going to hear good news, right?"

He glanced at her, shrugged again. "Yeah, I guess."

She stared at him for a few more seconds before stalking away. Halfway down Lafayette, pressure began building behind her eyes. She tried to imagine Razz finally caving in, using the cash from his next buy to get some cheap place by the docks, finishing his degree, getting a job at Malleus or maybe Winters-Armitage Labs. Maybe something that made him have to leave Oceanrest and go somewhere else, somewhere far away from Frank and the Québécois and whatever things crawled between the trees after dark. She tried to imagine him applying for a job at some greasy spoon shithole in town and asking if he could move back into Samedi's room or just crash on her couch. She tried to imagine him saving up and moving into an attic space over some retired Denton lady's garage and scraping through a program at the university.

But when she looked back down the street from the corner of Lafayette and Black Watch Hill, saw him tiny in the distance, skinny frame leaned back up against the truck, wrapped in a blanket he'd probably picked out of someone's garbage, all of that fell apart. What jobs were there anymore? What jobs were there for a kid who spent most of his weekly income on canned goods and didn't own a computer and didn't have a high school diploma? What old, white Denton lady was going to let a black squatter live above her garage?

She swallowed a lump that had collected at the back of her throat and steeled herself against the pressure behind her eyes. She told herself that he'd listen this time, that he'd finally make good on the promise he'd made so many years ago and just take the damned test. She told herself that Oceanrest showed signs of recovery, that new offices meant new jobs, that one of those jobs could belong to Razz. That maybe she could talk Shoshanna into getting him *something*.

She turned down Black Watch Hill and tried to stop thinking.

CHAPTER FIVE

Queasiness plucked at Paul's innards—something weird in his resurfacing sixth-sense, combined with the leftover dizziness of his head wound. Or perhaps it was the faint nausea of being trapped in the precinct for too long, as if he'd been thrust back into a former and forgotten life.

Or maybe the fact that Virgil had stuffed them in an interrogation room, since he needed the conference room to go over the day's assignments.

"I don't know if Virgil told you," Simon said, splaying copied crime-scene photos and other paperwork over the table in the center of the room, "but I asked for you by name. I heard about your last case when I was at BAU. Do you remember Dr. Fitzgerald?"

Paul finished his Styrofoam cup of cheap coffee. "Shouldn't he be retired?"

"He isn't. When I caught the assignment, I asked him if he knew anyone in the area. He gives me your name, and I ask for you at the regional office down in Boston. They have no idea who I'm talking about."

"That was the point of moving." Paul offered a taut, thin-lipped smile, his joke not a joke at all.

"So I find out *you* retired. You're a teacher now."

"Professor."

"Right. Professor."

"So what's the case?"

"The regional office has been working on and off with local PD for years. It looks like there's an active serial killer in Oceanrest, and there has been for some time. To date, we've got records of eight victims spread over nearly six years, all of them exhibiting similar ritualistic wounds. Previous work between regional and OPD hasn't brought in a suspect yet, and here I am."

"Where's your partner?" Paul asked.

"Still at the regional office, coordinating between Oceanrest, Boston, and Quantico. I'm doing all the beat work for the next few days while we get everything in order. Except..." Simon hesitated over the photos and paperwork.

"Except what?"

"Except I don't think we have that long. The killer's schedule has been steadily accelerating over the past couple years." Simon plucked a last photo from the folder and put it on top of all the other paperwork. "The latest victim."

Paul knew what he'd see before he even looked.

(*help me I don't know what to do*
you're the only one who sees)

An eyeless face stared up at him, grisly sockets full of dirt. Scavengers and carrion feeders had already eaten away patches of skin, the flesh of her cheeks. Leaves and twigs ornamented her hair. Someone had carved symbols into her flesh, her forehead, her collarbone, the tops of her breasts.

(*a figure at the foot of his bed, a tongueless voice invading his thoughts*)

"Her name was Lucy McKinney," Simon continued. "Last seen two years ago in Toronto."

Paul's tongue swelled and cracked, too big for his mouth. He unstuck his lips. "Time of death?"

"Five to seven days ago."

"What happened between her disappearance and her death? What does evidence suggest?"

"Are you okay?" Simon asked.

"Fine," Paul lied. "Just haven't seen one of these for a while."

"Yeah," Simon said, though his tone suggested disbelief. "Well. Contusions and abrasions on the wrists and ankles indicate significant time in restraints pre-mortem. Malnutrition suggests possible captivity."

Paul lifted his eyes to Simon's, realized the younger man had been staring at him the whole time.

Simon answered the unasked questions: "The victims all showed signs of extreme sexual assault prior to TOD. The cause of death in each case has been blood loss, probably resultant of nine stab wounds to the sexual organs, as well as the removal of their tongues. The symbols you see were carved postmortem, generally across the clavicle and upper breasts, and also appearing on the thighs. All eight victims had their tongues removed. This is only the third victim with her eyes removed."

"What are the other commonalities?"

Simon didn't glance at the paperwork, his cerulean gaze fixed on Paul's features. "They all had missing persons cases and all but one of them had a criminal history. Solicitation, possession, possession with intent. One of them was even a CI."

"Race? Age?"

"Three black women, three Hispanic, two white. The youngest was twenty-three, the oldest was thirty-nine."

"Where were they from?"

"Montreal, Toronto, Quebec. A couple from Portland, one from Boston."

"You need to talk to the local mob," Paul said, stepping away from the table, from the eyeless ghost flattened against the photo there. "The local mob is Québécois, they've got ties to most of the places you listed. If these girls were prosts, drug dealers, anything like that, maybe you'll get a hit."

"How does that help?"

"Someone targeted these women, someone with ties to all of those cities, someone who dumped the bodies in the woods around Oceanrest. That sounds like someone connected to local crime. You get the right hits from the right people, you could start working up a suspect list, or at least a few good leads."

"What about the ritual nature of the crimes? The symbols? This isn't some mobster disposing of witnesses, this seems—"

"Religious," Paul interrupted. "Sure. I'm not saying it's not. But whoever did this, he's not wearing fanaticism on his sleeve. He's been active for almost six years, quiet, cautious, uncaught. He's good at hiding, he bides his time. The mob could provide good cover, and possibly a level of protection from police."

Simon nodded. "I'll talk to Virgil about a shakedown."

"Profile-wise, you're looking for someone with religious ideation, or some kind of dogmatic ideation with religious symbolism. You should see if you can dig up anything about the symbols carved into her body, see if they connect to any known religion, cult, esoterica. The racial and age disparity of the victims doesn't immediately yield any leads, but most of the Québécois mobsters are white, so that's a start. Has forensics been able to do any guesswork on the perpetrator's height, based off of wound location?"

"The victims were all prone at TOD, so it's hard to tell."

Paul inhaled between tight teeth and backed toward the door. "Well, I'd start with a shakedown, see if you can get some kind of lead off of a usual suspect." He paused. "I actually, uh, I have a meeting with the dean to talk over my next semester's lesson plan, so…"

"Why don't you take these with you? They're all photocopies, and it wouldn't hurt to touch base later."

Paul hesitated. "Sure."

He gathered the photocopies back into the manila folder and tucked it under his arm.

Simon rapped his knuckles on the tabletop. "I wanted to, um…I heard about what happened in New York."

Paul headed back to the door. "I have to get to this meeting."

"I just want to say I'm sorry about your daughter. Dr. Fitzgerald wanted to extend his condolences as well, and—"

"Thanks." Paul flashed a tight, obviously-false smile. "We'll talk later."

"May I ask what happened to your head, by the way?" Simon indicated the bandages.

"I fell off the ladder trying to get onto the roof deck. Banged it on the seaside railing."

Simon looked like he wanted to ask another question, but didn't. Paul thought he saw the shadow of a smirk slant across the man's face. He pushed the door open and exited the interrogation room, half worried that the Fed would follow.

Paul went down the precinct stairs, out the front door, and to his car.

He tossed the manila folder in the back seat, picked up the flask from the passenger seat, and took a slug of whiskey off the top.

He revved the engine to life with four turns of the car keys and got the hell out of there.

■■■

Deirdre dragged the kitchen table to the front door and pushed it flush with the threshold. With the latch destroyed, the lock warped, and the desiccated wood around them pulped, she didn't have many options for security besides jerry-rigging a barricade. So she wiped sweat from her brow and went back to the kitchen and started dragging over chairs.

Samedi watched, impassive. After she'd hauled the fourth and final chair from kitchen to foyer, he cocked his head and mewled.

"Right," she muttered. "Your room's a mess too."

She climbed the stairs and got to work. Randall's boys had snapped her broom in half, so she had to make do with a half-broom and a dustpan to clean the scattered litter and the dried, crusted cat shit. After twenty minutes, she'd collected most of the mess into a garbage bag and refilled the litter box. She didn't bother with the cat castle. Samedi didn't seem to mind, satisfied at least that his toilet worked.

She checked the basement next, levering the frame lock, undoing the deadbolt, and keying her way through the rest of the security. Plant scents and mysticism wafted up from below, accompanied by the burble of hydroponics. The plants, though living, hung their heads limp-necked, beaten.

"It's okay," she whispered, padding between the planters and stroking her fingers along dewy leaves and muscle-thick stems. "You'll be okay."

It could have been worse, after all. It could have been much, much worse.

She picked her way over to a storage closet and swung it open. A dozen velvet bags hung by golden string from hooks on the back of the door, each marked by alchemical and astrological symbols. Randall had stolen the crates from the stock shelves, but he hadn't bothered with the powders. Deirdre plucked a purple bag off a hook, a golden key and harp of Orpheus stitched into its front. Inside, she dug up a pinch of night-dark powder and put it beneath her tongue. It tasted of salt and campfire. She took a second pinch and buried it at the base of the dreamroot plant. Its narrow branches shivered in response, its plump fruit pulsed amber.

She pinched off a dreamer fruit and brought it to her lips.

"Randall Tyler Hill," she enunciated, careful not to swallow the powder in her mouth. She repeated it a second time in a whisper, like she was telling a secret to the sliver of flora in her fingers. "Randall Tyler Hill."

She put the dreamer fruit in her mouth and held it on her tongue. She focused on what Randall had said fifteen hours earlier.

(*"don't think we'll need much more, to be honest."*

"honey, we're all gonna pay…")

She bit down and the fruit turned to honey. She swallowed.

There would be weird dreams when she slept that night. Visions.

Her phone buzzed in her pocket as she climbed the stairs back up. Paul's number flashed on the screen.

"Hey," she answered.

"Hey," he replied, a murmur in her ear. *"How'd it go on your end?"*

"Not well. Nobody wants to talk. All I learned is that maybe Randall's a pimp. Maybe."

Paul chuckled humorlessly. *"I didn't do much better. He's ex-Aryan Nationalist, did some time in lockup for assault. I heard about the pimping thing too, so that's a lead."*

"If it's true, you can bet the Québécois know about it."

"It's worth checking out. I, uh, I have some other leads too. Randall was part of some weird church from the eighties and nineties, real big with his Aryan friends. The place burned down but it might still be worth asking about, especially since…" Paul trailed off. Ice clinked against glass in the background.

"Since what?" Deirdre asked. "And are you drinking?"

"Need to do something to shut up the ghosts." Paul coughed. *"Anyway, there's something else going on. I can't quite figure it out, but I think those kids with the cloaks are tied into some kind of…some kind of cult? There's a Bureau guy in town—"*

"This is a bad time to drink, Paul."

"Did Randall leave any downers behind?"

"I'll check."

"Well, unless I can get something to shut up these ghosts, whiskey will have to suffice."

Deirdre swallowed her response, all sharp edges and harsh words.

"I've got a day's worth of downers, still. Less, but I'm rationing. So yeah. I'll work the beat, see if I can't dig anything else up."

She took a moment, making sure the sharp words stayed down. "I'll check out the Québécois angle."

(*clink*)

"Are you sure you want to stay up there?" Paul asked. *"I have space for you here. I could take the loveseat."*

"I'm fine."

"Right. Well, if you need anything…"

"I'll call."

"I mean it."

"I know," she said. "But I'll be fine. Take it easy, alright? Don't wake up tomorrow too hungover to do shit."

"I won't."

"Uh-huh. Good night, Paul."

"Good night, Deirdre. Stay safe."

She hung up and pocketed the phone. Shook her head, knowing Paul would already be pouring another drink. Knowing he'd probably do it even if he had a whole bag of downers. She sighed, pushing those particular concerns aside for the more pressing ones. Rebuilding her bedroom, for one.

By the time she'd reassembled her squat into something resembling a home, the sky had bruised to twilight, burnt to night. She wiped more sweat from her brow, wiped her palms on her pants, and picked about her kitchen for something to eat. She settled on a pear, some jerky, and a glass of water for dinner. She double-checked all her plants, added a few nails into the boards crisscrossing the first-floor windows, and adjusted the furniture of her barricade. As she worked, the dreamer fruit began to fuzz her perceptions. Drowsiness weighted her eyelids.

She climbed upstairs and settled onto the torn sheets of her unframed bed. Put her phone on its charger.

Samedi padded into the room and mewled. The dreamer distorted the sound into a pitched rumble, feline thunder.

She got as comfortable as possible in the ruin of her invaded home and closed her eyes.

Something buzzed deep and low against the hardwood, but she no longer recognized the hum of her vibrating phone. The world abstracted against the dark screen of her eyelids.

The buzz came again, a beehive. A third and fourth time, equally unrecognizable.

Dreamer wrapped her in honeyed arms and cradled her into dreams and visions.

■■■

Paul leaned back in his roof deck chair and scrolled through the hundredth article about the Oceanrest riots he'd read since leaving the precinct. His head swam with overinformation, with remembered ghosts and desperate dead, with a serial killing case, with a day of rapid-fire intel. The whiskey wasn't helping, except with keeping the dead quiet. Oceanrest Rock & Blues radio streamed from a site buried under a dozen other sites. He reached the end of the latest article and went back to Google for more.

What the hell was he looking for?

July, 1997: a fight broke out between Aryan Nationalists and civil rights protesters outside Howland Butler's recording studio.

July, 1997: union strikers brawled with scabs outside a warehouse, police arrested eight.

July, 1997: a neo-Nazi slashed a teenager's face with a broken bottle. The PD arrested the assailant, but he got off with a probationary sentence.

Then quiet. From July 29th until August 16th, nothing.

August 17th: union strikers and strike-breakers clashed all along the docks. At the same time, a gun went off outside of Butler's recording studio, a bullet striking a protester in the neck. For a weekend, absolute chaos descended on the city. By August 20th, twelve people were dead, twenty-seven wounded, and twenty-one arrested. Butler's recording studio and church had both burnt down. Fire had gutted half the trailer park by US Highway 1. And a fog that had hung unnaturally about the late summer weekend lifted just as unnaturally. "Oceanrest fog," the *Chronicle* called it. "Trickster's fog," according to a Google search.

One conspiracy nut blogged that the fog had *caused* the riots, had somehow infested the minds of Oceanrest residents.

Paul gave up on that particular site.

His cursor hovered over a link to a YouTube video, an old VHS-quality recording of one of Butler's sermons. He didn't hit play, felt somehow afraid to. As if hearing the man's voice would be a kind of brainwashing, as if the long-gone reverend's words would plant some kind of seed in his subconscious...

The Oceanrest Rock & Blues streaming site skipped, cutting off one song halfway through and abruptly switching to the next.

Jim Morrison sang about how *People Are Strange*.

The night before, a ghost had appeared at the foot of his bed. Lucy McKinney had been her name, once. Her killer, or killers, had gouged out her eyes, carved out her tongue, and buried her somewhere in the ever-expanding forests outside of town. Her spirit had lit his room, hovering at the foot of his bed. She'd found him for the same reason they all found him—she wanted peace.

But there were only so many times he could fail before he gave up trying.

He refilled his rocks glass and kept scrolling, searching for some lead on Randall buried in twenty-year-old half-truths.

His phone buzzed on the tabletop, and Virgil's name flashed across the screen. He set his drink back on the plastic table and picked up.

"Hello?"

"Paul," Virgil said, straight to business, *"I did some digging for you regarding Randall Hill."*

"Yeah?"

An intake of breath through a microphone. *"Look, whatever it is you think you're doing, I think it'd be best if you stopped."*

"'scuze me?"

"I had some of my men put his name to some CIs, a few buddies of ours from north of the border. You're right about one thing, he's a dangerous man."

"So you're going to move on him then?"

A pause.

Paul snorted. "You're kidding me."

"All we have is hearsay," Virgil explained. *"We have no actionable evidence to bring against the guy."*

"What about your guys with the Québécois? You can't arrange for them to *find* some evidence?"

"The situation is complicated."

"Bullshit," Paul spat, one of the puzzle pieces snapping into place. "Randall's connected to the mob and you're letting them tie your hands."

"It's complicated—"

"So, what, you do nothing?" Paul stood on booze-wavered legs, plucked up his drink, and walked to the edge of the roof deck. Beyond the marina's halogens, the Atlantic sloshed black. "You just let this psycho go?"

"I'll keep digging, but unless we find something actionable—"

"You want me to sidecar on the serial slaying case, right? Well, this is the quid pro quo. Open a case on Randall and I'll work as an asset."

"Paul—"

"You want to be the marionette on the Québécois' strings? Go ahead and dance for 'em. But I'm doing this."

"Christ," Virgil muttered. *"You're a bastard of a mule when you've been drinking."*

"Been called worse," Paul said. "So. Where do we stand?"

Another of Virgil's long-suffering sighs crackled over the line. *"Alright. Since you plan to play gumshoe, this is what I can do for you: I won't bring you in for anything you're not caught at and I won't tip anyone off to anything I don't know about. You stay under the radar, you stay out of trouble."*

Paul nodded along with Virgil's words. "Will do."

"One last thing, teach,*"* the last syllable came sharp as a razorblade, *"if you come across anything in the way of evidence, anything that might be cause to pursue a formal case or make an arrest, you come to me immediately. You're a civilian, not an enforcement officer, not a licensed PI, and certainly not a goddamned vigilante. Understand?"*

"Understood."

The line clicked dead, and Paul pocketed the cellphone. Car keys jingled in his pants and his fingers went from phone to keychain. He took them out and peered down at them in his palm.

Virgil had helped him out more than a few times since his arrival in Oceanrest. As tenuous as their friendship had become, Virgil remained a reliable ally.

Nearly four years earlier, Paul had downed most of a bottle of whiskey on his lonesome, gotten into his car, and torn around the abandoned side streets of Squatter City. He'd gone up to US-1 and out to Jonesport and Machias, turned back around, and blew through cloudy night back toward Oceanrest, crying the whole time. The cop who'd pulled him over had given him a black eye and a bruised cheek, but the ticket had been worse. Operating under the influence. Driving in excess of 30 MPH over the posted speed limit. A list of minor traffic offenses a foot long. Almost certain jail time.

Virgil helped broker the deal wherein Paul Somers kept his license and the ticketing officer avoided an assault suit.

Paul had just wanted to know what it might've felt like, at the end, for his daughter. What it might've felt like before the crash.

He jerked his arm back, nearly launched the car keys into the sea, stopped just short of letting go. He needed the car, now more than ever. The idea flattened him. His arm fell limp to his side, the keys back in his pocket. Draining the rest of his whiskey, he settled for hurling the glass into vast ocean darkness.

The bottle followed shortly after, though he stumbled in the throw and ended up breaking it on the end of the pier.

He made his way back to the laptop.

He didn't learn anything important.

Story of his life.

CHAPTER SIX

US Highway 1. A gray snake of concrete writhed past her. The Oceanrest exit let off onto an artery road, two lanes on either side of a double yellow line, a dying pulse bloodletting into the sea. Before the iron lung economy, there'd been a trailer park by the highway, and an ice cream shop, and a very large church. Their razed bodies curled in shallow graves, their bones hidden in underbrush. A monster licked the skulls empty, scavenged the flesh.

Teeth clattered against teeth, claw against claw. Hungry things fought over rubble and salvage.

Mountains moved. Vertebrae aligned. The black sea of the cosmos rippled.

Deirdre crawled over cold dirt, panting, her calves tattered by jagged teeth, skin sore from sandpaper tongues. Behind her, a pair of hungry jaws gaped forever. She screamed at the sight of their bottomless throats. Their bodies uncurled in sun flare, a scream of light ending in darkness.

Zoom out.

Warehouses rusted, windows broke. Vermin bred in the walls. A graffiti artist found a homeless man discolored with frostbite, ice-skinned.

Time passed. Warehouses shed exoskeletons and became artist lofts. Collapsing Victorians and colonials slouched into their roles as homeless shelters. The suburbs hunched into Squatter City. Malleus Industries International relocated its North American East offices to Oceanrest. Highrises sprouted overnight, a newborn downtown squealing in glass and neon. Oceanrest shivered out from its old skin. Everything became something else, eventually. Seeds sprouted in a hydroponic basement and stems of mystic flora crawled from tender earth.

do you hear me, Deirdre? a voice whispered from behind a too-thin wall.

This was not Gaea, this was not Luna.

This voice had no vined arms, no deep soil, no warm sun.

This voice scared her.

She stumbled through coils of vapor, no longer bird's-eyed on the city but fish-lens'd somewhere new. She clambered up Escher stairs and pulled herself into the stomach of a warped tower. Words pressed against the insides of her skull and none of them were hers. Bellowing beasts roared over each other, vying for dominance. They gnashed teeth, hissed. Their war banged a frenzy in her head. She pressed on. Somewhere above, a prophet sat on a holy throne, his face a squid.

One of the voices in her head belonged to the priest. Which one?

let's make a deal...

Not that one.

Who owned that voice?

Or what?

She reached up, rung after rung on an endless ladder. Pulled. Panted. Pulled.

A clawed hand grabbed her calf and skewered the muscles there.

She screamed.

Dirt silenced her. Raw dirt, stuffed in her mouth, down her throat. She clawed her way out of a shallow grave. Trees loomed overhead, branches knit to hide to the skies. A truck rumbled down a nearby street, headlights pointed south. A voice whispered inside her skull. The voice of a vast shadow, of a thing scraping its way through a paper-thin wall.

what do you want? It asked, It with a capital "I."

your enemy has an enemy, dear Deirdre.

The voice could deliver desires on silver platters, courtesy of its silver tongue, but the server was the one being served. The consumer, consumed. The shadow, honey-tongued, lured victims to Its jaws by granting djinn wishes.

It, with a capital "I," was one of three voices in her head.

One of three monsters.

One of three.

The high priest prophet put on a magic show, a shadow play. He puppetted shade-shapes against reality, gestured at their illusory forms, made them flesh. One hand waited behind his back, a hungry blade sleeve-hidden. He dug a barbed tongue into frightened hearts while the audience watched the puppet show. He licked bones. He lived inside the ribcages of old dead, sucking dry the marrow.

From the docks, she saw Paul's houseboat rise and fall on slow Atlantic waves. A woman stared at her through the marina-facing window. No. The woman didn't stare—couldn't. She had no eyes. She'd felt her way to desperate hope on instinct after digging herself out of a shallow grave. They'd cut out her tongue, turned her skin into a dress of grue and glyphs.

The woman's tongueless jaw unhinged, and a shriek slit the firmament.

...

Deirdre jerked awake, her hand reflexively latching onto the grip of her revolver. Her eyes flew wide on the wreckage of her room, iron sights leveled on the door, hammer back, ready, ready, ready—

Sweat soaked into her stained mattress. Silence hissed in her ears.

"The dream," she whispered, launching off the bed to the floor. She burst through her bedroom door and crossed to the bathroom, kicking aside moisturizers and hair products she hadn't cleaned up the night before. She had to take notes, write as much of the dreamer vision down as she could before it dissipated from her memories. Why the bathroom? She spun back toward the bedroom, remembering notebooks and pens.

Something wet and slimy smeared the arch of her foot.

Toothpaste.

On impulse, she snatched the tube from the tiled floor and squeezed a worm of blue onto her fingertip. She pressed it against the bathroom mirror and scrawled out a letter, then another, and another, trying to hold onto fraying images even as they vanished before her. The tendons in her hand flexed and twitched, English glyphs forming half by thought and half through some act of automatic writing.

Stepping back, she dropped the tube. Stared at the scrawl of pasted letters smearing the glass.

Tongue writhed from the ashes too,
they f e a s t and h o w l and e a t s
two beasts, three?, one tastes the sky,
eats until the sunshine dies

The sense of it fragmented from her mind, dissipating beneath the pressing reality of the waking world.

"What the hell *does that* mean?" she asked.

...

Paul groaned over the bleat of his alarm, slammed the snooze button, and crawled to the edge of his mattress. Four hours of sleep. He gulped a breath, burped whiskey and gin. The wound in the side of his head throbbed. His clothes felt filth-crusted, miasmic. He yanked them off and tossed them in the hamper. Couldn't quite get the image of fungal spores out of his head.

"Come on," he muttered to himself. "Don't be a fuckup."

He chuckled.

"Well…don't be *more* of a fuckup."

He went to the sink and swallowed three brown ibuprofen pills and two beer steins full of water.

The clock told him it was 9:15 AM and reminded him that another alarm would go off in ten minutes. He snapped the alarm off and found a cup of coffee at the bottom of a three-day-old carafe. He drank it without sugar or milk and grimaced through the mashed-cigarette flavor, slapping himself on the cheeks a couple of times for good measure.

The docks were livelier in the morning. The sun set the sea alight and flashed off the sails of fishing boats. Men who usually seemed gray-faced and ancient looked younger, rejuvenated by the summer breeze, throwing baggage aboard ships or dragging lobster traps out onto the docks. A long-haul truck rumbled toward one of the few still-operable warehouses. Paul opened the window above the sink and let the sound of the day wash over him. Days like these made it easy to imagine the way Oceanrest used to be twenty or thirty years earlier, the idyllic El Dorado Virgil talked about.

He opened his eyes as wide as he could and let the salty air sear them awake.

He got dressed and went to the bathroom. Splashed cold water on his face and examined his worn, exhausted eyes in the mirror.

For a second, he thought he saw the white cloth of the eyeless woman's tunic, but it was only his towel. Still, he cursed in surprise and reddened with embarrassment. Just a towel. He laughed at himself.

He went to his ashtray and plucked up the half-joint of sixth-sense depressants waiting there. He lit up, took a couple hits, and snuffed it. There wasn't much left, maybe two or three drags, if he was willing to burn his fingertips for them. Unless Deirdre had more to spare, whiskey would indeed have to suffice.

Breakfast came in the form of three spoonfuls of peanut butter and a glass of souring milk.

Then he got to work.

■■■

Deirdre found Samedi batting her phone across the floor. She shooed the cat away, unplugged phone from charger, and checked her messages. Her blood froze at what she saw.

A series of texts from Razz's burner phone.

'hey D, Frank says u were looking 4 Randall—same guy from ur place?'

'asked around a little & think I can help'

'see? so Im not some fkn dumbass dropout w/ nothing going on. I can handle myself. I can help.'

Her mouth opened in silent scream. She typed a response, *'Razz DO NOT get involved with this.'*

No answer.

She typed, *'Not kidding, Randall is a dangerous man, I don't care who you think will have your back, STAY OUT.'*

Samedi clawed at the doorframe.

Razz didn't answer.

Deirdre paced, frantic. Typing so fast she missed some of the letters, *'This is my business Razz I wll handle it myself DO NOT GET INVOLVD.'*

Nothing. Samedi stopped clawing and cocked his head, staring at her.

She called Razz's phone. It rang to voicemail. She hung up, tried again. Voicemail. A third time, steam building up in her chest, smoke in her throat, feeling a fire might explode inside her and turn her to dust. Voicemail. She squeezed the phone until the casing creaked, restrained the urge to smash it against the wall.

'COME HERE TONIGHT WE HAVE TO TALK.'

She paced in tight circles, kicking frustration. Samedi watched, impassive. She ran her hands through the sweat-frizzed hair crowning her scalp, pulled until it hurt. Razz, foolish Razz. A kid. A goddamned kid still trying to figure out the world around him, even just the *town* around him. And Randall?

She shivered.

"Don't look at me like that," she snarled at Samedi. Samedi gave a small growl of his own in response and went back to scratching the doorframe. She leaned against the wall clutching the phone so hard she was surprised it didn't break. Breath came quick and heavy to her lungs, trying to put out the cold-hot burn caged between her ribs.

Had Razz not heard her yesterday? Had he completely missed the message?

Had she failed so spectacularly in expressing it?

She shook herself off, pushed away from the wall. There were leads to follow, questions to ask, doors to knock on. If she could get to Randall fast, if she could dig his whereabouts out from under some Québécois' fingernails, she could handle the situation before Razz found himself in the middle of it. If she could do that, then the David Winters problem solved itself, and the Razz problem—

The phone rang in her hand. She whipped it up, hoping to see Razz's name flashing across the screen.

'RANDALL' the phone screamed.

Hand shaking, she swiped the "Answer" icon and brought the device to her ear.

"What the fuck do you want?" she said, low and quiet, steeling her voice against a quaver.

"*Deirdre, I just wanted to drop you a line regarding our recent disputes and make sure there aren't any hard feelings between the two of us.*" She could hear the smirk in his voice.

"Fuck off."

"*Ah, so I see that there* are *hard feelings. Well, if you're upset about the product loss, I promise I will pay for all of it in two weeks.*"

"Not enough."

He chuckled. "*I think you misunderstand the balance of power in this relationship. I already have what I want, you see, and I'm going out of my way to offer to repay you in due time so that you might eventually have the things that you want as well.*"

"Someone out there knows where you sleep."

"*I see I've put you in a mood. Please, understand that these matters are mere trifles. Well, I ain't in the mind to preach, so I won't go into that subject just yet. Let me frame this in a way easier for simple minds to understand: I hear that my name has graced a lot of lips this past day and so, and a man is liable to be pissed off about that kind of thing. Should my name keep passing lips, I'll bring all manner of hell down on you and yours.*"

"You son of a—"

"My momma was, in fact, a bitch. But am I making myself clear? Your friends have been asking after me and I aim to stop them, with extreme prejudice if I must. I'm calling to recommend, dear Deirdre, that you fuckin' drop this shit now, before people have to get hurt. People that you may have particular affection toward. Your buddy Paul, for instance, or that kid'a yours."

His words hollowed her skin, emptied her innards. Only cold remained.

Her lips fought for syllables and found none.

On the other end of the line, Randall laughed. *"Cat got your tongue? You always did have a thing for strays, huh? Well if you'll excuse me, I got some business to attend to. Be smart, Deirdre. I'd hate to see you hurt."*

Click.

She dressed in a hurry. Quiet-soled sneakers, athletic pants, black tee-shirt, leather jacket. She stuffed the snubnose in a hip holster, attached it to her waistband, and stormed downstairs. She flew past the barricade down the length of the main hallway to the kitchen and out the back door.

Froze.

A pocket knife pinned a photograph to the door.

An instant photo taken of Razz at a suburban house party. The tip of the blade had been driven through Razz's photo-captured chest.

"Stop now," Randall said in dark red ink on the back of the picture.

Someone had taken this photo in secret, unobserved, a white face in a mostly-white crowd.

Deirdre crushed the photo in her hand and threw it back inside. She closed and locked the back door and went into the woods, pretending not to be afraid.

CHAPTER SEVEN

"That's an awful dangerous question for a man from away t'be asking."

The odor of fish and salt and hard-worked sweat stewed about the old man. He smelled of Oceanrest's history made manifest. A lobster trap hung from his scarred hands, an erubescent crawl of crustaceans within.

Paul wet his lips. "I'm not here to judge," he said, holding his beaten memo pad up, "I just need information."

"A'yuh? And why'd someone need information 'bout something so long done?"

Paul weighed his response, scales tilting in his skull regarding which institution the seaman would disdain more—the police or the university. He stepped farther onto the pier, staring up at the man on the deck above. "I'm working with Virgil LeDuff. There's reason to suspect the, ah, the serial murders are somehow tied to Butler's church."

The old man tossed the lobster trap aside. "That so?"

"It is."

The old man daggered his eyes to scour Paul's face. "Who are you, then? You don't look like a cop."

"I'm a profiler."

The man scratched bristling salt-pepper scruff. "Like on the TV? The wife's always watching those shows."

"Sort of," Paul said, dodging the truer "not at all."

"You think you'll get closer to catching the sonuvabitch if you learn about Butler's church?"

"We do."

The old man smacked his lips and nodded. He went around to the pier-facing ladder and climbed down to Paul's level. "Name's Wallace. Captain

Wallace. This here trawler's called Diane, after my daughter. Unnerstand what I'm saying?"

"Of course," Paul lied.

Wallace snorted, spit over the pier side. "So what's it you want to know?"

Tattoo removal scars marred Wallace's knuckles and the backs of his hands.

Paul opened the memo pad. "How many people would you say attended Butler's services every week?"

Wallace shrugged. "Not enough to fill every pew in the place, but more'n most people would admit nowadays."

"Our records suggest that Butler was tied into a gang of Aryan Nationals for most of the nineties. Would you be able to confirm that? Or do you know anything about it?"

Wallace stiffened, his face taut with restraint. "A'yuh, I can confirm that. Butler had a pretty fair number of strings to pull before things fell down on him."

"You attended his services regularly?"

"You trying to say something?"

"Not at all. I just want to make sure you're a reliable source of information."

Wallace grunted. "A'yuh, I attended pretty regular for a while. It was a different time."

"Of course. And the content of Butler's sermons…?"

Wallace's scarred hands vanished into overall pockets. "He was the usual fire and brimstone type. A thumper, yeah? But he had sort of a hypnotic personality. It was hard not to listen to him. Hard not to buy into what he said. 'Specially considering the troubles."

"Troubles?"

"You know, everyone going out of business, losing jobs down every wharf and pier…it's not wrong to want answers."

"What kind of answers did Butler offer?"

"About what you'd expect from a bible thumper with Aryan friends."

"Anything you remember specifically?"

Wallace's gaze distilled to a glare. "No."

Paul closed his memo pad for what felt like the thousandth time that day. "Well, thanks for your help."

Halfway down the pier, Wallace called after him. "Wait!"

Paul stopped, turning back.

Wallace stood with one hand outstretched, a look of pained embarrassment across his face. "Goddammit." He dropped his arm back to his side. "You come back here and…and I'll tell you what I know."

Paul raised his eyebrows, walking back. "What is that, exactly?"

"Look, I just want to be clear…I never had any hate for the coloreds or anything, not any Jews neither. My wife's part Indian. So before I say anything about anything, you ought to know that."

"Right."

"I wasn't dragged into it on account of personal reasons. Lots of folk ended up down Butler's church on account of they were scared, not 'cause they were hateful. And on account of Butler being…being strange in certain ways. So lots of folks, myself as one of 'em, weren't there on account of…of what those protesters accused us of. You know?"

Paul gave a halfhearted nod. "Uh-huh."

Wallace glanced around, as if searching for people within earshot. The nearest people Paul could see were three piers away, taking down sail on a schooner. Still, Wallace gestured him closer, hushing his voice. "Now I know you're an educated man, Mr. Profiler, but there's parts of Butler's past that aren't on the records. Things that need a different sort of smarts to see into."

"Such as?"

Wallace chewed on his response, beckoning Paul farther down the pier. "You know the old Blackwood place? Out north of Denton?"

"I know it."

"You ought to go up there. A girl lives there now. She knows these things better'n I do."

"What do *you* know?"

"Butler wasn't just a preacher. Some of the Aryan boys weren't just thugs, neither."

"What do you mean?"

"Butler had his hands in something evil. It's how he roped so many folk into the congregation. He had a kinda gravity. You felt he knew things about the world that you didn't, and not just in holy matters."

"What other matters are you referring to?"

Wallace took Paul around the shoulders and guided him seaward. "Butler plucked strings with the Quebecs, the Aryans, even the cops. There's those of us around who think he caused the riots, back then, or at least made 'em worse than they ought'a been. Some of us even say he did worse than that."

Paul frowned. Wallace had changed tracks at some point, veered away from the central questions. "Did you know a man named Randall Hill?"

Wallace's arm dropped from around Paul's shoulders. "R-Randall Hill?"

"Yeah."

"I knew him. Very close with Butler, he were."

"What do you know about him?"

"Used to be very big with the A.N., very big with Butler's crowd. Something happened involving him and this colored boy, he ended up in jail a few years. Got back out just before the riots, which I'm not certain is any coincidence. But that's hardly half the matter." Wallace pursed his lips, his face wrinkling around them. "Are you a man of any kind of faith?"

"Excuse me?"

"Are you a Christian man? Jewish, something?"

"Agnostic."

"You superstitious at all?"

"Not particularly, no."

Wallace shook his head sharply, as if disappointed. "Go up the Blackwood Estate, ask for Nora."

"I will, but right now I'm talking to you."

"If you're after Randall, asking stupid questions after Butler's old burntdown church, you're not talking to me any longer. Not now, not ever. I got a daughter, for God's sake. I should'a let you walk away and kept my head down, but…" He glanced back at the docks again, and this time he saw something. His eyes went wide. "You're in deeper trouble than you know. Wait here."

"What? What are you talking ab—?" Paul started to ask, but Wallace was already gone, climbing up the ladder into the trawler.

Paul stood there, stock still in confusion. Turning back to the docks, his head spinning with Wallace's aberrant behavior, he saw what Wallace had seen—three rough-looking men coming down the pier toward him, clad in uniform. They wore bulky jackets, jeans, and jackboots. Aryan pride inked their skin.

The guy in front had an Iron Cross tattooed over his Adam's apple. Flanking Iron Cross, Paul recognized Isaiah from the attack at Deirdre's. The third boy was new, his fingers tattooed with unreadable scrawl. Behind the boys, tailing them at a dozen yards, Randall climbed out of an age-rusted pickup truck.

"That's the guy," Isaiah confirmed to Iron Cross.

"You Paul Somers?" Iron Cross yelled anyway.

"Who?" Paul asked.

The third thug whipped out an asp baton, extending it with a snap.

"Really wish you'd listened," Isaiah said earnestly.

Iron Cross reached into his jacket pocket and came back out with knuckle dusters. "Black pussy ain't worth it, buddy. No pussy is."

Randall walked calmly down the pier, slipping between his leather-jacketed comrades like water through a sieve. "So, you're Deirdre's action man." He smirked, sizing Paul up with theatric disappointment. Started tugging a thick pair of workman's gloves over his hands. "You're full white?"

"Excuse me?"

"Parents, grandparents, all that? What are you? Gyppo? Jew?"

Paul glanced between the four men, trying to ignore hot sweat beading his skin, cool adrenaline pulsing his veins. "If you'll excuse me, I need to check in at the precinct."

Randall held up a gloved hand. "I don't think you do, actually."

The kid with the baton smirked, smarmy.

Paul moved to leave, and Randall put a hand on his chest.

"Anglo-Saxon," Randall said, pushing Paul back a few inches. "An Anglo-Saxon with a doctorate degree doing some homeless pussy porchmonkey's shufflin' dirty work. Don't you have any pride?"

"Faggot-ass white knight," Baton snickered.

"Keep quiet," Randall barked. "I'm talking."

Baton went quiet.

"Get out of my way," Paul said.

"Afraid not, Paul Somers," Randall replied. "See, my name's been tumbling from your lips non-stop since our last chat, and I don't like that kind of attention."

Paul rushed for an opening, trying to slip through their blockade, but Randall grabbed his arm with serpent speed and threw him hard to the ground. Paul hit the pier face-first, all air exploding out of him in a *whuff*. He scrambled on hands and knees until a boot came out of nowhere and crashed into his ribs, flipping him over.

Laughter roared around him.

"I'm sorry, Paul, I am, but you know what they say—spare the rod."

Baton came down with the asp hard on Paul's guts.

"So consider this an object lesson. A learning experience."

Another boot came out of the blurry world and smashed his ribs again.

Paul groaned for air, rolling back onto his front and managing to get on hands and knees. His airless vision pulsed, the world fading to a narrow glimpse of jackboots, lobster traps, crates. He maneuvered on all fours, blood boiling against the Aryans' laughter.

Paul got focus on Baton's boots and kicked out at them. His shoe met Baton's leg mid-shin, and he heard something crunch beneath his attack. Baton's laughter cut into an animal yelp, and his body slammed to the ground next to Paul's. Paul scrambled to his feet, spinning to keep his eyes on the Aryans.

Randall lifted his eyebrows. "Now you really fucked up."

Randall nodded in Paul's direction.

Isaiah and Iron Cross charged.

Paul backpedaled from the attack, but the maneuver was pointless. They were on him in seconds.

CHAPTER EIGHT

Deirdre headed toward La Femme Rouge through the woods. Deciduous leaves whispered in the summer breeze, conifers silently needling. An ever-present mist coiled around her ankles. Her phone's screen showed one bar of service, and no new messages from either Paul or Razz. She adjusted her leather jacket against the eternal chill of the forest, fingered the frame of the binoculars she'd brought.

La Femme Rouge was the Québécois' headquarters, a three-story square of all-white building that had once been a hotel. The lowest floor served as a bar and "gentleman's club," the second floor as a brothel, and the third as the offices of the mob itself. Nobody trifled with La Femme Rouge, nobody visited trouble upon it.

So it came as a shock to see three police cruisers pulling into the parking lot when she reached the tree line looking out on the property.

"What the hell is this?" She leveraged into a crouch, kneeling in a blanket of leaves and pine needles. She lifted the binoculars and scoped the scene through the lenses.

Six cops climbed out of the vehicles, approached the entryway to La Femme Rouge. Two of the officers lagged behind uncertainly, clearly unsure if it was wise to approach a slumbering dragon. The guy in the front kept a hand on his holstered pistol the entire time.

The leading officer knocked on the front door. Waited. Knocked again. He glanced up at the forest, and for a second Deirdre thought his eyes found hers, that he'd spotted her somehow from a hundred feet out. A cool shiver rolled down her spine, and she felt something tug at the back of her jacket. She spun with the sensation, dropping the binoculars, and went for her snubnose.

Nothing there, of course. Just conifers and deciduous boughs, birds flitting between branches.

Just a slight dewy mist whispering over earth.

She shook herself off and picked the binocs back up from the forest floor. The lead uniform was speaking to several indistinct figures inside. The cop lifted a piece of paper in front of the open door and muttered something short and sharp. The shadows within the dim structure shifted, and two men stepped out onto the porch. They were dark-haired, wearing jeans and rumpled plaid button-ups, weapons hip-holstered. They undid their belts, holsters included, and handed them back to the shades behind them. Then the police led them toward the squad cars.

Deirdre's brow knit at the scene. The two Québécois got into the rear of one of the cruisers. The doors were shut behind them, and the vehicles pulled out and headed toward town.

Just like that, they were gone. However many Québécois had been in La Femme Rouge ten minutes ago, there were now two fewer.

Small blessings.

"Thanks," she said, as if Gaea or Luna could hear.

She crept the tree line around the rear of the building, out of sight of the front-window adverts and the pre-noon barflies, and slipped the binoculars into an inside jacket pocket. She closed her eyes and summoned the energy for a cantrip, a quick little charm she'd picked up as a kid. A spell to go unnoticed, a small piece of magic that drew gazes away from her.

Most of her spells followed that theme: to go unnoticed, unheard, unseen.

Such had been her childhood, until she'd hopped the train to Oceanrest.

She felt the spell ignite, a flexion of magic briefly tightening her musculature. A gasp of exertion parted her lips.

She crossed toward the building's rear entrance, trusting the curtains of the back windows and the nature of her charm to keep her unnoticed. As expected, the door was locked, prompting a second spell—*silence*, a cantrip that muted all noise within a few feet of her body. That one took a little more effort, causing a sweat to glisten her brow. She wiped it off with the back of her hand, wiped her hand on her jeans, then fished out a pair of lockpicks and got to work.

The lock undone, the door swung in with barely a whisper, old hinges quieted by her magic.

Her sneakers crossed soundlessly over the hardwood floor, not a single plank creaked beneath her weight. She dropped into a crouch and hugged the wall of the tight, dark foyer, moving toward a wide intersection a few feet away.

Voices carried in from the bar area to her right:

"…Somalians, down by the docks there."

"Didn't think they'd come 'round this far."

"Business is business, eh?"

"Well tell 'em to go back where they came from."

"Somalia?"

"Portland."

Laughter followed. Deirdre tilted her head around the corner and saw a battered hardwood hall running five or six feet before opening into a barely lit lounge. Precambrian beer and a decade of Maine winter mud stained the floor, black grime separating each scarred plank from the ones around it.

"You get Virgil on the horn, yet?" one of the voices asked from out of sight.

The reply came in French.

Deirdre shifted from her crouch and turned left toward a wide stairway leading up. At the top of the stairs, she stuck close to the wall and rose to her full height. She almost turned the corner when she heard a woman's voice:

"Marcy, shit, I can't sleep on this stuff…"

"Stop pacing, you're just wiring yourself up."

"I got the jitters."

"Come in and sit down."

She froze, focusing her energy on strengthening her charms, channeling pure willpower and physical exertion into magic. She knew a spell that could render her invisible for a while, but the effort would lay her low too quickly, wouldn't leave her any energy for the trip back out.

Under her breath and quieted by cantrips, she prayed that the women would stay away. Footsteps padded through the second floor toward her, then away from her again.

From around the corner, the woman continued. "I don't like it, Marce. What'd he give us?"

"Just some speed, okay? Come here."

"I feel real fucked up."

"Just come here. I've got you."

A door closed somewhere in the hall. Deirdre's whole body relaxed at the sound.

She turned the corner into the second floor. Chandelier lights hung from the ceiling, stained glass shards draped from a hundred strings. All the bulbs were off. Deirdre crept beneath them down the hall to the next and last staircase, the one leading to the top floor, the offices of the mafia high-ups. The place where they'd keep their books, and hopefully a paper trail for Randall Hill.

She paused outside one of the dozen doors lining the hallway and listened to one woman comfort another. She wondered what stories wrote themselves across the bedsheets in so many rooms, how many of them ended in jittery pacing up and down an unlit hall.

But there were more pressing concerns.

She picked the lock on the next staircase and ascended to the windowless third floor.

More doors, more overhead lights unlit. The de facto offices of the city's wealthiest criminals.

"Time to get to work," she muttered, knowing no one heard her. She padded past the first few doors without bothering with the locks. She tried to focus on her sixth sense, but the cantrips kept distracting her. Magic was exhausting work. The quick-and-dirty magic of cantrips even more so. Sweat beaded down her ribs and wet the fabric at the base of her spine. Psychic stimulants would have helped, but she hadn't bothered with them. She'd been too panicked, too rushed to find the next lead.

The first lock she picked led into a security lounge.

A wall of screens flickered black-and-white footage at her from across the room. Three empty chairs sat facing each other. She stepped into the room and leaned toward the screens, each of them showing a different section of the building. Five cameras covered the bar and lounge from different angles, four more covered the grounds, two on the parking lot, two facing the inbound road, two on the second floor hallway. She pursed her lips. Her spells wouldn't hide her from security cameras.

She closed the door behind her and started searching for recording hardware. It wasn't hard to find in the small space: three desktop computer towers in a thicket of wires. She frowned at the steel cases and got to work getting them open. Electronic guts greeted her after she pried off their shells. She unraveled them into their basic parts. As soon as the first guard opened the door, the Québécois would know someone had broken in, but at least they wouldn't know it had been *her*. She tucked recovered hard drives into various jacket pockets until they were heavy and bulky with weight.

She opened the door slowly back onto the third floor. No sign of life awaited her.

The next door showed her a luxurious bedroom, an empty four-post California King and an armoire she chose not to open. She imagined the door directly across from it would have a facsimile room, reserved for Québécois members or some special VIP list of clients. She checked the read-out on her phone and found it was already 11:02 AM. It wouldn't be long before people started showing up for a drink. Wouldn't be long before someone came up to the third floor to conduct business…

An office waited behind the door of the third lock she picked, a wide desk with heavy books stacked on top of it. A grin crossed her face. File cabinets, multiple dictionary-thick ledgers waiting face-open on the desk, and a single stack of cash as a cherry on top—all the cliché of crooked accounting. Closing the door behind her, she got to snooping.

She flipped through the open ledgers, red and black names and numbers, jotted notes as to who owed who how much, and found no mention of Randall. The second ledger held more of the same. Frank's name appeared a few times. It looked like he was getting into debt again, even with his work for the Québécois. Deirdre shook her head, moved on to a third ledger. Stopped.

A padlock on a drawer by her feet winked up at her.

She wiped sweat from her brow, bent low, and returned to her picks. Once she'd wrenched it open, the drawer proved to contain a second set of books.

She brought the newfound ledgers up to the desktop with the others and flipped one open.

An entirely different set of names and numbers. This time, Randall Hill showed up. Frequently.

But why two different sets of books? Deirdre's brow furrowed at the question. It wasn't as if one set of ledgers held legit holdings and the other set showed criminal holdings. Both sets had multiple books of each. So why would there be multiple sets? Why the padlock? Unless someone was skimming from the company coffers. Unless…

A key scraped the lock outside.

Deirdre closed her current ledger, moved to the side of the door, and flipped off the lights.

The door swung open. A middle-aged white man with wispy brown hair stepped in, flipped the lights back on. Deirdre dropped her palm to the grip of her gun as the man walked deeper into the room, not even glancing at her. At least…not until he got to the desk and saw the extra ledgers.

The accountant whirled around, his eyes taking a second longer than expected to find Deirdre and focus on her.

She wrenched her gun from its holster.

He got his own gun out at the same time.

Their barrels pointed at each other, neither fired. Fingers hesitated on triggers.

"Who sent you?" the accountant asked, eyes plate-wide and skin panic-pale. "I said *who the fuck sent you!*?"

CHAPTER NINE

Paul leapt back from Iron Cross' first swing, but the kid kept running. Paul threw up his hands but the knuckle dusters went between them and mashed his sternum. He stumbled back from the blow, barely keeping balance, suddenly aware of the exact length of the pier and the depth of the sea below.

"Grab him!" Iron Cross yelled.

Isaiah closed the distance unbelievably fast. Paul swung out, trying to remember his boxing training from years ago, but his follow-through was weak. He clipped Isaiah's chin to little effect. Isaiah ran into him hard, football tackle, and the two of them slammed into the pier. The kid with the baton limped his way toward them too.

Behind them, Randall's voice taunted, "Us whites gotta have each other's backs, you know. Gotta stick together."

Isaiah tried to wreathe Paul's body with his limbs, but Paul bucked him off and scrambled to his hands and knees. Sunlight cut the water about five feet away.

A lash of pain snapped across his back, and he dropped face first back to the pier.

"I don't want to have to hurt you," Randall said. "But you've gone and betrayed the team."

Paul got back on his feet and spun around fist-first. Baton backpedaled, put too much weight on his injured shin, and collapsed to his knees. Paul moved to press the assault, but Isaiah was already on him from behind, grabbing at his arms. Paul groaned, thrashing and yelling. "I'm with the fucking cops!"

Iron Cross reappeared from Paul's periphery, and a blast of pain hammered Paul's guts. Air fled his lungs, his shouts choked to silence.

"You're not with anyone," Randall said, appearing as a mere shadow in Paul's dizzied vision. "We checked."

Paul gaped fish-lipped for air. Isaiah threw him forward and Iron Cross tripped his legs at the shins. The pier rushed up to meet him, another blow against his beaten body. Paul scrabbled on the planks, driven by flight response and adrenaline. Baton must have gotten back up—another lash of pain sliced against Paul's scapula.

"My advice?" Randall huffed. "Keep your head down. This whole thing will blow over in no time."

Paul's throat gagged for words but couldn't find them.

"This doesn't affect you. Doesn't need to, at least."

A boot crashed into his ribs, put him on his back. His lungs reopened and sucked air.

"Fuckin' faggot," Baton said.

A glob of mucus saliva spattered Paul's cheek.

"Peter!" Randall said. "We don't *spit*."

"He kicked my—"

"I don't care what he did. Savages spit."

Paul's mottled vision cleared, revealing the silhouettes of his assailants. He saw Baton/Peter's limp, saw the kid turn toward Randall. He swung himself over onto all fours and threw his weight into the side of Baton/Peter's legs. The kid went over the pier side and splashed into the Atlantic.

Randall laughed.

Iron Cross hammered dusters into Paul's back and sprawled him out again.

Then shotgun thunder boom-crashed from overhead and everything went silent.

"You leave that man alone," Wallace growled from the trawler, "or I'll put you down where you stand."

Iron Cross and Isaiah backed away, while Peter treaded water for the pier side ladder.

"Chris Wallace? Is that you?"

"Randall," Wallace said.

Paul pushed himself up to all fours, groaning against the bruises and abrasions flaring across his skin. Standing straight ached him head to toe, but he managed it. Isaiah and Iron Cross retreated to Randall's shadow; Wallace stood on the trawler deck clasping a shotgun. Peter clambered up the ladder, soaked and dripping seawater.

Randall's smile glinted sunlight. "Well, I'll be. You got rid of the tattoos."

Wallace's grip tightened on his gun. "I don't want you here. None of ye."

"You married that *injun*, right?"

"That's none of your business."

"Kids," Randall said, not bothering to look at his cohorts, "why don't you wait in the car?"

Iron Cross, Peter, and Isaiah went back to Randall's truck. Peter glared overshoulder at Paul as he limped away.

"I'm—I'm telling you to leave," Wallace said, a stammer draining the threat from his words.

"But this is a reunion," Randall answered, still smiling. He stepped forward, closer to Paul and Wallace both. "Christopher Wallace, long time no see. The years haven't been too kind to you, looks like."

"You're not welcome, you—"

"How's that daughter of yours?" Randall interrupted. "She oughta be, what, eighteen, now? Seventeen?"

Wallace's lips went limp.

"She get your genes? Your sister was a real looker, gods rest her soul."

"Don't talk about my family," Wallace barely whispered.

Paul staggered forward, trying not to cradle himself. Trying not to show the extent of his pain.

Randall's smile shone bright and terrible as a burning corpse. "Well, you take care, Chris. Give your wife and daughter my fondest regards. You live over on Crescent View, right? Nice neighborhood. Good schools." He winked. "I'll send a card."

Randall turned and walked back to his truck, as casual as if he'd just dropped in for a drink.

"Thanks," Paul said, after Randall's truck had pulled away.

Wallace glared down at him from above. "Don't thank me, just get the fuck out of here. Go up the Blackwood place if you want answers. Don't ask me another goddamned thing. I ever see your face again, I can't be held responsible for what I'll do."

■■■

Paul found Simon waiting inside the car park on the far side of the harbor, standing between the entry gates and his car.

"Dr. Somers," Simon said, waving him over. "If you have a moment?"

Paul hid a wince, too aware of the fabric touching the abrasions and bruises blooming across his skin. "I have to get going."

"It's about the case."

Paul dug his keys from his pocket. "You found something?"

"Maybe. I've been digging through some old files, and there might be more to this than we thought."

"There always is." Paul toyed with the keys, hoping the sound would give Simon a clue.

"This might not even be our killer's first series."

Paul stopped jiggling the keys.

"We found some unexpected similarities in previous unsolved cases," Simon continued. "Not exact matches, but close enough to warrant suspicion. Two victims between 2006 and 2011, and three between 1994 and 1997. In both cases, no further victims showed up. The trail went cold. No bodies, no case."

1997. The year of the riots. A coincidence? Of course not. It couldn't be. And what happened in 2011?

"That would make the killer pretty old, by now. Assuming a typical profile."

"Or maybe we're not dealing with a lone wolf," Simon replied.

"Have you shared this with Virgil?"

"He's interviewing Québécois guys. We're meeting later to review our findings."

Paul nodded. "Good, good. Say, would you be willing to look into something for me? Off the record."

Simon arched his eyebrows. "I guess that depends on what you're asking."

"I have a theory, call it a hunch. Could you see if anything, I don't know, *noteworthy* happened in Oceanrest in 2011? Especially anything involving violence, crime..." he shrugged off the rest of the thought, uncertain how much of his own theories he wanted Simon to know.

"Why would I do that?" Simon asked. "Did you find anything?"

"No. Like I said, it's a hunch."

The two of them stood apart from each other for some time. Paul fiddled with his keys, and Simon stared at him with fathomless blue eyes.

"I'll see what I can find," Simon finally said, stepping aside. "I'll be in touch if anything comes up."

"Me too," Paul agreed, stepping around Simon toward his car.

He heaved a breath of relief when he got his engine started, inexplicably happy to have a steel frame between himself and Simon.

He waved to the younger man through the windshield as he drove away.

In the rearview, he saw Simon stare after him for quite some time.

■■■

Paul knew the Blackwood Estate. He'd heard more than a few whispers about the late Ambrose Blackwood, as well. Oceanrest wasn't a small down-east town, having over half the population of the Portland metro area, but the populace whispered the way denizens of a small town would. Back in Queens, Paul's neighbors had been more or less happy with ignoring each other. In Oceanrest, rumors were exchanged like ivory combs.

Ambrose Blackwood was a recluse, an academic, and last in the long lineage of the Oceanrest Blackwoods. Paul had heard more about his sex life than his professional life. The rumors were typical of any recluse. Ambrose was a "queer," a "pedo,"…Paul had even once heard he was a "eunuch."

He'd never met the man personally. He never would, what with the late Ambrose Blackwood being "late."

Before his death, Ambrose Blackwood had brought an underage homeless girl to Oceanrest. This seemed to confirm the rumor mill's allegation of pedophilia, but Paul had a gut instinct there was more at play than simple sexuality. The girl, probably this "Nora" that Captain Wallace mentioned, inherited half of the entire estate upon Ambrose's death. When it happened six months earlier, Oceanrest buzzed about it. It was old news now. Besides, even the most fervent gossip rarely spoke ill of the dead.

Paul went the long way around Denton to get to the short curve of Blackwood Drive and the offshoot private drive coiling off of it. Castine elms flanked the curlicued road, massive with age, branches outreaching, planted before he'd even been born. Up ahead, the massive Blackwood mansion crouched amid manicured foliage.

The private drive opened into a tight asphalt circle in front of the mansion's facade, an age-moldered fountain sitting in the center. Paul threw the vehicle into park and got out next to the fountain. A film of algae grew across the stagnant water, an angel standing over the pool pouring air out of an empty urn. Decades settled over the angel's wings in mottled black and green.

Paul approached the off-white steps, heading for the double-doors of the building's entry.

"You don't have an appointment," a voice said.

Paul spun, a flash of Neo-Nazi boot jerking through his memory.

"Look like you seen a ghost." The man stood six feet tall with broad, muscular shoulders, gray hair at the temples, no wrinkles in his face. His eyes glinted gold, his skin a shade of burnt sepia. But more than his physical presence, Paul noticed the man's mismatched garb. A Red Sox cap, a bulky Boston University sweater, and urban-camo cargo pants. A large pistol was in an open hip holster, a smaller one in a shoulder holster, and a large shotgun rested at the man's feet.

"I'm, uh, I'm h-here to see Nora," Paul stammered, his mind already working on the metric of the moment—how fast he could get back in the car if he needed to, what the chances were that he'd escape unharmed.

"I assumed as much," the man said, right hand frighteningly close to his hip holster, left hand loosely holding a pair of hedge trimmers. He tossed the trimmers aside. "Name's Victor. I'm the gardener here. Have been since just about thirty years." He smiled, bright white gleaming in the sun. "I'm also the doorman."

"Uh-huh." Paul glanced between the man's various armaments. "The doorman."

"Indeed," Victor said. He stepped around the bulk of a freshly-manicured bush. "Mostly I take care of the bushes, the hedge maze…." He reached up left-handed to adjust his baseball cap against the sun, his right hand still poised at the hip holster. "Whatever needs doing."

"I was told to come here."

"By who?"

"Captain Wallace?"

"Not a bad guy. Not a great guy either."

"I need to talk to Nora."

"About what?"

"I'm working with the police."

A chuckle came from Victor's lips. "No shit?"

"No shit."

"Unfortunately, that ain't an answer to my question."

Paul balked. "Excuse me?"

"What are you here to talk about?"

"A possible suspect in a murder case," Paul said. Victor raised his eyebrows but made no reply. Paul sighed. "I'm looking for information about Randall Tyler Hill, maybe regarding an old church in town."

"Alright. Wait here a second." Victor reached down and grabbed the shotgun from the grass—a matte black, military-looking piece of hardware that the apparent BU alum handled casually. Victor leaned the barrel of the gun against his shoulder and brushed past Paul to the double doors of the mansion entrance. A ring of keys came out of the man's pocket, and the doors swung open. Victor passed through, and they swung closed again.

Paul sat on the hood of his car, arms folded, masking a grimace of pain. He peered out from the circle of drive surrounding the fountain, past the hedges and bushes toward the vast, rolling yard of the estate. A guest house sat a few dozen feet out, but other than that it was clean-cut grass and neat-trimmed bushes all the way to the woods.

The mansion doors jerked open again a few minutes later. Victor leaned out between them. "Better come in. You want coffee?"

"Sure."

"I'll show you to her first. Wouldn't want you to get lost."

CHAPTER TEN

Deirdre felt her silence cantrip strain against the man's shout.

"Who are you?" the accountant yelled.

"You got the wrong number of books."

"You don't know shit."

Deirdre funneled energy into her misdirection charm, her heartrate rising as she poured herself into the spell. "You're already fucked, buddy."

"Says who? Some dead bitch?"

She gasped with effort as she pushed more energy into her misdirection spell and zig-zagged around the desk toward him. His gun went off, a sharp pain rushing through her tendons as her silence cantrip worked to quiet the bang. He missed. She swung around the desk and came at him, leading with the butt of her revolver. He spun to meet her, another loud blast shuddering her lungs and muscles as her magic worked to hide it. Missed again. The two of them collided. She came down on his skull with the pistol grip, drove her knee up into his groin.

He collapsed. She kicked him in the ribs a couple times, drove her boot down on his hand until he let go of his gun.

"Help!" he screamed. "Somebody help!"

Sweat poured from Deirdre, as her body worked to keep the spell from disassembling. She gave his hand another stomp, then put her knee on his spine and knelt on top of him. Pressed the mouth of her revolver against the base of his skull. "Shut up," she spat. "Shut the hell up!"

"You don't know who you're fucking wi—"

She grabbed a wispy lock of his hair and yanked, making him yelp. "Shut up. And get ready to answer some questions."

"You're not one of us," he gibbered, "you're not *one of us*. You're in deep here. They'll kill you."

With her hand still clasping his hair, she pulled his head off the ground and slammed it back down. He whined, high and plaintive.

She panted with effort, used her gun-hand to wipe sweat from her brow, then placed the barrel back where it was. "You've got extra books. A lot of math going on there. Like you're covering something up, hiding something from your own guys. So it sounds to me like you're in deep too."

"Nobody's gonna believe you. Luc won't believe you."

"You better start being real cooperative here, or I swear to the moon and the Earth that I'll give the cleaning crew the hardest job of their lives."

He didn't have a response to that one.

Deirdre took cleansing breaths through the long pause that followed. "Alright," she said, "here's how it's going to work. I ask questions, you answer them, I let you live. I won't tell anyone what you said, you don't tell anyone…" she paused, chuckled dryly. "Hell with it, you tell whoever you want. Tell 'em some random girl with a gun broke into your headquarters, got into your office, pinned you, and made you squeal. See how that little confession works out for you."

"What do you want?" he asked.

"Randall Tyler Hill."

"Oh, Jesus…"

"Jesus ain't here right now."

"You're looking for that psycho?"

"I am. Where is he?"

"I dunno. Maybe Jacques knows, I don't know."

"Jacques works with him?" Deirdre hadn't heard of a "Jacques" before, but context filled in the blanks. Jacques wasn't Luc. Jacques wasn't "the boss." That was why the accountant needed two sets of books. Something happening, factions splintering in the mob. The accountant playing both sides of a dangerous game.

The accountant groaned. "Jacques' people and the Aryans work together."

"Doing what?"

"Prostitution. Debt collection. Name it."

"*Specifics.*"

"People get in debt to Jacques, Randall comes up with…arrangements. Daughters and nieces mostly. Girlfriends. Randall came up with the idea. Back before we helped the cops deal with the Aryans, he was their big money-maker. Now he works with us. Jacques just did with the drugs, the gambling, the protection racket, all that. Not the money it used to be, though, and too many people don't pay up."

"So you kidnap women?"

"Luc won't make new business. He's too cozy."

"Where does it happen?"

"Motels. The bed and breakfast, sometimes. Mabel's place."

"Where do you *keep* them? Before you sell them, where?"

"I don't—"

She dug the barrel into his skin hard enough to bruise it. "Where?"

"I dunno."

She yanked the butt of the gun back again, brought it down on the man's head. He yelped. Easier for the cantrip to conceal, much easier than a gunshot. "Talk."

"I-I-I dunno," the accountant stammered. "I swear I don't know. Nobody knows."

"Bullshit."

"Jacques knows, nobody else."

"Habits? Hobbies? You've got something on Randall or else you wouldn't work with him, so what've you got?"

"Addresses, names. His whole crew."

"You scared of him?"

"He's insane. We got his kid, he's got a son in Portland, we keep an eye on him. If we didn't have that…"

"Are you scared of him?" she repeated.

"Y-yes."

A drop of sweat fell from her forehead and splashed onto the back of his scalp. An oppressive quiet grew around them.

"Think carefully about this next one," Deirdre whispered, craning forward to get her lips close to his ear, pressing the barrel harder against his skin. "Are you scared of *me*?"

He swallowed, licked his lips. Faint tears glistened around his nose. "Y-yes."

"Are you scared of Luc Grenier?"

The accountant nodded, his head scraping hardwood.

Deirdre removed the barrel from the man's head and stood up. "You can't play both teams. I don't know what Jacques has on you, but you better get out from under it. Randall's not crazy—he's a monster. What he does isn't insane, it's *monstrous*. I'm going to walk out of here now. Don't follow. When I'm gone, you're going to pick up the phone, you're going to call Luc Grenier, you're going to call the police, you're going to call everyone, and you're going to tell them everything you know about Jacques and Randall Hill and the women you've been *selling*. Get it?"

The accountant sobbed, curled up around his wood-scraped face and his crushed hand. The scent of urine wafted from his body.

"Don't fuck this up," she said.

In a fetal position now, he whined from the floor.

She hesitated at the door, revolver aching in her hand. It would be easy, she knew. The silence cantrip would argue with her, that would be the real effort, but the act of pulling the trigger would be easy. The man had fixed the Québécois books for years, which meant he'd been overseeing the sale of kidnapped women for as long as Randall had been doing it.

But killing a Québécois employee wasn't the ending of a thing, it was the beginning of one. If she killed this one, what then? Would she go after this "Jacques" person next? Where would it end?

A woodchipper, she told herself. It would end in a woodchipper.

She disengaged the hammer of her gun and slipped it back into the holster, pushed the office door open, and stepped into the dim light of the third floor.

She double-checked the hard-drives in her pockets and made her way back to the stairs and the exit. The two women she'd heard on the second floor had gone silent, hopefully free and clear of their earlier trip. She crept onward, down to the first floor, and was almost to the back door when a flannel-clad man turned the corner.

At first he turned away, reaching for the handle to the men's room. Then he froze. Turned back slightly.

"What the…?"

She dug deep into her bones and came up with her most desperate cantrip—*invisibility*. The spell tunneled through her, every muscle arguing with the exertion. In a soundless blink, she vanished. The silence cantrip covered her panting exhaustion, her heart slamming against her sternum with the effort of burning through so many spells.

The man in flannel turned around, squinting at dimness and shadow. "Huh."

Deirdre groaned from the demands of the invisibility cantrip, the silence cantrip muffling her voice. She moved slowly, painfully, for the exit. Put her hand around the knob, her clothes sweat-stuck to her skin. She glanced back at the man in flannel.

"Guys?" the Québécois man called out to the bar. "Uh…"

"What?" a voice yelled back.

"Never mind. Just…got a weird feeling."

"You piss yourself?"

"Fuck off."

The man turned back to the restroom.

Deirdre got the back door open and stumbled out of the building. She tried to run for the tree line but her legs felt weak and shaky. She limped at a bare jog, her muscles tired-cold. A man by the parking lot smoked a cigarette, gaze idly resting on the forest. Deirdre strangled a scream in her throat, pushing forward on willpower and adrenaline.

She could feel her energy bottoming out, the cantrips unraveling second by second.

The smoker had a gun. The men inside had guns.

A cramp sliced at her calf, her throat tight against the responsive shriek, muffling it to a strangled grunt. She limped. Close. So close.

She released the misdirection cantrip first, feeling the tapestry of the spell fray and collapse.

The cigarette man squinted in her direction. Was her invisibility charm already failing?

Her thigh shuddered, searing, the same leg as the calf cramp. An animal sound escaped her lips and she knew her silence charm had started dissipating. The cigarette man stepped away from the building, his hand hovering at a hip holster. Had he heard? Could he see?

She breached the tree line, but exhaustion had driven her vision narrow and blurry. Twigs snapped under her desperate feet, narrow branches whipped at her sweat-slicked face. She pounded on, listing hard to her right, focused only on her last remaining cantrip and the hope that she wouldn't crash into a tree trunk.

She fell face-first, landing genuflective before an oak. The invisibility spell came apart like dry leaves blown on hard wind. She collapsed to all fours, pawing over dirt.

She crawled. Forward, forward. She urged herself on, no energy or adrenaline left, scrambling along on willpower and hitched, heaving breath.

Up ahead, a massive rock jutted out from a small hillock, overgrown with brush and moss. She groaned and pushed toward it, hoping for shade and shelter if not safety. It couldn't have been more than twenty feet away, but the journey seemed vast to her aching body. She reached it in seconds or minutes or hours for all she knew, and collapsed beneath.

Her vision clouded, blue and black and violent, and the rhythm of her racing heart deafened her.

All around, branches reached down.

come back to the earth, leaves whispered on the wind. *come back to the earth and sleep.*

She pushed herself as far beneath the outcropping as she could and curled up, heaving.

Her eyelids fluttered.

come back to the earth and sleep.

And she did.

CHAPTER ELEVEN

Victor led Paul through an enormous foyer, through a threshold between two regal staircases, and down the main hall of the mansion. He'd lost the shotgun at some point, which Paul liked, but his right hand never ventured far from the hip holster. "I don't think I caught your name, Mr. Works With Police."

"Paul Somers."

"Nice to meet you, Paul. I hope you don't take offense at my, ah, wariness."

"I guess it's part of your job."

"Uh-huh."

"I won't lie, you gave me a jump when you came out of nowhere out there."

Victor chuckled. "I didn't come out of nowhere, you just didn't see me."

"Same thing."

"No, it isn't." Victor came to a stop at an enormous door-less threshold, somewhere near the center of the mansion by Paul's judgment. Over the bigger man's shoulder, he saw a vast, expansive library; three interlocked rooms, each three floors high, navigable by ladders built on brass rollers. Books overstuffed every shelf. Music hammered from inside, punk-industrial.

Victor flashed his too-bright smile again. "Hope you like loud music."

Paul's lips parted at the sheer enormity of the place, and his jaw all but dropped when he saw the confusion of the floor.

Besides the ladders rolling through each of the three rooms, the place looked unnavigable. Someone had lined up rows of file cabinets, desktop computer towers, piles of tape recorders and boomboxes, crates of CDs, floppy discs, VHS tapes, DVDs…someone had built a veritable maze of stacked recording paraphernalia and archival detritus. A library within a library.

He noticed something else, something that felt similar to Deirdre's cantrip buzzing through his skull or the voices of the dead. Maybe if he'd gone without the puff of downers that morning, he'd be able to place it. But he hadn't.

"She's in there." Victor pointed toward the center of the archival maze.

"How do I—?"

"Labyrinth," Victor said, by way of unhelpful explanation. "Means it's unicursal."

"Sure," Paul muttered, not bothering to hide his sarcasm. "Thanks."

Victor clapped his shoulder. "Don't do anything stupid."

Paul shrugged Victor's hand away, stepping into the maze between two file cabinets. He followed paths at random, trying to figure his way to the center. Overhead, three chandeliers hung from the ceiling, their brilliant lights blurring painted script beyond them. Paul peered up every few feet, hoping to use them to navigate his way forward. He wondered what symbols were painted on the ceiling, what glyphs roofed the library wall-to-wall. Lost in his curiosity, he tripped over a knee-high stack of DVDs, scattering jewel cases.

"Guest?" a young woman called out.

"Paul Somers."

"Take your next left, then a right."

He followed her instructions, and like the minotaur, at the center, she sat.

Paul found her in lotus position, perched on a desk with an office chair full of books next to her. Her fingers danced along the keys of a matte black laptop, logo-less.

Her hair was a bleached-white nest atop her head, the roots auburn, the sides and back shaved to the scalp. Gemstones glittered from her eye sockets, the exact colors escaping him. Clothing salvaged from thrift stores and garbage cans cloaked the rest of her body, hiding it in a tattered cloud. Silver glinted at her neckline. Hoodie sleeves rolled up to her elbows revealed narrow wrists and pinched white scars. Paul averted his eyes before he could get a good look.

She stared at him for a long time.

He opened his mouth but couldn't come up with something to say.

She raised her eyebrows, reddish-brown clashing with her hair, and gestured for him to speak.

"Captain Wallace sent me."

She set the laptop aside, closing it. "I know."

"I'm looking for information."

She lifted her arms, indicating the breadth of the library, and declared with self-parodied drama, "I'm surrounded by it!"

He flinched at her lightness, her inappropriate degree of humor. "You know anything about Randall Tyler Hill?"

She fiddled with the slender silver chain around her neck. A cross dangled on the end of it, a symbol Paul found confusing against the canvas of her aesthetic. "Depends on what you're looking to find out." She inclined her head, indicating the bandage peeling from the side of his scalp. "I take it this is a personal thing?"

He nodded, feeling the bruises growing across the rest of his body. "More personal by the hour."

"Oookay. So what do you wanna know?"

"You wouldn't happen to know where he's hiding out, these days, would you?"

"Nope. His family had a little house up by the old trailer park, but it burned down. So did the trailer park."

"In the '97 riots."

"Bingo."

"What about Howland Butler? Know anything about him?"

She slipped the crucifix necklace beneath her hoodie collar and stood up. "Absolutely. Ambrose has—had—a sizable file on that particular preacher." She crossed to one of the countless file cabinets and yanked open a drawer. Tabbing through the folders, she continued, "Howland Butler and Randall Hill had a kind of master-apprentice thing going on before the fire. Like the Sith."

"What?"

"From *Star Wars*? The Sith?"

"No, I got the reference, I just…" Frustration steamed beneath his skin at having Randall's violence pinned to something so casual. Or maybe he'd just spent too many hours being jerked around with nothing to show for it.

"Sorry. Just a salient metaphor. I didn't mean to, I don't know, *diminish* whatever happened to you, or whatever." She clicked her tongue against the roof of her mouth. "Sorry, again. I don't talk to people a lot, so, you know."

"I guess not," he forced himself to say. "So, what do you mean by 'master-apprentice thing?'"

She pulled a file from the cabinet and returned to the desk, plopping it down open-faced by the laptop. "Howland Butler was an ex-con-man when he started his weird revival tent shtick in New Hampshire. His bio *in brevis* is that he was a big-time scam artist, con man, and general 'rambler.' Cops were pretty pleased when they cuffed him…and less pleased when the sentence came down. Three years, virtually a slap on the wrist considering all the scams he'd perpetrated. Anyway. You know the way it goes, the whole 'born again' thing, hardcore evangelism, et cetera, et cetera. Fast forward a few years and he goes from a single tent, to a few tents, to a little church north of Oceanrest and, eventually a huge church and a regional radio show. He might've gone national except, y'know, fire."

"Uh-huh. So where does Randall come into it?"

"Oh, you know, black magic. What's all traditionally referred to as 'the dark arts.'"

"What?"

"Oh, yeah, Butler was deeeeeeep into that stuff. The whole Jerry Falwell fundamentalist thing was probably just a cover. Like I said, he was a big-time scam artist. He talked a mean game though. Racism, misogyny, homophobia, the whole bible-thumping fire-and-brimstone song and dance. According to Ambrose's notes, Randall was his right-hand man, his Guy Friday, and Randall's connections with the Aryan crew gave Butler an 'in' with Oceanrest's grittier, grimier crowd, and access to things that an upstanding preacher-type wouldn't usually have access to. And Randall got the inside scoop on the world of monsters and magic."

Paul nodded. "So Ambrose was taking notes, keeping track of them. Did he happen to uncover anything a little more useful? Like what they might've been doing?"

"A few theories but nothing concrete. There was a lot going on around that time, and not only in Oceanrest. Ambrose was a globetrotter, and Butler's coven kept quiet enough to end up on the backburner…until they weren't anymore."

"Butler's *coven*? I thought it was a 'master-apprentice thing?'"

"Oh yeah, Randall was definitely his number one pupil, but I'm sure some of the rest of the crew learned a trick or two too."

"What happened to get Ambrose's attention? How'd Butler come off the back burner?"

"Like I said, a few theories, nothing concrete. Details are vague. It looked like Butler's influence was spreading a little too wide, and his message became a little too violent, and Ambrose began to suspect he was involved in some heavy spellcraft."

"How heavy?"

"Heavy. Ambrose thought Butler posed a threat to the town, maybe even the region. He was digging into it, snooping around wherever he could, but…" she shrugged, a jerk of narrow shoulders, "…then the riot happened. Butler's church burned down and, well, you know the rest. Within a couple years of that, all the Aryan types had either flown the coop, joined with the Québécois, got arrested, or, um, 'disappeared.' Butler grabbed a handsome insurance settlement and vanished. Ambrose had nothing left to investigate."

Paul itched at the stubble bristling across his face. A question tugged at his lizard brain, but what was it?

Nora flipped a few pages around inside the folder and turned back to him, a smirk sliding across her features. "Hey, Paul, you know what you forgot to do?"

"What?"

"Pretend like you don't believe in magic."

■■■

Birdsong. Rustling leaves. The distant murmur of the Atlantic.

The last of the previous night's dreamer flashed images of a forgotten vision against the back of Deirdre's eyelids: an open rib cage, a tongue where the heart should lie; old Roman columns; double-doors flung wide; monsters hidden in the shifting shadows undulating on the walls; White Room, White Room, White Room; a throne inhabited by an ancient lich, lips open to reveal plaqued fangs…

Deirdre opened her eyes to mid-afternoon. Persistent gray-white mist hugged her. Where was she?

(*a redheaded woman spitting and screaming, Randall's fingers clasping her hair; here was the voice of a god, here were the teeth, the throat, a kingdom rising; a woman crying, trying to pull him back out of her, and he pretending she was jerking him off; a kingdom rising, a priest with a crown of tongues*)

Beneath her body, a history of twigs and leaves and pine needles and dirt. Somewhere deep down, rich soil, the Earth's mantle, and a million years' of lost history digested in rock. Overhead, an outcrop from dirty hillock. Branches reached both to sky and soil. Sun filtered through summer green leaves.

(*a handshake, a black bag, a kingdom rising—its castles made of broken bone, its power made of rending flesh, here is a kingdom of predation, here is a kingdom of fangs; here, a crown of tongues; here, a prophet-priest on a throne; in the White Room, the cost of building a kingdom)*

Deirdre shot up, the last of the dreamer nightmare dissolving from her mind. She nearly knocked her head into the roof of her makeshift shelter, and bent low to make her way back into the sun. She stood to her full height and brushed dirt and forest history from her clothes. She'd worn herself too thin keeping the cantrips going for so long on too little sleep, too light a breakfast, too much adrenaline. If she'd had her wits about her, she would have taken sixth sense uppers before leaving home, but her wits hadn't been about her. Why?

Razz. Razz was missing, doing something stupid, doing something *dangerous*.

Trying to help her.

She checked her gun in its holster, the hard drives in her jacket pockets, her lock picks.

She started walking, or limping, rather, back toward Squatter City.

(the teeth of a hungry god, a stomach churning with corpses)

CHAPTER TWELVE

Twilight purpled the sky when Deirdre found herself pushing Frank's door open again. It felt somehow heavier without the lock she'd busted off the day before.

"Frank, I need to know if you've seen—" she stopped short, finding Frank's limp form nestled in his sleeping bag. Plastic food wrappers surrounded him. A rubber hose wrapped his left arm, the syringe discarded in nearby dust. A bagged brick of off-colored heroin sat half-hidden under dirty clothes. Frank's mouth hung open, showing off old fillings and caps, remnants of a life Frank had long left behind. A life with dental insurance.

"Son of a bitch," Deirdre muttered, crossing the room. She bent over and took Frank by the shoulders, shaking him. "Wake up." She gave him a second shake, this one hard enough to send his head lolling in a lazy circle. "Wake up!"

Still nothing. Membranous drug-sweat glistened his brow.

"Goddamn you."

She crouched low and used her thumb and forefinger to peel open one of his eyelids. Kinked red capillaries crawled from his socket, but worse was the faded purple stain coloring the edges of his sclera. The sign of someone in the midst of a dreamer vision.

And where did Frank get dreamer?

How obvious an answer.

Frank let out a low groan and his head rolled from her grasp.

When she reached for his face again, Frank's arms rose like wave-brushed seaweed, pushing back. "Frank, I need to know where Razz is." She stretched the eye open again, watching the pupil dilate and contract. "Where's Razz?"

"The Mouth of God," Frank mumbled. "The gut of a hungry temple, steaming. Claws against the wallpaper."

Something about his words softened her voice, weakened her grip. "What the hell?"

"The beast, the beast…"

Lips pursed, she peered back through the door. Then she remembered Razz's idiot texts and his insistence on helping, on proving himself. She remembered Randall's threats, Razz's radio silence. She turned back to Frank, hauled him from the wall, and slammed him against the floorboards. He jolted awake, arms suddenly strong enough to scramble backward, his body a tangle of confused limbs and half-open sleeping bag. "Deirdre?"

"I need to know where Razz is."

Frank's eyelids fluttered, drug-glassed. "I dunno."

"What about that girl? The girl with the face tats. Olly."

"The spic?"

"Where are they?"

"The monster…"

"When was the last time you saw them?"

"Just now…" he muttered, already drowsing. "They were heading into the…into the…"

"Goddamn it! I need to find him, Frank. I need to—"

His eyes were closed, again, his head tilted back and to one side. "Just look back down where the tongue goes away."

Frank nodded comatose, heroin and dreamer swimming in his veins. Deirdre clutched the grip on her revolver, squeezing it as tight as she could. Frank didn't have a sixth sense. He didn't believe in ghosts or monsters and only occasionally referenced the weirdness of the forest or the Oceanrest fog. Frank didn't know about dreamer, and even if he did, he'd deny it till the day he died. Yet there he was, sclera purpled by its presence in the folds of his brain, and a whole brick of heroin dusted in dreamroot gold beside him.

Which meant Randall had given him his daily bread. Which meant Frank had cut some kind of deal.

"If he gets hurt, Frank, I swear to the moon and skies and the fucking Earth…"

But he couldn't hear her, anyway.

At the threshold to Frank's room, she slammed his door and kicked it hard until the wood at the bottom splintered around her foot. She left Frank's door busted and hanging wide, went down the rickety steps of his squat, and turned toward Black Watch Hill.

She got her phone from her pocket. The screen had cracked at some point during her time at La Femme Rouge, but it worked. She sent a series of texts to Razz, praying for a response.

'Please text back so I know you're okay.'

'Please tell me you're okay. I don't even care about all the other stupid bullshit, just tell me you're safe. You and Olly.'

She stared at the screen for a long time, standing on the corner of Lafayette and Black Watch Hill, but no answer came.

■■■

Paul sipped the coffee Victor had brought him. Nora's own mug steamed unattended on the desk, the girl flitting from file cabinet to bookshelf and back again.

"So, Ambrose never found out what Butler was actually up to?"

Nora jerked her eyes his way. "Sort of. He knew Butler and some of the Aryan crew, the immediate coven, were in the cult business, but no details. They were pretty good at staying tight-lipped, maintaining plausible deniability."

Paul inclined his head to the growing documentation piling the desk. "So what's all that?"

"Related information," Nora said, pulling yet another manila folder. "Including my own research."

"Your research?"

"Duh? I'm an archivist. A researcher. Ooh!" she snapped her fingers. "An investigator! I know what I'll do—I'll have someone put windows in the front doors of the house and etch my name into the glass and write 'private investigator' under it. I'll drink too much for my own good and have a constant five o'clock shadow and..." She turned to survey Paul. "Huh. Look at that."

"Not funny."

"Maybe a little funny?"

He shook his head, lips creased into a stern line.

"Sorry," Nora said, too casual to mean it. "But I do research things, yes. I also *investigate* things. For instance, Wallace mentioned you were working with the police, or claimed to be, so I made a few phone calls and listened to recordings from a few *bugs*, and I figured out you were tapped to help with the serial killing case."

Paul's eyebrows twitched up. "What are you, a spy?"

"More a fly on the wall. Essentially harmless. You think Randall is tied into that?"

"More and more, yeah."

Nora began pulling pages from the various stacked folders. "Okay, so. How much do you know about the workings of magic?"

"Nothing?"

"Right. Okay. You can categorize spellcraft into either cantrip or ritual magic, and either major or minor fractals. Don't interrupt, please. So, the first thing to know is all magic needs fuel. If you're powerful enough, or born with natural aptitude, you can fuel *some* magic off of pure energy and will-power. Get a good night's sleep, a hearty breakfast, et cetera, and a born-witch or a well-studied sorcerer can pull off a few tricks, though a little external fuel doesn't hurt. I mean, all blood magic needs blood to function. Thus the name, duh."

Paul gestured her to get to the point.

"Excuse you, have some patience. So where was I? Oh, cantrips. They tend to be major fractal magic, sometimes even plainly visible, and that makes them pretty demanding. If someone over-exerts themselves with cantrips, they can cause all kinds of havoc. Spell failure, which isn't so bad, or spell release, which is very bad. Plus unconsciousness, either way."

"Is this related to Butler?"

"What did I say about patience? Geeze. No. What Butler was doing was ritual. That's good and bad. Most spells can be turned into ritual spells, which lets the spellcaster use less energy per hour to build up a more powerful spell. Get it?"

"No."

"Okay, we'll stick to the basics. Cantrips fast, rituals slow. But rituals can build up a lot of power over time, whereas cantrips can't. You can build up a ritual for days, weeks, months…years. And while cantrips *mostly* run off of musculoskeletal and neurological capacity, a witch or wizard can fuel a ritual from a number of different sources. If they're using sex magic, they throw an orgy. Blood magic? Raid the Red Cross. But the biggest spells, the Fat Boys of sorcery…they take real sacrifice."

"Human lives."

"Not always, but, yeah, most of the time. How many victims are we talking about?"

"Eight."

Nora whistled, long and low. "Wow. That's, well, a lot. Actually, a frightening amount." She found the photo she was searching for and held it up toward Paul. "You know what this is?"

Paul gagged back a rush of gut-slap revulsion. "Is that a fucking lynching?"

"Yes. This is something human beings are capable of doing to each other. Consider it a metaphorical human sacrifice to a specific ideology—an ideology of white, male, heteronormative supremacy—but also, in this case, a *literal* human sacrifice." She flipped the photo around to look at it herself. "What year was this? They didn't even wear masks…"

"What were the sacrifices for?"

"They were trying to create a plague."

"Why?"

"Why do you think?" She showed him the photograph again. White faces showed white teeth.

He averted his eyes to the ghost of his image murked in coffee.

"It didn't work," Nora said. "That's one of the issues with using human sacrifice as a fuel source—it tends to get noticed. The spell these guys were working up required six sacrifices. They only made it to three before they were stopped."

"Stopped?"

"Two were arrested. Three, um, 'disappeared,' though the word is very much in quotes. This one," she tapped one of the smiling faces in the photo with a long fingernail, "was beaten to death by Atticus Stokes and Calvin LeDuff while trying to drag an unconscious black boy into the back of a car."

"LeDuff?"

"Virgil's dad, yep. He even stepped in when the cops tried to arrest Stokes. Calvin wasn't particularly progressive, especially by 60s standards, but he knew evil when he saw it. Of course, these days, evil has learned to hide better…" she paused as if to go on further, but didn't. She cleared her throat. "The Blackwoods and the Ashers had a hand in dealing with the coven as well, counter-magic and hexes and all that. Someone, an unknown third party, took a more direct approach. Thus the 'disappearances.'"

"An unknown party?"

"Probably a witch hunter or something."

"There can't possibly be that many people involved in this shit."

"There aren't," Nora said. "Maybe one in ten, twenty thousand people. But they do tend to gather in specific regions. Oceanrest is a big one. Giza, duh. The whole Transylvanian region. Parts of Louisiana. The Andes."

"Not New York?"

"I mean, there're nine million people living there, I'm sure some of them know a little magic. Even at, say, the odds of one in *fifty* thousand, that's still—"

"Why here?"

Another folder flipped open. "Oceanrest is weird."

Paul chuckled earnestly for the first time in a while. "No shit."

"Before the Ashers, Oceanrest settlement's founding family, the place already had a rep with the Wabanaki. Penobscot and Abenaki tribes figured the whole region as essentially haunted. Allegedly, however many thousands of years ago that the original First Nations folk showed up here, they found an abandoned Stone Age era town. Or Bronze Age, maybe."

"Excuse me?"

"*Allegedly*," she stressed. "There is some evidence, but very little. We'd be talking about something like Stonehenge or the temples at Ġgantija, maybe even older. Not the same thing you'd think of as a 'town' in modern parlance. The Ashers started the settlement anyway, despite warnings, and waves of French and, later, English settlers showed up to help them."

"How does this relate to the Randall thing?"

"You're here for information. This is information."

"It's unrelated."

"Nothing is unrelated," Nora replied, her voice sharp for a fleeting, shocking instant. "This place is a cat's cradle of secrets and tangents, the threads all wound together and knotted up. The Ashers founded this place pretending to be good Christians, but Ambrose's notes suggest they were *deep* into the dark arts. Same with the Blackwoods. Which begs the question of *why* so many sorcerers feel drawn here. Have you heard of 'Oceanrest fog?' Or maybe 'Trickster's fog?'"

"Sure," Paul said, his head starting to spin.

"Ambrose had another term for it. 'Concentrated meta-paranormal accelerant,' which is a fancy way of saying it makes weird stuff weirder. Cryptids, evolutionary and supernatural aberrations and mutations, all the various creatures inhabiting the secret shadows of Oceanrest's—"

"Hold on a second—"

She arched auburn eyebrows to her bleach-damaged hairline. "You mean you believe in magic but not in monsters? Keep up, Paul. You do have a sixth sense, right?"

Paul's mouth hung open.

"I mean, everyone does, kinda, but some people really *feel* it. Psychics, mediums, witches, et cetera. Most people just have 'gut feelings,' but people like you," she tilted the folder toward him, "you've got a whole extra level of perception. 'Para-normative,' they call it. You ever get the feeling, looking out at the Atlantic, that something's looking back at you? Or that there's things you don't want to see moving around the woods at night?"

Paul fumbled for a reply but found none.

"Well, you'd be right. And the Trickster's fog gets them wound up, some-times to the point that they end up getting seen by normal, upstanding citizens. Always a problem. Ugh. Trickster's fog also correlates with radio distortion, power failures, mechanical and electronic malfunction, GPS and navigational failure…and these are just the phenomena Ambrose *researched*, so there's likely other effects."

"And this relates…how?"

"Stay with me here, Paul. It's a meta-paranormal accelerant. It's unique to the region. What does that imply about the region?"

Paul shrugged. "I give up."

"It's full of weird. I know it sounds crazy, but maybe it *attracts* weird. I don't have any stats to quote, but I have enough personal experience to say there are twice as many—maybe *three times* as many psychics and witches in Oceanrest as there are anywhere else I've been. Per capita, I mean. Anyway, you want to know how it ties into Randall."

"Yeah," Paul said, frustration creeping into his words. "That would be nice."

"If Randall's really saving up sacrifices to fuel some major ritual spell, he'll probably want to wrap the casting when the fog comes back in. According to Ambrose's calculations, we're due for it. Overdue. But hey, the San Andreas Fault is due for a bout of light cataclysm, too, so maybe Ambrose was wrong."

A memory floated across Paul's mind, Randall calling out from Deirdre's yard the night he raided her house.

(*"but the stars are right and the fog's brewing up and there's not much more need for the niceties"*)

He frowned. "I don't think he was—"

Nora set the current folder down, sat on the edge of the desk, and picked up her mug. "It gets worse."

"Worse?"

"A lot of magic keys into important numbers. Three, as per the organization of triunes and trinities, or seven, as per sins and virtues. Or nine, as in the number of universes connected to the world tree, or the root number in *longshen*, or a triune of trinities, a completion of three threes."

"Or the number of victims Randall will have after the next one."

"Bingo."

"So he's doing something worse than a *plague*?"

"A regional, genocidal plague," Nora corrected. "And maybe not something *worse* but definitely something *bigger*. Which is probably worse." She ran bird-bone fingers through the coarseness of her hair. "I'll see what else I can dig up. I'm sure I'll have more by the time you come back."

"Come back?" Paul repeated. "You seem pretty sure of yourself."

"You seem pretty caught up in the kind of subject I know a lot about, so…" she shrugged. Theatrically.

"We'll see."

"If you come back late, ring the doorbell nine times."

"What about your 'gardener?'"

"His name is Victor," Nora corrected. "And he doesn't work twenty-four hours a day. Remember: nine times."

"Will do." Paul set his mug on top of a nearby file cabinet and turned back toward the winding corridors of data sprawling the library. At the threshold of the archival labyrinth, he paused. Remembered rumors itched at his curiosity, a prickly question needing answer. Or maybe it was just the impulse *to know*. He peered back at Nora. "Can I ask…what exactly *was* your relationship with Ambrose?"

"Kind of like a master-and-apprentice thing." She paused, then Yoda-voiced: "Always two, there are."

"Huh. Funny."

"I try."

He walked the path back to the front of the house, his head swimming in information. It was difficult to imagine Randall Tyler Hill as some kind of sorcerer, but maybe that was the truth. It made sense in the context Nora provided him. It made sense in the context of Deirdre's missing stash too. But if Randall planned to set off some enormous spell…what would it be? And if he only needed one more sacrifice, if he only needed the fog to roll in…how could they stop him?

He stepped down from the mansion porch and went for his car. As soon as his shoes touched asphalt, the realization struck him—the thing he hadn't been able to place about the mansion, about the library. Not only the presence of magic humming in the air, but an absence of something too. The dead. Crossing from the double doors of the building to his car, the distant chorus of rasping ghosts crept into the back of his mind. He flinched at the static fuzz of their innumerable voices.

Glancing back toward the paint-chipped estate, he muttered, "How the hell…?"

help me, a familiar voice rasped, far away and in his head at the same time. *help me I don't know what to do.*

Worse was the quieter, more distant voice: *dad…*

Paul started the car and got directions to the nearest liquor store.

CHAPTER THIRTEEN

Deirdre stopped walking before she reached her house.

WA-LAB2, the black sedan's license plate read. Shoshanna's body-guard stood on her porch, his unblinking gaze surveying the length and breadth of what had once been a legitimate street. Deirdre almost felt his eyes on her, a crawling discomfort worming across her skin. She braced herself for what would surely come next.

Deirdre had met Shoshanna early on in her Oceanrest career, not long after she had laid claim to the slouching squat she still called home. Those years took a lot out of her. She hadn't understood the demands of her decision when she'd fled her parents' apartment for the train station; hadn't imagined the desperate scavenging of her late-teen homeless existence. But she worked her way up. Oceanrest's underbelly tangled and knotted with politics, not to mention the less-political hierarchy of the squatters themselves, and once Deirdre had managed any degree of success, those politics and hierarchies sniffed her out.

One day, answering her door expecting to come face-to-face with Québé-cois threats, Deirdre had found Shoshanna on her porch instead. Her sixth sense had gone wild just looking at the woman. Shoshanna was something powerful. Not a witch, she'd figured out, but something else tethered into the magic of things, into the secret energies of the world. How Shoshanna had found her remained a mystery, but given the benefits of their meeting, Deirdre never pressed for an answer.

But after the previous day's clash with David, after the fight with Razz, after everything else…

There wasn't time to spare on conversations, on politics, on anything. Protecting Razz mattered. Getting her stash back mattered. Increasingly, stopping Randall mattered. But this? How could this matter?

Deirdre waved to Shoshanna's bodyguard as she approached. Something about him always struck her as *wrong*—not merely supernatural, but *wrong*. Maybe it was the man's absolute silence, or the way he stood without ever shifting weight or fidgeting, or the way he seemed to observe the world from some great distance, as though he himself were not truly part of it.

"Lurch," she greeted. "Where's Shosh?"

He opened one of his bone-crushing hands and pointed to the backyard.

"She let herself in?"

He nodded, soundless, and folded his hands back together.

"Great. Thanks."

He turned his attention back toward the street.

Deirdre's skin relaxed as she made distance away from the enforcer. She went around to the back of the house and found the back door unlocked, slightly ajar. A tea kettle howled inside the kitchen beyond. Deirdre pushed her way inside just as Shoshanna turned off the heating element on the stove, the kettle's wail simmering to a sizzle-whisper.

From the shadows of the squat's main thoroughfare, Samedi watched.

"Give me your set of keys," Deirdre said.

"I'm sorry for letting myself in but—"

Deirdre held out her hand. "Keys."

"Tea?"

"Give me your—"

"I brought dinner. It's in your den, along with the tea cups, because… well, you've got a barricade in your foyer, and no furniture in the kitchen."

"You can't just come and go whenever you want."

"I know. I'm sorry."

Samedi arched into an aggressive stance and bared his teeth.

"He'll fuck you up."

"Deirdre, please."

"You can't come in here when I'm not here."

"I'm sorry, but…" Samedi hissed and Shoshanna turned toward the cat, pointing a slender finger at the feline's face. "Don't," she said, and Samedi stopped. The cat's face scrunched in loathing, but no further sound emerged, and the animal padded away down the hall. Shoshanna turned back toward Deirdre. "I brought dinner. I made tea."

"I don't have time for a social call."

"This isn't strictly social."

"I guess that explains the breaking-and-entering," she said, meaning *no shit*.

Shoshanna picked up the tea kettle and carried it by the heat-resistant handle toward Deirdre's den. Deirdre locked the back door before following.

In the den proper, two plates of bulgogi steamed between twin mugs, and Samedi stood on the couch, no longer hissing but still looking pissed off.

Shoshanna poured the mugs full and took the kettle back to the kitchen.

Deirdre sat in the larger of the armchairs and peered over at Samedi. "Same."

The cat made a noise of disgruntled disapproval.

"When you called me, you told me there'd been an accident. Then we discovered you'd been robbed. But now…" Shoshanna drifted back into the room and sat on the chair facing Deirdre. "I know I shouldn't have let myself in, I know that was wrong. But your place is…what happened here?"

"Some speed freaks. Neo-Nazis."

Shoshanna sat up, alert. "What? Are you okay?"

"What do you think? Fuck no. You look at my room?"

Shoshanna averted her eyes. "They made quite a mess."

"They trashed the place. They made off with *everything*."

"We could provide security."

"I don't want that."

"David thinks—"

"Tell David he can suck—"

"He has anger issues," Shoshanna interrupted. "The way he acted yesterday morning was unacceptable. But he does have a valid point. Our facilities are highly secure, redundantly so, and we could protect you."

"I'm not going to start working at—"

"The pay would be substantial but more—"

"I'm not the nine-to-five type, and I'm—"

"—important, the security we could provide—"

"—not working for your fucking cokehead brother and—"

"Deirdre, please, think about—"

"—his goddamned bodyguards, who, by the way, threw me into a wall."

Shoshanna stopped talking. Folded her lips into a barely-there line. Sighed. "What happened was bad." She reached over to take one of the mugs, blowing steam from the top. "I haven't seen him react so brashly since…well, years ago. He hung up before I finished explaining everything."

"Don't defend him, okay?"

"He's my brother."

"Right."

"I won't defend what he did yesterday."

A pause followed. Shoshanna sipped some of the tea. Deirdre craned forward to pluck up the plate of bulgogi and the chopsticks next to it. She didn't want to be hungry but all those cantrips at La Femme Rouge had left her starved and aching. She went at the plate of beef bulgogi like a lion bearing down on a gazelle.

"If David tries to cut you off, it's going to take me time to make that right. Time, and possibly lawyers. And you might be without utilities, without *anything*, for weeks in the meantime."

Deirdre swallowed the mouthful of meat-sauce-vegetable and wiped at the corner of her lips. "I'm here because I want to be, Shosh. I live out here because I choose to. You get that, right?"

Shoshanna nodded, using her own chopsticks to push food around. "Yeah."

"You know anyone by the name of Randall Tyler Hill?"

Shoshanna's brow trenched. "Maybe. I don't think so."

"Been hearing that a lot."

"I'm on your side, Deirdre." One of Shoshanna's hands crept over the arm of her chair, ventured toward Deirdre, almost touched. "I'll do anything I can to help you, but I need you to trust me. Work with me. I need you to tell me the truth, the whole truth. If I'd known the extent of the damage here, maybe I could've done more, maybe I could've…"

Deirdre peered over at the other woman, not quite meeting her eyes. "There is something I might need help with."

"Oh?"

"You have any truck with the Québécois?"

"Some. Not much."

"I, um…I screwed up."

"What happened?"

"I broke into La Femme Rouge, following a lead, and, ah…I almost killed their accountant. I don't think he'll be able to make me, but if he does…"

"You want me to see if I can clean it up?"

Deirdre nodded.

A small chuckle breathed from Shoshanna's lips. "That might be a tough clean."

"They'll chop me if they find me."

"They're not barbarians. I doubt Luc's first course of action would be to have you *chopped*, as you delicately put it."

"They've killed over less."

"They won't touch you."

"You sure?"

Shoshanna withdrew her hand, returned to her food and tea. "Not entirely. But I could make it so if you were willing to part with your anonymity."

"I don't like the idea of being a known quantity."

Shoshanna took a bite of beef. "Well…did you find anything worth whispering about?"

"I did. Some splinter faction in the mob is working with the old Aryan Nation crew. Someone named Jacques is involved with what I'm pretty sure is a human trafficking ring. The accountant is fixing the numbers to hide it from Luc. Either he's playing both sides or Jacques has some heavy hex on his ass. Metaphorically."

A slow, pristine smile carved its white way onto Shoshanna's face. "That's very much worth whispering about. Did anyone see you besides the accountant?"

"I don't think so."

"I can work with this."

Shoshanna stared into space, her usually-sharp eyes glossy and distant. Her brow crinkled and she started mouthing words to herself, as if practicing a monologue.

"Hey, Shosh?" Deirdre asked, breaking the silence.

Shoshanna blinked, back in the room. "Yes?"

"Thanks."

Shoshanna's smiles tended to be practiced, rehearsed. Deirdre imagined that, back when Eli Winters ran the family and their business, he made her stand in front of mirrors smiling at her reflection over and over again until it turned out just right. So when the genuine article appeared, showing off the smile lines and the promise of very-soon crow's feet, Deirdre knew it.

This was such a smile.

"Of course," Shoshanna said.

They talked for a while longer, until Deirdre's plate sat empty, Shoshanna's half-empty, and both mugs were drained to tea leaves. Shoshanna excused herself to deal with Luc Grenier and the Québécois and her brother. Once she'd left, Deirdre went down to the basement, picked out a velvet bag, harp and key, and plucked a dreamer fruit.

"Razz," she whispered to it. "Razz."

It turned to honey on her tongue.

CHAPTER FOURTEEN

Paul cracked the top off the whiskey bottle before he got out of the car and took a long draught off the top. Two gulps burned down his throat. He grimaced at the afterbite and shook his head. The chatter of whispers grew quieter in the boozy aftermath, but he could still hear the voice of one ghost desperate for his attention. Lucy McKinney, a specter peeled free from Simon Perdue's photographs. Lucy McKinney, who'd driven him to speed his way to Deirdre's, whose appearance in his life had led him into this mess.

(help me. they stole my words. I don't know—)

He took a second heavy slug of whiskey, popped open the car door, and slipped out. The rasp of the restless dead quieted beneath booze, and soon they'd evanesce in amber drunk. He started down the sidewalk toward the harbor, the marina. Home. He tipped the bottle back a third time, recapped it, and clutched it around the neck within its brown bag.

He wrangled his phone from his pocket, switched the bottle to his left hand, and called Deirdre.

"Paul. Hey."

A brittleness to her voice.

"Hey. You okay?" he asked.

"Not really." She cleared frailty from her throat. *"What did you find out?"*

"We're in deeper shit than we know."

"How deep?"

"Deep. Serial murder, maybe human sacrifice…more than a couple of able-bodied goons willing to work someone over." He passed a vagrant hidden in the shadows of an abandoned storefront alcove and tightened his grip on the whiskey. "This is over our heads. Way over our heads."

"It's too late to turn back."

"I know."

Deirdre sighed, short and heavy. *"Randall's tied in with the Québécois. Debt collection, prostitution, human trafficking.... He might be able to call in favors."*

"I don't think he needs to."

"Find anything else?"

"A lot," he said. "More than I can frame in a few minutes on a phone. We stumbled onto something big, maybe something old. Randall's tied into this church, this old coven, apparently, and I think he's aiming to wrap up what they failed to wrap up however many years ago."

"We'll stop him."

"We should get someone else involved."

"You're thinking of Virgil?"

"I'm thinking of SWAT teams."

"How do we arrange that? Can you get Virgil to open an official case, make some kind of move for us?"

"I got him to agree to make a move if we can find some kind of actionable evidence."

"But he won't do anything until we put in the work for him?"

"It's complicated. If we can find something…"

"We haven't found anything yet."

"I just don't think we can do this without backup."

"You can't show up at the precinct talking about magic." A long pause followed. *"I want Virgil in on this as much as you do, but if he won't open a case, if he won't take the initiative…"* Deirdre hesitated. Sighed. *"Keep Virgil in the loop, but don't count on him. If the cops really wanted to help people out in Squatter City, they'd be helping. Besides, too many badges might turn this thing sideways. We don't know how many are on the Québécois payroll. Or Randall's, for that matter."*

"I'll do my best."

"Paul?"

"Yeah?"

"Watch yourself out there. Stay safe. I…just stay safe, okay?"

"Yeah. You too."

"I will."

The line disconnected, and Paul switched the phone for the brown bag. He took a shortcut between two abandoned warehouses to reach the harbor proper and started toward the marina. Dead voices whispered in the back of his mind and he had a fourth slug of whiskey to muffle them.

help.

Lucy's plea came as a bare whisper, fading along with his sobriety.

"I'm doing my best," he muttered.

The docks were quiet, which made the dead sound louder. The sea lapped at the shore and a waxing sliver of moon sliced through cloud cover. Stacks of crates, barrels, and other sundry supplies cluttered the piers and wharfs. Ships sat empty, where they sat at all. On the far side of the harbor, a couple lights glowed in the marina. There were guards and patrolmen, and the rare pass-through from Oceanrest PD, but in the main it was empty, desolate, dark.

He uncapped the whiskey, sipped it, capped it again.

He passed under an age-jaundiced streetlamp, and jumped when the crate next to him exploded. The thunder of a rifle shot broke the night and sent him staggering sideways.

He spun, dizzy in shock and booze, and searched the darkness for his assailants. He found them passing under sodium light—one man with a knife, another with a gun that could have been any long barrel from any hunting hobby shop in the country. The knife-wielding one ran toward him, blade glinting in the wharf side lights. The one with the rifle moved leisurely, certain.

"Fuck," Paul panted, already sprinting.

For the second time in half a decade, and the second time that week, he wished he had a gun.

He spun back around just in time to dodge out of the way of a stack of boxes someone had left at the end of a pier. He whirled from the crates and half-tumbled, his foot crashing down into a lobster cage. He fell face-first, somersaulting over concrete, the whiskey bottle banging his head where the still-healing wound shot fresh pain through his body.

A rifle thundered and pitted the cement six inches from his face.

Paul rolled onto his side and scrambled for the cover of some nearby crates and boxes. Somehow, he still had his whiskey in hand.

A bullet splintered wood from the crate by his head as he hunkered down.

He set the whiskey bottle aside and got to work trying to free his foot from the lobster trap. Some of the wire mesh between the woodwork had torn his pants and scored narrow cuts along his leg. He bent over, pulling at the mesh around his calf. The wire was stronger than it looked. The work was slow going and the knifeman would be on him soon.

"Shit," he spat, lifting his leg to bang the trap against the concrete. "Shit, fuck! Who still uses these things?"

He tore at the mesh with hurting fingers and slammed the trap against cement until it began to break apart. Panting with exertion, he pulled the contraption from his leg and hurled it into the sea. Grabbing the whiskey bottle, he made to leave cover, but a lightning strike of a bullet put that idea immediately out of his mind. The knifeman's shoes slapped concrete, getting closer.

He fumbled the cap off the whiskey bottle, desperate, and poured it around the base of the crates and boxes and the wooden piles of the pier. Fumbling through his pockets, he came up with his plastic lighter and sparked it. Although the booze caught, the flame spread slowly, taking its time to crawl to the wood and even longer to start chewing at it.

Capping the whiskey again, he peeked out from cover.

They were younger than he'd originally thought. One was maybe thirty, the other early-twenties, barely stubbled. The younger one wielded the knife, now only twenty feet away and closing. The older wore the typical clothes of a Québécois goon, blue jeans and plaid. The younger wore a gray-black cloak half-open over a leather jacket. One of Randall's.

The fire started to catch. Not the conflagration he'd prayed for, but it would have to suffice.

Grabbing the whiskey bottle, he crouched low behind cover and made his way to where the cement dropped to the sea. It wasn't a long fall to the waves, but it wasn't a short one, either. He glanced back at the slow-growing flame. No time.

The knifeman kicked aside some of the flaming crates and swung at the air. He snarled, feral, and backpedaled from the growing fire. His face twisted in the flame's glow, his eyes glinting wild as he saw Paul crouched at the end of the dock. "Over there!" the knifeman yelled, breaking into a sprint again.

Paul leapt into the water.

His body seized with the temperature, his muscles wrung taut by the wet chill. He thrashed his way above the waves with struggling strokes, teeth already chattering, and sucked in air. Salt water stung the small cuts in his legs, burned inside the healing wound in his head, and prickled the abrasions covering his torso. Kicking away from the dock, he took long, lopsided strokes toward the end of the nearest wharf, unbalanced by the weight of the whiskey still held in one hand.

"There!" the knifeman cried.

A bullet crashed into the sea mere feet away. The knifeman jogged along the dock, keeping pace with Paul's desperate swim, calling out his position.

Another bullet, closer. Paul reached for the next wharf, arm over arm, unbalanced, breathless.

A third bullet sliced the sea and the knifeman let out a giddy giggle. "You almost got him!"

Paul kicked, stroked, kicked, managing to put the concrete wharf between his body and the rifleman, but the kid with the knife leered overhead, ready to strike as soon as Paul went for the ladder.

"Come on up!"

The cold Atlantic sapped at Paul's tipsy strength. It tunneled his tendons, frigid and hungry.

"You don't look so hot," the knifeman mocked. "Better get to dry land."

A wave rolled through, sloshing salt water into Paul's mouth. He spat, heaved for air, and swam. The knifeman cackled overhead, following alongside. Paul thought about letting go of the whiskey, straightening out his balance in the frigid bay, but the bottle was his only feasible weapon. Not that it would do much good against a rifle.

"Bring me that sidearm!" the knifeman called. "I'll plug him, myself!"

Kick, stroke. Gag. Paul put distance between the knifeman and himself. Another ladder led from salt sea to harbor, but the knifeman would beat him to it. A tethered boat had an ocean-facing ladder; maybe he could climb aboard there. He swam for it, even as another gunshot split sky and splashed feet from his body.

A cramp spasmed down his arm, under his scapula. He groaned, head dipping below water. His drunk stomach flipped and twisted. His heart rampaged between cramped, cold-brittled ribs.

Another bullet, this one tearing fabric from his clothes, stinging his skin. Had he been hit? Glanced?

He thrashed to the surface, spat up acid bile, and kicked feebly toward the boat, the maybe-promise of escape.

"Think you nicked him, that time!" the knifeman called. "Come on, gimme the pistol. Gimme!"

The rifleman responded, too distant for Paul to make out with his ears full of seawater. He hazarded a glance back to the docks and saw the knifeman having a hushed conversation with the rifleman at the opposite end of the wharf, reaching for a pistol holstered on the rifleman's hip. Paul pressed on.

Closer…

Closer…

Another wave washed over him, his drunk and frozen limbs unable to fight against it. It rolled him under, scooped him up, and tossed him into concrete. He scrambled for the surface, pawing against the pebbled cement, trying to ignore the hot pain in his arm, the numbness of his torso, the burn of salt in his every wound, the knot of booze and panic in his guts.

His head broke the surface and another bilious upchuck surged out of him. The bottle of whiskey bobbed a few feet away from him, and he realized at seeing it that his hand had turned to distant prickliness. He reached out with his good arm and snatched the booze from the sea, glancing back at the docks.

Where had they gone?

The thought grabbed Paul by the throat and squeezed.

The answer came as gunfire, a series of staccato blasts from the dark harbor. A scream in knifeman's voice. What the hell was happening? Paul pushed from the rough concrete of the wharf and swam for the boat nearby.

Fifteen feet away. Just fifteen feet. His chattering teeth and seizing muscles screamed with every stroke.

On the docks, another shriek…of pain? Something else?

Paul reached, stroked, kicked. His vision tunneled, his periphery a blurry gray-black as his body began to give up. The ladder was ten feet away now. Closer.

More gunfire.

Paul strained, reaching into a growing darkness with dying fingers. He found purchase, the smooth cold of steel rungs. He gripped, pulled his corpse-heavy body to the ladder. He tried to lift himself up but couldn't. He got halfway up and fell back into the sea, guts churning with booze and saltwater. He pushed himself halfway up, again, and tossed the whiskey bottle onto the deck of the ship, then splashed back down.

Another scream echoed in distance, the knifeman's voice again. Shoes against asphalt.

Paul looped an arm around one of the rungs and floated, panting and shivering. He stuck one foot against the bottom rung and hung there, not having the strength to haul himself up. Barely having enough to avoid falling back into the waves.

Another gunshot, the scrape of shoes losing balance. A sickening silence.

Paul heaved for air, urging his body to move, urging his muscles to push him up the ladder…

"Dr. Somers?" Simon Perdue called from the darkness. "If you can hear me, please call out!"

***

Deirdre, a voice from nowhere said. *Deeeeeiiiirrrrdddreeee…*

Rats in the walls. Roaches under floorboards. Legs scrambled to press out from the wallpaper.

More in Heaven and Earth than is dreamt of…

if you'll let me hijack your feed for one second, I think we could help each other. The voice was chemical-sweet, carcinogenic, a pool of oily promise cooking in a silver spoon. Its silky bravado reminded Deirdre of stories about devils and demons, about dark fae spirits feasting on firstborn children after a handshake and a trick.

She uttered dream-speech, a moon-spell she wove from her own consciousness.

"No," was the name of the magic.

if that's what you want, but I'm warning—

The voice cut off.

Dreamer tendriled through the folds of her brain. She drowsed, half-awakened by the psychic intrusion. She glimpsed her ceiling, shadows squirming against shadow. Darkness copulated with itself. Her eyes drifted closed again, the voice half-forgotten as unconsciousness dragged her down.

Sunlight through leaves, a perfect shade of summer green. The back of her eyelids?

Nobody ever asked how dreamer worked. Not even Deirdre.

The dial tone of the universe. Nebulae swirled and danced to static-fuzz. Stories layered the world from its core to its surface, one piled on top of the next. Soil covered secrets, whispers grew into budded plants. Deep, deep down, a truth beneath every tale. Soon, too soon, a monster at the end of every story.

Razz held Olly's hand, approaching a big Denton house backgrounded by darkness. Young humans gathered within, a communal ritual played through by every generation since ape-hood. A tribe clustered around fires, in caves, in ancient cities undiscovered, exchanging stories, drinking fermentation until dizziness. A party. Razz let go of Olly's hand, dug a plastic bag from his pocket. Pills passed between palms. A throb of teens and UMO freshmen writhed through every room, their eyes tinged by alchemy.

A boy in a popped collar watched Razz from a distance. White polo shirt, checking his watch. Everything went as expected. He arced a white sphere toward a triangle of red cups, missed. He didn't care about the game, he was there to hunt. He shrugged at his teammate, drank watered down beer, glanced back across the party for his quarry.

White polo shirt, checking the latest text on his phone. Smirking.

It was time.

Razz watched the boy in the popped collar, watched the polo shirt. Did he know that death watched back?

The party melted from the vision. A song from the waking world tickled Deirdre's awareness. She fumbled to shut it up, her lips parting around vague truth. Something important called from the other side of dreaming, but nothing so important as the dream itself. Razz followed a boozy reaper into the woods, easy enough with the moonglow shining off the polo shirt.

That was the point.

In the deep, dark ocean, anglers used light to lure in their prey.

CHAPTER FIFTEEN

Paul tightened the thick blanket around his body and waved off the EMTs like buzzing flies. "I'm fine."

"You should have that checked out," a female EMT said, indicating the bandage she'd wrapped around his head, a replacement for the one he'd lost at sea.

"I did. I'm f-f-fine," he stuttered in his shivering, scowling at how weak he sounded.

"You could have hypothermia."

"I said I'm fine."

It wasn't true, but he didn't have time for an ambulance ride or a stay in the hospital. He needed a phone since his was ruined in the water, and he needed a good night's sleep. Persistently, the group of EMTs tried to coax him, giving up only when he snarled, "If I want help I'll ask for it. Leave me the fuck alone."

"You have to sign this," the female EMT said.

"What?"

"To show that you're refusing help."

Paul let one arm leave the blanket, jotted an approximation of his signature, and stormed off. He kept the blanket, wrapping it tighter as he left the ambulance behind. The EMTs muttered among themselves, but he ignored it.

Simon stood nearby, uttering curt reports into his phone, Paul's bottle of whiskey at his feet.

"…tried to shoot me," Simon said. "Yeah. One is still alive, he's on the way to Oceanrest Memorial. No, the other…" Simon nodded at nobody. "Yeah, I know. Paul's fine. A little beat up, but nothing serious. Of course. I'll talk to him."

Paul approached, doing his best attempt at a don't-fuck-with-me face.

"Right. I'll see you in the morning." Simon hung up, pocketing the phone.

"Can I get that back?" Paul asked, inclining his head toward the whiskey.

"Sure, just one thing, first."

"What?"

"I need you to fill out a report."

"Sure. Later."

"And Virgil wants you to come into the precinct tomorrow."

"No."

"No?"

"Did I stutter?" Paul grumbled.

"Paul, what just happened is a very serious—"

"Sure, whatever. I'll write up your report, go into the station, whatever. Can I borrow your phone?"

"Why?"

"I need to call someone."

Simon scanned Paul's face for several long seconds, then finally replied, "Fine."

Paul punched in Deirdre's number and turned his back on Simon.

Deirdre sounded drunk when she answered, *"A hole in the world, a billion limbs crawling out…"*

"Deirdre?" he asked. "Deirdre, are you okay?"

"Blue-eyed darkness, pale death. A hole…"

"It's Paul. I need to know you're okay. Listen, some of Ran—" he killed the name in his mouth, felt Simon's gaze on his back. "Tell me you're okay."

"There are holes in the world. The wallpaper. You've seen one, Paul, you know…"

"You're not making any sense."

"The static above the altar, it's a song. The hole is a window. I see you seeing it."

(a black room, darkness squirming on the other side)

Paul hesitated, the memory jarring him. "Deirdre—"

"Need to see," she interrupted. *"Need to dream."*

She hung up.

"Goddammit."

"You okay?" Simon asked.

He returned the younger man's phone. "I'm fine. Warming up, anyway."

"I'll need to take a statement."

"I need to get…" he trailed off, not wanting to talk about Deirdre or her house in front of Simon and not knowing quite why. "I can give a statement tomorrow."

"No, you really can't," Simon's voice hardened. "There was a possible attempt on your life, Dr. Somers, and one of the assailants was killed. The other's in critical condition. Listen, I don't want to push you, but when the investigation into my actions starts up I want things to be as cut and dry as possible. I need a written statement, a verbal statement, I need—"

"Tomorrow."

"I just saved your life."

Paul stood, nodded. "Yeah, you did."

Something gnawed at him about that, though exhaustion, booze, and the soul-sapping comedown of adrenaline occluded it.

"Look, I'll just take a quick statement back at your houseboat. Just to have something on the record. We can handle everything else tomorrow."

Paul pursed his lips, his brow trenched in question. But what question?

Simon bent low and scooped the whiskey from the ground. "Here. We'll head back to your place and get a preliminary. It'll take ten minutes. Twenty, tops."

"Let's make it quick, then."

■■■

Paul sipped his drink, a heavy pour despite Simon's objections, and tried to block out the aching concern about Deirdre's status. A growing, oily sixth-sense sensation sloshed and suppurated in his guts. Not the dead, but similar to the miasmic tang he'd smelled on his clothes that morning. He decided to kill it with drunkenness, as he did with so many other things.

"…and that's when you showed up, I assume," he said. Red pinpricks of blood blotted Simon's white shirt, more of them resting invisibly against his dark jacket. "I was in the water, didn't really see anything, but they stopped shooting at me, and the kid with the knife stopped chasing me around."

"The man with the knife," Simon corrected, his hand drifting toward the voice recorder between them.

"Sure. The eighteen-years-old-or-older male with the knife. Isn't that a leading question?"

"After I showed up, what happened next?"

"Shots were exchanged."

"You couldn't see the attackers fire at me?"

Paul huffed. "I was kind of focused on staying alive. I think I heard rifle fire, yeah."

"You can't be sure?"

"Not entirely." He took another sip and leaned back in his seat. "I went under, came back up, got tossed into the side of the pier by a wave. I think I heard rifle fire, small-arms fire…look, I know it's not exactly admissible but I'm certain they attacked you."

"Why?"

"Because they attacked me? Because they're crazy cu—" he cut himself off, halfway to the word "cultists" before he realized what he was saying—"crimi-nals. Québécois or Aryan militant Neo-Nazis or something."

Simon hit the red "stop" button on the recorder, brought his cerulean gaze to Paul. Nodded. "Strictly off the record, why would the Québécois be after you? Or the Aryans?"

"Long story."

"Considering the scrutiny I'm about to be under for saving your life, I think I might be owed a more thorough explanation."

Paul told the first lie that came to mind. "Debt."

"For what?"

"I'd rather not say."

Simon stared at him, ice-eyed.

"Would it help if I said I've worked something out with Virgil?" Paul asked.

"Depends on what you worked out."

"I'm a civilian asset in an ongoing investigation."

Simon gestured for more.

Paul sighed, sipped, slouched. "Alright. A couple nights ago, some Aryan psycho cracked my skull. He's tied in with the Québécois, and for reasons I don't want to get into, the PD doesn't go after the Québécois lightly." Simon opened his mouth but Paul held up a hand. "I said I don't want to go into it. It's complicated and longstanding and I only know the surface-level shit. How it's working is: I poke around for actionable evidence against the Aryans and, assuming I find it, Virgil brings the hammer down."

"Strictly off the record…Virgil has no intention of letting you leave the precinct tomorrow."

"Excuse me?"

"You can't blame him. Two men just tried to murder you, men who were dedicated enough to the task to get into a shootout only a couple hundred yards away from an active marina. If the crime here is as *insidious* as you suggest, they won't be the last people to make the attempt. Virgil's going to press you into protective custody. If that doesn't work, he's going to cuff you."

"For what?"

"He'll have twenty-four hours to figure that out."

Paul shook his head and drained the rest of his drink. "Why are you telling me this?"

"I'm a federal agent, Dr. Somers. I don't work for Oceanrest PD."

"Still…"

"Because I need your help. Because there's still someone out there, kidnapping and killing women. Maybe multiple someones."

Ice clinked against glass, and Paul examined his drink's emptiness. "Did you follow up on my hunch?"

"About something noteworthy happening in 2011?"

"Yeah."

"I did. It turned over nothing."

"Shit."

"What aren't you telling me?"

Paul hesitated before answering. "Your killer, or killers, might be tied into the Aryan thing."

"What gives you that idea?"

"It accounts for dogmatic ideation and criminal ties. Six out of your eight victims are women of color. And…"

"And what?"

"And it feels like an answer that makes sense."

"A hunch isn't evidence."

"Which is why I didn't tell you." Paul stood up and gestured for the pier side exit. "Now, if you'll excuse me, I need to get some sleep. I just spent my day being threatened and shot at, and I have to wake up tomorrow and keep looking for evidence to hand over to you and Virgil."

Simon walked to the door, opened it, and paused. "There are connections between the Aryans and the Québécois. Some byproduct of faction infighting, some mid-rank mobsters unhappy with current management, making allies out of old enemies. So you're right, it's a good hunch, but we still don't have any evidence. No suspects."

Paul sighed. "You might want to look into Randall Tyler Hill."

"Who's that?" Simon asked, still standing in the doorway.

"Old Aryan Nationalist. Used to be a pimp, likely into human trafficking. He has the means and opportunity."

"I'll look into him. And, um, thanks for coming clean with me."

"Yeah, well, the sooner we handle this, the better. I'll call if I find anything else."

"I'll do the same."

Paul locked the door after Simon exited, waited until the g-man's sedan rumbled into the distance, then pivoted.

Wait.

He stopped mid-step. How had Simon ended up at the docks that night? And how had he ended up in the car park that afternoon?

How had he known which car was Paul's?

CHAPTER SIXTEEN

Deirdre tossed and turned and dissipated. Dreamer lurched her senses into too many bodies, none of them hers.

She stood in a room fogged with drug vapor. Everyone wore white. White Room. This was the White Room. Here, a hungry throat rumbled the walls, an endless stomach gurgle given voice. In the skull of Hell, a man sat on a throne, smiling as he supplicated a starving monster he couldn't understand. The crowned priest believed he had power, but in truth, power had him.

Her senses shifted, bent.

Razz ran from bonfire terror, glancing back at Olly's sweat-glistened face. "Come on!" he panted, half-tripping over roots and night-hidden bracken. Behind them, a circle of men cackled. A blur of pallor stalked. Their limbs moved panic-fast, legs pumping at the pace of hunted prey.

A bend, backwards.

White polo shirt took a cloak from someone's hands, donned it ceremoniously. A bonfire blazed in the center of the coven's circle. The smell of burnt meat tanged the air. A chant went up. One of the other believers stepped forward, muttering words, moving his hands in esoteric gestures. Another threw rune-carved bones into the flames.

Between tree boles, Razz and Olly crouched low, thinking they went unseen.

White polo shirt smiled, knowing.

A bend, backwards. Deirdre's senses dizzied, nauseous through time and space and perspective.

Randall came without sound, jerking off over the manacled woman's stomach. She screamed and thrashed the chains, shrieking words Randall didn't recognize. A spell, perhaps. He knew a few tricks of his own, guessed at the nature of the witch's magic, waved a counter through the air. It didn't take. What was she doing then, if not trying to hurt him? He shrugged it off, zipped up his pants. Drew forth the hungry blade.

Pre-Latin tongue shrieked and chains rattled. Her voice hurt his ears.

Soon there would be no more screams.

Randall walked around the side of the stained-fabric altar, took red hair in his hands. Yanked. The woman arched back at the force, spat more words, writhed. The tongue. He needed to cut out the tongue. All the other motions had been gone through, all other torture complete. He needed the tongue, and the rest of the boys would sink their knives into the womanhood.

A bend, rollercoaster-sharp.

Olly wailed when she saw the fire open up and give birth. Razz clamped a fear-taut palm over her mouth, too late. The cloaked figures turned toward them and laughed. Then the two spies flew through midnight darkness and reaching branches, pursued by an impossible thing.

Razz kept hearing Olly's shriek in his head long after it had silenced.

(*Shhh, they might hear you*)

Soon there would be no more screams.

In Randall's hand, the woman spat the last of her syllables, lips curled in hateful victory. Randall drove the blade into her mouth. Other knives found purchase elsewhere.

Soon…

Razz ran breathlessly, fumbling a number into his cellphone, Olly's shriek echoing between the walls of his skull.

Pale violence stalked them through evergreen and maple.

There was a monster at the end of the story. Olly screamed.

Soon, there would be no more.

■■■

Deirdre shot up clutching at her chest, her heart an off-rails freight train breaking over her bones. She screamed. Samedi yowled and fled the room, claws clattering on hardwood. She went for her gun in a blind panic and froze, remembering the dreamer vision. Nausea and flashes of nameless violence.

She leapt to her feet and flew into the bathroom, snatching the toothpaste, smearing more gel across the mirror.

The images frayed (*Olly screamed, Razz ran, fire opened up*) as she scrawled, half from memory, half through dreamer-driven automation. When the last of the vision vanished (*Randall's blade catching teeth on the way in*), she staggered away from the sink, collapsed against the toilet, and puked.

The mirror said:

Tongue writhed from the ashes too,
they f e a s t and h o w l and e a t s
two beasts, three? one tastes the sky,
eats until the sunshine dies
And below that:
Speaker, Devourer, Tongue.
Samuel and Lucy buy time.
old magic. bad deals. long con.
Razz called.

Standing from the toilet and pressing some of the toothpaste onto a brush to clean vomit from her mouth, she stared at the words. They didn't make sense, didn't fit together the way she wanted them to, though the last line struck her like a fist. It spun her around and sent her back into her bedroom, where her cellphone flashed a green LED to tell her she had missed messages.

She checked the voicemail first, phone pressed against her ear.

"*Dee, Jesus, uh, Deirdre, it's me, it's me,*" Razz panted, his breath harsh. "*I just—shit, look, Olly and me, we—we were digging around about that Ku Klux motherfucker and, shit—my crew knew the guy, and—oh, shit, oh Jesus Christ...*" Whipping branches, wind, breath in the mic. Another voice in the background, Olly's, said something she couldn't hear. "*We followed one of Randall's boys to this party and...we followed him into the woods. I think he knew. I think...*" More panting, dry wood snapping.

"Run," Deirdre whispered, swallowing toothpaste. "Shut the fuck up and run."

"*I saw a monster, Dee, a real fucking monster. It came outta the fire, like, like...I can't even describe it. Like the fire opened up and this thing came out of the gap. And Olly...*" (screamed) "*...it doesn't matter. We took off but they saw us, they all laughed at us, and this thing, this thing laughed too.*"

In the background, Olly yelped.

"*Come on,*" Razz said, away from the mic now. "*Come on, get up. Come on!*"

Deirdre's mouth went dry. Her lips, dry. Her insides, dry.

"Run," she said to an hours-old message.

"*I know a place we can lay low for a while, up on Adams Court. You gotta meet us, Dee. You gotta. I mean, this thing is real. It's fucking real.*"

They were running over concrete now, shoes slapping asphalt.

"*I'll text you when we get there, I'll call, okay? I'll—holy shit!*" a sound, distant from the mic but loud.

The voicemail ended.

Shards of crystal blossomed from Deirdre's ventricles, carved apart her veins. Her hand tightened hard around the cellphone, squeezing until the plastic creaked. "No," she muttered, "no, no, no, no, no…"

She turned the phone face over and checked the text messages.

Razz 1:22 AM: *'doing fine, D. got some safe places set up just in case, don't worry.'*

Razz 2:01 AM: *'got a lead w/ 1 of Randall's boys'*

She shook her head, kept reading.

Razz 3:48 AM: *'holy shit, there's a legit white power meeting out here.'*

Razz 3:57 AM—a picture message, seven young men in asphalt-shaded robes, spaced out around a flickering blaze. Deirdre couldn't make out any faces, save for one. The scruff and lopsided features of the kid who'd cracked Paul's skull with the butt of a rifle. Isaiah, was it? He was the closest to the blaze, caught mid-gesture, his hands blurred.

Razz 4:09 AM: *'what language is this?'*

The attached audio recording was too garbled and muffled to make anything out. Jolts of interference rived through the recording, underscored by the sound of crackling flame. The cultists' words were unintelligible, but Deirdre recognized the growing sound building up below their drone, the humming interference of old magic toying with new technology.

Razz 4:22 AM—another picture message, this one a blur of smeared color and senseless shape, whiteness like paste erupting from red-yellow blaze. A hint of delineation, the implication of a curve of skull topping the cloud of thick, gross cream. Shadows silhouetted other possible features, but Deirdre couldn't make sense of them.

The last text came at 5:27 AM, a three-digit number Deirdre knew would correspond to an abandoned address on Adams Court.

She texted Razz. *'Stay safe. Please text back if you're okay. On the way.'*

She picked her revolver up from the mattress, not bothering to root through her still-messy room for the holster she'd tossed aside before sleeping. She stuffed the weapon in her pants' pocket, slipped two full speedloaders into the opposite pocket, and attached a pocket knife to her waistband.

Samedi returned to the room and mewled, standing in the middle of the threshold.

Deirdre paused, squinting at the cat. "What?"

Meow.

Deirdre hesitated, wavering. She'd heard that cats connected to an unseen world, that one-eyed cats could see the future through their blinded socket. Then again, the woman who'd told her those things had a dreamer habit and a tendency to go through mushrooms with frightening abandon.

Samedi moved in a tight circle in her threshold, mewled again. Flicked his half-tail side to side.

"Yeah. Uppers are a good idea." Deirdre went to her lockbox, opened it, and fished out a joint of sixth sense stimulants. It would make her magic sharper, stronger, less physically exhausting to use. After the near-disaster at La Femme Rouge, a little boost seemed like a good idea. Especially if the people after her were capable of summoning some strange monster from *else-where*—not the kind of magic an amateur could pull off.

She lit the joint and inhaled crisp power. The smoke tasted of cool electricity, of ice and fire, of battery tips and the gross underside of coins left sitting for too long. Fresh vegetables and rancid meat. Energy and potential.

Samedi mewled, pawed at the side of the doorway, and walked off. Mewled again from farther down the hall.

"Oh," Deirdre muttered, adrenaline fizzling in the wake of mundane banality. "You just want to be fed."

There wasn't time for that. There was only time to move.

■■■

Paul's entire body ached. Bruises and abrasions scoured the skin between his shoulder blades and discolored the flesh around his ribs. The pain of his arms and legs was more distant, a post-workout soreness from swimming against the frigid waves of the Atlantic. The cut on his head, half-healed, re-opened and salted by the sea, throbbed dully.

His innards didn't feel much better. Leftover queasiness plucked at his viscera, a reminder of his puke-ups from the night before.

No hangover though. So that was nice.

His phone buzzed, buzzed, buzzed, and he groaned through full-body complaint to pull himself toward it. Peeling his eyes open, he reached for the device. 8:39 AM, the phone face told him, with two texts from Deirdre.

The first text read, *'I need your help. Randall's going after Razz, I need to get him somewhere safe.'* An address was attached, a place up on old Adams Court, a half-collapsed street in the older, more substantially ruined reaches of Squatter City. Paul slumped forward, pressing sleep out of his eyes with the heel of his free hand.

The second text seemed more concerning, reading simply, *'Come armed. No cops.'*

He set the phone back on the end table, stood up, and wavered on unsteady legs.

That miasma persisted, something stale and gross on the air. Not just confined to the hamper either, but infesting his every breath. What was it? He inhaled and grimaced at the scent of it. Not a nasal scent, a sixth sense scent.

The realization jolted him awake. The miasma wasn't normal, it was paranormal. Not just stale air, but the aftermath of some dark presence, perhaps the giveaway patina of some sinister hex laid upon him. Paul stood stock still next to his bed, his mind racing with possibilities.

Except he only knew as much about hexes and curses as Deirdre had told him, which wasn't much.

And if there'd been a dark presence in his home, well…the dead weren't uncommon visitors.

Either way, there wasn't much to do about it now.

He shelved the questions on the miasma and got dressed. He ate another breakfast of peanut butter and souring milk, drank cold mashed-cigarette-tasting coffee, and searched through the mess of his houseboat for his knife. A long, wooden-hilted blade, he slipped it into his back pants pocket, and was halfway out the door when he froze.

The sea breeze carried the whispers of the dead, and the ghost at the end of the pier lurched toward him.

Was it Lucy?

Worse, was it Cassandra?

Paul stumbled backward and slammed the door shut. He raced across the room and clumsily toppled his ashtray while rooting around for the last pinch of supernatural depressant.

The background static of the distant dead crescendoed in his skull.

(*where am I why is it so cold // please let me out // insides on the outside Jesus Christ all so red and white how did I open up // I don't know what to do*)

He needed the downers, a drink, maybe both.

He pushed his way through spilled ashes until he found the last of the roach, put it between his lips without thinking, and lit it with a plastic gas station lighter. Inhaled.

dad, a distant voice whispered. Her voice, Cassandra's voice. *dad why did you leave?*

He held smoke in his lungs until he couldn't anymore, wheezing and coughing silver haze. He stumbled across the floor to the sink and spat foul saliva. Brought the joint back to his lips and took another toke. The cherry sizzled back to his fingernails, threatening to burn him.

you owe me answers. you owe me that much.

Another coughing fit racked his lungs, Cassandra's voice drifting away on the smoke. The background static of the rest of the dead went silent, lost beneath psychic downers. Still, better safe than sorry. He lifted the last pinch of joint to his lips and pulled until the cherry bit his fingertips and he dropped the remnants in the sink.

A third coughing fit brought tears to his eyes, his lungs and face seared with the effort of vaporous consumption. He grabbed the edge of the kitchen countertop to steady himself, hacked for a few more seconds, and spat phlegm and gross into the sink. Panting through the quiet that followed, he filled a stein with water and guzzled it down.

"Not now," he muttered. "Please."

But he could no longer hear the dead, and any answer given never reached him.

"I'm sorry, Cass," he said. "I'm so sorry, but I can't…"

Could she still hear him?

It didn't matter. Or it did, but he couldn't stop to deal with it. He had places to be.

He double checked his keys and knife, and left.

CHAPTER SEVENTEEN

Ruined houses lined the rubbled asphalt of Adams Court like busted teeth. The most distal appendage of Squatter City, Adams Court had no legal residents, no rental properties, and barely even any squatters. One by one, the houses had all collapsed, leaving only a handful of semi-stable structures behind. Knee-and-waist-high grass, shrubs, saplings, and bracken strew the land, blurring eventually into wilderness.

Between 1982 and 2010, Oceanrest had lost over a quarter of its population. Adams Court had been an early casualty of abandonment, and so its ruination was nearly complete. Most of the streetside structures had hollowed into husks, and those still standing looked frail, attenuated.

Deirdre chewed her lip, glancing from phone to street and trying to figure out which of the still-standing squats matched the address Razz had sent her. One of the homes wore graffiti as a bruise, two leftover words from what had once been a three-word sentence. The remaining words were "GO HOME." Whatever the first word had been, lost when that side of the building had collapsed an unknown history earlier, Deirdre was certain it had been an epithet.

An engine rumble snapped her gaze back to Main Street, her hand diving for her gun.

Paul's car rolled to a stop a dozen feet away on the uneven crags of Main and Adams Court. The driver's side door popped open and Paul emerged with a clumsy stagger.

Deirdre lifted an eyebrow at the sight of him. "What happened to you?" she asked. "Your head…"

"Yeah, the cut re-opened." Paul reached up and absently brushed hair away from the new bandage. "Had another run-in last night. Some of Randall's goons tried to kill me."

"Jesus, Paul—"

He held up a hand. "It's fine. I'm still here. Not so sure about them."

Deirdre frowned. "After we get Razz, we can't split up anymore."

"I strongly agree."

"We'll need to put more salve on that wound. I could probably just close it myself with a couple cantrips."

"Better save your energy, if you're expecting trouble." He reached behind him to take out a large, deadly-looking hunting knife. "*Are* we expecting trouble?"

"Yeah."

"What kind?"

"Not sure. If we're really lucky, nothing. If not, maybe some of Randall's thugs. Or…"

"Or what?"

"Something worse. A monster."

Paul balked, a huff of amused disbelief escaping his lips. "A monster?"

"Yeah."

"Shit."

"We should move. Last I heard from Razz was over four hours ago. The house is down this way." She tilted her head westward and started walking. Paul followed close behind. She crossed over broken, uneven asphalt, sprouts of brush and tall grass breaching through the rubble, and searched for numbers on the wrecked houses. Halfway down the street, they came upon the worn visage of a two-floor colonial, the second floor only partially collapsed. Squinting at the front door, Deirdre picked out the address and started over the knee-high foliage toward the entrance.

"How did Razz get involved in this, anyway?" Paul asked.

"Frank's loose lips. The junkie asshole spilled the beans about our troubles and Razz…Razz wants to help."

"You couldn't scare him off of it?"

She shook her head, pushing past brush to the battered front door of the building. It hung diagonal across the threshold, pieces of wood busted away, doorknob missing, paint all peeled off, battered and moldy. Deirdre pushed in and the whole thing broke away, slamming to the floor.

Inside, anxious silence lurked.

The stairs to the second floor sagged half-ruined, the railing gone. To the left, a table sat overturned, legs broken, surrounded by toppled chairs.

More mold. To the right, an overturned armoire, pebbles of gleaming glass, more shards of splintered wood. Deirdre went straight, over creaking floorboards into what might have once been a kitchen. Most of the appliances had been stripped or looted, but an oven sat against one wall, doorless hinges gaping wide.

Overhead, desiccated wood creaked and groaned.

"Razz?" she called, her voice hushed by the oppressive quiet of the wreck. Only the wind replied.

"You sure this is the place?" Paul asked.

"Shh. Yes."

A tree branch reached through a glassless window. Fungus grew thick in a corner. Water damage and mold mottled every wall, peeled wallpaper down into rot-yellowed scrolls. Linoleum tiles had been pried up from the floor, underpinning scarred and marred.

The basement door sat on the floor in front of a dark rectangle of threshold.

"Razz?" Deirdre called into the dark.

"D-Dee? Deirdre?" Razz's voice called back.

Her body went nearly limp from the relief. "Are you hurt? Olly?"

"We're fine!" Olly yelled up.

"Alright. Can you come up here?"

A pause.

Razz asked, "There anyone else around? Anyone follow you?"

"Nobody followed us. And we're armed."

"And that—that *thing*?"

"No sign of it. It's broad daylight."

Another pause. The sound of movement against rough concrete, then footsteps ascending stairs. Razz appeared in the threshold and stepped over the useless door. Before she knew what she was doing, Deirdre ran to him, wrapping him tight in her arms. Squeezed.

"Oh my Gaea," she muttered. "Oh, Luna, oh, thank God, thank… you're okay."

Razz pushed against her, but she held fast. "I'm not fucking okay, man. You know what I saw last night?"

"I don't care," she said, pulling away, her hands still on his shoulders. "I don't care about monsters. You're okay."

"I'm pretty far from okay," Razz griped. "This thing came outta *nowhere*. Out of *fire*."

For a second, she almost told him. She almost just said the words 'I know, I'm a witch,' but a kickback impulse stopped her. She pursed her lips, let go of Razz's shoulders, and stepped back. "I saw. That blur, right?"

"It had arms, legs—it was all fucked-up looking, though."

"No eyes," Olly said, making Deirdre remember that Olly and Paul were still there, that they were still in a slouching squat on a ruined street. "The thing had no eyes but it looked at me. I felt it look at me." Olly shook herself off, adding almost inaudibly, "Coño rey del infierno maldito, qué chingados…"

"Randall's crew, like…they fucking *summoned* it."

Paul shot Deirdre a stern, heavy gaze.

"We'll handle it," Deirdre said.

"How? How you gonna handle a real goddamned monster?" Razz backed away sharply. "We're fucked, man. *Fucked.*"

"I know someone who might be able to help," Paul said, and Deirdre offered him a small smile in return.

"You *know* someone?" Razz asked.

"Yeah. She's…she knows a lot about this sort of thing. She might be able to help us figure out what we can do to beat it."

"For real? Like, you know a girl who knows about monsters and magic and shit?"

Paul nodded. "Yeah. For real."

"And you never mentioned this to anyone?"

"Would you have believed me?"

Razz paused, stroking barely-there chin stubble. "Nah, I guess not. But shit. Shit."

"What is it?" Olly asked.

Overhead, more groaning wood.

The hair on the back of Deirdre's neck bristled. She cast her gaze to the ceiling, the source of the creaking, and narrowed her eyes. Sixth sense sensation roared in her head, a rush of implication and instinct.

"Move," she said.

She pushed Razz out of the way and leapt aside as the ceiling collapsed. The sound, the dust of plaster, the broken wood, the shocked calls of Paul and Olly, the overwhelming volume and adrenaline of the moment made her stagger, slamming sidelong into the wall. When she regained her balance, she drew her gun.

The thing appeared jointed, osteological, a creature of bone and sinew, but it moved like drooping glue. It stretched out and fell from the ragged hole in the ceiling, a horrific whiteness of teeth and bladed limbs. Too many legs, three arms—one from the top of its spine, if it had a spine, the others from curdled-milk textured shoulders—and a vast jaw lined with rows and rows of jagged fangs. In the center of the serpentine tube of its torso, a red-black hole guttered to its innards.

Olly shrieked, backpedaling and stumbling over broken linoleum. She tripped, tumbled prone. Razz moved to help her up, gaining momentum toward the exit, but the Beast effortlessly reached out, plucked him up with a many-clawed hand, and tossed him into the doorless oven. The oven dented from the force of impact and Razz howled.

"No!" Deirdre turned her pistol on the massive Beast and squeezed the trigger.

She missed her mark in the movement and sound, bullet slamming into the cottage-cheese flesh of its torso, inches from the black-red pit centering its chest. It swiveled its eyeless gaze toward her, considered her, and turned back to Razz. It lashed out, unbelievably fast for a monster so gargantuan and heavily-muscled, but Razz managed to roll to one side, the Beast's claws scraping the floor. Deirdre took a second shot, the bark of the weapon deafening in the claustrophobic space. Her angle was off, this time—there'd been no chance she would have hit her mark from where she stood—and the second bullet buried itself in the Beast's shoulder, slowly absorbed in dripping whiteness.

The Beast's second attack slashed Razz's chest, tearing fabric from flesh and flesh from bone. Razz screamed as streaks of crimson opened to bare muscle. He fumbled at the back of his pants, grabbing for something as he rolled and scrambled away from the monster's raking claws.

Paul ran in to intercept the Beast's third attack. As the spine-mounted appendage shifted and mutated into a scorpion's tail, multi-segmented and pointed with a vicious blade, Paul rushed forward and brought his hunting knife down on the monster's back. The Beast turned toward the attack and swatted Paul to the floor.

Deirdre strafed across the room, trying to get sights on the Beast's black-red gouge, the clear weak point in its mystic animus. She squeezed off a third shot, loud thunder echoing in the vacant squat, and this one struck home. The Beast staggered back, a gurgling, wet growl rattling up its throat. It snarled tiger-like, eyeless visage swerving momentarily to Deirdre. Then, as if suicidally focused on one single task, it continued its attack on Razz.

A many-clawed hand rent flesh from Razz's body yet again. Another scream of pure anguish tore from the boy's throat, but Razz finally managed his way around the Beast's dimensions, ducking under a second blow and staggering toward Olly.

"Get up!" he shouted. "Run! Fuckin' run!"

Razz wrangled a matte black semi-auto pistol from his waistband as he moved, but didn't turn to fire.

The Beast's third appendage shot forward, stabbing Razz's right shoulder.

Paul, somehow back on his feet, grabbed the scorpion-tail arm with one hand, the other pushing Razz free of the bladed tip.

"Both of you, go!"

Razz groaned and shuddered, staggered to Olly, and started to help the girl to her feet. "We gotta—we gotta—we…"

Slick blood glistened in broad strokes over the floor and wall. Deirdre stumbled over tile-less underpinning, struggling to line up another shot. The Beast flicked its scorpion appendage hard and fast, crashed Paul into a wall once, twice, a third time. Paul lost his grip and collapsed.

Razz got Olly back to her feet, his face a twisted grimace of bloodsmear. Olly moved to support him, but he pushed her away, turning toward the Beast. He fired without practice, his aimless and panicked shots having little effect. The Beast lunged forward and dug long claws into Razz's torso. Razz shrieked, stumbling back with flags of ragged flesh hanging from his body. The pistol fell from his hand as he turned to follow Olly.

Deirdre's fourth shot buried itself in the Beast's red-black heart. This time the monster roared, a sound loud enough to make gunshot paltry in comparison, but still it ignored her attacks in favor of its quarry. It spun away from Deirdre and lurched hungrily toward Razz.

"Get away from him!" she screamed, firing a fifth bullet uselessly into its back.

Razz, Olly, and the Beast turned down the squat's main hallway, out of sight. Deirdre rushed across the kitchen to follow.

Razz screamed again, and Olly shrieked in high-pitched terror.

Deirdre rounded the corner to find Razz lying face-down in the hallway, Olly running for the exit. The Beast brought one of its several leg-like appendages down on the back of Razz's head, rebounding his skull against hardwood, and clambered over his bloodied body to chase Olly. It swiped at Olly's back, fell short, and then Olly was out the front door, tearing through overgrowth, out of sight.

Deirdre's sixth round went into the back of the Beast's head. Its skull jerked forward, and a strange squelching sound followed as the hole closed back up. The Beast shook itself off, hesitated at the squat threshold for a second, and shambled after Olly.

Deirdre ran for Razz, her shoes squicking over wet blood. She landed on her knees next to him and tossed her gun aside. She rolled him over face-up, and pulled him to her. Hot carmine everywhere. His life soaked into her pants. His face, a mask of twitching, gaping anguish, peered up at her, bleary eyes fading fast.

"Dee…" he croaked.

She pressed her hand to his blood-soaked chest, the wide gashes wrought by the Beast's claws. Dug into herself, deeper than ever before, as deep as she could imagine her existence reaching, and pulled out everything she had. A pulse of magic, pure energy and will, blew through her muscles. A healing cantrip, a small spell against massive wounds. She felt the power reach through the gashes, trying to stitch sinew and muscle back together, patching veins and capillaries…but it wasn't enough.

"What—what's that?" he panted.

Paul flew through the hallway behind them, chasing after the Beast as it chased Olly, but Deirdre hardly noticed.

"Magic," Deirdre said. She dug in deep again, sweat beading across her forehead. Another attempt, more magic pushed into Razz's body. She felt fissures in his ribs, slashes carved through viscera, felt her strength filling in the gaps, pulling him back together—but there was so much damage.

"Are you…?"

"A witch."

A third cantrip, deeper still, a growing ache spreading down her spine and through her muscles. The spell drove through Razz's body, into sliced organs and tattered flesh; the concussion from having his head slammed into the floor; the wreckage of his shoulder; the ruin of his ribcage; the punctured lung; the sliced stomach; rent intestines; so much else…

Too much.

"Dee…you a witch?"

She opened her mouth to answer but gasped for air instead. The magic wore through her, hitched her breath, drove her heartrate up, up, up…

She nodded, started digging for a fourth cantrip.

"Are there ghosts?" Razz asked, soft and distant, his eyes dulling, the light of all his futures flicking off one by one.

"There's ghosts."

"You think...do you..."

"Stay with me. Come on, stay with me."

Razz coughed red spatter.

The fourth spell made her yelp with pain, her body pitching over Razz's, her muscles straining against her bones. Sweat and tears slicked her face. She panted, swallowed hard, and started focusing on a fifth attempt. A dizzy spell washed over her, a headrush of purple, black, navy.

"Stay with me!"

His eyelids lifted halfway. "You gotta...gotta stop 'em, Dee..."

She pushed the spell through again and the room flickered dark black and purple dizzy.

She imagined. In the stretching darkness of the seconds-long full-body wrack, she imagined Razz's futures, so many different futures. She imagined him sleeping on her couch, selling stupid product to stupid people, but making money. She imagined him living over a Denton woman's garage, working at a diner. She imagined him at UM Oceanrest, a diploma scrolled in his hands, smile as bright as the moon. She imagined him older, twenty-something, thirty-something, forty-something, anything, any other age but this.

But then she felt his lungs heave, his heart pound, his throat struggle for air, and all of it fell apart.

"Promise..." he choked on the word. "Promise you'll stop 'em..."

His eyes fluttered again, and closed.

Blindness crept on her from all sides, exhaustion tunneling her vision. A sixth attempt gutted her, patching the hole in his lung but still not enough, still not giving him all those years a life should promise.

"Please..." she prayed, sobbing. "Please, please..."

No answer came.

CHAPTER EIGHTEEN

Paul sprinted through reaching weeds and overgrown grass, panting to catch up to the Beast and Olly. He saw the pale white grossness of the Beast's back shamble through overgrowth, heading for the wreckage of another squat in the distance. Clutching the blood-slicked pistol Razz had dropped, he gave chase.

"Please, don't be out of bullets," he muttered, though he didn't slow to check either chamber or mag.

He saw a flash of dark hair and human body dart hard left, saw the Beast lunge at Olly and miss. Olly screamed, sprinting now toward the tree line and the wilderness beyond. Cursing, Paul changed course, finger pressed against the trigger guard of the pistol, eyes locked on the two figures ahead.

"Help!" Olly shrieked. "Help, fucking help! Somebody!"

Paul picked up the pace, ignoring the building heat and soreness twining through his legs.

Olly spun around, dodged one of the Beast's swinging arms, and moved away from the tree line again. The Beast's scorpion tail lashed forward, cutting her off. She whirled again, her panicked yelp tear-choked, and tore into the woods. The sound the Beast made as it followed resembled something between insectoid chittering and laughter.

"Fuck it," Paul muttered. He burnt his legs hard toward them, slowing to a stop a dozen paces away. Bracing into a shooter's stance, he lifted the pistol toward the Beast's back and fired two shots. The bullets planted themselves in the monster's flesh, and the Beast paused for a second to swivel its eyeless gaze over its shoulder at him (was that a smile?) before continuing its pursuit.

At least he'd bought Olly a couple seconds' head start.

As Olly and the Beast entered the tree line, Paul broke into another run. The burn of his lungs and his heart in his chest was nothing compared to the desperate ache he'd felt the night before, but the fatigue was becoming harder to ignore. He began to heave and groan, and a cramp threatened to cluster through his gut.

Branches whipped around him. Twigs snapped underfoot. Thick boles bristled from the ground. Every few seconds he had to reorient himself in the woods, spinning in circles and half-arcs, searching for a glimpse of Olly or the Beast. He took off to his left, his right. He spun in a circle, went back. The wilderness grew more confusing with each turn, and he could tell from Olly's ragged cries that her sob-strangled breath was running out.

"Help, please, help!"

He whirled around and ran toward Olly's voice. The promised cramp stabbed through his right side, a rough grunt escaping his lips.

He caught a flash of white between tree trunks, lifted his gun, and fired.

The Beast snarled but didn't let up.

"Here! Over here!" Paul yelled, hoping to draw both of them out.

Sneakers through leaves, footsteps approaching. He heard Olly's panting sobs, her uneven stride. He took a second to check the magazine and pistol chamber, happy to see even the few bullets he had left. Five bullets were better than none. Listing in the direction of his pulsing cramp, he jogged toward Olly as she jogged for him.

He saw her, just a few yards away, leaning forward, one hand clutching shallow wounds in her side. The Beast followed right behind, its inhuman jaws wide open, rows and rows of ivory teeth slavering in a grotesque smile. It lashed out with its scorpion appendage and cut another shallow wound down Olly's back. Olly yelped, falling forward at top speed, hitting the ground and sliding through dewy leaves and browned evergreen needles.

Paul slid into the shooter's stance again, squared off against the Beast, and fired, aiming for the black-red pit at its heart.

Five bullets rapidly became two.

The bullet that missed vanished into oozing goo, the entry wound sealing in sucking slop. The two that hit spattered viscous black-orange fluid from the Beast's guttering pit, gross-colored ichor. The monster reared back from the impacts, bellowing so loud, so goddamned *loud*. It staggered back, a flue of black-orange spewing from its maw.

Paul rushed toward Olly.

The Beast hesitated, hacked up another glob of gore.

"Come on, come on, get up!" Paul ran to Olly's side but didn't offer her a hand, leveling the pistol sights on the Beast.

Olly pushed herself to a crouch and staggered forward.

The Beast backpedaled a few more clumsy steps, its multiple leg-like appendages twitching and quivering under its weight. It turned toward Paul. Paul knew it could see him, somehow—that it could smell him, even—and being scented and seen by a thing with neither nose nor eyes rattled him.

"Go!" he yelled at Olly, not bothering to break his gaze from the Beast. "Go, I'll catch up!"

Her fleeing footsteps receded in the distance.

A low grumble came from the monster's many-toothed mouth. It tilted its head side to side, as if finding the thing before it curious, bemusing.

"Come get it. I'm right here, come on."

A low series of clicks came from the Beast's throat, followed by that hideous laughter again, that awful insect-swarm laughter.

It turned its back on Paul, and its flesh began to bubble and shift. Strange shapes pushed against its pale skin, its insides reconfiguring. Its torso hinged forward, its many leg-like appendages twisting together and combining, cording into four back-bent legs. Its arms shifted, becoming another set of legs. Its scorpion tail moved down its spine from its original location between its shoulder blades to the more traditional location at the root of the backbone.

Paul staggered away from the shifting mass, the Beast becoming a new monster altogether, its face elongating lupine, the black-red pit shifting from its now-hidden chest to the center of its forehead.

It turned to give him another insect-chitter snicker, and then loped through the trees, rapidly gone.

Paul stood frozen for several seconds, his eyes wide in disbelief, his breath coming in ragged pants.

As the shock of what he'd witnessed faded, the ache of his legs and lungs came to the fore. He swayed backward, knees creaky and weak, and lowered the gun to his side. He limped to a nearby elm and leaned against the tree trunk, laboring to catch his breath.

As the pain of his exertions faded, he teetered away from the elm bole and headed in the direction Olly had fled. His head moving on a swivel, he scanned for some hint of the girl. Where was she? Still groaning and heaving for air, he pushed on.

"Olly!?" he yelled.

He repeated the call. Once, twice, three times. He found her after a few minutes. She shivered, curled with hands clamped to knees, fetal in a dip of earth between exposed roots. Her shallow wounds colored her shirt red, but she didn't seem to notice. Shaking, her wide eyes focused on nothing, she folded in on herself, teeth chattering around whispered words.

"It's real," she whispered. "It's all fucking real. How? How?"

Paul knelt next to her. "Hey."

"It's real. All of it."

Paul put a hand on her shoulder.

Her head jerked toward him. "How?"

"We have to move," Paul said, trying to keep his voice even and calm despite his exhaustion. "We need to go back and get Deirdre."

"R-R-Razz?"

(a flash of sprint-past memory; Deirdre craned over the boy's body, hands against deep bloody grooves, magic spilling through the air)

(Razz's hand clamped vicelike around Deirdre's forearm)

(Paul's shoes squeaking over so much blood, so much goddamned blood)

Paul swallowed. "I don't know."

A high whine pitched through Olly's throat, fresh tears filling her eyes.

"I'm…I'm sorry. Maybe he's okay, I don't know. We have to move."

Olly's throat jumped as she choked back bone-deep sobs.

Paul put an arm under her and helped her unfold herself. Helped her back to her feet and looped one of her arms over his shoulder. She leaned hard to one side, the side where the Beast had struck her, where her shirt glistened damp and red. Paul glanced behind them as they moved, expecting to see the Beast coming up on their tails, but nothing followed them through the woods. Even the birds had gone silent.

"Wrong way," Olly muttered. "Turn left."

Paul listened, changing course, and found himself at the tree line a minute later. They left the wilderness and limped through the overgrowth of empty Adams Court toward the address they'd just fled.

"My car is over there," Paul said, jerking his head eastward. "Can you make it?"

"Yeah."

"I'll get Deirdre and…and Razz," he lied. "You get the car running. If that thing shows up, take off."

"No."

"Yes."

"I can't leave him."

Her words sapped strength from him, and he could only imagine their effects on her. He shrugged her arm from his shoulder and pulled his car keys from his pocket. "Take these. We'll be there as soon as we can. If that thing shows up, drive to Deirdre's."

Olly took the keys. "I'm not leaving—"

A long, loud wail cut Olly off. Paul whipped his head toward the ruined squat. Deirdre's anguish cut through the whole world. He pushed Olly eastward, already running. "Just go! Fucking go!" he yelled over his shoulder, a cramp faltering his stride as he sprinted in Deirdre's direction.

He didn't know if Olly listened or not, didn't bother looking back as he flew through whipping weeds and brush and grass. Didn't look back as his foot went through a woodrotten porch step or as he crashed through the squat's back door shoulder-first. He didn't look back until he saw the wreckage before him.

He'd never seen Deirdre cry before.

For every crime scene photo and tattered spirit he'd seen, for every ruined corpse and wretched ghost, nothing had prepared him to see this. To see the deep lines etched in her face, the streaks of her tears somehow worse than blood. To see her craned over the limp body of a dead boy, clutching him to her like she might resurrect him by want alone, by sheer will and desperate prayer and the anguished contents of her very sobs.

Then, suddenly, he looked back—not to see if Olly had listened, nor to see if the Beast had returned, but because a surge of embarrassment wrenched his gaze away. This moment was not for him to witness. Head bowed, he angled himself half-away from the two people collapsed in the hall of the squat. From the one person. His mouth turned dry, his throat a mucous mess, and he shut his eyes hard against the world.

Deirdre howled again, one long, stretched-out denial, sob-soaked and pain-wormed, and collapsed into the wall behind her. Paul knew without looking that she still held tight to Razz's cooling flesh, that she cradled his cracked, bruised skull in the palm of a desperate hand.

He turned back, battling against the muscle-taut impulse to lower himself to the crimson-slicked floor and pull her into him. He opened his eyes but couldn't quite bring himself to look, let alone to move. He stood frozen, dueling impulses tearing at his sinew—the urge to go to her, to wrap her up, to bring her to her feet, and the stronger sense that this moment didn't include him. Couldn't.

Finally, he stepped forward. Worn wood croaked under his foot and Deirdre sucked in a sharp, wavering breath, as if only then noticing his presence. She closed her eyes tight, leaned her head back against rotting plaster, and fought for air against hiccups of sob-hitched inhalations.

"I'm...I'm sorry," he whispered, cursing the words as soon as he'd said them. How often had people said those same words to him, and how little difference had it made? He took another step, the toe of his shoe finding tacky blood. "Deirdre—"

"Don't," she said sharply. "Don't say it. Please."

He nodded, though she couldn't see it. He let her live in silence until her breath evened out, until the tears had been fought back, the anguish internalized. Then he took another wood-creaking step and lowered himself to the floor next to her. "We have to leave."

She shook her head. "I'm not leaving him here."

"We'll come back."

"I'm not leaving him. I'm not..." her breath faltered again, and she folded her lips taut.

"We're still in danger. That thing could come back any time."

Deirdre opened sob-reddened eyes. "I know. Just. Can I...for just a minute, could I..." she shook her head, dispelling the thought. She unwrapped Razz's body from her arms and began to stand up. Once she stood, she didn't peer back down. She walked past him on shaky legs, her body worn from magic and pain.

He reached out after her but fell short, his fingers trailing inches behind.

CHAPTER NINETEEN

The drive to the Blackwood Estate seemed eternal in its silence. In the passenger seat, Deirdre pressed her forehead to the window, her shoulders seizing up once in a while around a strangled sob. In the back, Olly sat belted tight, her gaze focused on some invisible thing in the middle distance, her face slack.

Paul pulled up to the fountain and parked.

"You brought guests." Victor's voice took him by surprise as he left the car.

The armed gardener came from around one of the columns fronting the mansion's double-doored entrance.

"We were attacked."

Victor's gaze tracked from Paul's face to the unmoving passengers beyond the windshield. "You lost someone."

"Yeah."

Victor adjusted his Sox cap, bunched up his cheeks, and looked to the horizon for answers. He drummed his fingers against the grip of his hip-holstered pistol. Nodded. "Alright. I'll go get Miss Nora. You wait out here." He backed toward the mansion, hesitating at the doors. "She's not too good with…emotions."

"That's fine."

Victor gave a single bob of the head, turned his back, and vanished inside.

Paul let out a breath he hadn't realized he'd been holding. He went to the passenger-side door and opened it. Wordlessly, Deirdre unbuckled her seat belt and climbed out of the car. Her clothes were soaked with blood, deep-hued stains that would never come out.

Paul opened Olly's door too, but she didn't move.

He searched for something to say that wouldn't be cursory, shallow, but he knew firsthand that no simple words would suffice. He passed behind

Deirdre and settled his weight against the side of the car hood, watching her as she wrapped herself in her arms and stared blank-faced into distance.

Olly finally unbuckled and eased herself from the vehicle.

The mansion doors creaked open and Victor stepped out, Nora in tow, fidgeting with the cross around her neck.

"Um. So, um." Nora moved ahead of Victor down the front steps. "I heard you guys were…I hear you, um, lost…" Her eyes flicked from Deirdre to Olly to Paul to the ground. "The mansion is pretty safe, if you want to stay here."

"Nora," Victor said, the tone of a chiding parent.

"There's, like, sixteen bedrooms, Vicky."

Victor sighed.

Nora clucked her tongue against the roof of her mouth, turned back to Paul. "I'm, um. I'm sorry. That sounds stupid. But…"

"Stop," Deirdre said, quiet and loud at the same time.

"Sorry, sorry," Nora said. She tangled the necklace, untangled it. "I don't—what do people say, when something like this happens?"

"Usually nothing," Deirdre replied flatly.

Nora shifted foot to foot, peered at Paul with raised eyebrows.

Paul shrugged.

"Okay," Nora began again. "So. Okay. We've got coffee and food and some beds. You can stay here as long as you want to, or, I don't know, *if* you want to. But, um, and I know this might seem like the wrong time, but I *do* need to ask someone about what happened, just in case I can—in case I have files on the, um…"

"I'll do it," Paul offered.

"Okay. Okay, alright. Victor, you can make sure they're set in their rooms?"

Victor nodded.

"Right. So. Follow me, I guess."

Deirdre broke her long stare at nothing and took Olly gently by the arm. Nora led the way back inside, Paul following closely. Deirdre and Olly drifted behind, out of sync with the rest of the world. Victor brought up the rear, his hand rested on the grip of his hip-holstered pistol.

●●●

In the library, Nora questioned Paul for a long time on the details, each question a sharp, intellectual jab at a fresh tragedy. Nora queried as academic, as distanced observer, an obsessed archivist, not as a teenager with scars criss-crossing her arms. Paul stalked from the experience with frustration bubbling beneath his skin.

He reminded himself with every step up the stairs to the second floor that Nora had given them shelter when every other place seemed dangerous. That they were essentially strangers to her, and she'd done it anyway.

Still.

Upstairs, on the second floor (and how did one get to the third floor?), Paul followed Nora's directions to Deirdre's room. He hesitated outside the door, his arm extended, frozen mid-knock. He pursed his lips, trying not to think about the way she'd looked holding Razz's body, her face twisted in an agony he could never unsee.

"Paul?" she asked, muffled by the door.

He blinked. "Uh...yeah."

"It's unlocked."

He turned the handle, pushed. The room beyond seemed *almost* cozy, curated for comfort yet somehow missing the mark. Everything inside was vintage or antique, plush and cushioned. An old bureau, a worn set of drawers, a 19th century writing desk, a four-poster bed...all seemed lived-in and warm, but somehow not welcoming.

Deirdre sat on the floor, her back pressed against the bedframe, staring at her palms.

"Hey," Paul said.

"Sixth sense uppers." Deirdre reached up and touched the side of her head. "I took some earlier. It's how I knew you were out there."

"Oh."

"I just can't..." she shook her head, dabbed at tears that weren't there.

"I know." He closed the door and sat on the floor across from her, his back to the antique bureau.

Deirdre's gaze drifted to his. Her eyes were caverns, dark, endless. "They killed him. They killed my..."

"We'll get them back."

She flinched. "We won't get *him* back."

"No."

"Why didn't we...why didn't I..."

"Those questions are never going to have answers. Trust me."

She ran a hand over her forehead, grabbed a palmful of hair. "How did this happen?"

"Randall Hill," Paul answered. "There's nothing we could've done to—"

"There's *plenty* we could've done," Deirdre snapped, tugging at her hair. "So many times I should've just told him the truth, and then maybe he'd still be staying with me and…"

"We couldn't have stopped Randall from going after him."

A long silence. Deirdre took deep breaths, her shoulders shuddering against the body's impulse to weep.

After minutes that felt like hours, Deirdre brought her tired eyes back to Paul's. "You can see them. You can talk to him."

Paul balked at the words. "I—I—you mean the dead? The ghosts?"

Deirdre let go of her hair, nodding. "You could go back there and see if he's there, if he's still here after…after—"

"It doesn't work like that."

"But if he is, you could. He knew who Randall's boys were, he knew their names, maybe where they lived. We could—"

"I don't just choose which ghosts I see," Paul interrupted. "I don't find *them*, they find *me*."

"But he could, and then—"

Paul stood up. "I can't just turn it on like that."

"Just stop taking the downers, stop drinking, stop—"

"He might not even be there. Not every victim becomes a ghost, you know. Not every—"

"He *might* be!" Deirdre stood too, mirroring him.

"I don't know how ghosts are made, what keeps a spirit here after the body is dead, I don't know if—"

"You told me they go insane, they forget what it was to be alive, they forget everything, they live in pain and—"

"You're asking me to embrace a fucking *curse*!"

Embers lit behind their stares, the two of them smoldering.

"What are you so afraid of?" Deirdre asked.

"I'm not afraid, I'm—"

"Bullshit."

"I'm following the available leads."

"What about that murder victim you talked about? You said you thought it was related. Is it?"

"I…" he trailed off, searching for some excuse.

"Answer the goddamned question."

He dropped his gaze to the floor, backing away. "Yeah. I think so."

"So what the fuck were you doing, getting drunk, taking downers, avoiding the problem while Razz put himself on the line? What the fuck scares you so much you'd rather let a boy die than deal with it? There's a victim you saw *days* ago, a victim who *wants* to talk to you, who already found you, but instead you've been doing…what, exactly?"

"I dug up as much information—"

"What the fuck are you scared of?!"

"My daughter!"

The silence following their words gutted the walls. For a long time, the sound of their breath was the sole sound in the room, perhaps in the entire mansion.

"Your daughter?" Deirdre whispered.

He sagged into the desk of drawers, easing his weight against old wood. "She died a few years ago, back in New York. I was working a case and… and the guy was still out there, killing women ages fifteen to twenty-one. My daughter was sixteen. I kept having nightmares where I went to her room and she was gone. I hadn't been home in days. Me and the detective leading the case, we just slept in the office, when we slept at all. I hadn't seen my family in…weeks. And she always had problems, even when she was just a kid. She'd been getting worse. A lot worse." He fingered the place where he'd once worn a wedding ring, however many hangovers ago. "She died in a car crash. A drunk driver."

Deirdre's eyes asked the only possible follow-up.

Paul nodded. "She was the drunk driver."

"Jesus."

"I don't know how it all happened, what all happened…I don't know how long she'd been drinking or…" his gaze bored into the floor. "I'd, um…I'd started taking speed. Because of all the late nights working the case, me and the lead detective, we went doctor-shopping and got some prescriptions. We even picked stuff up from a friend of his who worked Narcotics." Had his mouth ever been so dry? He coughed. "It got bad. Really bad. And I guess she must've snuck out with one of my prescriptions because when they finished the tox screen, she was positive for alcohol and amphetamines in her bloodstream. So much of either one the coroner was surprised she hadn't just overdosed." His chest tingled, cold and hot. "She went through a guardrail at over fifty miles per hour. Four people died, including her."

Deirdre sat on the mattress, limp. "You see her?"

"She was the first one I saw. I woke up at my desk and she was standing over me. Her face was…" he reached up toward his own visage, but there was no gesture to communicate the ruin of his daughter's face, the architecture of human expression rendered so utterly inhuman. "I screamed. I thought I was hallucinating, having some kind of waking nightmare. But I got the news just minutes later, and…"

"You never saw anything before?"

He shook his head. "I heard things when I was younger, but…I'd never *seen* anything. Not before then. It was like it started just so I could see her."

Deirdre stared at him, saying nothing.

"I started seeing them everywhere, hearing them all the time. Only drinking made it bearable. And people…fuck, people. We started getting calls at the house, people calling to tell us our daughter *got what she deserved*, calling to tell us how evil it was that she *killed* those people, telling us she was a murderer, like she was as bad as the psycho putting bodies in Flushing Bay."

"I'm sorry," Deirdre whispered.

"We got an unlisted number. Someone spray painted the front of our building. We got new e-mail addresses. But even after the strangers stopped hounding us, after they found some other awful thing to move onto, there was always someone asking…my wife's clients, our friends—people I *thought* were our friends—asking all these questions, looking at us like…like they knew we'd fucked up somewhere, like we'd ruined our child and they wanted to find out what we'd done so they wouldn't do the same thing."

Deirdre stared at the floor, shaking her head.

"My wife, my ex-wife, she used to joke that I'd spend more time with them if they were dead, if they were crime scene photos. Not so funny, after."

Deirdre brought her eyes back up to his, glassy and drained and hollowed. "I'm sorry."

"You didn't know."

"Razz…Razz was mine. He was…"

Paul nodded. "I know."

"I wouldn't ask you to do this if…" She crooked her hand in a gesture trying to make sense of senselessness.

Paul stared at Deirdre, at her eyes focusing and unfocusing on a ghost she'd never see.

A memory unearthed itself: the way his wife had looked in the weeks following the news, the way she looked at things but never really saw them.

The way she always seemed to be staring at something he couldn't make out. The broken-down pits of her eyes, high on painkillers, opiates, staring at the wall, silent tears streaking drug-slacked cheeks. Maybe that had finished them off even before the divorce papers. Neither of them could live with what happened and neither wanted to watch the other one die so slowly.

He'd spent years trying to blind himself from ghosts, but other people would have given their eyes for a chance to see one.

"You're right," he said. "I should've done something sooner."

Deirdre's eyes stormed. She stared at him, fury and pity and mourning all at once.

Her gaze told him that she understood, but that understanding wasn't forgiveness.

"We can still stop Randall. I'll talk to the victim tomorrow. We can go to the squat, see if Razz is there somehow, if there's anything left."

Deirdre folded her arms, pressed her lips together, said nothing.

"First thing in the morning, let's stop at your place and pick up some psychic stimulants."

Her eyebrows jumped up. "What?"

"If we're going to do this, I want to do it right. I've already screwed up enough."

A brief glow glimmered behind her storm. "Alright."

"I'm…" What could he say? "I'll see you in the morning."

"Yeah. See you then."

CHAPTER TWENTY

Dreamer had a way of lingering in the bloodstream, especially after multiple uses. It left tatters of dreams and visions as it dissipated, the comedown a rapid-fire spam of images, all narrative gone.

Deirdre's eyelids movie-screened, nonsense footage reeled through a dusty projector.

A priest on a throne. A building of bones. A tongue.

Terrible whiteness shivered and drooped, warping and transforming in monstrous adaptation.

A dog whimpered. A woman whimpered. A man snickered. A priest wheezed, a crown of tongues and broken teeth on his head. He pointed a crooked finger and added another tongue to the headpiece. A blaze ate through steel and flesh, cooked meat on the air.

A serpent uncurled. Insect legs scratched at wallpaper. A war chittered between swarms.

How did any of it relate?

Dreamer gave no answers, only hints.

A hole in the wall, rats sniffing at it from the other side. Tiny claws scrabbled at wood. Something awful lurked in the darkness.

The priest reached out and gripped the wallpaper. Peeled it down. On the other side, an infinity of starving mouths.

■■■

Deirdre awoke to a shrunken world. The vault of the heavens had collapsed under the void and the fundament of the mantle had splintered and crushed.

This was a world without Razz.

She dressed zombielike, donning borrowed, baggy clothes. She stared at herself in the mirror and tried to imagine a future that mattered. All of it seemed so much narrower, now. So much less.

Victor fetched her wordlessly, an entire conversation held with door-knock, door-open, and a long, silent gaze. He put his hand on her shoulder and gently guided her into the hallway. His were the eyes of a man who knew the claustrophobia of loss, and knew too that no words were powerful enough to lift the sky back into place.

He led her downstairs and into an unexpectedly renovated kitchen, an oasis of modernity in a time-warped, antique mansion.

The kitchen table, a long six-seater set with plates of breakfast food, was unoccupied save for one other person.

Nora sat at the head of the table, eyes bag-bruised and bloodshot, her plate already a mess of leftovers. She sipped coffee with cream and paged through a dusty grimoire. She glanced up from the book only when Deirdre pulled out a chair and sat down. Nora stared for an awkward beat, as if unsure if Deirdre were truly there.

Nora coughed unnecessarily. Sipped her coffee. Asked, "Are you a witch?"

"Excuse me?"

"Sorry, I just never actually met one before."

"This whole house hums with magic."

"You don't need to be a witch to use magic. Besides, it's all inherited."

Deirdre glanced back at Victor, the man a shadow in the kitchen threshold, but he just shrugged, folded his arms, and watched.

Nora sniffled. "I don't mean to pry. Well, I mean, I guess I do. But most magicians and sorcerers and whatevers aren't actually born with expertise."

"I wouldn't know. Never attended Hogwarts."

Nora flinched as if hearing a dirty word. "Okay, so I don't think that joke makes sense within the lore of the books? And, yeah, I guess most magic types in real life *are* self-taught, but, um, what I mean is, what Ambrose *said*, was that people like you—" Nora froze. Her face blanched. "Witches, I mean. 'People like you' as in 'witches.' Um, so you and your fellow witches," emphasis, now, on *witches*, "you can cast spells naturally?"

Deirdre spooned bacon onto her plate, thanking sacrificial pigs. "Uh-huh."

"They call them 'cantrips?' Like, you don't need a grimoire or a spell book or a bunch of fancy runes or, like, chicken bones or anything?"

"Sometimes I use chicken bones." The joke was dust stirred by dry wind.

"But there are some things you can just *do*. Like, just by focusing on something and trying kinda hard? Like, with your sheer willpower?"

"Yeah."

(all her energy screaming through her bones and sinew, Razz's wounds stitching shut not fast enough)

(not fast enough, not well enough, not anything enough)

"That's cool," Nora said, as if commenting on a band. "Ambrose said natural-born witches make the most powerful sorcerers. Or, um, sorceresses, I guess. He said he'd introduce me to a couple he knew abroad, but…you know. He didn't." She forked cold-looking egg into her mouth and chewed.

Victor made an amused sound from the threshold.

Nora's eyes flicked to him. "What? What is it?"

"I told them you were bad with people."

"I'm not bad with people."

"You aren't great with them," Deirdre said, crunching on a strip of bacon.

Nora forked more egg. "Whatever. It's special to meet a witch, is all."

"You want me to get the other one?" Victor asked.

"Yeah, thanks," Nora replied, nodding to Victor as he moved off. She glanced back at Deirdre furtively and poked at the food on her plate. "I'm sorry if I haven't been, I don't know, *comforting*. I know it's hard to lose someone you're close to. When Ambrose got on that plane…" she twitched her shoulders, exhaled shakily. "I never found anyone's kind words and positive vibes to be that helpful."

"They aren't."

"I know Victor…well, that's his story to talk about, not mine."

Deirdre opened her mouth to ask, but found that Nora was right.

Nora sniffled. "Anyway, you and Paul are welcome to stay here. Olly might."

"I've got my own home. Besides…" Deirdre hesitated over the next part.

"I'm not going to try to stop you," Nora said. "I mean, I don't always do so well at relating to people, but I can read them okay. I know you and Paul plan to see this through. I know there's nothing anyone could say to stop you. And I know that if I tried to stop you non-verbally, you'd never forgive me."

Deirdre stared at the birdlike girl heading the table, her eyes narrowing. "You're right."

"I'm an archivist. My whole life is about knowing things and figuring other things out."

"So what did you figure out last night?"

"I'll tell you as soon as your partner gets here."

"My—"

"Like Hap and Leonard. Riggs and Murtaugh. Somerset and Mills."

"Stop listing."

"Okay."

They fell into bacon-crunch, fork-scrape nondialogue, each one glancing at the other every few seconds until Victor and Paul arrived almost five whole minutes later. Paul gave Deirdre a nervous half-nod before sitting, spooning cooling eggs and a pancake onto his plate. Victor remained at the door, surveying.

"Coffee?" Paul asked.

"Right." Nora pushed herself from her seat and filled two mugs from the nearby carafe. "Cream, sugar?"

"Doesn't matter."

"I'll have a spoon of sugar," Deirdre said, not bothering to voice her preference for tea.

Nora made the coffees, brought them to the table, and returned to her seat. "So," she began again, "I have a few possibilities for what you, er, *encountered* yesterday. Probably the worst news is that whatever coven you're gunning for, Randall Hill and the Howland Butler Throwbacks, they're far from amateur."

"Figured as much." Deirdre crunched bacon.

"The thing itself, this 'Beast' as Paul called it, is either a summoned entity or some kind of construction, neither of which can be done with a magician beginner's kit."

"How do we kill it?" Deirdre asked.

"That depends. If it's a summoned entity, the easiest thing would be to unsummon it."

"How?"

Nora shrugged. "I dunno, I don't practice magic."

"Okay, what are the other options?"

"The second easiest way works for both types of monster. Well, mostly. There are exceptions."

Deirdre gestured for her to get to the point.

"Okay, okay. Unless it was summoned and then unbound, which I doubt, then killing the person who summoned it *should* unsummon it. If it's a magical construct, killing the person who created it *should* make it dissolve.

Though, again, if it's unbound, that changes things. But if it's unbound, it also doesn't have to listen to its master's commands, so…"

"Randall and his people have a power fixation," Paul said. "They wouldn't summon or create anything they wouldn't be able to control."

"So that's the best method. Whoever led the summoning or creation ritual, just kill that person."

"You do realize you're telling us to murder someone?" Paul asked.

"They tried to murder you first. And they're trying to do worse than that, if they can."

Paul and Deirdre both raised eyebrows, waiting for more.

"Right," Nora said. "I buried the lede. How much do you guys know about pre-colonial Oceanrest?"

"Not much?" Paul said.

"Okay. So, there are stories among certain Wabanaki archivists and conspiracy-obsessed archaeologists that Oceanrest was once a place of ancient spirituality, for, well, reasons unknown. Like Göbekli Tepe, you know? Paul, you remember what I told you last time, about that Stone Age township?"

"Can we skip the exposition?" Deirdre asked.

Nora frowned. "It's actually more backstory."

"We have things to do."

Nora sighed. "Okay. The point is, from what Ambrose gathered from these First Nations archivist-types and the crazy-conspiracist academics, these way-long-dead guys were very into the supernatural and had a pretty grim pantheon of entities that may or may not have some kind of extant manifestations. We've dug up a few names—"

"What does this have to do with Randall?"

"I'm going as fast as I can," Nora said. "Excuse me." She cleared her throat dramatically, then proceeded. "Some of their deities had very simple names. The Speaker, The Devourer," she stared very purposefully at Paul, "The Hollow One."

Paul's whole being tightened at the name. He stopped eating.

"Some had more complex titles. She Who Crawls Within, The Eater of the Veil, The—"

"Very orally fixated," Deirdre noted.

Nora steamrolled forward. "The Queen of Behind You, which might be a bad translation, The Teeth and Claws in Shadow…there are over a dozen of them. I think Ambrose listed sixteen at last count."

"Are they real?" Paul asked.

"If they are, they're not literal deities, though I guess within a certain spectrum of interpretation—"

"Are they real?" Paul repeated, harder, sharper.

"I think Randall aims to find out."

A beat passed.

Deirdre leaned forward. "Excuse me?"

"Paul's serial murder case—the new one, I mean," Nora said, as if there were other likely possibilities, "they're sacrifices like we thought, but now I know what kind of spell they're for. I found it last night while I was going through all of Ambrose's notes and all his old dusty books on magic and summoning and blah, blah, blah…"

"What did you find?" Deirdre pressed.

Victor shifted in the threshold.

"If you hack into the police database and snoop around, which, of course, I would never do, and if you have a lead from a friend of yours who thinks the crimes are related to magic and mysticism," she tilted her head towards Paul, "you'd be able to figure out what sort of goings-on might be going on. The ritual, the removal of eyes and tongue, the harvesting of human suffering and sacrifice, the blood, it's all a preparation for a huge ritual spell. An *enormous* ritual spell. The places the bodies were dumped are like those connect-the-dots puzzles in books—they make a glyph. When the glyph is complete, and the rituals are all complete, and all that magic they stored up is ready to explode, well…they're going to tear a big old hole in reality and summon one of these things through it."

Long, scared silence.

Nora rubbed one eye with a balled hand. "It's hard to figure out since the records are all based on oral history and BCE artifacts, but they're probably going for one of those 'orally fixated' entities, based on the shape of the glyph. The Eater of the Veil, The Speaker, The Devourer…"

"What happens if they succeed?" Paul asked.

"Who knows? If the entity in question is literally real, it will become materially extant on our physical plane. If it's not, well…they're still going to set off an incredibly powerful spell, one that could distort spacetime and let loose any number of supernatural side effects. Either way, I'd say it's bye-bye Oceanrest and probably a decent chunk of Maine with it. Maybe not a literal, worldwide apocalypse, but definitely a metaphorical, regional one."

Paul's wide eyes screamed to Deirdre from across the table.
"We have to go," he said. "Now."

■■■

"A couple years ago, I helped Virgil on this serial murder case," Paul explained
as he drove. "He'd done a pretty big favor for me, so I agreed to do the profile
on that Static Killer. I figured it would go faster if I skipped some of the
profiling work and just talked to the victims, so I spent about forty-eight
hours without downers or drinking, trying to sift through all the spirits to
find someone he'd killed, but none of them had left a ghost behind.

"I don't know how he did it. I would understand if it were only one or
two victims—not every murder victim becomes a ghost—but this guy had
killed four people that we knew of, maybe even a fifth. I couldn't wrap my
mind around the idea that none of them ended up left behind. I went back
to the downers after that, and the drinking, and I did the profile work the
old-fashioned way, but I couldn't stop thinking about how he did it. *How* he
killed so many people and left no ghosts behind. But now…I don't know.
Maybe it was related to this human sacrifice angle."

Paul shook his head, looking lost, barely hitting the brakes in time to
avoid blowing through a red light into oncoming traffic.

"You think these things are real?" Deirdre asked.

(*let's make a deal*, a chemical-sweet voice muttered in her memory.)

Paul drummed his fingers on the steering wheel, muscles tight around
his jaw. "I don't know. But I saw something when they arrested him…
something…"

"What was it?"

"I couldn't say. Nothing. But not 'nothing' as in 'I didn't see anything.'
'Nothing' as in…a very hungry void."

(*a canvas of black behind the wallpaper*
an infinity of hungry mouths)

They drove the rest of the way to her squat in silence, Paul's hands white-
knuckled on the wheel.

CHAPTER TWENTY-ONE

Deirdre couldn't shake the feeling that they were being followed. Turning onto Lafayette, she thought she'd even glimpsed a car tailing them, but then Paul laid on the accelerator and tore rumbling down the uneven street. The only thing constant in the rearview was the ruination of Squatter City. An old woman rattled a shopping cart down the sidewalk, bags overstuffed with found bottles. Somewhere behind closed doors, Frank dosed himself with dreamer-laced heroin.

She turned her attention back to the road ahead. "You sure we need the uppers?"

"I'd rather have, and not need."

She nodded, uncertain he was right but feeling too brittle to argue.

Paul cranked the wheel and revved the engine, swerving onto Black Watch Hill. The high-noon sun knifed through the windscreen and Deirdre squinted against it. Here, even Squatter City slouched. Here, nature retook its land. Deirdre's gaze wandered back to the rearview mirror, though she still couldn't find a word to label what she expected to see.

Paul pulled the car up along the side of her property and killed the engine.

Deirdre popped her door open and stepped into overgrowth.

There was a scent in the air at once familiar and foreign. She knew she'd smelled it countless times before, but its presence now seemed strange.

She drew her revolver and opened the cylinder. All six shots were loaded. She closed it again and flicked off the safety.

"Something wrong?" Paul asked.

"Maybe."

She crossed ankle-high grass to her front porch, listening for something out of place, but heard only rustling leaves and singing birds. Still, some dozing part of her nascent sixth sense ached within her, and she cast another glance back at the turn-off onto Lafayette. There was a rusted coil of old steel, the boughs of reaching trees…and perhaps a shadow under leaves, but impossible to tell.

"Smell that?" she asked, barely loud enough to hear.

"Smell what?"

She stepped up onto her porch, inspecting the damaged wood where shot had tattered her door latch. She inched forward, put one hand in the center of the door, and listened.

Nothing.

"Maybe we should go without the uppers," she suggested.

"Alright. Let's go."

Realization came as a series of three painful blows. One, Samedi wasn't waiting for her, wasn't mewling or pawing the door, perched on her porch, or pacing the hall. Samedi was missing. Two, the scent she'd caught on the air was diesel exhaust. And third, when she pushed on the door, however gently, the hinges creaked. Her barricade had been taken down.

Deirdre had time to warn Paul, yelling the word, "Trap!" before it happened.

The door swung in, a cloaked figure wrenching it open before retreating fast into her den. A second boy, armed with a hunting rifle, stood twenty feet down her main hallway and lifted his weapon when he saw her. She caught a glimpse of some other object on the floor between them, but didn't have time to make out details before the boy yelled out, "Lie down!"

Deirdre launched herself to the side of the threshold as gunshot cracked the air.

Paul backpedaled, stumbled, and went for the car. "Come on!" he yelled, yanking a blocky semi-automatic pistol from his waistband.

Razz's pistol, she recognized.

Rushing back toward the car, Paul swerved and ducked. A volley of gunfire spat from the backyard, peppering the hood and passenger side of the vehicle. Paul ran back her way, fumbling the pistol's safety.

"You got two choices, Deirdre!" Randall called out from the side of her house. "Either you two put down the guns and let us take you peaceful-like, or you and your new boyfriend get what's really coming to you. I'll give you ten seconds to make up your mind."

From his crouched position in the grass Paul shook his head at her.

Deirdre pursed her lips.

It wasn't a happy ending either way. But at least if they fought back, they could make the bastards hurt.

And if they could get inside, they could arm themselves.

"Five seconds!" Randall called.

Deirdre cranked the hammer back on her revolver and spun around the threshold. The cloaked boy twenty feet away lifted his rifle to his shoulder again, too slow. Deirdre squeezed the trigger twice, punching two ragged holes in the kid's chest. The rifle clattered to the floor as the cloaked boy fumbled at his wounds, groping at his own blood in disbelief. His knees hit the hardwood and he fell sideways with a high whine.

The second boy came back from the den with an aluminum baseball bat. Deirdre spun her sights on him and squeezed the trigger, but the bullet barely grazed his shoulder as he charged her. He swung down and swatted the gun out of her hands. She yelped from the shock, the jolt of the blow tunneling her wrists and aching up her arms.

"Alright boys!" Randall called out. "Do what you gotta do."

The baseball bat came in and blew the wind out of her. She stumbled forward and grabbed the boy's lapels, trying to close the distance so he couldn't swing again.

Paul crashed into the two of them from her periphery. His whole body swung in, cracking the boy's temple with the butt of his gun.

All three bodies crashed to the floor.

Breathless, Deirdre tried to untangle herself from a confusion of limbs. In the dimness of the hallway, she couldn't see her gun, but fumbled for it along the hardwood while the melee raged around her. She pulled herself from between bodies, a stray elbow cracking her head as she disengaged.

A few feet away she saw a bear trap gaping toothy before her. She'd almost put her arm right into it. She drew her hand back and sucked air.

Had the baseball bat broken a rib?

She wrestled herself to her feet, hearing wet blows and male yawps behind her. Her revolver lay about a foot away, pushed up right against the wall. Taking a second to balance herself, she went for it.

"Move!" Paul yelled from the melee.

She pressed herself against the wall in time for the two brawlers to crash into the opposite side of the hall. Plaster cracked where they smashed into it. It appeared Paul was winning, at least. Crimson claret masked the boy's face, and Paul had his forearm pressed into the boy's throat.

She bent for the revolver again and this time picked it up.

Paul spun from the wall and hurled the boy down. The kid's arm landed directly in the bear trap. Steel snapped and meat tore.

The hallway filled with shrieks.

The screams roused the bloody heap of the other boy, who reached with carmine-smeared fingers for his rifle. Deirdre stopped him with a third bullet, this one slicking red across the hardwood and crumpling the rifleman into a limp heap. Paul put his foot into the bear-trapped boy's face until the screaming stopped, then switched his pistol for the long gun.

A shadow fell across the dim light from the porch, and Deirdre whirled toward it and fired.

The bullet blew fabric off a third cloaked figure's arm and sent the silhouette whirling from the doorway.

"Come on, Deirdre," Randall called from the unseen side of the porch. "Don't be a damned fool."

Something slammed into the back door of the house.

(gluelike flesh and mutant muscle, the Beast heaved its grotesque body against her sanctuary)

"See?" Randall said. "We got you surrounded."

Deirdre reached into her pocket for spare bullets, loading them into the revolver cylinder one at a time.

Paul checked the safety on the rifle and leveled its sights on the doorway.

In the kitchen behind them, the back door bucked again.

Deirdre reached for her keys, remembering the reinforced basement door and its countless locks, but they'd been lost somewhere in the scrap, in the chaos and melee of the trap and the brawl. She cursed, bringing the barrel of her gun to bear on the threshold ahead even as she glanced back toward the kitchen.

A third impact hammered the back door, and an awful, screeching snarl came from behind it.

Randall appeared in the threshold for a split second, and Deirdre and Paul both fired. Neither bullet hit, and Randall vanished again. The back door thumped against its reinforced bolts. Randall reappeared, big-mouthed semi-auto in hand, and squeezed a round off before disappearing. Paul and Deirdre missed their second volley, but Randall's shot struck home. Paul tumbled back, his white shirt blooming long vines of red down from his left shoulder.

Deirdre reached for the wound, already focusing on her healing cantrip.

"Stay focused!" Paul snarled.

Randall took that as a cue, leaping through the threshold. Muzzle flash lit the hall as Randall squeezed off two more rounds, both punching through Paul's torso. Gouts of gory claret spattered the floor as Paul stumbled backwards and fell.

Deirdre whirled toward Randall and returned fire, but the abrupt twist of her body and the speed of her movement threw off her aim. One bullet went wide and buried itself in a wall. The second hammered Randall's chest and sprawled him out—but there was no blood. Then two more cloaked figures were in the hallway, charging her, and the kitchen door began to scream on breaking hinges. She lifted her gun and fired off a third round. One of the cloaked figures spun from the impact, but again, no blood.

The other cloaked figure smashed her arm with the butt of a shotgun. She crashed sidelong into the wall and dropped her revolver. Rebounding from the blow, she dove at him, hoping to replay her earlier grapple. However, this boy was better prepared, and bashed her sternum with the stock of his weapon.

She fell backward, landing on a body that was either Paul's or the dead rifleman's, clutching the searing pain of her chest.

The shotgun stock came down on her again and her lungs voided.

"Call off the dog, Isaiah," Randall's voice rasped. "We got the bitch handled."

The thumping at the kitchen door stopped.

"Now get her bagged."

Deirdre kicked at her assailants, but her blows were weak without air to support them, and soon the boys were on her. A boot came down on her pelvis and sent her writhing on the hardwood. The airless world blurred and faded, her vision a pulsing whorl of darkness and dimness. Distantly, she heard Paul's voice wheeze out bloodied words.

"Forget him, just bag the bitch and let's go!"

Her gun was inches away. She reached for it with feeble fingers.

Black fabric was pulled over her head, string tightened around her throat, and she was instantly blind. Reflexively, she reached for the rope at her neck. A bolt of rage clarified the world for an instant, her senses coming to her long enough to get her hand on the gun. It didn't last. Before she could turn on her back to blind-fire on her attackers, a boot came down and crushed the weapon from her grasp.

She shrieked, lips stinging against coarse fabric. Groping hands found her in the darkness, grabbed her legs and arms, and hauled her up. She felt the air around her beaten body as they carried her back onto the porch and into the yard.

"Deir...dre..." Paul called after her, his voice muffled by his own blood.

"Paul!" she screamed back, wrestling against the hands that carried her.

"Shut up!" one of the boys yelled.

"Sorry," Isaiah said, "but you brought this on yourself."

The diesel fumes grew stronger. She heard a door squeak open and an engine rumble to life.

"Get her in the back," Randall said.

Another door opened.

Deidre thrashed, freeing herself from the clutching hands long enough to faceplant in bracken. She rolled onto her side and a boot swept in and exploded against her ribs. She crunched up against the blow, blind with starlight pain. "Fuck you!" she screamed, "Fuck you, fuck you, fuck you!"

Another kick threw her onto her back.

The black curtain of fabric tore away.

Randall smiled down at her, aglow in the noonday sun, pointing the huge-mouthed pistol at her face. "I think you've done about enough fighting now, ain't ya?" She glared up at him past the barrel and he chuckled. "This would'a all been easier if you'd just kept your head down. But since you had to go cunting around in our business, we figured we might as well make you a part of it. Right, boys?"

At least three other voices joined his snicker, maybe four.

"You're a son of a bitch," she spat.

"We already covered my momma being a bitch. And pa was a bastard."

She moved to get back to her feet and another kick sent her reeling.

Randall shook his head. "See, boys? It's in their nature to fight. There's violence in their blood." He turned his focus back on her as she spat on the grass. "We got plans for you, Deirdre. Big plans. Oh, it'll be beautiful. I always did kinda like you, in earnest. I think it's a fitting compliment that you'll get to be there at the end of things, when the circle finally gets broken. Too bad what'll have to happen to you..."

The black bag found her again, and a pair of handcuffs bit into her wrists as they wrestled her into the back bed of the truck.

"It's like they say in that big Christian bible of theirs, isn't it?" Randall slammed the gate of the bed shut. "'Thou shalt not suffer a witch to live.' They was right about that much."

Boots on the truck bed told her she'd have a guard for the trip.

"Why don't you get some rest, huh?" Randall taunted. "You'll need it where you're going."

The truck doors all slammed shut some seconds later, the engine snarled, and the vehicle started its journey.

Deirdre reached into herself for a healing cantrip, hoping to ease some of the beating she'd taken. She felt the magic gathering inside her, funneling away whatever was left of her energy and sent the spell coursing through her body. Wounds began to stitch themselves back together, bruises retreating and healing, blunt force trauma reversing. She wasn't sure how much good it would do, considering the situation, but it was better than nothing. She made a second attempt, hoping to get herself back into fighting shape.

She tried to gather the energy for a third attempt, but she was sapped. Dizzy faintness washed over her.

And then: sleep.

...

Paul grimaced through deathly blur as the boys carried a thrashing Deirdre to the front door.

Randall stayed behind a moment, glaring down at him.

"Deir…dre…" he rasped, reaching for the rifle inches away.

"Paul!" she screamed.

("Shut up!")

Randall, or the blurry figure Paul thought was Randall, shook his head. "Too bad 'bout all this. Have to hand it to you, you put up a hell of a fight." He crossed the floor, bent down, and tore the rifle from Paul's enfeebled fingers. Nudged Paul with the toe of a boot. "Well, I guess I'll see you in the great void, brother. 'til then." Randall pantomimed a tip of the hat and headed away. "Get her in the back," he called out as he vanished.

Paul groaned, pulling himself along the floor. His whole body throbbed, burning cold. Deirdre's revolver lay another few feet on. There were still bullets in it and if he could just…

A wash of blanketing unconsciousness crashed over him.

The world fuzzed to gray, then color again. The hall reasserted itself. The revolver was a foot away. His legs still worked, he dimly knew, and he pushed himself up onto his knees. Red rivulets flowed from his chest, outletting tributaries of gore along the floorboards. On all fours, he managed to get to the gun.

He coughed bright red.

"Deir…" he groaned with effort as he pushed himself to his feet.

The world shuddered and he fell sidelong into the opposite wall.

His muscles strained. They screamed to move him over the unconscious body of the bear-trapped boy, railed with anguish against his steps toward the porch. His shirt soaked red, and his thoughts no longer made any sense. He remembered Cassandra when she was a child, racing Lego cars along a stretch of kitchen counter in Queens. He remembered her when she was fifteen, wearing long sleeves every day. She could still laugh though, even in the depths of her growing angst. He remembered her laugh.

Paul was dying.

It seemed terrible, the way things could just end.

He stumbled down the porch steps to the shin-high grass and fell, landing on one knee, bent over so his off-hand balanced him. Butchery seeped from his wounds, droplets of cruor dotting his pants. He remembered brushing a killer's blood off with a knit cap. An engine rumbled to life somewhere in the vast distance. He pushed himself back to his feet and almost fell over again.

A shadow approached from the forest, a shadow in the shape of a man. A second shadow followed, much larger, not in any shape at all.

Paul tried to call out, but he choked on the words. He spat red into the green below.

He'd met Deirdre by accident. His alcohol tolerance had gotten too high for liquor to sufficiently block out the dead, so he'd switched to cannabis. Razz had been his dealer, back when Razz lived with Deirdre. Paul had stopped by the house for a pick-up, saw her reading in her den, beautiful. At first she'd wanted him to take Razz in himself, but he lived on a houseboat. Deirdre became something like a friend. One thing led to another, and a few months later, he'd told her the truth. She'd already known, somehow.

He stumbled around the side of the house and smelled diesel. An engine revved distantly, tires rolled over grass. A massive white monster sank into wilderness, vanishing. He made it a few more paces and collapsed, sagged against siding.

A shadow trailed him, its own shadow growing like day-devouring night.

He focused on the shadow and lifted the revolver, pivoted away from the side of the house. "Get away," he tried to say, but couldn't.

His hands shook. His legs shook. His single shot went wide into the woods and the recoil sent him crashing back into the side of the house and then down, down, down to the ground. His vision pulsed and the high sun flickered like a dying bulb. His body went slack and limp and he realized his breath came in wet wheezes and mangled coughs. His chin was slick with blood, his torso soaked with it.

He was dying.

A shadow approached. It seemed terrible. A second shadow followed; an ending.

The backs of his eyelids were painted pantry doors. Beneath that darkness, forgetful black. Void.

Beneath that?

A hand touched the wound in his right lung. The sensation that rolled through him was similar to Deirdre's healing cantrip, but different. Deirdre's magic felt overflowing; this felt *hungry*. Deirdre's magic felt as if it was giving him something, this felt as if it might take something away.

A sharp breath came into him, alive.

A shadow stood, familiar features hinted by noon sun. The second shadow billowed and undulated, eating light.

"Shhhh," the smaller shadow whispered.

Paul's eyes fluttered closed.

The vaster darkness tethered to the smaller shade smiled an invisible smile.

More cold, icy magic wormed into his wounds.

don't go dying on us now, an aspartame-sweet voice whispered. *we've still got work to do.*

"Get some rest," the smaller darkness said. "Tomorrow's the big day."

Unconsciousness swept him under.

CHAPTER TWENTY-TWO

Paul's existence blurred. Fractured reality came to him in glimpses and flashes.

Bodies dragged away. A trunk closed.

Hefted into arms, taken upstairs.

Dark murmurs. Shadows that moved on their own.

Noontime purpled to twilight and blackened to darkness. The air reeked of bleach and cover-up. He got back to his feet but dizziness spun him down again. A shadow put its hands over his eyes and closed them. He fought against bad dreams, nightmares of wide-open mouths eating their way through the meniscus of reality. Of tentacles and claws, an uncoiling serpent, infinite spider legs. Of mismatched parts patchworked senselessly together.

Cold magic stitched his wounds. This wasn't the hopeful warmth of Deirdre's cantrips, nor the natural acceleration of her salves, this was the precision spellcraft of patient darkness. His health wasn't a gift from a caring friend, it was a necessary part of a plan he wanted no part in.

we'll talk again soon, Pauly, a sickening-sweet voice muttered from the bones of his skull. *we've got business together.*

He groaned denial, semi-conscious.

The sickening sweet thing chuckled in alien tongues. *it'll all make sense soon. trust me.*

The shapeless nightmares melted into fantasy dreams. The dreams would have been joyful had they not been so impossible.

But Cassandra was dead and Razz was dead and Paul knew from experience that the dead did not have futures, only pasts that repeated until madness.

What was crueler—the shriek of impossible nightmares, or the gleam of equally impossible hopes?

•••

Deirdre's memories sundered, the rest of the concussed day whipping past, the night unraveled.

The truck parked in a forest-eaten lot. Old bones had been lashed together, two long-dead things fused into one undead monstrosity. They dragged her into its maw, down its throat, into its bowels, and then lower still, down into its boiling groin. Fumes filled the air—psychic drugs. Sixth sense uppers, burnt dreamer, supernatural stimulants—she inhaled vaporous mysticism with every breath.

What had happened to her clothing?

She rested on a foreign bed. Bodies moved in the room around her. They rarely spoke, and only two voices stuck in her memory. One of them muttered comfort in her ear, long fingers caressing tears from her face. Why had she been crying? She cried because the dead did not have futures.

A distant voice muttered in her head with a sandpaper tongue. Not the aspartame voice of her past visions, but a new one.

She hated this one more than the last.

Food went into her mouth. She chewed, swallowed. Shadows and shapes drifted through blurry vision.

Where was she?

Exhaustion and confusion ached her bones. She needed rest. Sleep.

"Everyone's lost on the first day," the kind voice told her. "You'll feel better in the morning."

"Where am I?" she asked, out-of-body.

"It's the vapors. We inhale the vapors like ancient oracles. You'll be okay. You have the gift, and people who have the gift adapt to it."

"Who…?"

"Shhh," the voice whispered. "You'll feel better. I promise."

She believed the voice.

She slept.

•••

When Deirdre awakened the next day, eighteen hours gone in a smear of barely-there memory, she first noticed the smell. Her eyes closed, body still sleep-groggy, she knew the smell. The drug vapor of sixth-sense uppers and burning dreamer fruit. Airborne molecules kissed the pores of her skin. Vaporous magic and psychic residue spoored the air.

She opened her eyes to dimness, a cement-walled basement with a dirt floor, furnishings of wood benches and rusted steel cots. Through the humid clouds of mysticism she saw zombie-like figures shuffle aimlessly. She could see the womanhood in their silhouettes, she could scent them in the mist. Their number vibrated in her spine: she was the ninth occupant of a room built for nine. The number nine seemed important. Thinking of the shape of the numeral made her imagine a human body curled in repose.

The mattress beneath her was well-used. Its fabric held the stories of many other women. Its springs could speak volumes of them, the shape of their bodies, the weight of their hearts, the length of their tales. Yes. The springs could tell her how long it took a human soul to rust.

"Where am I?" she asked, far away from herself.

"This is the white room."

(White Room)

The other woman stared at her from a nearby bench. She sounded young, and was, but in the wear of her voice Deirdre could tell she was *old enough*.

The springs creaked a tale as Deirdre sat up. "Who are you?"

"Mali. We met yesterday."

"I don't remember."

"I know. You were hurt and overwhelmed. You're acclimating now."

"What the hell is this place?"

"A dungeon. Tongue calls it a convent, but Tongue lies."

"Tongue?"

"He says he's the voice of the gods. He can talk to us in our heads, sometimes even hear our thoughts without us saying them."

"A psychic?" Deirdre asked.

"I like your name," Mali said, changing the subject. "You told me it was 'Deirdre.' You picked it yourself."

Deirdre moved to the edge of the mattress. The bedsprings cradled her in apology. "I was sixteen. I read it in a book and I liked the story."

"My mother chose my name. I'm named after one of my grandmother's grandmothers. My mother's dead, now."

"I'm sorry."

"She hit my grandmother for teaching me. It's bad to hit your parents."

"It's worse to hit your kids."

Mali left the bench and moved through billowing vapor to sit next to Deirdre. Deirdre saw that she was pale but not *white*. Dark-haired and slender, her features smooth-young, betrayed by old, wounded eyes. In Deirdre's heightened sixth-sense, Mali smelled of copper and senescence and ozone.

"You garden," Mali said.

"You smell like blood."

Mali nodded. "Grandmother always said it wasn't how magic happened that mattered, but how you used it."

Deirdre knew little of sorcery and history, but the sixth sense stimulants and dreamer in her veins filled in blanks.

Blood magic. Spellcraft hewn from bloodshed, power accrued through opened veins and human sacrifice.

It was the kind of power people killed for, or killed other people for having.

"I've never met someone like you," Deirdre said.

"Me neither, except my grandmother. I'm trying to teach some of the other girls," she tilted her head to indicate the room, the shuffling women somnambulant, "but most of them are barely conscious. There's a couple who can do some small tricks. Maybe they'll be able to do big ones one day. Rituals."

Mali wore a white tunic. Deirdre realized she wore a white tunic too. The mattresses were white, once, and the walls still were.

(White Room)

"It's hard for them to learn," Mali said. "They weren't born with it, and the vapors make them forgetful."

"Why are you teaching them?"

"Maybe if they learn enough, we can use it. We can get out of here."

"Are we the only witches here? The only ones born this way?"

"No. There is one more."

Three makes a trinity, Deirdre thought for some reason, *and nine makes a triune of trinities.*

Mali leaned forward. "Tongue calls them all witches and says they are unclean, but Tongue lies. There are only three of us and the rest are normal women. Some of them have been learning, but only small things. They don't have it in their blood. They don't have whatever Tongue needs for the altar. He keeps them here because he hates them."

"How long have you been here?" Deirdre asked.

"A long time."

The other voice from her tattered memories came through the mist. "She has been here eight years. I come just after."

Deirdre turned to the new arrival, a middle-aged woman with a strange accent. History walked crow's feet around the angry embers of her eyes. Her hair hung in near-black curtains, framing her face.

"That's Marisha," Mali provided. "She got here just after me."

"Many have come and gone. Since we were first, I think perhaps they save us for last."

"Eight years…" Deirdre's voice drifted into mist. "They've been doing this almost a decade."

Marisha snorted. "They have been doing this for centuries."

Marisha's magic escaped Deirdre's sixth sense. It was a magic of not-there-ness, a promise unfulfilled, the magic that made people look at someone's left hand while the right hand performed the trick. She smelled of nothing in particular, save the hint of maybe ozone from a different source.

"I never learned much magic," Deirdre said.

Marisha smirked.

"Not many people do, even if they're born with it." Mali reached out and took Deirdre's hand. "I was lucky to have a teacher, even if my parents tried to stop me from learning."

"How did you end up here?"

"My father sold me," Mali answered, her voice casual despite her words. "He owed many dangerous people a lot of money, and my mother had died expensively. He thought I was evil, and my grandmother wasn't around to protect me anymore. Someone offered to fix everything."

"I was kidnapped," Marisha said.

Mali's hands drifted to Deirdre's face. The young woman's touch was gentle, exploratory, an archaeologist's brush around lost civilization. "You're beautiful," she said, her fingernails running the length of Deirdre's hairline. "Your thoughts are so sharp, though. If Tongue catches them…. Can you hide them?"

"No."

"Like Lucy. She was here before you. She had knife-thoughts. You could feel them on her skin. She was a witch too, like us, her veins full of magic. She fought them when they came for her. Nasty spells that carved sigils in their bones. They collared her, injected scripture into her veins, even took her to Tongue, but she just had knives, knives, knives."

"What happened to her?"

Mali's hands withdrew, dropping down to Deirdre's. "They used her for the ritual. The altar. They took all her magic out of her and used it for…for something else."

"What do you mean?"

"You don't want to know what she means," Marisha interrupted. "The ritual, evil. What they do, vile. We hear the screams for hours."

"They took her magic out of her to fuel something. To feed it." Mali's gaze turned to the mist, and Deirdre saw the faint outline of a scavenged steel staircase suggest itself from vapor. "It's something sleeping, something dead but not dead. Something in a shallow grave."

As if responding to her notice, a set of steel double-doors swung open at the top of the stairs, banging out of sight.

Randall appeared at the top of the staircase, bandaged and probably salved with her own stolen supply. A massive, cruel grin painted his expression as he started down. Behind him, two boys in asphalt cloaks followed, rifles first. The bedside conversation ceased, and all the shuffling women trapped in that place stopped moving, as if by being still they might go unseen.

Randall lifted a familiar black bag, shook it. "Deirdre, it's time for an ablution."

"Fuck you," she snarled, standing.

Randall chuckled, his cheeks bunching in terrible glee. "Oh-ho, that's cute." He peered up at the boys following his wake. "Sounds like maybe she ain't learned her lesson, boys."

Mali put a hand on Deirdre's arm. "Please. Don't get hurt."

Deirdre battled against a feral snarl, the muscles of her face agonizing to restrain her rage.

"Please," Mali pleaded quietly.

Randall came down the stairs, the boys close behind. A knife sat on one hip, a large-mouthed pistol on his other. The black bag hung limp in his hand, the scared breath of uncounted women still trapped in its fabric. "I'll hurt you if I have to, you know. You already showed your true colors, Deirdre. Violent, uncompromising…hell, you wouldn't even take my offer of an IOU."

"You attacked me. You killed—"

"What happened to the boy was unfortunate, but you had every chance to stop it. Hell, he had every chance to butt out of things himself."

Only Mali's hand around her wrist stopped her from charging him.

Randall's smile widened. "I warned you fair and square. I told you what would happen if you decided to make this a big deal, and you made it a big deal. I gave you a chance to bail, and you rejected that chance. You even got your new boyfriend and that little kid'a yours to dig into things on your behalf."

"If it's the last thing I do I swear I'm going to kill you."

A rusty saw of laughter ripped out of him. "You ain't gonna be killing anyone now. No guns, no weapons, no kevlar…that's what Isaiah and I had on back at your place, you know, when you thought you put me down. Kevlar."

Marisha joined Mali, the older woman's hands gently coming down on Deirdre's shoulders. "Don't be stupid, girl."

"You heard the old bag," Randall said. "Smarten up. I'd hate to have to put anyone else down on your account."

Deirdre spat in his face.

Randall wiped the gob of saliva off his cheek. "See, that's why your folk always lose. Men, white men especially, we know how to keep our cool. Cunts, colored cunts especially…you lose your cool at the drop of a hat. Every month you go out of your goddamned minds."

Mali had to use both hands to stop Deirdre's balled fist from lashing out.

Deirdre inhaled, her breath smoldering to smoke in her body. "Alright, fine. Let's walk."

Randall's smile glinted the shade of sun-bleached bone. He held out the black bag. "That's more like it."

CHAPTER TWENTY-THREE

E ye burn, irritation; Paul's existence itched beyond sleep.

Fuzz batoned his face, a swell of allergy.

He sneezed himself awake. Samedi mewled panic and scrambled into the detritus of Deirdre's bedroom.

Paul jerked up, not quite hearing the clatter of steel against hardwood. He fumbled for the wounds that should have killed him; he discovered shrinking scabs, rough scar tissue. The twice-bandaged head wound remained unhealed, however, still long and rough and scabrous. Pushing himself from the mattress, he rose on shaky legs. A set of clothes hung from the door. Not quite the right size but close.

Samedi mewled again, prowling the wreckage.

Paul rubbed his itchy nose, sniffled, and went to the clothing. A loose pair of slacks, a white button-up and undershirt, athletic socks, and heavy-duty hiking boots had all been left for him to find. Not by Deirdre, his fragmented memories of the ambush confirmed that much, but by someone.

Who?

In one of the pants' pockets, he found a phone. His phone, or at least the same model. With his contacts programmed into it.

How?

He went downstairs, Samedi following after him, and scanned the house. Faint bloodstains lingered in the wear-and-tear of the hardwood, but only if he really looked for it, and no such evidence persisted on the walls. The scent of bleach reached him through allergy-blocked sinuses.

Razz's gun sat on the floor. Deirdre's too. He took both of them, one for each pocket, and continued searching.

His car sat outside, paint and chassis bullet-marred. A bright sun beat down on the unused garage, the sprawl of wilderness around him, the empty porch, but the hard light showed nothing unexpected, nothing that served as a clue to what had happened. He made a circuit of the house, pausing around the far side. A queasy sixth-sense miasma hung in the air, the leftover aura of some dread entity.

But it wasn't a lead, and there were no other clues to follow. He did another round along the perimeter and returned inside.

Samedi mewled at the foot of the stairwell, went up a few steps, and came back down. Mewled again.

Another memory went through him—his agreement to take the sixth sense uppers, to talk to the dead, to help track down Randall.

To see if some part of Razz remained beyond the wall of death.

Paul followed Samedi back upstairs, careful and quiet. He paused at the second-floor landing and waited, listening for some sign of life, some signal that his suspicion wasn't unfounded. No such signal presented itself.

Samedi scratched at the wall outside Deirdre's room.

"Hold on, hold on."

The cat hissed.

"I said hold on!"

Samedi stared at him one-eyed for a few more seconds, made a guttural feline noise, and paced down the hall to his own room. The scratching continued, now against an actual scratching post. Paul shook his head and moved back to Deirdre's room, scanning the area for her stash, for the drugs he'd promised to take to—

The lockbox caught his eye.

As did the keyring Samedi had dropped before waking him.

He glanced back at the hallway. The cat had brought him the keys? Or…?

Nothing made sense. He'd been dying and someone—something?—had saved him. Who, or what? And why? Through what mechanism? The questions crawled chittering within the walls of his skull, their insect-legs scratching his thoughts. But Samedi's mewling brought him back to the present, the lockbox in his hand, the drugs inside the lockbox. The weight of his promise. Deirdre had been taken in an ambush, dragged kicking and screaming from her own home. The responsibility for that laid, in part, on his own inaction, his own failures, his own myopia.

He keyed open the lockbox and stared at the collection inside.

One rolled-up plastic baggie of psychic downers, two rolled-up baggies of psychic uppers, a glass phial packed with cannabis, a prescription bottle of painkillers, and another with a label he recognized halfway through reading it.

Dextroamp-amphet ER 30mg cap.

He remembered tossing a bottle just like it to the lead detective during the many late nights they'd turned into early mornings.

There was money in the box too, but he didn't bother with it.

Paul stared at the collection of drugs, his heart rumbling. Thoughts raced through his head. The oil-slicked seaweed color of the downers caught his eye, and he brought it out of the lockbox and held it up. A grimace mired his face at the sight of it. He went to the bedroom window and threw the bag outside.

It was a long time before he went back to the lockbox. Longer still before he got himself to do what he knew had to be done.

...

The handcuffs bit into Deirdre's wrists, her hands angled tight and awkward over her waist. Pressure squeezed her joints. Darkness surrounded her. She felt the breath of dozens of other people stiff in the fabric of the black bag over her head. The drug vapor followed her wherever the men led her, fuming up through vents in the floor. How far had she walked over tile and steel and old, cheap rugs? She was two floors above wherever the white room was, but the men with the guns in her back had led her in circles through the rest of the structure.

She could barely make the scent out through the black bag fabric, the scent of prey anxiety underneath all their sweat and musk and gunpowder.

"Alright, get her in the tub."

Hands grabbed her. Calluses scraped her legs, thick fingers clamping down. She yelled and kicked but they already had her off the ground, her body suspended in fog and vapor. She swung her arms and someone grabbed them, pinning them across her body.

"No need to be loud about it," Randall muttered, terribly intimate. "A little bath never hurt nobody."

Cool water lapped at her tunic. She froze, mouth open, and stopped fighting. The men lowered her gently into the water, as if handling something fragile. The tub felt hungry for her. Her skin goosepimpled when her legs went in.

"There we go," Randall cooed. "See? It's not so bad."

"T-T-Take off the bag." Her teeth chattered.

"'Fraid I can't do that. It'll be easier to focus with it on."

The water soaked her tunic, soaked her skin, soaked her bones.

There was something off about it, something syrupy. It took her pores a few seconds to figure it out, once the gooseflesh had opened back up to drink in the liquid. They'd boiled some of the uppers in the water before pouring it in the tub. Dreamer-juice too. Her skin sucked it up, adding to the buzz of her sixth-sense high. The porcelain of the tub vibrated around her as she sat curled in its center. Magic hummed.

Something bristled at the back of her mind.

let me in, dear Deirdre.

It was not the voice from her dreamer visions. It was a new one, one that sounded human.

"Who are you?"

The men in the room stifled chuckles in the backs of their throats.

I am Reverend Tongue. I want to help you wake up to the future.

"Where am I?" her voice quaked in a way she wasn't used to, in a way that embarrassed her.

Tongue's words tickled her brain stem. *limbo, if you will, dear. both physically and spiritually.*

"Deirdre," Randall said, "we're gonna have to ask you to lie down."

"Why?"

you're going to engage with a spiritual hallucination, Tongue answered, *just listen to Mr. Hill's instructions and lie down.*

Deirdre shook her head. Tongue was inside her spine, his words vibrating in the nerves between her vertebrae. A psychic invasion that made her teeth itch.

"No." The denial came out as a whisper. "I'm not lying down for you."

Randall sighed, faux-frustration masking glee. "Well, boys, might as well not waste any time."

Deirdre tried to stand up, to launch herself from the tub and run through the twisted maze of wherever, but the men were already on her. The rough hands of four men, including Randall, found her limbs and pushed her under the water. The black bag soaked through and stuck to her face, a second skin with no features, and she opened her mouth to scream. Water rushed in and she gagged and spat.

"Just stop fighting, Deirdre." The water turned Randall's words into a low thrum. "Lie back and it'll all be okay."

She bucked against their hands and flung her head forward, bursting from the water to gulp air through soggy fabric. Her lungs cried out. She sucked in a wide-mouthed gasp and a hand that smelled like gunfire and masturbation grabbed her jaw. She screamed, but lost the words against the wall of palm as it plunged her back under.

She held her breath, thrashing weakly.

The hand pressed the back of her skull to the base of the tub.

what do you want?, Tongue asked, the same words as the voice from the vision but not the same voice. *you want to live, right?*

The water bubbled around her. Magic vibrated along the surface of her skin. Her heart boomed in her chest, thundercrack after thundercrack. She yelled closed-lipped against the palm over her mouth. The tub tightened around her, smooth porcelain shrinking to cocoon.

what are you willing to do to live?

what are you willing to give up?

don't you want the pain to end?

The fingers clamped to her legs disappeared, ghost-hands fading like age-bleached photos. Only the one over her face remained, solid as unworn steel.

Burning air escaped her lips. Blackness swam in blackness behind her eyelids.

Even Tongue's voice was far away. *what are you willing to do?*

CHAPTER
TWENTY-FOUR

Deirdre burst from the water, gasping.

Her uncuffed palms found smooth stone.

Her eyes found stalactites silhouetted by dim light.

She hauled her body from the water and onto the stony shore, panting. Her tunic clung to her. Rolling onto her back, she stared up at an ornate ceiling, stalactites growing down from ancient architecture. Older than Oceanrest. Older than Rome. Old enough for the Earth to have reclaimed it many times over, for Gaea to have found it and lost it and found it again, for the whole structure of it to have been absorbed into unmapped caverns.

Her legs shook as she clambered to her feet.

The ceiling hovered thirty feet over her head, and the floor of the cave stretched half as long as her street. The underground lake, deep and lightless, was the size of her house. It was so vast even her breath echoed, the sound of every gasp coming back to her a hundred times.

The water hummed. It wasn't something she heard, but something she felt through her feet and the bones in her legs. Something deep down under the lake resonated up through the floor of the cavern and into her. It called to her. It sang through her ribcage.

A tunnel opened to her left, yellow glow spilling warmly down.

Tongue's voice: *come up into the light, dear. come up and pray with me.*

She wiped lake water away from her face, squinted up at the brightness above.

I'm sorry it had to happen like this, my child, but awakenings are always difficult. why don't you come up here and pray? I want to talk to you about your future forever. about the beautiful thing awaiting us all.

Bubbles swam to the surface of the lake and popped. Each one carried a word inside, a whisper of air caught in the cavern.

come

down

here

and

breathe

It wasn't Tongue's voice. It was the one she'd felt in her head during her dreamer visions, the saccharine sweet silver-tongued darkness.

Tongue's words down from the tunnel: *why don't you come on up here? dry off. we wouldn't want you to go back in the water after what just happened, would we? it wouldn't be safe.*

"Tongue lies," she whispered.

come, child, come to me. there will be no lies when you enter the light.

She shook her head and backed away from the tunnel. The cool air of the cavern stroked her skin. Darkness draped its arms around her shoulders. The floor hummed and she could feel a voice deep under the Earth.

come

down

here

and

breathe

She walked to the edge of the lake, bare feet on smooth cool stones, and peered into the water. Only her reflection peered back, hints of face and a block of uptop hair silhouetted by the light from the tunnel, all of it familiar yet somehow different. The reflection rippled, its lips distorting into a grin, its eyes glinting wickedly. It vanished, leaving a place for her to fit.

you don't want to do that, dear Deirdre. you don't know what kind of things lurk in such darkness and depth.

Tongue was right. She didn't know what waited at the lake bottom, what foul thing owned the aspartame voice of her dreamer visions, but she knew exactly what kind of man waited for her in the beckoning warmth and light. She knew exactly what kind of man reached out to her with such soothing words, exactly what kind of man smiled sunshine and talked gospel while women were beaten and raped.

She took a deep breath and dove down, down, down...

...

The sun drooped lazily westward and the dead grew louder. Paul felt them strengthen in the coming night, heard their voices crescendo. Felt some of them reach out for him.

How many ghosts skulked about the city?

Some spirits couldn't remember dying, lived in denial of their new nature for as long as they could. Others remembered nothing *but* dying, obsessed with their endings. All of them, eventually, forgot themselves. Eventually, some became frighteningly powerful.

He finished the first joint of psychic stimulants and ground it out. His newfound phone blinked at him, one light green, one red. He had new messages and low batteries. When he woke up the screen, he'd missed ten calls from Virgil and three from Simon Perdue.

He put the phone aside and assessed his armory. Deirdre's revolver, three speedloaders, a pile of spare bullets, Razz's pistol with two bullets left and no spares.

Was he going to call them back? It seemed wise to do so, considering what little he could remember of Randall's ambush.

He guzzled water from a tall glass he'd found in Deirdre's kitchen. The uppers dried him out and he'd had two glasses already.

He picked the phone back up.

the vines grew through me, wrapped me up and buried me, one ghost wept in the distance. *please...*

there are shadows here, moving where they ought to be still, another called out.

Ghosts were sad, trapped creatures.

He focused past the growing whispers of the dead and punched in Virgil's number. The line rang three times, four times, five...

It wasn't Virgil who answered, it was Simon. *"Paul?"*

"Simon? Where's Virgil?"

"In a meeting." Something buzzed under Simon's baritone, static interference fuzzing the reception. *"Where are you?"*

"What do you mean?"

"We've been trying to get a hold of you for two days."

"I, uh...I had to get a new phone. Mine died in the harbor." A warbled distortion made Paul wince.

Simon cleared his throat. *"Did you find anything?"*

"Maybe."

"Maybe doesn't cut it."

"I'm following a lead. I think I'll have something at the end of it."

A wave of static broke over the line, drowning the first half of Simon's sentence. *"…out of time. This is a very serious matter. Virgil thinks you should come to the precinct and go over the facts…"* The static returned again, crackling the rest. Paul got the gist.

"Absolutely not. Like you said," (he assumed), "we're running out of time. I don't have spare minutes to drive to the precinct and review paperwork. I have a lead, I'm tailing it."

Not that he could have driven to the precinct in any case, his engine having caught several bullets.

Simon's sigh distorted through the earpiece. *"We need actionable evidence."*

"I'll have it soon. Tonight."

"What's the lead?"

"Randall and his people. I'm almost sure they're tied into your killer. I'm close to a location."

"Where?"

"Near US highway one," Paul said, not certain of more and unwilling to guess without consulting Lucy's spirit.

"I'll take some people out there, see if we can…" More static hissed.

"Say again?"

"We'll take east of the exit, you take west. We can meet—"

"There's something fucking up the reception," Paul muttered. "When do you think—"

The call dropped. Paul tried the number again but only got a busy signal. A third time yielded a brief ring, two words exchanged, and a sudden disconnect. Sighing, Paul turned the phone off and pocketed it. He'd turn it back on and try again if and when he found something new to report.

He lit a second joint of sixth-sense uppers and went to Deirdre's boarded window. Outside, a turbid, silver-white fog swaddled the wilderness. If the phone interference and sudden clarity of the dead were any judgment, Paul guessed this was Oceanrest's "Trickster's fog."

That meant Randall would make his move tonight, probably sometime approaching the colloquial "witching hours."

Paul saw the fog as somehow alive, in his sixth-sense. A living creature crawling its way out of the bay, up and over the rocky coast, stretching limbs northward, tendrilling appendages around tree trunks, reaching over forest floor, pulling itself toward…

Toward what?

He exhaled mysticism and shook himself off. Fog wasn't alive, not in the sense of having motive or intent. Not in the sense of having appendage or body or mind. That was the drugs distorting his perceptions. Had to be.

More voices of the dead reached through wilderness and mist, his strengthening sixth sense making their sentences more cogent, more understandable.

come to the Black House, a small choir sang out. *come to the Black House and let us out.*

He pushed their voices aside, tried to pick Lucy out of the crowd of spirits. He reached out as best he could, as best he knew how, and took a deeper drag on the joint. By the time Lucy found him he'd be able to converse with her as naturally as he would with another living person. Would she have yet figured out how to disguise her mortal disfigurement? Or would he see her as she'd appeared in his houseboat those days earlier, eyes weeping blood and tongueless maw gaping?

He shivered, and warmed himself with another drag. This one burnt in his lungs and sent him into a coughing fit, wheezing and hacking through silver exhalations, doubled-over and clutching his knees. When the fit subsided, he wiped burnt tears from his eyes, and froze.

There.

A shape hovering in the den's threshold, pale in his periphery.

He turned slightly, felt the threat of different tears quiver his eyelids.

The background sound of all the dead retreated as she spoke, proximity giving her power.

you can't run away, this time.

She had her mother's long fingers. She wore long sleeves over secret scars.

Paul dashed the cherry of the joint against the boards crossing the window. Nodded without looking at her. "I guess not."

■■■

Deirdre's lungs burned with held breath. Her muscles yearned for oxygen, her throat begged for air. She kicked, stroked, kicked. How far down had she gone? Opening her eyes to the fathomless lake, she found only darkness.

not far, now, the not-Tongue voice from her visions told her.

She kicked again, surged through water, and found the rocky outcrop of the lake's bottom. She grasped stony protrusions and pulled herself along the lake floor. Her lips ached to open.

almost there.

Kick, pull, kick, pull...

She couldn't hold out anymore.

A wall of white bubbles burbled from her lips. She gave a final kick and reached out. Her throat flexed and gagged—*inhale*, it pled. She fought the urge even as numbness prickled her limbs, and exhaustion threatened unconsciousness. But as her body went soft and frail and limp, she gave in.

She opened her mouth and—

Air. Somehow, air. At the bottom of the lake, beneath an unknown depth of cold, dark water, she found air. She sucked it up, rejuvenated, and pulled herself along the craggy floor until her hands found something new.

A gap. A slender scab opened up in the world's mantle. Somehow, it shone darker than the darkness. She brought her eyes to its lips and peered inside.

Nothing. The kind of nothing Paul had talked about—not an absence, but a waiting, hungry presence.

"What are you?"

No water flooded her mouth.

hello, Deirdre, the too-sweet tone purred, buzzing up the marrow of her vertebrae and singing along the skin of her eardrums. *you can call me The Speaker.*

"You're the thing they're trying to summon?"

A sugary chuckle of cold amusement. *if I were, would I be hiding down here?*

Her mind brimmed with a thousand questions. "What—what are you then? Who? And where?"

let's address more pressing issues.

"What are they trying to summon, if it isn't you?"

my competition. the Devourer, they used to call It, though I'm sure the 'Good Reverend Tongue' came up with a more palatable name.

"Why should I believe you?"

you are experiencing a psychic vision brought about by near-death brain chemistry, dreamer, psychic stimulants, and Tongue's magic. you're in a liminal place. this is a gap—real and not, on your side of things and on mine. a hole in the wall, with so many vermin fighting to get through it.

"The fuck are you talking about?"

we'll skip the exposition. you should believe me because I had to work very hard to find a gap in Tongue's wards. you should believe me because I've been trying to reach out to you for days. because I want to make a deal.

"Bullshit."

why don't you listen for a second before passing judgment?

"You're a liar."

no, I'm a deceiver. there's a difference.

"I'm out of here."

where to, might I ask? Tongue's prayers? the White Room? the sacrificial altar?

Deirdre hesitated at that, suddenly aware of the weight of the water above her, the promise of anguish back in the physical world. "Okay. What's the deal?"

She felt the thing smile, felt its tar-heroin lips curl up. She felt it pulse through her veins.

I want your help to take down Tongue and his little cult. I need an inside agent. you're inside.

"What's the catch?"

you'll be a satellite. I'll need access to your brain meat, that buzzing, beautiful thing inside your skull. I need a working relationship.

"Sounds like possession to me."

no, not nearly so permanent. but the deal would be ongoing, a 'talent holding' arrangement, you understand.

"Brass tacks, Mephistopheles. Where comes the tragical history?"

I'll spare you the spin, Deirdre, I know we don't have time for PR and pretty talk. it goes like this: we work together to dismantle Tongue's wards, open up his little sanctum to my dismantling wrath, and I help you avenge your lost son, free those kidnapped women, and otherwise canonize you as a witch heroine. after our first deal is done, crossed and dotted, we assume a more traditional relationship. I can give you power and knowledge and a little more bang for your mystical buck, and in exchange I ask for a little service and some small access to your brain space.

"No."

nothing too intrusive, I promise. at least, not without extenuating circumstances. just a little access to your dreams and dreamer visions, maybe a few whispers in the waking world now and again. a small—

"No way."

you won't find a better deal. you won't find anything else so eager to help you out.

"I don't care." She pushed herself away from the scab in the world. "I'm not dealing with some twisted Mephistopheles motherfucker just because he's my enemy's enemy."

in your traditional mammalian sense, I'm sexless. an 'it' not a 'he.'

"Go to Hell."

I've been. it's not very impressive.

She kicked off toward the surface of the lake.

why don't you put your ear to the walls of this place, hear what my competition has to offer? maybe you'll change your mind.

She opened her mouth to reply, but she'd left whatever safe bubble of air she'd been in and water rushed between her lips.

let me know if you have second thoughts. we'll be speaking again soon. very soon...

■■■

She erupted over the side of the bathtub, gagging for air, and rolled onto hard floor. She gasped through the soaked black bag and choked on drops of water falling from the fabric. Spat, jerked her head around, and heaved against rising nausea.

"Now that wasn't so bad, was it?" Randall asked.

she is a born witch, Tongue's voice returned to her. *and untamed by the offering of solace. she will be a good sacrifice.*

Steam wisped from her skin, commingling with the vapor in the air. Callused hands grabbed her, hauled her back to her feet. Her soles slipped on spilled water.

Randall chuckled. "Having a little trouble there?"

"Fuck you," Deirdre panted.

"Get her back to the White Room, boys. Don't be too rough with her. We don't want to damage the goods before the ceremony."

Hands pushed and pulled on her, and she wrestled against them. "You ever hear the Speaker, Randall?"

Randall snorted. "I hear the words of many gods. The Reverend hears them all, and translates."

"The Reverend fucking lies."

A fist caught her face and spun her weightless, the grasping hands of her captors her only support against the force of the blow. She froze in the aftermath, the pulsing heat of a bruise ripening beneath her skin. She worked her jaw against the pain.

"Get her out of here," Randall growled.

Tongue's voice crept into her mind like a thief. *you'll have to forgive Randall. he's not used to women who have forgotten their place in the world, especially coloreds. he's never figured out the value of gentle education, the value of restraint when dealing with our inferiors. but he's a forgiving soul, at heart. you could learn from that.*

CHAPTER TWENTY-FIVE

hy did you run away? Cassandra asked. *why do you keep running?*

Paul couldn't bring himself to glance at her face, didn't want to know if she'd grown strong enough as a spirit to recast the ruin of her visage. He dropped onto the couch and stared hard at the coffee table between him and the ghost of his daughter. "I don't know. I'm sorry."

sorry? the clarity of her voice made him long for downers, made him despise the growing strength of his sixth sense. *is that all you have to say for yourself?*

"I can't tell you how sorry I am. But right now—"

you're kidding me. right now? it's been five years and you still—

"I promise. I promise after I find Deirdre, after tonight, you can have me. Whatever you want to say, whatever you want to do, I know I deserve it, but please let me do this first."

why?

"Please."

no. you left us. you just left *us. you left Mom all alone and me...you saw me, I know you did, and you kept seeing me, and I kept reaching out and you pushed me away, drank and smoked until you couldn't see, and then you left. look at me.*

His skin bristled at the cold of her. "Cass, stop. Please."

is that how you always lived? did you always run away?

"Cass."

'cause you did it like you had practice.

"My friend needs me."

I NEEDED YOU.

now

look

at

me.

Paul forced a shuddering breath through ragged lungs and looked.

Cassandra Somers hovered just feet away from him, sixteen years old (almost seventeen), sixteen years old forever, until she went mad, or dissipated into death, or whatever other fates awaited ghosts. Her dark hair coiled in a slick ribbon down one side of her head. Her mother's green eyes glittered in her renewed face above stern cheekbones, her jawline mirroring his own. Floating inches off the ground and half-translucent, her stare carved him open, a jagged blade. Her lips moved and the voice in his head almost synced up with them.

why did you leave?

"I just…there was nothing left. You were everything to us."

before then, Dad. before. Mom hadn't seen you for days and I hadn't seen you for weeks. weeks. she thought you were cheating on her, you know. probably still does.

and me, fuck, Dad, why couldn't you ever just listen to me?

Words crumbled inside his chest, the threat of a sinkhole in his heart. "I—I—there was a killer, Cass," he stammered. "A killer going after girls, girls like—"

like me.

"Like you. Killing them, dumping them in the bay, and I—I was scared, I thought if I could catch him, if I could do that, I could fix everything else, that everything else would make more sense."

you know what that year was like, for me? at school? you know what those weeks were like, when you barely came home? they threw eggs at me. they painted the word 'dyke' on my locker.

one of my friends had to pick me up at a party after the kids there pushed me into a closet and blocked the door with a desk. that's not a fucking metaphor, Dad, that's something that actually happened to me in Forest Hills, in a tiny walk-in closet with the lights off and no room for me to breathe and them laughing about it and you didn't even pick up your phone

my friend had to come into the party and punch the host and move the desk and carry me out

"Cass, I didn't—"

you were scared about a stranger? what about the people who weren't strangers? what about me?

He'd thought these things a thousand times already, after it was too late. Drunk and alone, he'd gone through a thousand versions of this dialogue in his head and he'd never come up with the right words, and now was no exception.

I know you weren't cheating on Mom. you were doing drugs with your detective buddy, looking at crime scene photos until the amphetamines got the better of you and then walking the streets until dawn grinding your teeth like an addict.

"I was trying to solve the case."

the case was an excuse and you know it. you didn't want to come home, so you didn't. but, hey, you caught the killer, so I guess you get the blue ribbon. but how could you see my arms and think a killer's knife was more important than the razors you left in the bathroom?

Her arms were like Nora's. Pinched-lip scars sealed against secrets.

Paul searched for an answer in his hollowing innards.

What could someone say to the dead to earn their forgiveness?

"I was scared."

She laughed, cold and cruel. *you were scared? then what was I?*

"I didn't mean…I didn't know about the party or your locker or any of that. All I knew was that you'd swiped a bottle from our liquor cabinet, that you'd snuck some pills from one of my prescriptions, that you were a teenager, maybe a troubled one, that you were experimenting or…" the words crumbled in his mouth, syllables fragmented from meaning. "I knew you were hurting but I never knew why."

you didn't ask.

"I'm sorry, how many times can I say—"

never enough.

Her sigh gusted through his innards.

you thought Mom would handle it. you figured you could lay low and wait for it to blow over, that your lovely wife would figure it out without you. that she could put me back together even as she fell apart herself.

she was scared, too. she was so sure you were going to leave us.

and, surprise, surprise…you did.

Paul stood up, pulse too fast and body too tense to remain seated. He crossed the floor, nearly tripped over an ottoman, and caught himself against a bookshelf. A pair of books tumbled from the shelves. He panted against a dizzy world.

when I tried to reach out to you, after…do you know how fucked up it is to realize that you're dead? that you're a ghost?

He shook his head, trying to choke down a tear-crafted teratoma cancered in his gullet.

I wish it had been Mom. I wish Mom ended up with the sight instead of you. she sucked at fixing things but at least she tried. she would've kept trying.

"I'm—"

sorry. yeah. you said.

The teratoma birthed a wretched sob, a strangled keening. "I would've talked to you if I'd known."

'if.' but you didn't care to find out, did you? you pretended things would sort themselves out, or that you'd figure out your family if you could figure out your job. it doesn't work like that.

and what about after? I'm dead but I'm still…here. and I found you over and over again, I always found you, and you just drank and smoked until I was easy to ignore. and then your tolerance got too high and your doctor told you the liver tests weren't coming back so great and you left.

"The city was full of ghosts. I couldn't sleep without being drunk, could barely even walk around. There were so many of them and they were all so loud." His knees shook, his legs weak. What could he say? What could someone say to the dead to earn their forgiveness? "I'm sorry I left. I was an idiot, I was caught up in all those crime scene photos, and I never snapped out of it until I saw the photos of you, the way you looked with broken glass all around you, all the blood…"

you left Mom, left the apartment, left your job; you cut your losses with a handful of signatures and ran away.

Her cold aura leached the heat from his tears. "It wasn't just that, it wasn't you or your mom—it was all those phone calls and the e-mails and people calling you a *killer*, calling you a *murderer*, and all those fucking people whispering all around us that their kids would never end up like that, that their kids were some kind of fucking saints, that we'd fucked up and ruined you and—and—and maybe we did, or I did. I did fuck up, but I just couldn't take it. That shithole city and all its ghosts and your face the way it looked in those photos, I just couldn't take it so, so yes, yes, I ran away."

He fell back from the bookshelf, tripped over the same ottoman, and went down. He crashed to the floor in a single second of full-body pain, gasping at the suddenness of it.

because why, Dad? at the bottom of all your excuses, why?

What could someone say to the dead?

did you not think that Mom got those voicemails too? those e-mails?

He pushed himself up to his knees, genuflective. "I didn't want it to be real. After all those nightmares, walking to your room and back, again, out on the streets on speed—and we got the guy, but it was too late, because all my nightmares had already happened. And I couldn't stop hearing all those voices in my head, couldn't stop seeing all those bodies…and then there was your mom just staring, just *staring* at the walls, so fucked up on painkillers she couldn't even hear me talking and I couldn't live like that. I just couldn't."

that's what you think the truth is? that you just couldn't handle it? that there was no other way out?

Cassandra's voice was so quiet in his head he couldn't tell if it was full of pity or wrath.

He collapsed forward, hands clutching her jeans, jeans that weren't physically there, not entirely, but held him up like taut string, and sobbed. The texture existed in the sixth sense, denim as a cloud, as a concept, but between his fingers, against his tear-slicked cheek, it was as real as flesh. As Earth and sky and the deep Sargasso Sea.

what did you think would happen? what did you think would happen to Mom? do you want to know what happened to Mom?

He shook his head, shivering from cold and despair and marrow-lapping sobs.

of course you don't. good or bad, it wouldn't matter. you left. that was the end of the story for you.

but like every other asshole, you don't think about all the people whose stories have to keep going.

She flicked her pale, translucent wrist and a pulse of pain spiked his hand. He let go of her not-quite-there jeans and fell back, tailbone hitting the floor. He peered up at her with tear-streaked cheeks and bloodshot eyes, his mouth quivering with unsaid words.

we're not finished, she said, her tone harsh, uncompromising. *but I'll let you do whatever it is you need to do for your friend. maybe you'll actually help someone, this time.*

Maybe he didn't deserve forgiveness.

So he wept. He collapsed against the floor and sobbed the way he hadn't since the day after the funeral. Snot and mucus sobbing, heaving lungs and whining, reedy breaths. And he stayed there, weeping on the floor, until after Cassandra had left and the silence around his animal despair served as its own unremitting condemnation. He stayed there until another presence oozed through the wall and a second aura of cold death came to find him.

Body frail, he pushed himself up to all fours.

"I'm sorry," he whispered.

help me, Lucy McKinney beseeched.

"I'm so, so sorry…"

A hand found the back of his head, slender fingers frigid in his hair. *you're the only one who hears me, and I don't know what else to do.*

Paul wiped the tears from his face and gazed up at Lucy, at the eyeless sockets pleading down to him. "Where are they?" he asked, brittle-voiced.

the church, Lucy told him. *the thing that rose from its grave, hungry. we have to hurry.*

CHAPTER TWENTY-SIX

Water dripped down Deirdre's legs as she stood in the White Room. Her hair frizzed in vaporous humidity.

"I think they will start soon," Marisha said, seated on the edge of Deirdre's cot.

Deirdre knew from Paul's suspicions and flashes of remembered dreamer vision exactly the thing Marisha referred to.

(cum spattering stomach)

(Randall's hand pulling hair)

(knife driven into mouth)

"What did you see?" Mali asked, closer to Deirdre and quieter.

Deirdre scoured the unfinished basement wall. "An underground cavern. A darkness with teeth. The Speaker."

"You didn't make a deal, did you?"

"No. How did you know he—it—offered one?"

"It's been trying to get inside this place for a long time. Ever since Tongue made the magic that keeps it out. It's reached out before."

Marisha grunted. "It reminds me of bad fairytales my grandmama used to tell."

"Tongue lies," Mali said, "but I don't trust The Speaker either."

"Don't trust things you can't see," Deirdre said, still staring.

Mali followed Deirdre's eyeline to the age-cracked cement. "What is it?"

"A hunch." Deirdre stepped away from Mali and crossed the drug-misted room, feet padding over soft soil. She reached the wall and pressed her palms against it, felt its unfinished roughness. Something hummed through the warmth-hungry surface of it. The resonance reminded her of The Speaker, but different. Hotter, if that was a thing a hum could be.

She closed her eyes and lowered her drying forehead to the cement, dreamer and sixth sense uppers pulsing through her veins. Blood cells communed with the unknown and the unknowable. A deep breath filled her up, focusing her on the magic woven through Tongue's church, the unseen thing humming in the walls.

She inhaled.

Exhaled.

Inhaled.

And jerked back, screaming. She spun from the surge of sensation, dizzied by brutality and grotesquery. Mali caught her before she collapsed, Marisha joining shortly after. Deirdre panted against the memories, the terrible millennia compressed into that single second.

The Speaker had a voice of chemical sweetness, a silver tongue telling pretty lies. The Speaker sang a lullaby of deals and promises, scams and swindles, pleasant deceptions and falsehoods. Cloying. Sinister. Untrustworthy.

But the voice in the walls of Tongue's church sang no lullaby. Its ongoing, everlasting snarl beat out the rhythm and tattoo of war, of gas chambers erected over the remains of torched villages that were themselves built on the killing fields of forgotten tribes. It growled a song that spasmed and throbbed in the nastiest parts of her, a guttural chant overlaid by drums and death whistles. A war cry. A child gurgling to death on its own blood. A rape. A genocide. A bomb burning ghosts into the sidewalks. The Devourer's mouth was a field of mass graves, hungry for more flesh.

eatkillshitrape the hymn growled over and over again, without cease, without stop, without end.

Deirdre's consciousness flooded with unbidden images. Her foot on a man's throat; her gun against a man's head; her hand wrapped around power; her seat atop a throne of yellowed bone, a kingdom spread out below her in bloodstained wasteland. In return: offerings, worship.

Worship: apes eating their own young, faces smeared in meatjelly.

Worship: jackbooted soldiers marching over corpse-strewn battlefields.

Worship: a father staring at the severed hands and feet of his own child.

Inside her gut, an instinctive gospel heaved itself into her diaphragm. The scripture said there were two kinds of people in the world: predators and prey. All other truths were secondary. Deirdre could be a predator in exchange for worship. If not…

She teetered against Mali and Marisha's buttressing, wanting to free herself from the whole world all at once.

She jerked forward, hunched, gagged. Puked up ramen and bile and bathwater. A dry heave gutpunched her, the impulse to unpoison herself not recognizing the difference between physical and spiritual poison. She lurched. Spasmed. Struggled against the best efforts of her fellow inmates to collapse.

"What's wrong?" Marisha asked, panicked.

Deirdre remembered her dreamer visions, two monsters trying to gut each other, all claws and fangs and sandpaper tongues. She had met them both now.

"Get her to the bed!" Mali yelled.

Her body moved through space. Her mind reeled with the savage testament of a bloodthirsty god. She puked, empty-stomached.

Why couldn't she throw up all these terrible things?

She turned over the edge of the mattress (when had they gotten her to the mattress?) and spat red into the soil floor.

The world came back into focus around her. Marisha and Mali had gotten her in bed and now stood at either side of her, concern aging their features. Deirdre panted for breath, panted against the airless vacuum of such massive death, and tried to settle her innards. Each convulsion of her heart echoed a detonation in her mind, a replay of a cloud frothing its head up high, spilling over a screaming city.

"What happened?" Mali asked. "What did you see?"

She shook her head.

Mali lowered herself down and put a gentle hand on Deirdre's cheekbone. "Whatever did that to you, you should not suffer it alone."

Deirdre shook her head again, freeing Mali's hand. "No. It doesn't matter. I'll live. Just…"

"What?" Mali pressed.

"We have to stop these men."

From behind her, Marisha responded, "Yes. Good. We knew this. The question is, *how?*"

■■■

The last rays of sunlight set Lucy ablaze, made her look like a beacon of light and fire. A wisp leading him through quiet woods.

The stories of men who followed wisps never ended well.

Still, Paul followed. His sixth sense blossomed in his skull, flowering in psychic stimulants and some strange interaction with the fog. The dead grew louder, and Paul bit his tongue to distract himself from them. Behind them, his car rotted roadside, punctured in gunshot, unusable. And so he'd gone on foot, while Lucy floated inches from the ground.

He took a drag from another sixth-sense joint, exhaled another fume of silver into fog. Was it possible to overdose on magic? He took another puff. It didn't matter. As long as he got to Deirdre before he died, nothing mattered.

He wouldn't run away this time.

Not again.

Lucy led him west through abused and derelict neighborhoods. Tree limbs and coiled vines wrenched apart man's architecture, rendered civilization to decay. On Adams Court, Paul tried to focus, tried to see if he could hear Razz's voice whispering among the others, but there were too many spirits, and it was impossible to tell.

Go home, a house told him.

Go home, it warned.

But Lucy led on, and Paul followed.

They left the ruins of Squatter City and entered the wilderness proper, the vast sprawl of evergreens and maples and elms and spruces and all other foliage wild and mad, sprouting from Oceanrest's uncommonly rich soil at lunatic angles, vying for the setting sun.

Fog mantled the woods around them. Oceanrest fog. Trickster's fog. A dense pea-soup mist, half-opaque, humming in his sixth sense. The psychic uppers keyed him into its resonance, the strength of its supernatural nature. His arm hair vibrated, his skin goosepimpled. Lucy delved into the gray-white curtain.

follow closely, she advised.

"Yeah," he muttered, distracted by the memory of Cassandra. By the weight of his failures, both now and then, threatening to flatten him forever.

Oceanrest isn't a normal town. never was.

"I know."

Shadows moved within the mist. Silhouettes crouched, deformed, humanoid and non; they maneuvered his periphery, watching from between the trees. They gave him and Lucy a wide berth, spying and hiding and waiting for nightfall. He'd heard stories about creatures living hidden in the woods, but he'd never believed in monsters. Not until he'd seen one. Now every story seemed possible. Was that a good thing, or a bad one?

He took out his phone and turned it on. In the interfering fog, reception was spotty. He called Virgil's number five times, never quite connecting. He called Simon's next. Two calls. Three. Finally, on the fourth, he got a passable connection.

"*Hello?*" Simon said through garbling static.

"Simon! Can you hear me?"

"*Wh…?*"

"Can you hear me?"

"*Yessss,*" static slurred sibilance to the end of the word. "*What did you—*"

"Randall is at Howland Butler's old church!" Paul yelled, as if volume would make up for interference. "I repeat, at Howland Butler's church!"

Fuzz and static. Electric crackle. A squeal of interference. Something else he couldn't quite place.

"*Kksshhh,*" Simon seemed to say, the actual words blanked away.

Paul kept repeating: Howland Butler's church, Howland Butler's church, Howland Butler's church…

The line disconnected. He typed the words into a text message and sent it. The message failed. He kept sending until his phone abruptly died.

Lucy glanced back at him. *don't yell. you do not want to find out what things might be listening.*

The admonishment sent a cold shudder through his bones. He nodded. They moved on.

The dead hissed in his ears, different voices cutting over each other: *Jesus get him outta there! // please just put it down // this is what It wants! I'm going to give It what It wants!*

Paul stuck close to the shade ahead. "How many people died out here?"

too many, Lucy answered. *but that's not the worst of it.*

"What do you mean?"

you already know.

("The things," remembering Nora's words again, "*the things living out in the woods.*")

monsters and myths aren't the worst. ghosts and ghouls are just the beginning. there is evil here. true evil. and it's been here for a very long time.

He turned his sixth-sense away from the trail of thoughts that followed. What did she think he already knew that was worse than monsters?

("The era of man is at its end")

("There's a war going on behind things, beneath them…")

He shivered.

there is a thing called the Strangling Tree. there is a thing called the Willow of Masks. there is the Black House. the Asher Farm. you did not pick a good place to live, seer.

"Can you read my mind?"

when I was alive, I could do so many things…now it's all so vague. my memories burn like dry leaves.

"They shouldn't be."

yet, they are.

"It takes most spirits decades—"

and, yet, they are, she repeated forcefully.

Somewhere in the distance, a beautiful voice, seductive, called through the whispers of the dead to reach him. *who do you want to be?* it asked. *come and mask. you can be whoever you want. come mask. live the dream. stay with us and you can live the dream forever.*

"What the hell is that?"

the Willow of Masks, Lucy answered. *do not listen to it.*

"Get me out of here," he said.

that is the plan.

■■■

"There was a boy, once, who wanted to help us," Mali said quietly, seated in a lotus position next to Deirdre's bed. "He was a born witch, like us, but he was a boy, like them, and he was white, like them, and so they allowed him freedom. He said he believed what they believed, until he didn't anymore."

"So it always goes," Marisha said.

"When I was the only one here, he would bring me food," said Mali. "When Marisha came, he brought food for both of us. He went to the ablution pool and communed with the things he found in his visions. He told us he would help us, that he would set us free."

Marisha snorted.

Mali shot a glare at the older woman. Marisha shrugged, muttering an under-the-breath apology. When Mali returned to the story, her gaze drifted to middle-distance, building a stage out of mist in her mind. "His name was Samuel. I believe he loved me. He looked at me sometimes the way Randall's clients look at me, but more often he looked at me differently. He looked at me the way my father used to look at my mother, the way some of the men at the docks look at the sun glowing over the ocean. I know he wanted to do what he said he would do.

"In a different world, I think I would've liked to kiss him. But I'm not sure about the world we've got. I don't even know if I like kissing boys in the world we've got, or maybe if I'd like it more if so many of them hadn't kissed me like they were chewing meat. Maybe if he'd kissed me, I'd know what it was supposed to be like. What it would feel like to be kissed like a person."

Something heavy and languid stirred in Deirdre's chest.

"One night he came to us, to me and Marisha and that woman whose name I can never remember, and he said he had to leave Oceanrest. He said he had a plan to make things hard for Randall, for Tongue, but that he wouldn't be able to come back for a long time."

"What happened?" Deirdre asked.

"We are still here," Marisha said.

"There were gunshots that night," Mali explained. "And an explosion. We don't know if he lived or died or who might've gotten hurt."

"We are still here," Marisha repeated, sadder. "And I do not think he is coming back."

Deirdre straightened up. "So we save ourselves."

"There is no plan. You say we live or die, but you have no plan. You say we fight, but Samuel fought already."

"We aren't him."

"No, we are not. He had magic and guns, we have only magic."

"They need us," Deirdre said. "They need a sacrifice. If they kill all of us, they don't get a sacrifice."

Silence. A beat.

"They're going to kill us," Deirdre said. "Whatever rituals they do, whatever horrible things they plan to do to us before they cut out our fucking tongues and dump our bodies, that's how it ends. We are going to die here. We can die begging for mercy, or screaming curses, or on our knees crying like children, or we can die fighting."

Another long silence. Sacred silence, prayer silence. The silence of hope enduring against hopelessness.

Marisha nodded. "Fuck it. I am too old to die scared."

Something glowed through Mali's tarnished eyes. "Yes. Thank you."

"I will die for this, but if it can be avoided, that would be better. Which brings me back to point one. We need a plan."

Deirdre peered through the coils of drug smoke at the stairs leading up from the White Room. They were narrow, fit for no more than two men standing shoulder-to-shoulder.

"That's the only way in?"

"And the only way out, yes."

"Whoever comes to get us, they have to come through that door. They have to come down those stairs."

"Yes," Marisha repeated.

The hinges on the doors were rusted and loud. The men carried guns with long barrels, rifles and shotguns, their only handgun in Randall's holster.

Deirdre exhaled drugs into the drug-rich air and allowed herself a soft chuckle. "I have an idea."

■■■

Darkness crept across the sky.

Paul glanced into the distance. "What the hell is a Willow of Masks?"

a wise man won't endeavor to find out.

Paul forced the dozens of other questions back down his throat. He'd heard countless rumors and folktales during his tenure in Oceanrest, but the idea that some of them were literally true still seemed faintly impossible. Or the idea *had* seemed impossible, until the Beast had drooped its hideousness down from a hole in a ceiling. Paul blocked out the other references Lucy had made and focused on the task at hand.

The thickening fog and psychic stimulants gave Lucy more depth. She seemed almost material now. Paul could see how blood once pumped through her body; where veins and muscle and sinew once wired her together. He could see how she'd once been human, alive.

The rest of the world followed suit. The chorus of the dead grew louder. The sense of being watched by unnatural things grew worse.

He could even feel Cassandra follow in their wake, waiting to see if her father had grown up.

The restless dead crowded the back of his mind. They strained to be heard, clawing through graves at the back of his skull. *hear us,* they pled. *please, hear us.*

And some of them merely chorused giddily *you, too, soon.*

"We have to get out of the fog," he said.

Lucy shifted direction slightly, and kept floating on.

After a few more minutes, they came out of the mist along a stretch of barren road. Paul could feel its route beneath his feet, could envision it stretching through the woods and into Oceanrest proper, one of the main avenues cutting through town all the way down to the sea.

this way.

The fog followed along on their left side, wreathed between every tree as far as he could see. The road was clearer, the mist thinning beyond the tree line. The voices of the dead receded, becoming unfocused radio chatter cutting in and out of his head.

In the distant hiss of their voices, he heard all the reasons why he needed psychic dampers: *no please don't hurt me please no please // the fog rolled in and brought Them with it // there's things I can't see but I know they're real...*

(*you too, soon,* they chorused together. *you too, soon.*)

He balled his fists and focused on Lucy's hair, the crimson color coming back into it as his sixth sense sharpened.

Up ahead, a black sedan appeared from the mist. It sat crooked along the shoulder of the road, passenger-side door hanging open. A rhythmic *ding* repeated from inside, the only sound Paul had heard since sunset besides the rasp of unsettled ghosts and the promises of inscrutable entities. Paul broke away from Lucy to approach it, knowing where it was from even before he saw the Virginia license plates. The keys dangled from the ignition. A digital read-out on the dashboard read "Door Open" in narrow orange letters.

He circled around the car to the passenger's side and saw grue glistening on the grass. "Blood."

something's not right with this car.

Paul bent down, tracking the claret splotches to the tree line and beyond. Broken branches and kicked-up divots of dirt. Someone running? He pursed his lips. Had Simon and Virgil gotten his text? Had they followed up? Whose blood slicked the dewy grass beneath his feet?

something's wrong.

He checked the tires and found no visible damage, and none to the frame. What drove it off the road?

we should keep moving.

"Hold on." He closed the passenger door and crossed back to the driver's seat. Keys in the ignition, battery fine, tires fine. His jaw worked at the idea. Why the hell was it *there*? His teeth pressed against his lower lip. It didn't matter. None of it mattered. Getting to Deirdre mattered. "We'll take the car."

it's wrong.

He slipped into the driver's seat. Lucy was right, there was something off about it, something in the air that set his teeth on edge and tickled the reflexes of his lizard brain. A familiar sensation, a dark miasma, choking wrongness.

All the voices vanished, just like at the Blackwood mansion. The chorus of the dead couldn't reach him inside the car.

Lucy's voice came in like talk radio crackling between frequencies.

something's wrong with it.

He opened his mouth to answer but glimpsed something in the rearview that stole his breath. A flash of white between tree trunks, a pale movement glimpsed in twists of fog. A queasy recognition turned his guts. He cranked the keys in the ignition and the engine growled to life. "We're taking the car."

I can't...can't get in...

It wasn't just the miasma. Not just the wards against the dead either. Something else, something in the air. "Get in front of the car then, or next to the window."

we can walk.

"No, we can't."

Another flash in the rearview, closer. The paleness, the vile, curdled texture of it, moved toward them.

something's coming, Lucy said, her body translucent again, blinking in and out of his periphery.

"I know. We won't outrun it on foot."

Lucy wavered, considering. In the rearview, the Beast gained form, heat-white and enormous, emerging from mist, slavering milky drool. Lucy floated to the hood of the car, her almost invisible body serving as a guiding light.

okay, she said. *then we leave.*

He threw the car into drive. The car jerked away from the road shoulder just as the Beast crashed through the tree line. It walked on six legs now, its scorpion-tail appendage properly placed, its sapient torso wielding two sapient arms and two massive pincers. It lashed out at the trunk of the vehicle but fell short. It roared at its fleeing prey, the bellow quivering Paul's innards.

this way, Lucy said, as if indifferent to the monster.

Paul nodded, fear stealing his words, and accelerated. It was lucky Simon's car had been there waiting for them. Simon's car, with its air heavy, sweet and carcinogenic. Simon's car, abandoned on the side of the road. Just in the place he needed it to be.

Paul had never personally been set up before, but he imagined this was what it felt like.

Simon, always where he needed to be, when he needed to be there.

Even now.

Somehow.

CHAPTER
TWENTY-SEVEN

Rusted hinges wailed. The doors thundered open.

Three boys stood at the top of the stairs. Deirdre recognized the rearmost, the soft-spoken Isaiah, his rifle stock still scabbed in Paul's blood. The other two were strangers, one wielding a rifle, the other a pistol-gripped shotgun. None were older than twenty-five, in her estimation.

The kid with the shotgun took the lead. He pointed the barrel toward Mali. "You're up first."

Deirdre rose from her mattress, repressing a soft delight at the shifting of the boys and their guns. She walked to the foot of the bed, stood there, and watched them. She focused on a cantrip, watching if any of them noticed the smallness of the charm.

"Come on," the shotgun kid jabbed the barrel in Mali's direction again. "Let's go."

is something wrong, Luke? Tongue's voice echoed in her head. *is the Dawn-land woman giving you trouble?*

"No, sir," the shotgunner, Luke, addressed the air. "I got it all under control."

good, then let's waste no further time. the altar awaits.

Luke stepped forward, lifting the barrel to Mali's head. "Last chance, witch."

"Luke," Isaiah called, the rearmost of the group. "Lower the gun and grab her."

Luke took his eyes off of Mali to glance back at Isaiah.

That's when they made their move.

Magic sliced the air, a jolt of sharp energy crackling through mist. The Mali in front of Luke evaporated, and the real Mali, squeezed between the mattress and the floor, reached out, grabbed his ankle, and wrenched him off his feet. Luke yelped, hitting the ground, shotgun flung from his grasp. The two boys on the stairs lifted their rifles.

Four Marishas burst from the drug vapor and rushed the steps, one of them dissipating immediately as a rifle bullet shredded the illusion.

Deirdre funneled energy into her own cantrip, casting a spell to go unnoticed. Eyes slid away from her. So did aim. She darted sidelong around the bedframe, kicking Luke in the side of the head on her way to the stairs. Behind her, Mali clambered out from under the bed, crawling on top of her would-be assailant, lips already moving as she worked more magic.

Another volley of gunfire erupted, and a second Marisha disappeared.

Mali did something to Luke that drenched his face slick crimson.

"Hit the alarm!" the last boy yelled up to Isaiah.

Deirdre blew through the last illusory Marisha and crashed into the yelling boy's body. Rifle blast echoed in the tight stairwell. They crashed into the wall, wrestling. Deirdre grabbed the rifle barrel, pointing it up; with her other hand she grabbed the kid's throat, squeezing. A second blast rang in her ears, a slug piercing ceiling.

Isaiah fired. The pistol-grip went off, either in Marisha's hands or Mali's.

Deirdre drove her forehead into her opponent's nose. A bright pain flashed her vision, a grueling crunch kissed her ears. The boy screamed, losing his grip on his rifle. She drove a knee into his groin, felt the flesh there crush and flatten. From above, Isaiah fired again. Someone yelped in the room below.

Deirdre spun, letting the rifle tumble down the stairs as she grappled the boy as a human shield.

More gunfire, seemingly from every direction at once. A flare of pain lit against her ribcage. The boy gasped in her grip, begged some word she didn't hear.

A final volley of gunfire, more wounded cries, and the doors slammed shut. Outside, Isaiah hammered the floor with his feet, fleeing. Deirdre whirled around and sent her semi-conscious opponent tumbling down corrugated iron steps. He landed sprawled in the hard dirt at the bottom.

Marisha stood over him, two violent roses blooming over her tunic. She held the rifle in her hands.

"Please, please," the boy begged, words reddened by the flood of cruor from his nose.

"How many people begged you 'please?'" Marisha asked.

Then the rifle went off, and the kid stopped begging.

The deed done, Marisha dropped the rifle, staggered back, and leaned heavily against the concrete wall. Her hands pressed against the worst of her wounds, and she sagged, coming to rest crumpled on the dirt.

Deirdre rushed down the steps, met Marisha at the bottom. She pressed her hand over Marisha's, applying pressure against the mouth of the wound. "I can help."

She triggered her healing spell, pushed her will into Marisha's ragged wound. Like Razz all over again. The extent of it, the ragged punctures through her body, the havoc wrought. Tatters of organs hemorrhaged blood, her biography unraveling inside of her. But there was a chance. It wasn't as bad as Razz, and she felt rested and ready. The air itself stewed in supernatural stimulants, her body hummed with a level of power she'd never felt before.

Marisha grabbed her wrist, vicelike. "Don't."

"I can save you."

"No!" Marisha snapped, scolding. "You can't. You need your energy, both of you." She turned her head toward Mali, citing some agreement they'd made long ago. "You can't waste it saving some old woman. Not if you want to save the others."

The other women had fled to the far walls and corners of the room, crouched down, hunkered, whimpering. Deirdre only just then noticed them again.

"We can't leave you," Mali said, joining them.

Marisha's body coiled tight, her grip threatening bruises on Deirdre's wrist. "I am old. I was buried here years ago." She withdrew her hand and used it to cup Mali's face. "Whatever small future I still had before me, it is yours now. I give it to you. Travel, love, explore, do whatever you do, but don't wait in this crypt with me so you can be buried at my side. If you don't act now, they'll throw that door open again and shoot out your legs. They'll drag you to the altar and win. So go."

"But—"

"Shut up!" Marisha yelled. "You owe this to me. You owe me the hope that you will win. Tell me, Dawnlander…how much will it take to blow their little house down?"

Mali glanced up at the overhead door and pressed her teeth against her bottom lip.

Marisha grinned. "This, I allow."

The smell of copper and iron tickled Deirdre's nose, wafting up from Marisha's life all over her hands and from Mali's skin too. The perfume of her magic.

"In your name then." Mali reached down and put her hand over Deirdre's.

"I don't care whose name," Marisha muttered.

Hot blood boiled against Deirdre's palm, scalded through her skin and into her bones. The heat ran up her marrow and she realized that Marisha was much older than she looked, that she'd been there too long, the second of Tongue's acquisitions almost a decade earlier, after the ashes off his old church painted the forest black. Marisha had been a lone hitchhiker, an explorer caged away.

Now she was magic.

Mali closed her eyes.

The force of it erupted outward, echoed in Marisha's blood and Deirdre's veins, lighting up the vapor, pricking their skin...

Blood magic. Raw. Powerful. Violent.

Mali's eyes opened, whites and irises and pupils flashing ichor-red.

Rusted hinges screamed as the spell tore them apart. The door exploded into rust and shrapnel, blades of old steel knifing into the room beyond.

"Hurry," Marisha ordered. "I want to be alive when you end it. I want to *know*."

Deirdre cast the healing cantrip again, sweat beading down her back and burning her own minor wound. It wouldn't save the old woman, but maybe it would keep her alive long enough to see the White Room tumble down around her.

"Go!"

Deirdre picked the dropped rifle back up from the floor and handed it to Marisha. "If anyone makes it back here, shoot them."

Marisha chuckled, nodding. "I know."

Mali went for the pistol-gripped shotgun next to Luke's blood-drenched carcass. The boy's body twitched, reddish bubbles sniffling from his claret-streaked face. Mali picked up the weapon and considered the dead or dying creature at her feet.

"I'll handle him," Marisha said. "You save your ammo."

Mali considered, nodded.

From somewhere above them, a fire alarm rang out.

Isaiah's voice shouted something muffled and unintelligible.

"Here," Mali said, holding the shotgun toward Deirdre. "You'll need it likely more than I will."

Deirdre took the weapon, its weight tombstone-heavy in her palms. "Okay."

From the floor, Marisha coughed weakly and stared at the two women at the foot of the stairs. "Finish this."

Deirdre nodded, turned away, and flew up the steps two at a time, barrel first.

■■■

Paul whipped the g-man sedan hard down the curl of asphalt, trying to ignore the growing hum of magic in its frame.

Then the radio turned on by itself. It scrambled and fuzzed through the stations and track listings and settled on a song by The Doors. "My Eyes Have Seen You."

Paul bit his tongue, tried to keep his focus on Lucy through the windshield.

Paul, a silver tongue mused over Jim Morrison's. *Paul Somers, are you listening?*

He tilted the wheel along the curve of road, minutes from his destination. Wispy figures shambled in the fog, silhouettes he knew would be much more hideous if not for the car's strange wards.

I'm here to help, Paul. I'm here to make an offer.

Paul took one hand off the wheel and punched the radio's power button. It turned off.

Two seconds later, it turned on again.

My Eyes Have Seen You.

just give me a minute, doc. we'll be done by the time you park.

"Fuck off."

we haven't even been introduced.

"I said 'fuck off.'"

He lowered the driver's side window and stuck his head out into the whipping wind. The too-sweet voice and Jim Morrison's lyrics faded beneath the crescendo of the dead. Outside of the car's resonant wards, Lucy appeared bright and near-human. The ghosts moving through the fog grew shape and form, flesh and sinew. They reached toward him with crooked fingers, beggar palms, desperate claws.

help us, they rasped in his head. *help ussss…*

(*you, too, soon*)

"Lucy."

She turned her eyeless face toward him, worse given the coloration of the living.

"We need to go faster."

She nodded and turned back to the road ahead. Paul pressed down on the accelerator, bringing the car's engine to a grinding roar. Wind whipped his hair back and he closed his eyes. Old dirt sprayed up from the asphalt and peppered his face. He tried to turn his sixth-sense toward the rolling road, away from the chorus of the dead. The last exit was coming up on Highway 1, his last chance to turn off before he got to where he was going.

...you too, soon...

He ducked back inside the car, opening his eyes in time to see the bright green exit sign blur by. The next turn-off was his, a small suburb of Oceanrest whose name no longer mattered, its population long since reduced to single digits. Except for Randall's cult.

Jim Morrison sang from the speaker.

The other voice was louder. *you sure you can handle this on your own, buddy?*

Paul's knuckles paled on the steering wheel.

been trying to reach out to you for a while, you know, but you keep killing your sixth sense. I could teach you how to use it better, how to get a firmer handle on it. wouldn't you like that?

Paul glued his eyes to the fading, glassy form of Lucy through the windshield and kept one ear by the open window. The dead hissed after him, but their voices receded when he pulled up to the old church road and turned his headlights to the woods.

After the 1997 fire, nobody had rebuilt the little pocket of Oceanrest northwest of Highway 1. Like the rest of the dying city, it was abandoned to nature. Since then, even the exit ramp had been conquered. Tall weeds and mounds of dirt and grass cracked the asphalt. Paul followed it down toward the old church. Off the ramp was even worse, unmaintained roads gone to potholes and rubble. He slowed the car, careful and cautious over the jagged concrete.

The song changed, another by The Doors; lyrics originated by Howlin' Wolf. "Back Door Man."

I was a big fan of the Lizard King. I whispered to him in his dreams, showed him some of the possibilities he could've opened up in the world. too bad how it all turned out. he would've made a good agent, maybe even a prophet. but Mr. Mojo Risin' wasn't in the cards.

but you, Pauly, you're special, too. we saw you through that hole in the wall, saw you when you helped drag away the Static Killer.

"Look, whatever the hell kind of monster you are? Shut up."

if you insist. good luck with your suicide mission. I'll be around when you change your mind…

The voice retreated to silence; the music played on.

The church reared its hideous visage through the trees and fog long before the road's winding appendage curled to it. Waxing moonlight gleamed along its monstrous architecture, and fire glowed from behind half-broken windows. Paul's eyes widened at the sight of it, even in brief glimpses.

"Jesus Christ," he whispered, knowing the name held no power here.

The front half of Butler's mega-church had been rebuilt and refinished, aged and half-crumbled but proud. It wore the blackened marks of its fire-eaten past with the confidence of a scarred warrior and gaped shards of stained glass from its toothy mouths.

The rear of the church bristled, twenty-five trailers or more fused and lashed and welded and rebar'd into some non-Euclidian cathedral of the damned. They'd been bound together by infernal surgery, steel and magic and melting heat, a maddened Escher structure built at lunatic angles.

He made the final turn toward the parking lot and turned off the headlights, half to go unnoticed, half to go blind.

Lucy hovered by the open window.

this is where they do it, she whispered in his head. *this is where they want to welcome up the end.*

He took one hand from the steering wheel to touch the grip of Deirdre's revolver in his pocket.

The song switched over again, and Jim Morrison began singing about The End.

The end of everything that stood.

■■■

Deirdre and Mali came up from the White Room into the gutted body of a double-wide. Deirdre froze at the recognition of the thing for what it was. She could see where kitchen appliances had been pried from the walls, how the cultists had repurposed the thing into an anteroom. The whole trailer tilted on an incline, heading up.

They ascended into another gutted double-wide, this one leveled out. A table and four chairs sat in a corner, an aborted poker game laid out on top.

The doors were welded shut, and a ragged hole had been carved in the ceiling, letting out a spiral staircase of corrugated steel and catwalk materials. Overhead, she heard yelling voices, their words lost beneath the warble of the fire alarm.

Tongue's voice sandpapered the back of her skull. *my children, please, you know not what you do. this is a quest of vanity, of naive self-importance. your power is small compared to the powers of gods, you must know this, you must—*

"Get out of my head!" she screamed, pushing back against his intrusion, battering at his psychic assault until it quieted. She stood panting in the room, a sheen of sweat on her forehead reflecting her spent effort.

"We have to save our energy," Mali reminded her.

"I'm sick of hearing him."

"Me too."

Deirdre approached the scavenged spiral staircase slowly, angling the shotgun barrel upwards, trying to see into the room above. She thought she heard footsteps and voices below the klaxon screech, but wasn't sure. "This is a choke point. There'll be guards at the top."

Mali's gaze lowered to the graze at Deirdre's ribs. "I could try a spell."

"How much will it take out of me?"

"Very little. I'm going to do something small."

Deirdre reached down, touched the barely-there graze. "Will it get worse?"

"Yes. But not much."

"Okay…" she wavered, uncertain, but nodded. "Do it."

Mali's touch was gentle around the wound. Her palm pressed slowly into Deirdre's skin, molecules meeting molecules. Deirdre felt when Mali started to draw energy—a faint headrush, a vague reflexive panic, an urge to peel Mali's hand away and flee—but she remained still and steady, taking deep breaths against the impulses of her lizard brain.

The moment passed.

"Alright," Mali said. "Here we go."

The young woman mouthed a series of alien syllables Deirdre did not recognize, and her hands flicked swiftly through a series of sharp gestures. With the last syllable of the spell, Mali sent her gaze upward through the ceiling, and her eyes flashed bloodshot red.

Someone started screaming. A body hit the floor.

Another voice yelled something panicked.

Boots scrambled overhead.

Deirdre rushed the stairs.

CHAPTER
TWENTY-EIGHT

The parking lot sat in silhouette and moonlight.

Nature had ripped it apart from beneath, saplings and brush splintering concrete as they fought for light and air. Parked among the crags and conquering wilderness, three cars glittered moonbeams. Farther on, Randall's truck sat right before the church facade, geared up to drive hard into the mouth of God.

this is as far as I can go, Lucy said.

More wards. More magic. More bullshit.

"I'll do everything I can," Paul said. "I promise."

please…

He knew what she would say next, felt her halfway say it in his head. A request to which only one answer existed, to which any other answer would mean pulling up anchor and drifting down the seaboard to another dying town, pretending his history didn't exist.

"I'll finish it."

She faded into night, another spirit caught on the wind. Another voice in an endless choir.

Inching lightless toward the church, Paul spotted two men sitting on the cathedral steps. They wore shoulder-slung rifles and passed a joint back and forth. One wore an asphalt cloak, the other a leather jacket with swastika patches on the shoulders. Both of them grinned, shit-shooting, and laughed.

After a toke on the joint, the cloaked guard turned toward him, squinting into the darkness.

Paul flicked on the headlights.

Both of them leapt to their feet, shrugging their rifles off their shoulders and into their hands. Paul slammed down on the accelerator and the car jerked into motion, engine red-line roaring as it rumbled across the battered lot.

35 MPH.

Jim Morrison wailed through the car radio to the accompaniment of tires screaming against asphalt.

One of them strafed to flank him, rushing toward a car parked up ahead.

45 MPH.

The guard in the cloak used Randall's truck for cover, levering his rifle over the hood.

The leather jacketed one started firing as he strafed, still crossing the lot.

Bullets spiderwebbed the bullet-resistant glass by Paul's head. They sang from the reinforced frame.

Paul cranked the wheel sideways.

55 MPH.

Rubber wailed.

A bullet punched through crippled glass, part of the windshield caving in.

Jim Morrison shrieked.

Headlights glared on swastika patches, on *totenkopf* symbols.

60 MPH.

Paul ducked down, barely able to see through the fissured windscreen.

His target saw the oncoming maneuver and broke into a sprint for cover.

The jacket back gleamed "14/88" whitely in the headlights.

65 MPH.

Jim Morrison's voice melted into a long, warbling wail, all lyrics devolved into animal keening, human pain. The boy ahead of him chanced a glance back, late-teen features illumed death-scared.

The front fender caught him just below the waistline, and only about six feet from safety. The boy's pelvis shattered and his body twisted and spun through the air, rolling over the hood of the car and crashing into the ragged mess of parking lot behind. The boy ragdolled along the cement lot, bones breaking on impact, tumbling in jerky, fast-forward motion until he tangled himself up in his splintered limbs and went limp, a heap of dismantled human architecture.

Paul slammed on the brakes and spun the wheel.

The scream of tires finally overwhelmed Jim Morrison's voice.

50 MPH.

The car swung wide, curling 180 degrees, still going.

Burnt rubber stank the air.

35 MPH.

The car spun toward impact, another vehicle seconds away, a sapling off to the side.

A bullet blasted the back window, cracked it into cobwebs. The car frame shuddered over uneven crags, tires and axle fraying, coming apart. The seatbelt dug into Paul's skin, straining against his weight.

He yanked up on the emergency brake, spun the wheel hard left.

20 MPH.

The car listed, threatened to turn. The front tires dug in, rubber smearing asphalt. For a second, gravity gave up, only sheer speed and straining seatbelt pinning him down.

0 MPH.

The headlights lit up the splintered body of the first guard.

He released the emergency brake and switched back to the accelerator. Another bullet tore through the windshield, whistling by his ear. The car loped back across the lot, half beaten. The second cloak-garbed guard stuck close to the church, alternating his stance between the steps and the cover of Randall's truck. Paul frowned.

THUMP-UMP.

The leather jacketed body went under his tires and Paul slammed the brakes. A bullet cobwebbed the driver's side window inches from his face. He threw the vehicle into park and loosed his seatbelt, climbing to the passenger-side door to push it open. Blood pooled around the crooked body behind him. A rifle with a half-empty mag glowed in pale moonlight near the back fender. He dove to the ground, scraping his hands on uneven crags.

A high trill rang out from inside the church.

A fire alarm?

Paul scrambled across the war torn lot to the rear of the car and snatched the dead boy's rifle from the moonlight. Wet blood kissed his palm along its grip. He wiped the gore on his pantleg and pressed his back to the tire well at the rear of the vehicle. Another bullet yawped against the reinforced frame.

From the tree line, the chorus of dead rasped, *you too, soon.*

He gulped dread and tightened his grip around the gun.

The last of life drained out of the body crumpled beyond the rear of the car. Would the dying guard soon join the chorus of ghosts? How long did it take for the spirit to rouse itself from the cage of bones?

Another bullet bit the car frame. He brought himself up in a crouch and peered through the rear passenger-side window. The church glowered overhead, the visage of a hungry deity. The second guard stood on the steps behind Randall's truck, rifle-barrel pointed toward him.

Soon...

He spun around and brought the rifle over the trunk. Squinting through the iron sights, he aimed at the other man's chest, the curve of clavicle under the throat. A bullet whipped by him. He squeezed the trigger of the stolen rifle and felt its bark up through his shoulder. The guard dropped to the steps, hidden behind the bulk of Randall's truck.

Paul ran around the trunk toward the church.

Fog crawled toward the parking lot, wreathing the trees. A sea of whispers called from the woods.

you too, soon.

The guard was scrambling for footing, halfway back up, warped Kevlar showing through the tattered fabric of his cloak.

"Freeze!" Paul yelled, sights pinning the guard. "Stop moving."

The kid stopped moving.

Gunshots popped from inside the bloated architecture beyond them.

"Tongue'll get you," the guard muttered. "He's stronger than you think."

"Where's Deirdre?"

"Who?"

Paul hauled back and smashed the butt of the stock against the side of the guard's head. The kid's body crumpled limp and tumbled down the stairs. Paul watched for a few long seconds while the kid's chest rose and fell, waiting to see if he'd get back up. He didn't. With a nod, Paul tore the half-empty mag from the feed of the rifle and spilled the bullets down the church steps. He tossed the rifle aside and pulled Deirdre's revolver from his pocket.

He paused, hesitating.

The dead stood with the army of trees, lining the border of the lot. They stared at him between the boles, holding ranks in wait. But there was something else there too, something moving among the dead that he couldn't place. An anomaly. He stared into the fog, trying to keep his focus off the line of specters staring at him hollow-eyed. Something moved between tree trunks, something massive and powerful and not at all like a ghost.

Then the Beast appeared through the translucence of the warded dead. It leapt through their incorporeality in lupine form, its body a vile amalgamation of canine and insect. When it breached the tree line, it turned its faceless gaze toward him, its head marked only by the red-black pit in its center. Its too-long, over-toothed jaws parted in a vast, slavering maw, and it made a sound at once a wolf's howl and a human's shriek.

Paul gripped the revolver in white knuckles and ran for the double-doors of the church.

■■■

Deirdre squeezed the trigger and a bright flash of carmine spray followed. A throat, a lower jaw, the ridge of a clavicle disintegrated in buckshot. The boy who'd been at the top of the steps staggered, his tattered face warped and lost, stumbled backwards, and collapsed, the shotgun falling from his hands. The second boy rolled on the floor screaming, clawing ruddy tributaries from his skin.

Deirdre froze for a moment, sensing her victim's consciousness dissipate in vapor.

She'd only killed one other person in her life. It had felt different then. It had been a middle-aged predator, ice-eyed and heartless. This one barely looked old enough to drink.

Mali drove the heel of her foot into the screaming boy's face, silencing him, and retrieved the shotgun from the slick red pooling the floor.

Deirdre snapped back to the moment. Predators were predators regardless of age. "What kind of magic was that?"

Mali checked the boy's pulse. "I made him feel like there insects crawling around inside of him."

"Jesus."

Mali shrugged. "It's easier to play with perception than to make new reality."

But that hadn't been what Deirdre had reacted to.

"We have to keep moving."

"Which way?" Mali asked.

Three doors showed more gutted trailers and scavenged steel. In one trailer, a pair of fried eggs cooled on a hotplate. Other than that, only doors and stairs and more doors. "We'll start—"

A surge rattled the structure. The ozone scent of powerful magic reeked the air, the bristling electric sensation of a big spell crackled up her arms. This was no mere cantrip; the sheer power of the thing overwhelmed her, pressed as a weight across her shoulders. This was a ritual of years, a long plan fruiting.

"Tongue," Mali said.

"What the hell is he doing?"

Mali shook her head, unknowing.

The walls popped with heat, roared with static. Steel screamed, sundered, peeled away. Deirdre's sixth sense went wild, every impulse in her body recoiling from the *wrongness* around her. Reality unzipped before her eyes, floors and walls melting into some new Dali steelscape. Gravity twisted, shifted, plucked at her from different directions like groping hands. The beaded blood from their opponents rose from the floor and floated mid-air. Somehow, her feet stayed suck to the ground.

The trailer expanded, shrunk, and expanded again. The spiral staircase they'd come from grew, distorted, drilled down into the earth and up into the sky. Steps elongated, the spiral widening into a curve.

"What the fuck?" Deirdre yelled over noise and steelscreech and her own deafening confusion.

The spiral staircase ate the trailer, sucked up the walls and doors.

Mali clutched at her stomach, puked up dizzy bile, and leaned hard against the new curve of wall ascending the stairs.

Tongue's voice invaded her head. *you wage a war you cannot win. we have seen future days, we have seen providence, and—*

"I said fuck off out of my head!" Deirdre snarled, fighting nausea and psychic invasion both.

Tongue's voice dissipated, leaving behind only the faint hint of a yellow-toothed smile.

Deirdre panted, sweat trailing down her face, and joined Mali leaning against the curve of wall. "Only one way to go now," she said, peering up the ascent of stairs.

Mali spat, her mouth dry. "He was ready for this."

"Doesn't change anything."

"No."

Gravity threatened to shift, again, sucking at her innards, yanking her spine. Somehow, it didn't quite take. "We do this, or they win."

Mali moved shakily from the wall. "He's stronger than I thought…"

"Yes. And we have to fight him."

"Yes, we do."

They stared at each other for a long moment, aware of the gauntlet ahead, of their already-waning energy, of the vastness of the monument they were trying to topple, and they began their ascent.

CHAPTER
TWENTY-NINE

Paul flew down the aisle of what had once been a large church and was now a grotesque monstrosity. The pews still stood, fire-singed, age-worn, with hymnals and bibles strewn around like broken-backed birds. The dais held no altar, but instead a blood-and-fluid-stained mattress, iron manacles situated at each of its four corners. Beyond the fabric lectern, a wall that had once held an organ now gaped open around a long steel incline leading up into a gutted double-wide.

Paul chanced a glance over his shoulder and saw the Beast crash through the double-doors fronting the cathedral.

He sucked air into wracked lungs and hammered his feet up the steel incline into the bristling structure ahead.

Crashing through the threshold into the repurposed trailer, a wave of psychic nausea rippled through him. He fell sidelong into a wall, rebounded, and fought against a purple-black headrush.

who is this invader? a sandpapery voice asked. *my fellow believers, there is an intruder come upon us, an outsider come to aid our enemies! we are assailed from within and without and there is no room for mercy! cut out the witches' legs, hollow out this sinner-outsider, gut him wholly! tonight is a night of glory and we will not have it tainted by infidels!*

Paul fought against the psychic intrusion, fumbled half-blind for an exit, pulled himself through a tight door into another, narrower trailer. He stumbled, crashed into a table, and heard plates break on the floor. Doubled over, he heaved once, twice, three times, and finally managed to regain balance, to throw off his psychic attacker.

Behind him, the Beast roared.

Somewhere more distant, gunfire.

He struggled back to a jog, lost in a series of doorways and double-wides. The Beast snarled, no more than twenty feet away.

Despite a stitch slicing his side, he picked up the pace, clutching the unexpected spasm. He stepped through a doorway and headed for a scavenged stairwell. Behind him, the Beast broke the same table he'd run into, barely slowing down. Paul cranked the hammer back on Deirdre's revolver, struggling to straighten himself out, knowing he'd never outrun the monster.

A wave of energy thrummed through the steel around him, and a roar filled his head. Another wave of blinding dizziness washed his vision, and he rushed toward the remembered echo of gunfire, hoping only to make distance between himself and the Beast. Ozone filled his nose. Static buzzed the hairs on the back of his neck. His sixth-sense screamed, his lizard brain panicked, his body pumped adrenaline and flight impulse and the stitch in his side vanished from perception.

He puked when reality unraveled.

The room shrank. The Beast stood a foot away in one second, gone entirely the next. The room expanded. Steel shrieked itself to pieces, the walls unseamed. The floor gave out and Paul fell. Gravity vanished—he floated. Gravity changed direction, and he crashed into some ungrounded surface. The Beast shuddered through a wall, its body and the structure's architecture briefly occupying the same space, and then it disappeared again.

For a second, revealed in a spiral of sharded steel and twisted rebar, he saw a bathtub. Old-fashioned, claw-footed, filled with murky water.

Then the fickle source of gravity jumped and tethered him, wrenched him (down?) through a kaleidoscope of rust and steel and void, and crashed him hard into new ground. His breath burst from his lips, his body yelped in pain. He vomited again, ejecta swirling into weightless zero-g globules, floating before his eyes.

The ozone sizzled and faded. The spell completed, his senses began to reestablish themselves.

He stared at his own vomit, watching the multicolored globs orbit each other, dancing.

"What the hell?" he asked.

looks like the proverbial shit has hit the proverbial fan, the voice from Simon's car said, in his bones, in his head.

"What?"

the good Rev Tongue just punched a hole in reality itself. he's buying time, positioning himself for a tactical advantage. it doesn't bode well, Pauly.

Paul took his eyes off his own vomitus and rolled to his hands and knees, panting. "Where's Deirdre?"

the good news is, if the church is untethered from traditional physics, it's also untethered from about half of its wards. thus my long-distance call across enemy lines.

"Where's Deirdre?" Paul repeated.

would that I could tell you, doc, but I'm barely able to get a transmission through—forget reconnaissance work.

"Then fuck off." Paul pushed himself to his feet, shocked by the enormity of the landscape before him. The trailer seemed to stretch a hundred feet in every direction. Ovens and fridges piled up in obelisks. A massive hole gaped in the center of the floor, the entrance to a curving staircase, each step about a dozen feet wide.

you're probably going to want backup, the voice said casually.

He walked toward the waiting staircase, casting sidelong looks at the appliance-obelisks as he went.

do you know how to navigate a broken reality, by any chance?

He went for the stairs and gravity switched. His body whipped upside down, the stairwell suddenly overhead, his hand outstretched toward it.

things are different when physics breaks. the good news is, it's magic. the bad news is, it doesn't look like you know how to interact with it.

He jumped for the stairs and they drifted away. One of the obelisks creaked and Paul felt gravity rotating toward the sound, his body rotating with it. "No!" he yelled, kicking out as if swimming, not moving a single inch despite the effort.

Somewhere in the distance the Beast roared. Something clanged against steel. Gunshots echoed.

The sourceless voice smiled, smiled its teeth along the ridges of his spine.

want a tip, Pauly? we can call this one a freebie.

■■■

Deirdre and Mali slowed their pace. Running the marathon of stairs seemed unwise.

"He can't keep the spell going for long," Mali said between pants. "It's too big."

"That supposed to make me feel better?"

"Even as a ritual, this thing must burn a lot of fuel. It'll burn itself out soon."

"How soon?"

"Fifteen minutes?" Mali guessed. "Twenty?"

"Not soon enough then."

"Or…if we can find a focus, we could try to dismantle the spell."

"What's a focus?"

"Do you," *pant*, "not know," *pant*, "what a focus is?"

Deirdre snorted her answer.

"Shit," Mali said.

As if on cue, an inhuman keen echoed (down? up?) the stairs.

Deirdre shuddered in the blizzard of recognition.

(Razz's blood all over her)

(a thing the color of pure heat lashing out with claws and multi-jointed limbs)

(the light flickering behind his eyes as she begged begged begged)

She brought the shotgun to bear. "Back to back," she said. "When it gets here, aim for the black-red…thing."

"What?"

"There's a monster coming. Not metaphorical."

"What kind? My grandmother—"

"I don't know," Deirdre interrupted. "It's the kind you shoot in its weak spot, so shoot it."

Mali nodded, hoisted her shotgun, and pressed her back to Deirdre's.

For a long time, nothing happened.

Then came the footsteps, multi-appendaged, clattering clawed toward them, directionality obscured by echo and magic, except that they were clacking closer and closer and closer.

Then the breath, something like a horse's wheeze, hot and regular, steaming, humid, slavering—closer, closer, closer.

Closer.

Closer.

And then the Beast itself rounded its bubbling body into Deirdre's sights.

Its latest transformation had warped it into something sapient-arachnid, six-legged, two-armed, three-mouthed, its form an impossibility of appendage and dentition.

Deirdre fired, strafing sidelong to widen the space between herself and Mali.

Mali spun to face the thing, bringing her own shotgun to bear but not firing, screaming, "What *is* that!?"

"Just shoot it!"

Before their eyes, its arms melted and reformed, shifting from nine-fingered hands to elongate razorblades, double-edged, hacksaw serrated, each one five feet from tip to elbow. A tail came from its arachnid rear, dripping glue-like into the shape of a stabbing blade. The red-black pit gaped between the first and second mouths of its stretched sapient-serpentine torso.

Deirdre fired a second time, missed. Mali's first volley missed too, but smashed its topmost maw with buckshot, splintering rows of teeth into a jagged mess. The overcrowded dentition melted, bubbled, and began to reform. A sound between chitter and chuckle came from the monster's many mouths.

"Aim for the—the *thing!*" Deirdre yelled, taking a third shot and finally placing it where it needed to be.

The Beast snarled, off-orange ichor drooling from its pitted gouge. It swung its arms in wide arcs, surging toward them. Deirdre backpedaled from the slashing blades, panic stealing her breath as they came closer, closer, closer. Mali trailed behind, lining up a shot, and had to dive beneath one of the razor arms to avoid being cleaved open. The evaded blow clanged into the steel curve of wall, the sharp angle of the Beast's bladed bone sticking there.

Mali shot at the Beast's weak spot, and a burst of wretched gore vomited forth.

"Duck!" Deirdre called, noticing too late.

The second razor arm swung in, stuck deep into Mali's side, and lifted the young girl off the ground.

Mali screamed, dropped her shotgun.

Another chitter-chuckle came from the Beast's three mouths.

Deirdre cut it off with buckshot. Another regurgitation of wrong-shaded ichor spattered the floor, and rivulets of the same began to drool from the trio of maws. The Beast whipped Mali free of its arm and sent her tumbling up the stairs, until some strange force of broken physics grabbed her wounded, semi-conscious body and lifted her into mid-air.

Deirdre missed her next shot, diving forward before the razorblade appendage sliced the air above her. She rolled herself into a crouch and levered the gun toward her target again, only for the Beast to wrench free its occupied appendage and swing it her way at the last second. She tumbled sidelong, felt the sharpened edge of the limb pass centimeters from her body.

Her next maneuver wasn't so lucky. Retreating from swinging blades, she tripped over a step, lost her rhythm, and one of the blades grazed her, swiped fabric from her tunic, skin from her thigh. Only a flesh wound, but already bleeding bright crimson. She winced at the sharp pain, tumbled back. Rolled sidelong, dove forward, dodged another swiping blade, and ended up right back where she'd started. She lost focus in the rapid motion, gravity threatening to yank her sideways. She stumbled, avoiding another slash out of sheer luck and panicked clumsiness, and crashed into the wall.

By the time the fight made sense again, she stood in exactly the worst place: right between the Beast's blades.

The Beast chuckle-chittered, preparing its razored arms to scissor Deirdre in half.

Then it stumbled. Its eyeless face, all teeth, somehow warped into an expression of confusion.

All three of its mouths began vomiting blood. It teetered, all six legs drunk-dumb, and crashed sideways into the wall. Ribbons of viscous ichor unraveled from its lips, from the red-black pit of its weakness, and roped through the air, weightless in broken gravity.

"Finish…kill it…" Mali groaned, straining.

Deirdre brought up her shotgun, took a breath, and fired.

Buckshot rent the black-red pit, and the Beast's violent hemorrhage crescendoed into hurricane spew, ejecta bursting out in all directions, ropey strands and floating globs, spatter and spittle, bubbling foam, every orifice outpouring gore. It erupted vileness for several seconds, crashing through broken physics against floor and wall and ceiling, and finally it fell limp, curled against the wall.

Mali followed suit, her eyes fluttering and body going slack.

Deirdre threw her gun aside and rushed to Mali, who was again floating in mid-air. She grabbed Mali's leg and pulled her down, wrapped her up, leveraged her to the floor. "Wake up," she said, pressing her hand against Mali's fresh wound. "Come on, wake up…"

Sweat poured out of Deirdre as she cast the healing cantrip. Streams of it wept down her cheeks, beads rolled over her collarbone, a patina soaked her tunic. One cantrip. Two. She felt Mali's wounds—a punctured lung, severed cartilage between ribs, fissured bone—felt her magic strain against the injuries.

Her muscles groaned, her bones ached, her heart hammered in her chest, but Deirdre pushed.

She patched the lung. Sealed the fissured ribs. A dizzy spell passed through her, and she momentarily lost gravity, began to float—but the dizziness passed, and gravity returned. She gasped for breath, figured the sliced cartilage could wait until later, figured the parted skin and subdermis could wait too.

The worst of the damage dealt with, Deirdre sagged into a panting heap, caught her breath, and slapped Mali in the face.

Mali awoke with a scream, her eyes kinked in red capillary. "What...did it work?"

"Yeah. You'll have to tell me more about this shit when we have time."

"It's the strongest spell I know. Cantrip, at least. Well—"

"We'll chat later. Get your gun, we gotta move."

"Freeze!" a boy's voice called out.

Deirdre leapt for her weapon, but the boy's rifle barked and she froze out of instinct.

"I said freeze!"

Deirdre spun to face the boy. "You want me? You better kill me, kid, because I'll—"

"Shut up. Get on your knees."

Mali went for her shotgun, and the boy switched targets. "You too, Pocahontas. On the floor."

Deirdre glanced sidelong at Mali. Met her eyes. Nodded.

Mali dove for her gun.

Deirdre dove for the boy.

The boy tightened his finger on the trigger, turned the barrel toward Deirdre.

One step.

Two steps.

The trigger rolled back

The boy's knuckle flexed

and time

slowed

down

and

CHAPTER THIRTY

The boy's head exploded in bloodslick and skulltatter.

With all the sixth sense stimulants and psychic drugs in Paul's bloodstream he thought he heard the kid's last thoughts (*drag these fucking bitches to the altar* and then a millionth of a second later every neuron calling out *mommy* and then nothing at all for the rest of time) and the weight of that moment knocked the air from him.

The boy's body went limp, curled up, and floated to the ceiling.

"Paul," Deirdre half-whispered, visible through a floating mist of red blood and orange-ichored streamers.

"I'm here," he said, unsure. He took in the stairwell's carnage for a second, the Beast sagged and unmoving, the air filled with blood and shredded fabric, every surface gore-painted in black-orange and red. He stepped forward. The boy's misted life clung to his lips, a taste more familiar to maggots than men.

"I saw them shoot you," Deirdre said, hushed, her eyes shining with something besides mere recognition. "How did you…?"

"I don't know exactly," Paul admitted. "It's something we can deal with later."

"Yeah. Later."

Beyond Deirdre, a pale-but-not-white girl picked a shotgun up from the floor. "Paul?" she asked. "Deirdre, who is this man?"

"A friend," Deirdre answered. Then to Paul, "This is Mali. She's been here for a long time."

Paul averted his eyes from the younger woman. "I'm sorry."

"This isn't the time for 'sorry,'" Mali said.

"Okay, I'm late for the party," said Paul. "Do we have a plan?"

"We need to find a magical focus," Mali said.

"Or we have to buy time," Deirdre added. "Fifteen or twenty minutes."

"Right…and what is a magical focus, exactly?" Paul held Deirdre's revolver out to her as he asked.

"Thanks," Deirdre said, taking her gun back. "You bring spare ammo?"

Digging through his pockets, Paul replied, "I brought some speedloaders and a handful of loose bullets."

"It's hard to explain, but there must be several focuses in this place," Mali explained.

"Why would there be several?" asked Deirdre.

"Tongue, Randall, and Isaiah all practice magic. A focus helps, and it gets stronger with use. My grandmother used a special knife."

"But we don't know what these guys would use, and they'd probably keep it on them," Deirdre countered.

Mali winced, touching the mostly-healed flesh wound scoring her ribs. "Maybe so, but we need one."

"We don't even know how to get around this place."

"I have an idea," Paul said, not mentioning where the idea originated. "It took a while to figure out, after the spell went off, but there's some kind of psychic element to navigating this…wherever we are. Everything is kind of, um, *nebulous* at the moment. Gravity, directionality, the spell threw it all out of whack. That can work to our advantage."

"How?" Deirdre asked.

"Because it can be influenced by focus and willpower."

Deirdre's eyebrows arched. "And you know this…how, exactly?"

go on, Pauly, tell her about your new friend.

The sickly sweet voice from Simon's car smiled in his head.

Paul flinched. "Figured it out the hard way. I got here a while ago, actually," *liar,* "but couldn't figure out how to get around. Then it sort of just clicked."

Deirdre examined him suspiciously. "Uh-huh. So how's that help?"

"What if we concentrated on finding a focus?" Paul suggested. "If we can exert some of our will, influence the spell, maybe we'll sort of naturally navigate toward one."

"Doesn't sound like much of a plan," Deirdre said.

"We don't have a better one." Mali glanced at the blood on her palm, wiped it on her white tunic. "And there are still men with guns hunting us."

I could help with that too, Paul, the voice whispered. *not for free, though. you're plum out of freebies.*

"First thing's first—how are you guys holding up?"

"Just grazed," Deirdre said, gesturing to her thigh and Mali's ribcage. "And exhausted."

"Okay, so how about we—"

The Beast huffed. Its body shivered, skin shifting and curdling, bones crunching inside it.

The three of them all looked at each other. Then at the Beast. Then at each other again.

The Beast huffed, coughed, snarled, shuddered.

"We have to kill the person who summoned it," Paul remembered aloud.

"Shit," Deirdre uttered.

Its folded limbs twitched, its many legs shivered and scuttled. It coughed, hacked, wheezed.

Mali gripped Deirdre's tunic, already moving. "We have to run."

Paul plucked the dead boy's rifle from the floor before following, all three of them in complete agreement on running.

■■■

Deirdre led the way, flying up the stairs.

Behind them, the Beast snorted, snarled, and spat.

"It wasn't this long when I came down," Paul said between breaths.

"What?"

"It wasn't this long when—"

"How?" Deirdre's shout came ragged, desperate.

"I don't know, magic?"

Farther behind them, still too close for comfort, the Beast grumbled, growled.

hello, Deirdre, the Speaker purred in sucralose. *rethinking that offer about now?*

Gravity hiccupped and she stumbled, righting herself through force of will alone. Her thigh ached, stinging pain and burning muscle.

"Fuck off," she muttered.

"What?" Paul asked.

"Nothing, nothing. Keep moving."

Steps zipped past underfoot, but no landing appeared ahead.

Tongue's church is reality-poor, ward-poor, too. the offer's back on the table. given about twenty minutes, it'll be off again. this is a time-sensitive proposition.

The Beast roared somewhere below them.

"Focus on finding a landing," Paul panted. "Maybe we can influence the spell."

"I'm trying!"

am I interrupting your concentration?

Deirdre tried to push the Speaker out of her head, stumbled over the steps, and hesitated.

it'll take a little more work to kick me out than it did to kick Tongue out.

She slowed, breath eluding her.

look, I don't want to be too pushy, but your chances here aren't great without a little outside help. you've got a few spells left in you, sure, but you're running low on energy. Mali too. and besides the shapeshifting monster behind you, there's still the matter of all the guys with guns, not to mention a psychic sorcerer...

She gave the Speaker a second push.

alright, alright, no need to belabor the point. don't waste your energy bouncing me, Deirdre. save it for when you need it. I'll be here when you change your mind.

She gave a third push, got the voice out of her head, out of her bones, out of her awareness entirely. The endeavor staggered her, and ever-shifting gravity flung her sidelong to the wall. She banged her shoulder, rebounded, tripped. Paul helped her back to her feet, stabilizing her.

The Beast wheezed out an ugly chuckle, distant but closing.

"We need to focus," Paul said.

"I know." Deirdre righted herself, shook herself off. She tried to imagine a landing, any landing. Tried to keep the image in her mind. The Speaker had been right though—pushing the chemical-sweet voice out of her head took more effort than it was worth. She gulped for air, slowing her heart. Focused.

A landing. An end to the stairwell. Anything.

"Okay," Paul said. "Let's keep moving."

They ran, breathless. Paul clutched at his side. Deirdre grabbed his arm with one hand, half-dragging him with her.

The Beast snarled, closing in.

Closer. Closer. Closer.

"Fuck, fuck, fuck," Deirdre panted.

Focus, focus, focus.

And then a landing appeared, only a dozen steps ahead.

On the landing stood an asphalt-cloaked teenager with a rifle.

Mali tumbled as the bullet blew through her, crashing to the steps with a wounded cry. The boy lined up a second shot, barrel swiveling toward Deirdre.

Paul fired first, staggering the boy and stumbling him sidelong. Deirdre didn't pause to aim, just went from the hip and squeezed the trigger.

The Kevlar absorbed most of the force, but the vest was already half-useless from Paul's volley. The kid fell to the floor with a whine, letting go of his weapon in the tumble. Paul rushed forward and brought the stock of his gun down on the kid's face once, twice, three times—a spray of teeth floated the air, a burst of blood peppered his face. Unconscious, perhaps dead, the boy's body floated on broken gravity until it stuck to the wall.

Deirdre rushed to Mail, struggling to get the girl back to her feet.

The wound was center mass. Mali's mouth gaped anguish.

The Beast shambled toward them, so loud it couldn't have been farther than a dozen feet below.

Deirdre looped her offhand around Mali, grimaced against the weight pressing into her bruised arm, against her stinging thigh, and half-ran half-limped for the landing. Paul gestured them to hurry, eyes widening as he peered past them to where the staircase curled its descent. "Go, go!" he yelled, gesturing at a door Deirdre hadn't noticed until just then.

They burst through the threshold, lungs burning, panting for air.

A double-wide, furnished. A couch, a poker table, a few chairs, a desk—enough to set up a passable barricade.

Paul fired from the other side of the threshold, backed through the doorframe, and slammed the door. He put his back against it, bracing for impact. "It's right on top of us!"

Deirdre eased Mali to the floor and sprang into action.

Paul grabbed the nearest chair and buttressed the doorknob.

They went for the couch next. The desk. The poker table.

The door bucked in its frame as they set the table in place. The Beast roared on the other side.

Mali clutched her newest, bloodiest wound, face paling as her life oozed between her fingers.

The door bucked.

They piled as much into the barricade as they could, but they knew it wouldn't hold.

"Shit," Paul muttered as the door shuddered a third time, the structure of it already straining from the impacts. "We're just buying time."

Deirdre ran to Mali. She pried Mali's fingers from the newest wound and pressed her own palm against hot blood and reached into herself for another healing cantrip. Heart already pounding at near-maximal rates, muscles already straining with exhaustion—she dug in and pushed the spell through her aching body.

More damage, just as bad as the Beast's razorblade arm had done. The bullet hadn't hit anything immediately lethal, but stomach wounds killed. Deirdre didn't have the energy to spare, not considering the list of challenges the Speaker had laid out ahead of her, but she dug in anyway. Buying time. She pushed magic into the most pressing damage—the ragged hole in Mali's stomach, the broken capillaries, the shredded musculature...

No.

Too much. It was too much.

Patching the injuries properly would drain her, would leave her near-defenseless for whatever came next. Still, she bought time. That was good enough. It would have to be.

"You're not going to die," she whispered. "Not here. Not now."

"We need to keep moving," Paul said, backing away from the barricade as the door began to crack and bulge behind it.

Mali rolled sunken, red-tinged eyes to Deirdre. "The tub. I can use the tub." She bit down, gritting her teeth against the pain.

"We'll find it," Deirdre promised, hoping.

A large part of the door fell apart, one four-jointed appendage bursting through in the shape of a heavy club. Half a second later, a matching appendage battered another section away.

Paul rushed to Deirdre's side, the rifle strap looped over his shoulder. "I'll help you carry her."

"I'm...fine..." Mali said, the lie obvious in her grimace.

"Come on." Deirdre grabbed one of Mali's arms and Paul took the other. They hoisted her up and started moving.

The Beast battered down the door and started in on the barricade.

CHAPTER
THIRTY-ONE

Paul moved as quickly as he could considering Mali's lagging pace, the young woman's weight balanced between him and Deirdre.

not looking good, Paul. gotta say, not looking good.

He ignored the voice as best he could, focusing on keeping his feet on the floor and on putting as much distance as they could between them and the Beast.

"If I had a salve…" Deirdre shook her head. "Goddammit."

that's a stomach wound, Paul. your friend helped a little bit, but the girl's still dying. and I'm sure you know, for all the crime scene details you've read over in your life…well, it's not going to be a pretty death. the girl's going to die in abject agony, praying for numbness, conscious of nothing except pain.

Paul swallowed the urge to scream.

"The tub," Mali mumbled, her lips drunk with blood loss.

They kept moving, Paul falling into a slight limp with Mali's weight, the stitch in his side, his aching everything. They passed through a trailer that seemed to go on forever, only to end up at another catwalk staircase. They went down the stairs for what felt like minutes, only to end up at another surreal trailer-scape.

"What does the tub look like?" Paul asked. "So we can focus on it."

"We don't know," Deirdre said. "They kept us blindfolded."

They took a tight turn, a second one, hit a dead end, turned around to a completely different hallway, followed that, found another staircase, and started up.

"Where's the Beast?" Paul asked, conscious of time passing in silence.

"Behind us," Deirdre answered. "That's what matters."

well, the voice in his head began, *not soooo far behind you…*

Paul wanted to muffle the thing, to shut it up and push it back into quiet darkness, but he was afraid to take his mind off of gravity, off of surviving.

A plane of corrugated steel and ceramic tile opened before them. An obelisk of washing machines and dryers stood in the center of the room. The trailer looked to be fifty feet across and rolled out hundreds of feet ahead of them. Windows lined the walls, looking out on deep, endless dark.

"Fuck this," Paul muttered. "We need to figure out a better plan."

"Are you kidding me?" Deirdre snapped. "The thing could be right behind us."

"You need to rest, see if you can get enough energy to help her," Paul indicated Mali. "I need a better description of this tub to focus on. Come on, over here."

He and Deidre maneuvered toward the obelisk, seeking cover in its shadow. Mali rested her head back against the structure, breathing deeply, hands clutching her wound.

"She shouldn't be this bad," Deirdre muttered, examining the young woman.

"She's malnourished. She's been living in inhuman conditions for—"

"I'm sitting right here," Mali interrupted.

"Sorry."

come check out the view, Paul.

His eyes flicked instinctively to the broken windows, to the undulating darkness beyond them. He remembered.

(a spiral of painted branches, a hole in the wall)

(a void, an altar, a shifting nothing)

He shivered. "Okay. What do we know about the tub? Anything specific?"

you saw it, Pauly. the murky water, the clawed feet, the basin…

He tried to summon the image of it into his mind, the old-fashioned tub full of alchemy and magic and esoteric drugs.

I don't think you're going to pull this off by yourself.

Deirdre groaned with effort, all her muscles straining at once. The groan turned into a sharp, short scream, and she tumbled backward from Mali's body, landing hard on her tailbone. She panted, breathing ragged, her body sweat-slicked. "Okay," she gasped. "Mali, how do you feel?"

Mali grimaced, pushing herself up. "Better."

"Not better enough," Deirdre responded.

come on, help me help you.

"What about how it felt like in the water?" Paul asked.

"I remember." Deirdre wiped sweat from her forehead.

"Maybe that will help. Focus on what it felt like in the tub, both of you, and maybe…"

the problem you guys have, Paul, if you don't mind my pointing it out, is that all three of you are fumbling your way from one move to the next, while Tongue's been planning his plays for a long time. you see what I'm saying? you guys are playing checkers, he's playing chess.

you wanna know what kind of games I play?

"You're still bleeding," Paul noted, unbuttoning his shirt as he stepped toward Mali. "This might stanch the…you know."

look out the window. go on. call it a demonstration. I'm offering you a deal, you keep flipping me the bird without even listening to the terms, but you should know the kind of backup you'll have if you decide to sign. I'm not some two-bit poltergeist, I'm not some spirit wreaking havoc in a haunted home. I'm the big guns, baby. come and see.

"The internal bleeding is what's worse," Deirdre said. "I patched as much as I could."

Paul realized he was staring at the windows, at the darkness behind them.

you wanna know what you're buying into, right? keep looking.

And, for reasons he would never be able to explain, except that he'd always felt the intense impulse to know more, he kept looking.

Eidolons swam in the outer dark. Blacknesses squirmed and separated, becoming distinct entities. They had shape and were shapeless at once, form and formless. Even perceiving them shot fresh nausea through him, sent a new headrush purpling his vision. Something writhed in flat shadows, pressed its unfurling spine against the frail skin of the Earth.

Paul stepped toward the window.

The chittering swarm of somethings and nothings shivered and buzzed. Small things, vast things, human-sized, microscopic, gargantuan, the darkness teemed with unreal life. The Escher impossibility of entities simultaneously enormous and invisibly small, entities existing in multi-states and collective consciousnesses and sometimes without consciousness at all, entities whose own limbs operated independent of their minds.

Dozens of them. Too many.

look at the one right in front of you.

Until then, Paul hadn't noticed that one. But after the terrible, sickly-sweet voice brought the closest shape to his attention, he saw little else. It was teeth and talons and fire and mustard gas, it was ghosts scorched into Hiroshima streets, showerheads pouring poison into tiled rooms, and a grasp that twined itself around his own bones, a tongue that licked for marrow in his own spine, and a hunger he could feel in his own stomach.

that's the one, Pauly. they call that one 'The Devourer.' it helped make you. so did I. not on purpose, if it's any comfort.

An enormous monster of infinite claws and tendrils and sharpened fangs, boneless bones, spineless posture, a million tongues lapping up blood and more blood and never sated. Paul saw just one aspect of the Devourer, just one angle of its existence, and that glimpse sent rolling fury, revolted nausea, and absolute horror through his vertebrae, through his viscera, through his skull and his groin and his balls and through every joint of his body. Every part of him wanted to run away or kill himself, kill himself just so he wouldn't have to see it anymore, so he wouldn't have to see the parts of it that disgusted him. And especially so he wouldn't have to see the parts of it he liked, the idea of shattering teeth in his self-righteousness, of burning alive the people who'd called his daughter a murderer, of killing Randall's Neo-Nazi goons himself, of feeling their bones snap under a hammer, hearing their pleas as he pulled each individual tooth from their gums, of smelling the copper as he—

"Paul!" Deirdre's hand gripped his shoulder. "Are you listening?"

For a few seconds, Paul heard only war drums and war cries and the desperate screams of gutted children and raped women and men gagging on water through a facesucking towel. For a few seconds he heard only the low growl of infinitely grinding teeth and the wet smack of raw meat shoveled between bloody lips, he heard gunshots and bombs dropping and the cheers and roars of parade marches over the contorted carcasses of an enemy rendered inhuman by propaganda.

And then he heard the Beast's wall-shaking bellow, too close for comfort.

"Paul!" and he heard Deirdre's voice, the most real thing he'd ever heard before. "We need to move."

"Yeah," he said, dry mouthed and breathless. "Let's—let's go."

I'm of a similar species, if you will, the voice in his head spoke, silver tongued, *it's got a little more muscle than I've got, but I've got the brains, and the brains always win.*

The Beast roared again, closer still.

"I don't need help," Mali argued as Deirdre and Paul moved to support her.

"You don't need it," Deirdre said, looping her arm around the younger woman, "but it won't hurt."

so let me know what you think, Paul. I think we'd make a hell of a team.

Paul couldn't dig up the anger to argue, and settled for taking some of Mali's weight on his shoulder and running, though away from the Beast, or away from the things he'd seen through the window, he wasn't sure.

■■■

They kept running, Deirdre trying to focus on the sensation of the tub's alchemy-stewed water in her pores. Of the texture of the basin bottom against her head as hands pressed her down.

She tried to focus on these things even as the Beast bellowed its imminent violent approach.

In the aftermath of the Beast's belly-deep roar, a second vile noise rose—Tongue's voice.

repent and beg forgiveness and I shall bestow a gift upon you. we are set to welcome into the world a kingdom of god, pure and singular, and we shall set everything into its natural place, and you—

The Speaker's saccharine tones overrode Tongue's words: *blah, blah, blah. see how nice I am, Deirdre? I saved you the effort of shutting him up yourself.*

She didn't bother fighting off the Speaker's invasiveness, knowing how exhausting it was, how pointless.

"Stay focused," Paul panted to Mali. "Stay focused and the three of us can get there."

"I'm focused," Mali muttered, breathless herself.

I could get you there in three seconds, the Speaker told her. *if you sign on the dotted line, I could take Tongue's spell apart in such a way that you'd already be standing there. all you have to do is say 'yes.'*

Deirdre heaved for air, her body giving under Mali's weight, under her physical and magical exertion, under the burden of everything that had happened.

Mali lost her balance and all three of them staggered from the shift in weight.

Tongue isn't a two-bit sorcerer freshly graduated from minor chicanery. he's been working on his wards and his rituals and this particular spell for years, for a decade even. this is top-notch stuff, Deirdre, and it'll take more than a little elbow grease from an untrained medium, a witchy botanist, and a half-conscious Penobscot blood mage to monkeywrench things.

The Beast roared—twenty feet away, through a thick wall, running a long landscape parallel to their own. At least, that was what it sounded like.

"It's hard to focus on the memories with all the running," Deirdre said.

"Then we slow down," Paul replied.

"What about the monster?" Mali asked.

"It can't kill all of us. Tongue needs one of us for the ceremony."

two of you, actually, the Speaker said in her head.

She froze.

oh, I probably should've mentioned that earlier. that's why Tongue gave Randall the go-ahead to abduct you. in case Marisha or Mali pulled off the same stunt Lucy McKinney did.

What stunt? Deirdre thought to herself.

she used magic to kill herself before they could finish the ritual. did you not think it strange that Paul could see her ghost and not any of the others? you know, if he'd really committed himself to this, he would've talked to the ghost first. Lucy McKinney could've pointed you in this direction days ago. Razz would probably still be alive.

Although Deidre already knew this, a sudden shakiness quavered her body.

"What's up?" Paul asked.

She didn't hear him.

Lucy offed herself before Randall and Isaiah and Tongue could finish the ritual. she cost them a sacrifice—they need nine, they have seven. they need an extra body to make up for it, and they need it tonight. otherwise they'll have to wait a whole other year. longer.

Deirdre's head swam. Her knees shook.

She already knew, she told herself. And the Speaker was wrong. It wasn't Paul's fault.

Right?

the monster, this 'Beast' as you all think of it, isn't here to kill you. at least, not unless all other options are unviable. though, if Tongue's men managed to drag Marisha out of the basement before the crone kicked it, that would change things, but the odds on that look slim. in that case, the Beast would be looking to disable you, neutralize threats, et cetera. then the boys carry you off, rape and brutalize you, cut out your tongue, the whole song-and-dance.

Could they have saved Razz?

Deirdre wavered, fell to her knees.

"Are you okay?" Paul rushed over to her, knelt beside her, buttressed her.

Could they have saved Razz?

wrong question, Deirdre. well, maybe not 'wrong,' but certainly not timely. here's the timely one: how can you use this information to your advantage?

Could they…?

don't ignore me. I just gave you a freebie, a no-charge, no-strings-attached helping hand. a 'thank you' would be appropriate.

She'd already known, and yet…

"What's wrong?" this time it was Mali, her voice weak, weaker by the second.

if worse comes to worst, you could kill yourself and Mali, make Tongue wait another year, maybe as long as a decade. but let's look at other options: let me in, let me in, let me in.

"Hold on, hold on, hold on," Paul was whispering somewhere right next to her but also far away.

what do you say?

She blinked, her hand limp around the grip of her revolver. Razz was dead. Paul fucked up, but Paul didn't kill him. The Beast killed Razz. Isaiah killed Razz. Randall killed Razz. Up in the skull of this mutant church, plucking the marionette strings, Tongue killed Razz.

Or…

They'd all played a part.

"There!" Paul gestured to a yawning steel corridor. At the end of the tunnel, a tub waited beyond a threshold. "Come on!"

Deirdre blinked, felt herself pulled into two pieces. Half of her braced Mali's weight and followed Paul toward the tub, the other half screamed grief at the walls of her skull until the sound deafened her. Virgil had refused to open a formal investigation, refused to involve himself or his precinct in any of it. Paul had refused to talk to the victim, found anything else to do instead. What they'd done, failed to do, hadn't come about through malice, but it allowed malice its victory. Randall. Tongue. The Devourer. What divided indifference from malice?

They'd stolen Razz's future, all those possible futures. They'd made off in the night with every beautiful thing he could have done.

Deirdre? Speaker to Deirdre, Earth to Deirdre, come in…

She didn't want the Speaker's help. She didn't want anyone's help. When she did to Randall and Isaiah and Tongue what they'd done to Razz, she didn't want anyone else taking credit. She wanted to know it was her. She wanted them to know it. Not the Speaker. Not Paul. Not anyone else. Her.

A shriek trembled the length of the steel hall and the trio stopped to glance back.

The Beast lumbered into view, a grotesque, bubbling mass of white. Eyes and mouths surfaced and sank along its flesh, claws and tendrils lashed out and melted again. It heaved itself along on wolf legs, centipede legs, spider legs, each method of locomotion morphing to another.

I tried to warn you.

"Go!"

CHAPTER
THIRTY-TWO

They raced down the corridor as the Beast mounded its way after them. Mali slipped, lost pace. The three of them lurched and staggered. A new cramp scissored through Paul's body as he twisted to buttress the jerking weight. Gravity snatched him by the spine and wrenched him sidelong into the wall. He jammed there, stuck in broken physics.

"Run!" he shouted.

Deirdre hesitated for a second, long enough for the Beast to snarl and slaver and gain distance, and then she pulled Mali up and kept running.

Paul tried to think through the magic, tried to reorient himself in space. He needed his feet on the floor, not on the wall. He stared at the scavenged steel, the Dali trailer. Nausea ached through his guts and threatened his gorge. The Beast piled itself up and melted down, a rolling boulder banging down the corridor toward him.

Tongue's spell eased away, gravity shifting with Paul's concentration. His muscles burning, he stretched himself toward the floor. His heart pounded. Everything hurt. He groaned himself belly-first to the ground, gravity temporarily patched, and pushed himself to his feet. The Beast lumbered on, no more than a dozen feet behind. He sprinted after Deirdre—or tried to, slowed by exhaustion and the cramp flare.

The Beast gained, a tsunami of glueflesh and curdle.

Deirdre waited on the other end of the threshold, staring wide-eyed past him.

His feet hammered steel. Squelching squishing snapping noises followed, gaining.

He dove through the doorframe as a razored tentacle slashed at his back. He yelped and fell, landing face-first, pain singing the skin along his spine.

The door slammed—not a trailer door, but an old thick steel one with a vault crank. Deirdre shut and locked it as Paul fought for footing.

The Beast's massiveness thundered against the bulwark.

Paul stood panting, hands on his knees.

The Beast crashed into the door again and the steel whined in protest.

"We don't have much time," Deirdre said.

"No shit."

Mali had limped over to the tub and collapsed at its side, heaving for breath, bleeding. "I don't know if I…if I have the energy…"

"Dierdre, can you help her?" Paul asked.

Deirdre pursed her lips. "I don't know…"

"Shit."

"The spell…it'll run out of fuel soon…"

"How soon?"

"Five minutes?" Mali whispered, drylipped.

"We don't have five minutes." Deirdre stared at the door as the Beast howled from the other side.

Paul fell to the floor, drained. "So that's it."

Deirdre shook her head. "We can't give up."

Paul curled into himself, felt the speedloaders in one pocket, the lighter and joint in the other. He jerked up with a surge of adrenaline. "Sixth-sense uppers," he said. "You told me they made magic easier."

"I'm already running hot. The air…" she trailed off. The mystic fog had dissipated, diffused in the vastness of the trailerscape.

Paul pulled the half-smoked joint from his pocket, the plastic lighter with it. "Then we run hotter. You and Mali. We use this, you patch her, she takes down the spell."

"Then what? I'm scraping the bottom of the barrel already."

"We figure it out."

She stared at him for a long time. Smirked. Took the joint from his hand, and the lighter.

He smiled.

She lit up, took a long drag, and exhaled. "This won't be much of a push."

"Anything is better than nothing," Paul said.

She took a second drag, holding the fumes in her lungs as she crossed the room to Mali. "Here," she said in smoke, "take this."

you know what else is better than nothing? sweet saccharine asked him.

Deirdre and Mali burned away the rest of the joint, then Deirdre leaned in close to Mali and put her hands on the stomach wound. Mali's eyelids fluttered, her skin paled. The two women exchanged short, whispered dialogue. Mali nodded and closed her eyes. Deirdre muttered something underbreath and closed her eyes too.

The Beast hammered against the door again and the steel bulged from the blow.

Deirdre's body arched, her spine curling into a question mark, her shoulders bunched up. A groan rattled up her throat, shook and shuddered her, and seized her musculature. Burnt ozone wafted the air; pure energy. Mali's body spasmed and her eyes opened, breath flooding into her. Deirdre cried out and fell backwards, sweat-soaked and panting. She choked on air, spat a few times, and laughed. "How you feeling?"

Mali echoed the relief. "I think—I think I can do this. I need you in the tub. Both of you."

The Beast banged a nasty dent into the door and roared.

"I need blood," Mali said. "In the water. Your blood, both of you. And I need you to focus on something real. Memories. Things that really happened, things with a place and a time in your head. The stronger the memory, the better."

Neither Paul nor Deirdre questioned her instructions, conserving the energy of any potential curiosity for the trials to come. Paul kicked off his boots and peeled the bandages away from his head, removed the speedloaders and bullets from his pocket and set them on the floor. Bracing himself, he dug his fingers into his scalp and clawed the scab back open. Grimacing at the pain, he widened it, scratching and tugging the cut until blood dribbled and leaked from the wound. Only afterwards did he wonder if the slash along his back had been bleeding. More blood couldn't hurt, in any case.

He and Deirdre lowered themselves together into the water, their clothes sucking to them in the wet.

"Heads under," Mali said, kneeling, hands on the rim of the tub.

Paul took a big lungful of air and lowered himself deeper. Opposite him, Deirdre mirrored his actions, their legs tangling together in the center of the basin. Mali said something above the water, but Paul couldn't make it out.

Then Mali switched languages, grasped the lip of the tub, and began the spell.

Paul squeezed his eyes shut, trying to find the right memories to drag them back to reality. Trying to find something strong enough to tether him to the real world, obeying the laws of physics and chemistry and with gravity that didn't require attention to function.

Cassandra.

No. No, not Cassandra. Anything else.

But what else could work?

The darkness of his eyelids intensified, Mali's voice faded, and all fell to silence and calm.

This was the quiet of a church before a funeral.

No.

This was the quiet of void between binary stars.

And something was about to happen there.

■■■

Paul's heart jammed against his sternum.

Black space. No gravity.

Cassandra.

Things moved around him, outside of his reality, too big to understand, too small to see.

Voices whispered. They always whispered, coming in through every crack.

Speaker. Devourer. She Who Crawls—

Cassandra.

The Queen of—

Cassandra, he focused. Cassandra, the lost sum of his biography.

The movie screen lit up with memory, but the memory wasn't his (how?— or maybe why?)

Blackness resolved into nighttime highway. He sat behind the wheel, white lines whipping by like one endless stripe of cocaine. The world blurred around him, eidolons pulsing at the corners of his vision. Ghost cars rode alongside, New York license plates translucent in the sea of night. Jaundiced cabs wove between lanes.

Speed limit: 45 MPH.

Speedometer: 57 MPH.

A whirring sound thrummed from the world around him *wwwhrrrwhr-rrwhhrrrwhrr* and The Doors mumbled gibberish from the sound system. The road focused and unfocused, the windshield a camera lens unable to track distance. Sickness plumbed his stomach. A voice in the passenger seat shouted *look out!* and the windshield caught focus on a figure in the road, in his lane.

A man? Something else. Who? What?

He jerked the wheel hard to the left and created a question that nobody would ever answer, a question that drove him mad (*did she do it on purpose?*), and the hood of the car tore through rusted steel guardrail. The high-pitched monster-scream of metal on metal filled his head. His foot still rested on the accelerator.

An oncoming truck tried to swerve out of the way.

Impact.

Through the windshield, through the hood of the truck, both vehicles bucking and his body free. Her body. The side of his face smeared the truck grille. Who stood in the middle of the lane? His ghost tumbled across the asphalt and stared up at the night sky, at the vast blackness interrupted by faint and desperate light.

He fell through abyssal darkness.

In an unlit bedroom, he stuffed Deirdre's clothes into a backpack. A voice bellowed through the paper-thin walls. Another voice replied, pleading, trying to heal a fractured soul. No solace. No peace. He zipped the backpack closed and went to the window overlooking the awning of the shop below. Things would be better alone. The war could eat itself if she left—he, if *he* left (but he was her, then)—and the two voices could find their ways to opposite ends of the world. No reason to stay together without her binding them. Let it all unravel. Things were better when people were alone. Fewer strings, less screaming. There was comfort in isolation.

She wanted that.

Onto the awning, after the backpack. Tears vanished in the rain, down-pour from the cosmos.

A woman he didn't recognize spoke to him in a conference room. A man whose suit seemed like it might burst around him shadowed her, watching his motions (Deirdre's motions?) with dead eyes. The woman flirted with her smile and twisted power between her fingertips.

The room melted.

Everything blurred. Eyes unfocused. Everyone loses someone and everyone is lost.

His houseboat sailed on a sea of tears. Someone bought his ex-wife's wedding ring from a pawn shop and now a woman wore it somewhere on Long Island. Was there whiskey enough in the world to drown his mistakes?

Floating again.

Blood poured from the side of his head. The dizzy carousel of history blurred against the black screen of the universe. Oceanrest sagged on his shoulders. He vomited his daughter's overdose all over his shirt. Deirdre rode a train through his intestines, years earlier. Terrible entities that weren't gods but could be mistaken for them vibrated in his bones and reached many-dimensional appendages through holes in reality and prodded protozoa along experimental evolutionary pathways to see if they could create the perfect tool and look at that thing *what is that thing* that is an ape with anxiety and—

The dead whispered in his ears, tugged at his shirtsleeves, clamored for attention because he could hear them, see them, feel them, and so few people could and still they needed to be heard, to be seen, to be felt, and—

He stood in his houseboat and looked down at himself begging, please, help me, please, "Help me," his voice said, "you're the only one who sees and I don't know what else to do." He watched himself flee the scene, abandoning the victim in pursuit of selfish solace—

"Help me," Paul said.

"Help me," everyone said, losing and lost and—

Mali's magic seared through his body. His memories, his daughter's memories, Deirdre's memories, they collided car-crash in his head, scrap steel and screams and too many people remembering too many things and feeling so much how could anyone possibly feel so much? Deirdre rollercoastered to Oceanrest a dozen years earlier, her old name (not her real name, but her old name, the one her parents gave her) her old name was Imani Greene but she'd killed it on the train ride, deleted it a hundred times with a fat-tipped marker. Then her train derailed and blew through a rusted guardrail into oncoming traffic and his houseboat blew its truck horn and crashed into it and they sank to the bottom of the Sargasso Sea, his last drink a triple-vodka mixed with everyone's tears. How could anyone feel this? What could someone say to the dead? Why did people remember? What could be done when the past was immutable? Could they have saved Razz? Could he have saved anyone? Wasn't it terrible how things could just end? What if he'd just talked to his daughter? What if they'd, what if he'd, what if, how did, what could, what did, why, why not, why, why, why—

Paul blasted out of the water in an explosion, his body wracked with too many memories and soaked to the bone in tears and

drop curtain

full dark

his consciousness collapsed.

CHAPTER THIRTY-THREE

Mali's spell went off hard and fast. Deirdre burst from the water, over the side of the tub and onto the floor, gasping.

Paul exploded from the tub a second later, scrambling wet on all fours across the floor of the double-wide. He panted, gagged, and spat up bile and water.

Deirdre leapt to her feet and moved to help him up and—

He hit the floor limp and unconscious, his sole syllable of speech caught between pant and gag and going unheard.

Deirdre spun to Mali, whose own body leaned hard against the side of the tub, and asked, "What happened?"

Mali sagged, going limp, burnt out on magic. "The spell's unraveling. We did it."

she's right, the Speaker silver-tongued. *not much time left to negotiate.*

Mali sucked air, tried to push herself up, failed. "Just need to finish it, like we promised."

Deirdre rushed to Mali's side. "No, no, no. Stay with me, okay? Stay up. We can do this."

"They can't take us both."

what do you say, Dee-dee?

"That's not my fucking name," she snarled.

Imani. Deirdre. Dee, Dee-dee, whatever—why are you so picky?

"Green magic," Mali mused, droopy-lidded.

(Razz's eyes sagging shut)

(the softness of his face without him in it anymore)

"Stay with me!" Deirdre yelled.

Mali went limp, breathing shallowly.

as I was saying, with Pauly's lights out and Mali on the same road, maybe now we talk turkey.

The walls rumbled, contracted. The room was shrinking, reality returning. She realized she'd stopped paying attention to gravity and directionality altogether, that Mali's unconscious body didn't float or tumble. Physics functioned again. Tongue's spell frayed around her.

we've got one minute, Deirdre, the Speaker stressed, *then Tongue's wards go up and I go bye-bye.*

The Beast roared from behind the battered door. The hinges bent, near breaking.

It would be through soon.

And elsewhere, guns. How many guns? How far away? Where would Randall set up his defensive? His offensive? How many cultists were still standing? Panic-adrenaline seized her veins. Mali was unconscious. Paul was unconscious. She had two speedloaders Paul had left at the side of the tub. Nothing else.

"Goddammit," she spat, letting go of Mali's shoulders to grab her revolver from the floor.

so, chips down, end of the day, what do you say?

"Goddammit!" she yelled, whirling in circles, scanning the room as it transformed from surreal landscape to real double-wide.

the clock is a'tickin'.

■■■

Paul watched them from outside himself. Watched Mali sag, Deirdre yell.

Everything happened in slow motion.

down for the count, Pauly.

"What the hell is this?"

you're not using your brain right now, being unconscious, so I figured this would be a good opportunity to set up a tête-à-tête.

He saw the trailer rebuild itself molecule by molecule, everything so slow. He crossed the room to his body, kicked at it. His foot sailed right through.

not fun being a ghost, huh?

"What is this? Some kind of game for you?"

on the contrary, buddy, this is deadly serious. I'm just trying to help you see how serious it is. in Escher-land, you were in the middle of nowhere, but when the magic wears off, you're going to be in a physical location, and you have no idea where that might be. for all you know, Randall's already in the next room over, waiting for an opportunity to put Dee-dee down.

"That's not her name."

I'm only pointing out certain potentialities. you saw the size of the place from the parking lot. pretty big, but only one way in or out. so let's deal, right?

"That place I saw? Wherever it is? You can stay there. I'm not helping you get out."

you're thinking too big. I don't want your help busting out.

"What do you want, then?"

I want your help keeping the Devourer in. the Devourer causes enough havoc on your plane of existence just by virtue of its role in your evolution, not to mention the damage it does by just whispering—imagine if the thing actually made ground! nobody wants that.

here's the brass tacks, Pauly: I need Tongue to fail. so do you. and you want to get out alive, preferably with Deirdre and Mali alive to boot. I can make that happen. you probably can't.

"We don't need your help."

you do, though. because Deirdre would sooner eat her gun than be taken alive, and Mali's in no state to put up a fight. the fact of the matter is, at this point, Tongue's not going to have the necessary number of sacrifices. I'm getting what I want, regardless. what you want, however…

Rage burned him up. "You're ransoming them?"

harsh words, Pauly. that's your perspective on things. mine is different. I want them to live too, but my metaphorical skin isn't in the metaphorical game in that way. I'm looking for a deal-sweetener.

"Yeah? What kind?"

you let me in, Pauly. not full-time. you're no Tongue and I'm no Devourer. but I'm interested in getting your digits, to use the human colloquialism. and you never know, I might never even call you, that's a difficult thing to say even from my perspective—but I'm very interested in having your number, having access to that thing in your skull, and I'm willing to help you out in return.

"What do you mean?"

you let me whisper something to you every once in a while. let me give you a few words of advice here and there, maybe play around with your dreams. worst comes to worst, maybe I borrow you for a couple of days.

"Borrow me?"

you ever seen The Exorcist, *Pauly?*

Paul's eyes burned in his sockets. He looked from his unconscious body to Deirdre and back again.

I appreciate your confidence in her, but what do you think the Vegas odds would look like?

...

tick-tock, Deirdre.

That voice, deep down in her bones…

She almost missed Tongue.

She stared at Paul, hand so tight around the grip of her revolver she could feel her tendons going stiff. "Come on, come on…"

fire sale! all merchandise must go! one day only. a metaphorical day, that is. in the more literal sense, it's 45 seconds.

Deirdre laid Mali down by the tub, close to cover. It was the best she could do.

Another cantrip?

No, she might need the energy. Besides, with so little fuel left in her, she wasn't sure a cantrip would even get Mali back up.

thirty seconds! act now and I'll throw in a lifetime supply of cyanide!

She considered the cylinder of the revolver. Considered Mali. Considered herself.

She pointed the gun at Mali.

Pursed her lips.

Lowered it.

fifteen, fourteen…

She slammed her fist against the floor.

...

"What are you, anyway?" Paul paced angry circles, pulling his hair, boiling.

you already saw.

"No. That's impossible."

nothing's impossible, Pauly. what's that quote? 'even the word says I'm possible?'

"You talk like a used car dealer."

I'm translating my thoughts into something approaching modern sapient speech. compared to most of the primordial fogeys on this side of your reality, I'm on the cutting edge. if it would make you feel better, I could stick to King

James-approved Olde English, but what would be the point of that? if it would make you comfy, I could even stoop to showing you vague visions of an unguar-anteed future. but as long as your so-called 'sixth sense' is this wide open, and as long as you're waltzing through a hole some big-headed megalomaniac punched in the fabric of your so-perceived 'reality itself,' why wouldn't I take full advantage of the moment to chat with you directly? we're just two beings who both like Jim Morrison, hashing out a business deal.

"You said you helped create us, so you're, what, a god?"

no. we had a little bit to do with the evolution of mankind, but we didn't design you, didn't 'create' you, per se. we're more like scientists, fiddling with struc-ture, experimenting, dabbling. I mean, come on, Pauly. a god?

In ultra-slow-motion, in the material world, Deirdre stared at Mali, raised her gun, lowered it again.

"Go to hell."

I get it, you're angry. you just found out that mankind is tiny and the universe is indifferent, blah, blah, blah.

"You think I don't know that? Me, of all people?"

compared to who? come on, you don't have it all that bad. well, except for the 'imminent death' aspect.

"My daughter—"

let me break this down for you, doc. indifference is something you should pray for. you know why humans exist? because we accidentally triggered a series of evolutionary pathways by losing control of our own experiments. mankind is an accident. you are not what we envisioned. but somehow you apes ended up running the planet, so we work with it. we reach out. we whisper. we tell people secrets in their dreams. sometimes, we attract a follower, or a prophet, or a cult, but just as often you people lose your minds, go way off the rails from what we were looking for. you're shoddy tools, the lot of you. but you're what we got.

and we noticed you, Paul. back when you were reading encrypted psalms from a mad acolyte of the Hollow One. you noticed us, we noticed you back.

"The Static Killer," Paul muttered, the heat of anger cooling off. "What... what was in that room?"

suffering. a malignant universe. what was in that room, doc? the results of having something notice you. just ask Deirdre. Randall noticed the absolute hell out of her.

but it's too late for you now, just like it was too late for Deirdre as soon as Randall closed the door of his truck. sooner or later, one of us is going to figure out a way to get to you. me? I want dibs. I want a deal. the others aren't as nice as all that. you think the Devourer cares about deals? the Devourer doesn't know what a deal is. the Devourer's a big, strong idiot with very simple desires. you saw it, didn't you? what it wants, what it likes, what turns it on?

(sloppy splurt of scissored meat, sound of a blade pushed into viscera again and again)

(cry of starved bodies in a ship's hold)

(bomb drop, gunshot, the cheer of the victor over the contorted dead)

Deirdre fumbled with the speedloaders, but her tunic had no pockets. In slow motion, she cussed, crouched next to Mali's comatose body, and put her back against the bathtub. She closed her eyes. It looked like she might've been praying.

"Get me up!" Paul yelled, waving at her as if she could see him. "Use me as a human shield! Something!"

afraid of losing her? you've got a bad history of losing women you love. or leaving them. some of that is on you, though, you know?

The thing in his head smirked smugly at that one.

Paul gritted his teeth, clenched his fists.

Deirdre opened her eyes and stared through him.

The floor retreated toward the tub, the room folding in on itself. The Beast roared, the slow-mo effect dopplering its bellow through Paul's bones. One of the three sets of hinges gave out, tumbling away. The door bent, threatening to break open entirely. Across the room from Deirdre, a stairwell unfurled from the wall, a landing made of catwalk leading to an open doorway.

let me unload a theory on you. so, Tongue isn't an amateur. Nor are Randall and Isaiah. they've had years to plan out their little chess game. they have a tub, a focus they use for rituals, for testing witches, for brainwashing people…and they know it's full of magic herbs and magic resonance and power. and they have these spells, wards and protections and veils against outside notice, along with one big spell that blows a hole in reality for about half an hour.

and a spellcasting focus, unattended.

a focus that a witch might be able to use to break down the wards and protections and the big spell that blows a hole in reality. and they know where the focus is. they know where the chokepoints are. and they know that there's only one way out. see what I'm getting at?

There would be men at the stairway landing, or in the room beyond it. They'd have guns.

Opposite them, the Beast would come in from the flank.

Game over.

good. you're paying attention. so let me answer my earlier question. the Vegas odds would not look good. so what do you say?

CHAPTER THIRTY-FOUR

Deirdre watched a doorway form in the wall, a landing extend from the doorway, a short staircase unfurl from the landing.

Cloaked, armed shadows waited in the room beyond.

She ducked below the lip of the bathtub, considered Mali's soft breath. Couldn't do it.

seven seconds. six.

She just couldn't shoot the girl. Couldn't even do herself.

She wanted to die fighting.

four...

"I don't make deals with—"

I told you I'm not—

The Speaker's voice vanished, its toxic-sweet dulcet subsumed by the Devourer's endless growl.

(*killfuckeatshitrape*)

Grease and gunpowder scented the air. Drug vapor pumped up from floor grates. Voices murmured at a distance, footsteps hesitated at a threshold. She crouched in cover, hinged low, and sent up another prayer to Luna and Gaea and anyone else listening. Earth, Moon, Sky, Stars. Something, anything.

Her finger tightened along the trigger. A bead of cold sweat tracked over a hot patina of the same.

The Beast slammed into the door again and part of it collapsed. Its mutant curdling bristled beyond, an eye on a stalk rising asp-like to stare at her.

(*slicegnawfuck*)

Tongue's voice sandpapered her skull. *come, now, child. let us end this folly.*

(*killtakerape*)

"Come on, Deirdre!" Randall yelled from the room beyond the stairs. "We all know how this is gonna end."

"Then come fucking get it!" she screamed back. "Unless you're chickenshit."

Randall's laugh boomed from the stairwell. "Not chickenshit, Deirdre, just smart."

"What—" The rest of her taunt vanished when the door bucked open, snapped off its hinges.

The Beast slithered through the door on millipede legs, a serpentine body straightening sapient at the front. Four spiderlegs propped its humanoid torso up from its abdomen, attaching just below the gouge of red-black at its heart. Four shoulders hung from twin clavicles partway up its body, each limb warped into specific function. One shoulder gave way to a twine of four tentacles, another to a multi-jointed razorblade arm in the mimicked shape of a straight razor. The third arm ended in nine clawed fingers, the fourth in a bulbous, spiked club appendage.

It wore a head again, eyeless as always and possessed of a ragged crimson smile overburdened with teeth.

It snarled and began the trek across the floor toward her.

"Alright, boys!" Randall called from the landing. "Let's take her!"

Deirdre put her back up against the wall of the tub, lowered herself next to Mali's body, and pointed her gun barrel at the Beast's ichor-drooling gouge.

■■■

Paul's eyes flicked open. Facedown on the floor, clothes soaked and suctioned to his skin, the lights in his head turned back on. He blinked, and saw a discarded rifle (his?) a couple of feet away. Deirdre yelled something he couldn't quite focus on. He inched his arm toward the gun slowly...slowly...

Behind him, maybe ten feet away, maybe less, the door blew open.

Paul got his hand on the rifle stock.

Randall said something from a distance. Deirdre replied. Paul still couldn't quite make out the words and focused on playing dead long enough to execute his next move. He played his fingers slow, slow, slow against the gun stock, inching the weapon closer to his body.

The Beast growled, skittering a multitude of limbs against the floor.

That wouldn't be his target.

"Alright, boys!" Randall's voice echoed through the room. "Let's take her in!"

The Beast's too-many legs clicked steel. Through that noise, Paul heard the more important sound—boots against scavenged catwalk. Randall and his gunmen were stepping onto the landing on the opposite side of the room.

Paul sucked in a breath, snatched the rifle from the floor. He stood.

Pivoted, spun.

Drew sights.

Fired.

He put a bullet into the first cloaked figure he saw—a short, stocky boy, vaguely familiar. The boy bucked from the impact, yelped, and swiveled his own gun around toward Paul. Paul didn't bother trying to time the boy's counterfire, he just squeezed the trigger again.

The second bullet staggered the boy, who stumbled back into the other bodies emerging from the threshold.

Randall reached out, steadied Paul's victim, and shoved him toward the railing. "Walk it off, Zeke! Open fire!"

Deirdre's gun barked from somewhere near the bathtub and the Beast made a strangled sound and disgorged ejecta. Peter and Iron Cross raced down the steps, shotguns at the ready. Isaiah and Randall hung back on the landing.

Paul strafed sidelong, moved to intercept Peter and Iron Cross as they went for the tub.

Stopped mid-stride as Zeke finally got a shot off and buried a bullet four inches ahead of him.

Spun around as one of Randall's life-ending slugs caught him in his left leg and took him to the floor.

"Get the bitch!" Randall yelled. "This kike's good as dead already."

Paul groaned against the fire licking up his ruined thigh, braced the stock against his shoulder, and fired again. This third shot sprayed bright life from Zeke's throat and tumbled the boy off the landing to the floor below. Dead or soon to be dead, either way. Paul swiveled the rifle sights toward Randall, ignoring the anguish searing through his legs and the thunder booming all around him.

He fired and missed.

Somehow, Randall predicted his shot. The older man jerked out of the way and shielded himself with Isaiah's body. Isaiah caught the bullet in the left shoulder and yelped. The betrayal went unacknowledged, and Isaiah fired at

Paul without hesitation. A lance of heat lightning spasmed through his gut, spurting blood against the back of his throat.

His body pumped out a sea of numbing agent to make death more bearable.

Iron Cross changed direction, shrugging off Randall's orders to lower his shotgun barrel in Paul's direction.

Paul dove to the side as the gun went off, landed with a scream, and rolled to a kneeling position. He swerved his sights toward Iron Cross and squeezed the trigger.

Iron Cross yawped, kicked-dog, and stumbled sidelong, falling into a genuflect a few feet on.

Another blaze of hot death gouged Paul's innards.

More gunfire everywhere.

Paul's vision swirled purple-black, clouds of nothing creeping in. He struggled to get his sights up again, to get another shot, but couldn't quite see anything. The world vortexed around him, blurry and twisted, all fuzz and static and conquering darkness.

paging Dr. Somers, the Speaker said, sugar-giddy. *the desk has a special message for Dr. Somers.*

Paul coughed blood, slumped over.

More volume—gunshot, roar, deafening violence—and something else.

the cavalry has arrived. see if you can hold on for just one more minute. we can't raise the dead, but we can save the dying.

Numb fingers gripped the gun and he collapsed facedown.

Dark clouds ate the firmament. The sky bled black. Hot pain and cold death masticated his innards. His marrow stewed. His history ached for completion, begged for an ending. How terrible, the way things could just end.

Something vast and dark approached.

Squelching sounds, yelling voices. An epithet. Gunfire.

Feet pounding on steel.

And the dark thing, a sixth-sense presence, a late-stage cancer infecting the body of Tongue's church.

A miasma.

It said one thing in a language Paul had never learned but somehow knew.

It said "Stop."

∎∎∎

Deirdre squeezed the trigger and hit her mark. The Beast squirmed anguish and disgorged ichor.

It kept coming.

Behind her, boots pounded on the staircase.

A gunshot barked from an unexpected direction. Deirdre snapped toward it, saw Paul back on his feet, rifle raised, firing. It wasn't much, not with Paul standing in the open, but it was something.

She spun her attention back to the Beast and fired again, ignoring the gunfight in Paul's part of the room. The Beast bucked back, puked viscous ebon-orange, kept coming. She rolled to the side and dove from cover. A series of tentacles smashed into the tub, found her body gone, and began to wrap up Mali instead.

Deirdre lined up a shot and fired.

The Beast coughed more of its blood, pulled Mali into itself, and positioned the young girl over its red-black heart.

It snickered a cicada chorus.

More gunshot filled the air, and Deirdre spun around to take in the scene. Paul's shirt stained red with blood, his pants the same. She turned in time to see Paul dive to the side, evade buckshot, and put his own bullet into a neck-tattooed cultist's leg. Iron Cross screamed, staggered sideways, fell.

Another guy, cloak-clad and tattooed, charged her with a shotgun. "Hands up, bitch!"

She tilted her barrel toward the gunner and squeezed the trigger. The kid spasmed from the force of the shot and stumbled. He caught himself, blasted Kevlar visible through the ragged hole in his cloak, and swiveled his own gun toward her. "Fuckin' cunt!"

She dove to the side but still caught a few pellets in her right calf. A yelp burst from her lips. She landed, tumbled, groaned as she righted herself.

"Get the nigger bitch, Peter! Blow her fucking knees out!" Randall yelled from the landing.

Another blast from Paul's side of the room.

Deirdre spun, sighted the shotgunner, and fired again. This shot missed altogether. Peter swung his shotgun around for another shot and Deirdre darted to the side just as the gun went off and—

—blew a chunk of white meat from the Beast's club appendage.

The Beast, two feet from her, swung the remains of its bludgeoning arm into her ribs. The blow lifted her bodily from the ground, sent her sailing through the air, and brought her to the earth with a crack. She cried pain, white-knuckling her gun and rolling back to her feet, bruised bones aching.

Another shotgun blast, this one poorly aimed and peppering the ground beside her.

Paul's gun went silent, his body sprawled bloody on the floor.

"Give it up, Deirdre!" Randall yelled.

She spun toward him, lifted her gun, paused—

Isaiah.

(a picture message from Razz)

(the face at the head of the circle)

(the fire dancing over familiar features)

Adjusted her aim slightly.

"Shoot the nigger, Pete! Just shoot the nigger!"

She squeezed and fired, and saw flame kiss the air and a bullet whip through space. Isaiah's familiar features and his victorious smirk melted into vortex, into a meatgrinder, into a garbage disposal face suctioning his expression into steel teeth, his last thoughts tattered in shrapnel, his neurons silenced by lead and heat and speed. Isaiah's existence unspooled into red, white, gray, without detail or reference, as his body went limp from the neck down, his spine no longer receiving incoming messages. The teenager's corpse fell to its knees, then tumbled off the landing entirely and thunked against the floor, dead weight.

Behind her, Mali's body hit the floor.

The Beast retched and screamed, a strangled animal keen breaking the air.

Two birds, one stone.

Then Deirdre collapsed too, as one of Randall's bullets blew through her guts and laid her out. Heat tunneled out her lowest rib and tore through her organs and she went down, her revolver skittering across the floor like a scared roach.

"If you want something done right..." Randall muttered. "Fucking cowards. Aw shit, Peter, you *had* an opening."

"I wasn't sure I'd hit the legs," Peter said.

"We only need her alive long enough to do the ritual. Now Isaiah's dead."

"I—"

"Shut your fucking mouth. Say one more word and I'll plug you myself. Matthew, status?"

"Fuckin' kike faggot got my leg."

"Wrap it up and walk it off. We'll deal with it later."

"But—"

"Dress the wound and we'll deal with it later. Get the cunts cleaned up and complacent. Prep 'em. I'll get the Reverend." A pause. "Don't fuck this up."

Deirdre rolled over, every limb aching. Her gun sat five feet away. She reached a straining, screaming arm toward it and pulled herself along. Blood soaked her tunic, her skin, everything. A deep, gnawing hole in her body drooled away her life. Spat it. Puked.

Paul wheezed nearby. Coughed.

"Hurry up now," Randall said. "The nigger's still got fight in her."

"What about—"

"Fuck him."

Footsteps approached.

Deirdre reached, muscles wailing, bones aching, fingers straining for the pistol grip…

A boot came down on her hand.

She screamed.

Another boot came in at her ribs and flipped her over.

Iron Cross (Matthew) and the shotgun-wielder (Peter) stared down at her. Matthew's body angled to one side, his face a grimace of hidden distress. Peter's pain lived quietly beneath a sneer of revulsion.

"Alright," Matthew said. "I don't know if I can get hard for a jungle whore, but I'll sure as hell try."

Then a sound like dying stars ate the world.

The syllable came from a human throat but no human could have made it.

Her vision pulsed, gave way to darkness, and reasserted itself in flashes of neon. A cure for AIDs and a medicine only the rich could afford. Mechanized everything and endless unemployment lines. A future so bright it baked itself black. True power and true evil desperate to keep that power for itself.

The promise of a better world and the perversion of that promise.

Her body seized.

The sky went away. The room vanished.

It came back sharp and hard, consciousness as a gut punch. She sucked air, scrambled for purchase.

hey, Dee-dee, the Speaker purred. *looks like I'm here just in the nick of time.*

CHAPTER THIRTY-FIVE

Deirdre realized she'd been clutching her ears and when she pulled her hands away from them, her palms were bloody.

see if you can cling to life for about sixty more seconds, the Speaker said cheerily. *otherwise I won't be holding up my end of a very important bargain.*

She groaned through bullet wounds, slash wounds, countless bruises, left shoulder dislocation, magical and physical exhaustion, groaned through battered existence itself, and slowly inched toward her gun. Peter and Matt crouched nearby, hands clamped to their ears, blood leaking between fingers.

A gunshot echoed from the stairwell and Peter's head erupted.

Footsteps followed.

Deirdre reached her revolver, wrapped bone-tired fingers around its grip, and pushed herself onto her back.

The man descending the steps wore an ill-fitted suit over bulky Kevlar. He had sand-blond hair and sparkling-sea eyes, the jawline and cheekbones of an All-American superhero. He held a matte black pistol and a terrible smirk gleamed his face.

She lifted her gun toward him. "Who are you?"

"The cavalry," the man said. "The 'deus ex machina.' Mali knows me. So does Paul."

"Samuel?"

"Bingo. Or Simon. I had to change my name back in 2011."

Still quaking, Matthew lifted his wide, bloodshot eyes and stammered, "S-S-Sam?"

Simon/Samuel turned to the tattooed man. "Oh. Matt. I almost didn't notice you."

Simon/Samuel lifted his pistol, twitched his smirk into a smile, and squeezed the trigger. Flashbulb light disintegrated Matthew's head into modern art grotesquery. Matthew's last thoughts evaporated in crimson haze, Deirdre's dreamer-and-upper soaked brain catching their barest whispers before silence.

Matthew's body joined Peter's, limp on the floor.

Simon huffed, amused. "I used to babysit him."

Deirdre grimaced as she leveraged into a crouch. She tried to get to her feet but her joints warned against it. "What are you doing here?"

"I'm saving Mali. And I'm going to give you a little patch up and an offer."

"What kind of offer?" She meant it to sound harder, but coughed, a spurt of blood painting her lips.

"I'm going to deal with the worst of your wounds and get you back on your feet again. Then I'm going to stay here and tend to Mali and, if you agree to these terms, to Paul as well. Meanwhile, you're going to go on ahead and kill Randall." Simon described all this as if summarizing a TV episode. "Sound agreeable?"

Deirdre hesitated.

"It's the best deal you're likely to get," Simon added, the Speaker's voice saying the exact same thing in her mind.

considering the parties offering it, the Speaker emphasized.

"You're with—with that *thing*?"

"Yes. Obviously."

Deirdre looked him over, from blood-speckled shoes to neatly-combed hair. "You'll save Paul?"

"All you have to do is kill Randall. Tongue too, if you feel like it."

you'll have to make up your mind soon, the Speaker mused. *Paul Somers isn't long for this world.*

Battling pain, Deirdre rose to her feet. She wavered there, unbalanced, clutching her gun in taut-tendon hands. The words "fuck you" fought to the back of her teeth but she swallowed them like sour spit-up. "You save Paul, you save Mali…I'll kill Randall. You fuck it up, I'll kill you."

Simon grinned. "Sounds like a deal." He knelt down and put a hand over Paul's most ragged wound, muttering beneath his breath. A purple-black glow flashed between his fingers, and the blood staining Paul's shirt receded, vaporizing. "That'll keep him alive for a few more minutes. Now let me take a look at that." He nodded to where Randall's bullet had gored her.

"Go ahead," she managed, loosening the death grip on her gun.

He approached, holstering his own weapon and holding out empty hands. "It might feel different than you're used to."

"As long as it keeps me moving."

"It will."

Simon's magic, the Speaker's magic, felt cold and clinical. If Mali's magic carried copper and ozone, if it felt hot and electric, this felt frigid and slow. As Simon's healing spell worked at reassembling her organs, she felt at once its power and its origin's indifference. Her own healing magic was given as a gift. It was warm when she used it on herself, and she hoped it felt warmer when used on others. This was given as a deal, as cold as a smirking handshake.

She hated it. She hated more that it worked better than her own.

A wave of relaxation rolled over her as the wound stitched itself closed.

Simon stepped back. Sweat beaded along his product-slicked hair and rolled down his forehead. He wiped it away backhanded. "There you go. I gave you a little spare energy for when you run into Randall. He's only got the one trick, brute force stuff, but it won't hurt to have something in your tank."

"Yeah. He struck me as a brute force kind of guy."

"You'd know better than I would."

Deirdre didn't respond, she just brushed past Simon and started on Randall's trail. She grabbed a speedloader, started up the stairs, and paused at the landing. "You better damned well hold up your end of the deal, Samuel," she called over her shoulder, "or Simon or whoever the hell you are. Because if I come back and Paul's…if Paul's gone, or Mali, I will make it my life's mission to end you."

Simon smiled, apparently pleased. "I know you will."

■■■

With the church back to normal size, the density of drug vapor returned fog-like.

Deirdre sucked in lungfuls of dreamer smoke and sixth sense uppers. After the half-hour of feeling semi-normal, the slow crescendo of her sixth sense began to build again. It started in a faint realization of drumming, the perception of the Devourer's growl in the walls around her, of its war drums hammering through the church's foundation. It grew into further sensations, scents of brutality and savagery, the stink of scared and angry men.

A choice presented itself within thirty seconds of leaving Simon.

To her left, a declined trailer led into a church. To her right, an incline led to Randall.

you can leave, Tongue said, once again invading her thoughts. *just turn left, walk away. nobody will follow you. there's nobody left. you've made your point, you've won. why take further risk? just leave.*

She turned right. In part because she wanted Simon to save Paul; in part because she wanted to stop Tongue. But mostly because these people had taken away Razz's futures and she wanted the favor returned.

She climbed the steel incline to a makeshift staircase, and followed that.

Even after Simon's patch, her body ached. Soreness scored her muscles. Attenuation brittled her bones. Her left arm pulsed pain and the slice in her thigh stung constantly. She was far from dying, but still teetering on the edge of exhaustion.

She persisted.

The staircase flattened into yet another barren double-wide, this one with three doors.

Her eyes flitted from option to option, her brain desperately trying to assemble a map of Tongue's church.

The uppers and dreamer in her blood tickled her nose and jerked her head to the rightmost door. Randall's scent? Gunpowder, sweat, and blood. A jerkoff palm he'd pressed into her face to drown her. Yes, that was him, lurking, waiting, cowering. She crossed the room as quietly as she could, and gripped the doorknob.

Silence, save for her breath.

She dug into whatever reservoir of energy she had left, whatever her body and soul and mind could stitch together and whatever little bit Simon had given her as extra, and began to focus on a spell. Invisibility. Closing her eyes, she took a deep breath, filled her lungs, and focused on that desire to go unseen.

Magic shot through her, the effort of it plucking her tendons, twisting her musculature, burning her lungs. Her heart slammed against her sternum, but after everything else she'd endured, this was just another drop in a bucket. She choked a groan of exertion into a bare whimper, took a couple deep breaths, and opened her eyes.

She wouldn't be able to keep the cantrip active for long, not in her current state.

She moved to the side of the door, cranked the handle, and swung it wide, spinning into the threshold gun-first.

She felt Randall dismantle her magic with a single syllable and a gesture. Brute force, indeed.

The spell whiplashed out of her control and sizzled into nothing.

Her aura of invisibility disintegrated and she was left standing in the threshold of a long hallway, in a shooter's stance, undefended. Randall stood at an angle to the door eight feet away, his legs shielded by a kitchen bar counter.

Deirdre spun toward him—too slow.

A bullet finished the work on her left shoulder, pulping it to red spray and tattered flesh.

A second bullet missed.

She fired her own gun, finally.

Her shot grazed Randall's gun arm, barely a flesh wound, and pitted the wall behind him. The recoil jammed up the bones of her left arm and ignited matchsticks in her ruined shoulder. She yelped, recoil-pain and wound-pain hitting her brain at the same time, and leapt back as Randall's third shot blasted the floor.

She got a second shot, this one giving Randall a mirror-image wound to her own, his offhand shoulder erupting in blood and tendon and muscle tissue. But the sharp anguish of recoil rammed her bones again and she screamed and dropped her gun.

Randall took a fourth shot just as Deirdre leapt back through the threshold.

It would have gone right through her chest if she hadn't moved. It would have blown right through her sternum and sundered her heart.

Back in the three-door intersection, she pressed her spine against the wall and whined against the burning wreckage of her left shoulder.

"Come on! Just you and me now, right?"

"It's over, Randall! It's fucking over!"

On the other side of the threshold, behind the cover of a kitchen bar countertop, Randall gave a gallows-chuckle. "Come on, Deirdre. You ain't that stupid. It's never over, don't you get it? It's never gonna be over. The Devourer, these things? They exist, and they ain't going away. Only way this ends is if one of them makes it end."

Deirdre reached for her shoulder, touched the meaty rubble of it, and hissed anguish.

Her muscle fibers tugged at her like old vines pulling houses apart.

(come back to the earth and sleep)

"'course, it's over for both of us." Another coffin laugh wheezed from Randall's lungs. "You and me, Deirdre? It's over for us. I'll kill you, or you'll kill me, or Tongue'll…" he paused, snorted, spat. "My people or your people or the Québécois…one way or another. I gotta admit, it ain't the way I thought things would pan out."

Deirdre angled herself to peek through the threshold, searching the floor of the other room for her gun.

"See how I'm not reloading? You're givin' me plenty of time. But I'm a principled man, and I know it wouldn't be fair to give myself another seven shots when you've only got…how many you got left?"

"Enough."

This time the chuckle came as soft as air stirring up dust in a mausoleum. "That Lucy bitch really monkeywrenched us."

Deirdre glimpsed her weapon a few feet from the doorjamb. "Who?"

"Don't matter, she's dead. That old crone's probably croaked too, and our wards are down. See, if I kill you, we lose our sacrifice, but if I don't kill you, well, I guess you'll kill me. So I'm in kind of a rock-and-a-hard-place situation. But fuck it, I'm gonna kill you. No offense."

Could she get to her gun without taking fire?

She tried to do the math—the height of the kitchen counter that Randall had as cover, the angle of his line of sight, the position of the gun by the threshold…

"Hey, that kid? Raspberry or whatever?"

"Razz," she said. "His name is Razz."

"Well, it *was*," Randall replied.

The past-tense hurt worse than the gunshot.

"Razz," she repeated quietly.

"What kinda fuckin' name is Razz, anyway?"

Anger snaked through her viscera. She narrowed her eyes, dug inside herself to use the rage, the energy it gave her, shaping it into a healing cantrip.

Focus.

Left shoulder.

She released the magic in a surge of energy and it crumpled and died against another of Randall's counters.

Randall snort-laughed from the other room. "You're not much of a sorceress, huh?"

"What, you are?"

"You gotta learn how to cast quiet-like. I could feel that spell building up all the way in here."

She crouched low, moved to the threshold, glanced at her revolver. "You're no Merlin yourself," she called back, hoping to use the source of his response as a variable in her metric.

"Guess not," he said, off to the right of the doorjamb, still behind the waist-high counter. "All I know is counter-magic, but hey, it keeps you witch bitches in line."

"Except that Lucy beat you at it."

"She didn't beat me, she just did something I wasn't expecting."

"Oh, so she outsmarted you?"

"Not too smart to get dead."

She darted into the room and vipered her hand for the revolver. She snaked it from the ground, stood up, and pointed the barrel at Randall's wide-eyed surprise. Squeezed the trigger.

Recoil jittered her bones. The bullet took most of an ear off but missed the center mass of his head.

His gun came up inches from her chest.

CHAPTER
THIRTY-SIX

Paul's vision returned in fluttering blurriness. A ceiling, dim bulbs struggling for life, and an obscure visage above him.

"Wha...?"

"Give it a few seconds," the visage said. "I'm still saving your life."

Cold magic pulsed through him, sweetened his blood, knit his organs back together and dissolved the shrapnel inside him, turned a gaping wound into a small scar. A dark shadow smiled, charming yet chilling, at the back of his skull.

hey, Pauly. how's it feel to be alive? it was a close one.

The world clarified. The gutted, stacked double-wides came into focus, the decades-old lightbulbs flickering above. Simon's face asserted itself in his vision, a cerulean gaze kinked with exertion-inflamed capillaries. Sweat soaked Simon's blond hair and slicked his face, ran in sheets down his neck to his collar.

"The fuck are you doing here?" Paul asked.

"Saving your life. For the second, wait, the *third* time, I should mention."

"You've been planning this all along."

"It was one of several plans, yes. This was Plan B. You're welcome, by the way."

Paul scrambled away from Simon, pushing himself back to his feet. His whole body ached, but he didn't immediately collapse. "How did you know? How long have you been putting this together?"

"Oh, I've known for almost a decade," Simon said, cucumber-cool. He crossed the room to Mali's prone body and, next to her, a white-slicked carcass rotting in a pool of curdled milk.

"The hell is that?"

"That's Isaiah's little pet."

"It's a—"

"A dog, yes. Pets make good sacrifices for that sort of magic."

Paul blinked, unable to connect pet dogs and the grotesque Beast in his head. He went back to the earlier topic. "You've known about this for a decade? And you did nothing to stop it?"

Simon murmured a series of primordial syllables and pressed his hand to Mali's stomach wound. Purple-black glow flickered between his fingers. "I did plenty to stop it. I submit as evidence: it's stopped."

"Eight women died."

"Yes."

"What were you doing while eight women died?"

"Graduating. Quantico. Maneuvering myself into this assignment. I needed to be here myself. I needed to be sure." Simon removed his hands from Mali, wiped more sweat from his face, and turned his cold blue gaze on Paul. "You're not that different and you know it."

"You fucking monster."

"I opened multiple avenues of attack. A frontal assault, yes, because Randall and Butler need to die. But also an avenue for gathering evidence, creating narrative, building a case. To make sure that the surviving cultists end up either in prison or otherwise institutionalized, to make sure that this *ends*, and it doesn't come back in twenty years when one of these twenty-somethings turns into a forty-something who knows how to recruit more twenty-somethings."

"Like Randall," Paul said.

"Like Randall," Simon confirmed. "He recruited me. It was a second cycle. We can't allow for a third."

An unwilling chuckle escaped Paul's lips. "The hubris of that…"

"Of what?"

"To think that this is the end of it."

"It's the end of this cycle, in this city, in this region. That's enough."

Mali's eyes fluttered opened. "Samuel?"

Simon smiled down at Mali. "It's Simon now, but yeah. It's me. I came back like I promised."

"We thought—"

"I know."

Paul scanned the room, bent low, and picked his rifle up off the ground. He pointed the barrel at the back of Simon's head. "Where's Deirdre?"

Mali sat up, her own head whipping around to take in their surroundings. "Where *is* Deirdre?" she echoed.

Simon stood and turned toward Paul. "She went on ahead to finish things."

"You let her go alone?" Paul asked.

"She insisted. She wanted me to stay back here and make sure you and Mali were safe and secure."

"These men…" Paul shook his head. "Fine. Well, we're safe and secure now. So let's go."

Simon tutted, shook his head. "That wasn't the details of the deal, Paul."

Mali grabbed Simon's arm, hard, and squeezed. "We're going," she said, her teeth bared at his ear. "She saved me before you did. She helped me. Now I am going to help her. If you leave me to do it alone, then maybe you came back here for nothing."

Anger wrinkled Simon's face and his jaw tensed. Then his expression smoothed out and a new smile appeared. "Alright then. Deal done."

Paul jerked the rifle barrel toward the stairwell. "Lead the—"

"Lead the way, I know."

■■■

Deirdre dove to the floor as Randall fired

The bullet barely grazed her upper back, but it hurt like hell.

Face down, she scrambled for the threshold when Randall leaned over the countertop barrel first.

A bullet blew a hole through the floor an inch from her foot.

She made it through the doorway and darted sidelong, put her back to the wall, and panted through pain and panic and heart pounding exertion.

"My fucking ear!" Randall yelled. "Jesus Christ, I'm fucking deaf! You cunt, you fucking cunt!"

Deirdre chuckled shallowly. "I thought white men knew how to keep their cool."

Randall spat, slammed something hard into the kitchen counter, and spat again. "Fucking niggers. All gotta have names like 'Razz' or 'Li'l Biggie' or some stupid shit. That kid was gonna end up dead anyway. Some gangbanger or Québécois chopper or even a fuckin' cop. Someone would'a got him."

Wrath singed her bones.

"Oh, not feeling so funny now, huh?" Randall taunted.

Her face hurt from not roaring her rage at him, but she kept control.

"Yeah," Randall said. "That's what I thought."

A beat.

"Was it Frank?" she asked.

"Of course it was Frank," Randall answered. "We said 'jump' and Frank jumped first then asked 'how high?' You were an idiot to trust a junkie like him."

Dierdre nodded.

Tense silence followed. For a long time.

Then Randall said, "You know, I always thought you were better than the other ones. You were smart, you did good business, you kept to yourself…"

Deirdre bit back her reply.

"Look, I don't like your kind. Witches or bitches or coons, none of 'em. But you're alright. You did the best you could, considering the way you were born."

"This going anywhere?" she asked.

He wheezed his funeral laugh again. "Yeah. You know what they call you behind your back?"

"The Sheriff."

"Yeah. The Sheriff of Squatter City."

"That's not my name."

"No, but I bet Deirdre ain't your name, either."

"It is."

He cackled into breathlessness, a series of hacking coughs. "Bullshit. Your name something like Quallanda or Oogieclickin'boogie or some shit. What your parents called you?"

"Doesn't matter."

"Sure it doesn't, Sheriff. You believe that. People believe all kinds of crazy shit. People think the sky is *up*. The sky is *out* though, isn't it? We just feel more comfortable thinking it's up 'cause otherwise you gotta admit the whole world is a little speck of rock floating in the fucking dark."

Her breaths came shuddering and ragged, the pain in her arm and her legs and everything else running her down. "Wrap it up, Randy."

"Randall," he corrected. "Ah shit. I get it," and he did, apparently, because he rasped out another chuckle. "What I'm getting at, Deirdre, is that, well, we're both gonna die here. And seeing as that's all but guaranteed, I'd at least like to die with some goddamned dignity."

She snorted. "Yeah?"

"Yeah. I'm saying let's do it old-fashioned like. Pistols at dawn. We do a count-off, we turn our respective corners, we shoot. This hallway's gotta be... ten, twelve feet? That's about enough paces. Gotta be. I only got the one bullet left, and you know I ain't reloaded."

She sank into a crouch, testing the soreness of her muscles as she coiled them for action. "You always want to be a cowboy?"

"Before I even knew what a cowboy was."

"And you're sure you want to risk dying in a quick-draw against a lowly negress?"

"Like I said, it's not your fault the way you were born."

She thumbed the hammer back slowly, testing her legs. "I'm sick of all this talking," she said. "Go ahead. Count it off."

It would be the Sheriff of Squatter City versus Randall Hill, Québécois Mafia Pimp and Cult Lieutenant, a showdown in the darkness before the dawn, and all the dead were watching.

"Alright, Sheriff. We go on one."

"Go on one," she confirmed.

"Six," Randall began. "Five."

Three bullets in her cylinder.

And maybe...

Deirdre dug into the near-empty reservoir of her will and energy, trying for the smallest, easiest cantrip she knew. She closed her eyes and willed her strained body to make it happen, something subtle, so tiny, so seemingly weak that Randall might not even notice it. Her muscles strained with the effort and her wounds seared hot against her. She sealed her lips against a whimper.

"Four, three..."

A simple trick, to avoid notice. Not as powerful as invisibility, not as obvious as healing magic. But something useful when it came time to have a gun pointed her way.

"Two..."

The spell went off, a moment's dizziness head-rushing her vision.

It worked.

She smirked, dropping in her squat and readying herself for what came next.

"One."

Deirdre pushed off with the balls of her feet and launched herself through the threshold.

Randall spun around the bar countertop at the other side of the narrow hall.

Deirdre swung her arm toward him; he mirrored the motion.

For a fraction of a second, they floated, mid-motion, arms outstretched, feet maneuvering for stance—two deadly avatars squared off against each other, mirror images.

Both guns barked at once.

Randall's bullet sliced a red path along the side of her already-wounded arm. If her spell hadn't worked, it probably would have gone through her lung.

Her bullet blew through his right thigh, fracturing bone and slicing sinew. Every muscle in his leg spasmed at once, functionality torn asunder, and he collapsed kneeling to the floor. He clutched the wound, grimaced through scream-worthy pain, and peered up at her. "There it is, then," he said, voice reedy with anguish. "You win."

Then he raised his pistol and fired again.

The bullet spun her in a half-circle, skipped off the top of her pelvis, and lodged itself hot and terrible in her lower abdomen, tattering muscle and sinew and intestine as it went. She clutched the wound with her free hand, yelped against the hot anguish of it, and whined from the pain of shifting her ruined shoulder to grab it.

"Except I lied," he said.

He ejected the spent magazine, grabbed another from his pocket, and slapped it in.

Deirdre whirled back toward him and fired again.

Her shot blew through his right clavicle, sawing meat and bone, and when he squeezed the trigger a microsecond later, his pistol bucked from his grip. The bullet missed Deirdre by inches, Randall's aim thrown off by spellcraft and pain and a sudden weakness in his right arm.

Grunting, she stepped toward him, heat lashing along her left leg and up into her gut. She took another step. "I never told you how many bullets I had left."

He lurched to grab his pistol from where he'd dropped it.

She squeezed the trigger again, put a bullet in his lower back.

He reached his gun, grabbed it.

She stomped his hand with her right foot.

He let go, yelping.

She cracked the side of his drooping head with the butt of her gun and he fell over sideways, right onto the wreckage of his left shoulder. He keened when he landed, the combined pain of shoulder and leg and probably a tattered kidney coming out of his throat in a single, long wail.

She knelt in front of him. This time she brought the butt of her gun down on his jaw.

"That's for Paul," she said.

She hit him again, the cheek this time, because she missed his jaw. "That's for Olly."

She hit him a third time, though he screamed and sobbed now, and tried to pull his dying body away from her. "And that's for Mali."

He rolled onto his stomach.

She dropped her pistol, leapt on his back, and dug her fingers into the bullet hole she'd made there, feeling tendon and muscle and soft slick tissue squish-squelch underknuckle. She pulled. Hard. "That's for Marisha and Lucy and all those other women you raped, you kidnapped, you sold…" She jerked her hand so hard it hurt her knuckles, peeling the bullet hole wider, wider, wider even as he bucked and screamed beneath her weight. She felt meat part around her finger, felt something gelatinous catch on her nails.

"Stop! Stop!" he shrieked. "Devourer, Allah, Jesus Christ, whatever, just fucking kill me!"

Panting from her assault, she punched the back of his head, rebounded it from the floor, and struggled to stand back up. "No."

"I'm dying anyway."

"You are," she said, pushing against the complaint of every muscle in her body to walk over to his own gun and pick it up.

"You said—"

"You said you only had one bullet."

"Deirdre, please, you're better than this," he whined, pushing himself back on his side to look at her.

She thumbed back the hammer of the large-mouthed semi-automatic. "I'm better than this, huh?"

"You're the fucking Sheriff."

"I'm not the Sheriff. I'm not Imani Greene. I'm not Dee-Dee and there's no one left alive allowed to call me Dee. I'm certainly not a bitch or a whore or a cunt or a nigger. My fucking name is Deirdre." She pointed the barrel at his still-workable leg and fired. He spasmed, screamed again, and curled toward his newest wound. "And your name *was* Randall Tyler Hiller, but soon it won't be, because you'll be dead, and nobody is going to mourn you."

He was beyond words then, capable only of guttural syllables and slurred pleas and bright red coughs.

She ejected the magazine, tossed it behind the kitchen counter, ejected the cartridge from the chamber, and threw the gun out through the doorway. "You're going to bleed to death. It's going to hurt. You're going to die alone, knowing that we killed your coven and your followers. You're going to die knowing that I did this to you. Deirdre did this. All you had to do was leave me alone and let me live in peace. You didn't. Now I'm going to kill your Reverend and, if you haven't bled to death by then, I'm going to drag you all the way to Black Watch Hill, the actual hill, not the street, and I'm going to hang you there. And that…" she picked her own gun back up from the floor, "that's for Razz."

CHAPTER THIRTY-SEVEN

Paul followed Simon up the stairs, through a room, and up another spiral staircase.

"Where are we going?" he asked, rifle held at his hip but still pointed at Simon's spine.

"Up," Simon said. "Tongue lives in a trailer lashed to the roof of the church. Randall was heading up to get him, and Deirdre followed Randall."

"Well, pick up the pace."

They went through two more trailers, one of them inclined ramplike, until they came to a gutted double-wide with three doors. One of the doors hung open. A discarded pistol sat by the threshold, unloaded. Paul recognized it from Randall's holster. Simon bent to pick it up.

"Don't," Paul said. "Leave it."

"It's not loaded," Simon replied.

"Leave it."

Simon sighed eyerollingly. "Fine."

They went through the open door to find blood everywhere. A kitchen, full appliances, a bar-height countertop, and streamers and streaks and spatters of flesh and gore. Paul took it in slowly, struggling to force a clinical distance on himself to avoid panic.

"Deirdre will bleed to death, judging from the evidence," Simon said. "Randall's likely already—"

A wheeze cut Simon short.

Paul, Mali, and Simon all turned to the source of the gurgling sound. The wreckage of Randall laid on the floor, clothes tacky and stained crimson, face bloated with bruises, both legs and both shoulders streaming claret. He barely appeared human anymore. He wheezed again, a word lost in blood-choke and lung-ruin.

Simon tutted. "She was supposed to kill him."

"He's as good as dead," Paul replied.

"But not literally dead." Simon adjusted his suit jacket and reached for his holster.

"Don't," Paul said, lifting the rifle stock to his shoulder.

"Why not?"

"She left him alive for a reason."

"Unfortunately, the deal was—"

"I don't give a shit about your deal. Randall deserves as long a death as she sentenced him to."

"Look, I appreciate the Old Testament mentality, but—"

A low wail cut him off, a choked scream gurgling out in a blood-drowned throat.

Paul grimaced at the meaty tearing sound as Mali pulled Randall's tongue from his mouth.

Mali stood, dropped the tongue on the ground, and stepped on it. She glared over at Paul and Simon. "You weren't here. You didn't feel what he did to us. You don't get to make this decision."

Paul and Simon could only nod, speechless.

Mali bent down and tilted Randall's head so he wouldn't drown on his own blood. She lowered her lips to Randall's ear, put a hand on one of his wounds, and whispered something. Cast a spell on him.

As they followed Deirdre's path upwards, Paul wasn't sure if Randall would ever stop shrieking. He did, of course, not long afterwards, but Paul could somehow still hear it.

■■■

Deirdre stumbled on the incline. Her left hand prickled pins-and-needles, her left shoulder gnawed and gnashed. Her gut ached, the bullet boiling inside her. Her hip and her grazed calf gave her an uneven and unreliable gait. Her joints creaked, even the uninjured ones.

The world shuddered with every breath, her muscles pushed to breaking, her will shaken, her energy all but drained away. Only vaporized uppers and sheer stubbornness kept her moving. All else broke. The edges of her vision darkened and blurred, and her guts knotted in anguish. Every few steps, her gait gave out and she'd have to stabilize herself against a wall.

Still, she climbed.

Her dreamer-and-upper soaked brain played with her perceptions. The incline of scavenged steel, gutted trailers, and welded catwalks became a steaming throat, an organic thing, humid and odorous, exhaling the stench of shallow graves and stained mattresses with every breath.

Still, she climbed.

She wondered what Tongue would look like when she finally saw him. What a man could possibly look like who could do such things so guiltlessly. What a man could look like who could bend Randall's knee and recruit such a young-faced army to such a wicked, violent cause.

you'd be surprised how little convincing and recruiting it took, the Speaker said in her mind.

"I really wouldn't," she said aloud.

I suppose not. but don't expect to be impressed.

"Stay out of my head."

She didn't wait for its refusal or acquiescence—she willed it out. It took energy, energy she wouldn't have to fight or use magic later, but she was sick of uninvited guests and would tolerate no further intrusion.

She felt him up ahead. The crowned priest possessed by power, worshiping the thing that ate the world.

Up ahead, at the end of the throat, a chorus of serpents hissed at her.

She moved through the drug vapor and mist and found a simple door.

She pushed herself through the opening, around an ornament that was simultaneously a hanging light bulb and a uvula, and stepped inside. She entered the Mouth, the Throne Room, the Jaws of the Devouring God, or maybe just another in a series of countless double-wides gutted and lashed together with scavenged steel and magic, the bare skeleton of an illusory power. Tongue. The Devourer. God, the Devil, or nobody at all.

and there you are, Tongue's voice whispered in her skull.

There he was too.

Tongue sat on a wheelchair throne in stained once-white briefs, his legs a mess of scar tissue and atrophy. Wrinkles trenched his face around pitted, jaundiced eyes. Thin gray hair wisped from his scalp in frayed patches. Decades earlier he might have been handsome—he had the bone structure for it, the strong chin and jaw—but bad habits and the passage of indifferent time had stolen any charm from his features. His cheeks were hatchets pressed to skin. His fingernails, too long and scratching idly at the wheelchair armrests, glowed yellow under the dim overhead light.

A bulbous protrusion of plastic translucence and protuberant tentacles centered his face, dominated his expression.

Behind his throne, something large and bullet-shaped draped more tendrils down. Similar bomb-sized shells littered the rest of the room, shadowing Tongue like royal guards.

Serpents hissed, hidden in every direction.

Behind him, behind the broken thing in its little throne, a shadow shifted and warped, fading by the second. A chant issued from its darkness, the retreating cadence of the Devourer's endless drone. As the shadow faded, burning itself free of Tongue's throne like a photograph given to fire, she could feel the humming power of Tongue's presence fade.

Deirdre struggled on exhausted legs, wavering on her wounds. A chuckle forced its way from her lips, short and humorless. "You're Tongue."

I am beyond naming, now, he said in her head, his lips unmoving beneath the tentacular mask. *Tongue will be dead soon. Howland Butler too.*

She spat, blood and saliva mixing on the floor. "Good."

it is a pleasure to see you in person, Deirdre.

"Wish I could say the same."

He adjusted a red-knobbed lever with his right hand. The wheelchair(throne) whirred and jerked forward. The royal guard shadowing Tongue followed the motion and wavered once it stopped.

I so seldom meet people of genuine power. Randall knew one thing very well, true, and Isaiah showed tremendous potential, but I do not speak of magic. you possess something more important than mere magic. you have conviction.

"I don't have time for a monologue."

Tongue raised a withered, yellow-clawed hand. *please. if anyone is at a loss for time, it's me.*

Snakes hissed.

"Oh, yeah?"

had I the strength left within me to fight back, I could attack you with a psychic assault the likes of which you've never experienced. but I am an abandoned creature, now, and the fire within my spirit is guttered out. my men are dead, dying, or unconscious. your men are on their way to play cavalry. if you don't kill me, they will. if they somehow don't, then the Québécois will eventually find me out and tie up my loose end.

The tentacles on his face twitched, amused.

you look upon a dead man. allow him his last words.

She spread her stance, searching for balance. "Make it quick."

Tongue's head shifted slightly, all the tendrils moving in unison as he peered down at his sagging skin, his pale-grub body. *pardon my appearance. I was in the process of dressing when you executed your plan. given the direction things took, it seemed narcissistic to insist on vestments for my demise.*

"Alright, enough of that." She lifted the barrel toward his face, looped her finger around the trigger.

Paused.

Something was wrong.

Serpents hissed.

go on then. if you won't even allow an old man his last confession.

She flinched, squinted, staggered back, and groaned at the unexpected weight shot through her bad leg.

Snakes.

No.

Not snakes. Not bombs or royal guards, not tentacles (though the things writhing from his visage looked impossibly tentacular)—oxygen tanks, valves cranked open, filling the room with potential explosion. A face full of tubes to buttress failing lungs.

ah, you've noticed.

She grimaced and realigned her stance. She went to shove the gun into a pocket, realized she had no pockets, and dropped it. "Motherfucker."

first let me say that I bear no ill will toward women or colored people, Tongue began, delivering his own eulogy. *I adopted these philosophies as a means to an end. when I arrived in Oceanrest, there was already a certain degree of racial resentment and misogyny, and the extant Aryan Nationalist movement made finding a core group of loyal followers quite easy, given the proper ideological alignment.*

"You monster."

a con man, actually, and bound to no particular dogma. I played a long game, bouncing between the Speaker and the Devourer, plotting out my own end-game.

"I don't care," Deirdre muttered. "I don't give two shits about your life story. You kidnapped, sold, and raped women. You killed people."

the ritual requires sacrifices, and cults require loyalty. it was easier to thread my needs through extant dogma than it would've been to come up with something new. as for the sale of prostitutes and, yes, occasionally of slaves—that wasn't a requisite, but every organization needs revenue.

She grabbed one of his age-attenuated wrists from the wheelchair armrest and twisted it wrongways. A strangled sound croaked in the old man's lungs. "Listen to this, you ancient old bastard, it's over. You're right. Someone's going to kill you. Everything you did here, everything you hoped to do, it ends tonight."

His eyes widened, reddened with burst capillaries. A surge of dizziness blew through Deirdre's perception, a cloud of purple-black curtaining the world, nausea spinning up her innards. She staggered back, let go of his wrist, clutched at her stomach. She hunched forward and spat bile.

you think yourself some kind of hero, doing what you've done? you're only postponing the inevitable. the kingdom of mankind is at its end. do you think this is some terrible fate? look at the world around you. is this what you would settle for?

She snorted, spat again, and struggled to straighten up. "Yours wouldn't be better."

we could've wiped clean the slate. started again, anew, built a utopia—

"A utopia? For who?"

this would be a chance to try the human experiment again, with a real god, a real deity that people could hear and commune with. a deity that demands sacrifice and returns power. a deity that answers prayers in exchange for blood.

She reached out for him and fell short as his next psychic attack rolled through her. She roared, lashing back against it. Pushed him out of her head. Panted and heaved against his assault, against his very voice. "You're delusional," she uttered between desperate breaths.

and what of you? you believe you're saving these women? what sort of lives do you imagine them living after this? you're not saving them, you're damning them. you've done no justice.

Deirdre shook off the last of his assault, pushed his voice down until it barely whispered. She snickered. In her throat, the small laughter grew larger, louder, growing into a lunatic cackle that nearly toppled her from her teetering stance. As she laughed, he grew silent. The wheelchair whirred, backed away a few inches.

"You think I'm here because of justice?"

The wheelchair whirred, retreating.

The wheels knocked against oxygen tanks.

so execute me. pull the trigger.

She shook her head and stepped forward. Felt him press against her with psychic force and magic, felt the air thicken with resistance until she was pushing her way through swamp. "I'm not here for justice. I'm here because you killed Razz. I'm here because you kidnapped me. I'm not here for any reason except that you brought me here. You brought me to your house, and now I'm tearing it down."

so shoot.

Another snort of laughter tore through her dry throat. "After what you've done?" She thought she grinned, but her face was too numb to be sure. "After what you've done to me? To Mali, to all those women? To Razz? After everything you've done, you think I'm just going to shoot you? I'm not going to shoot you."

Her muscles strained. She felt something in her thigh go tight and stiff. Her left knee buckled. She stumbled, almost fell.

She shuddered a breath, glared, and limped forward with her left leg pain-straight. "I don't care if you believe their dogma or not. I don't care if you're a con man or a preacher or a cult leader. I don't care why you did these things, just that you did them, that other people did them in your name."

The wheelchair whirred, but there was no more room to retreat. Oxygen tanks clinked together.

She broke through his wards and stepped forward, close enough to smell him. Close enough to smell his age, the decades of sweat and cigarette smoke stuck inside his body. Close enough to scent the reek of all his cons, his scams, his tricks and plays and double-triple-crosses, his cheap swindles. Close enough to inhale the odor of rot exuded from his very core.

you have to understand—

"No, I don't."

She was close enough to reach out with her weak, wounded arm and tear the oxygen mask from his face. Close enough to blacken his wet red eyes and overturn his throne; to break his crown and choke the gospel from his lungs.

CHAPTER THIRTY-EIGHT

The drug-dense mist dilated time, stretched it around them.

Paul brought up the rear, trying to shut out the whispers that had crept into his head since Tongue's wards had fallen.

Every few paces, drops of blood marked their pathway up.

follow the red liquid road! the Speaker chimed in his head.

"Shut up," he growled.

alright, Pauly, if you insist. I'll save your digits for special occasions only.

The Speaker's silence felt more final this time, not as if the entity had quieted, but as if it had left.

He could feel Deirdre's strength coming off the drizzles and spots of blood like steam.

With Tongue's wards down, the whispering dead distracted him. *come to the Black House*, one voice whispered. *where's my baby? who took my baby?*— another soul spiraled in repetition, each cycle louder, angrier, more lunatic.

He closed his eyes, trying to push the sound as far to the back of his mind as he could.

But he had too many psychic uppers in his bloodstream. Too many amphetamines.

(*where am I? why is it so cold?*)

A few feet ahead, Simon and Mali bowed their heads together as they walked, whispering.

"You don't *have* to do anything," Simon told her. "I didn't come here to force you to…(*to what?* Paul thought, but he couldn't hear)…The Speaker doesn't do that to people."

"What then?" Mali asked.

"Whatever you want. Whatever you *really* want."

She said something else Paul couldn't hear. Something about a book?

"We'll talk about this when we're out," was Simon's reply.

Paul's sixth-sense pounded him with mixed messages. Magic vibrated along the lines of the structure, and every step sent him into near-vertigo as the Escher sensation settled back in. This had never just been a church, not since Oceanrest's economy folded and the Reverend gave scared men a finger to point. This was something else, or a monument to something else. Something that made him sick without knowing what it was.

"Are you okay?" Mali asked.

"I'm fine."

A throat. A trailer. A horde of vermin scrabbling behind wallpaper. A cathedral. A house of worship. A focus, psychic and magical, channeling raw fury, terrified hatred.

How long had Howland Butler's con played?

He could feel the Devourer in the walls, retreating.

(*fucktakekilleat*, it repeated, trailing off quieter and quieter and finally gone elsewhere, underground or out in space or through a hole in a wall between realities)

The Speaker chuckled through the architecture, no longer bound to Paul's head.

poor Reverend, the Speaker mused. *looks like you've made your last mistake. you pick brawn because you think brawn is easier to control, but the brains still win, Rev. I think you bought too much into that sapient English saying, about it being better to rule in Hell...*

"Faster," Paul muttered.

Simon glanced at him over his shoulder. "There isn't a rush at this point."

"I said faster."

Simon rolled his eyes. "Sure."

A wave of psychic energy rolled down the incline, another attack on the senses. Paul's vision blurred and curdled vomit churned up his throat. He choked it back down and spat sour saliva. Took a steadying breath, and picked up the pace, keeping his barrel leveled at Simon's back.

The inclined leveled out.

This was the skull of the church. These were the jaws.

Overhead, a light bulb was also a uvula.

"In," Paul said.

"He's on our side," Mali said to him. "You don't have to—"

"It's fine," Simon interrupted.

Mali looked between them as if struggling to decide who to chastise.

Simon entered Tongue's throne room.

Mali waved for Paul to go next, then followed.

Hissing filled the room. Hissing, and grunts, and airless gags.

Opposite the entrance, a wheelchair lay overturned amid a mess of oxygen tanks. In the middle of the floor, Deirdre was strangling Howland Butler, straddling the age-withered man, puke-up drying on her chin and his face, her expression a battle between anguish and fury. Slick red soaked her tunic, rivered her skin. Her muscles spasmed and seized as she clutched Butler's throat, her tendons twitching. Butler scratched at her with nicotine-yellow nails, clawing ruddy lines along her arms, but she remained immovable, knuckles seething rage around his last gasps.

Simon grinned.

Paul stepped forward, looping the rifle's strap over his shoulder. He imagined kicking the ancient priest in the side of his head, imagined the frailty of such an age-weathered skull.

But he didn't. It served no purpose. And watching Deirdre's back curve against Butler's reprisals, watching her bear down on him with all the pain and rage of loss, it felt selfish. This wasn't his fight, not the same way it was hers. He knew in his marrow and his gut and the thing throbbing between his lungs that only Deirdre could end this. It had to be her.

Still, he moved in close so that Reverend Howland Butler would see him over her shoulder before dying, so that Howland Butler could see that he was dying alone, and that Deirdre wouldn't.

Reverend Butler bucked against Deirdre, his psychic assault failing, his hands failing, his church failing, his everything…

Deirdre's gun sat on the floor by Paul's feet, and Paul bent to retrieve it.

Butler gagged and retched, his arms going limp and splayed wide.

Deirdre clung on, her chest heaving with effort, sinew threatening to burst from her skin.

Butler gave up a few more spasms and went slack. His eyes fluttered, widened, and sagged shut. Still, she held on, hands vice-clamped around the dying man's throat. Paul counted his heartbeats, allowing fifty of them to pass before he reached out and put a hand on Deirdre's shoulder.

She spun toward him and grabbed his arm. Her pupils shrank, grew, and shrank again.

"Paul."

"Deirdre."

She struggled to her feet, legs shaking. She'd lost too much blood, and all the drugs and nausea and exertion hadn't helped. She gripped Paul's shoulders and went limp against him, her weight jerking him forward. He steadied himself, barely.

"Mali," she whispered, unfocused eyes peering over his shoulder. "Paul. Mali. I…we…we did…"

She collapsed, her limp body falling deadweight. He staggered and tried to break her fall. He caught her for a second, crashed to his aching knees, and lost his grip. She fell before him, breath coming in shallow, ragged gasps. For a couple seconds all he could do was gape at her wounds, at the arrhythmic rise and fall of her chest.

Dierdre was dying. Quickly.

"No," he muttered. "No fucking way, no way in hell." He scrambled back to his feet and shrugged the rifle off of his shoulder, aiming it at Simon and Mali. "Get her up." His voice reminded him of the way Virgil sounded those years ago, the unexpected ferocity that spilled from his lips just before he smashed the butt of his gun into the perpetrator's face. "If she dies, now, I swear on everything decent in this world I will kill every fucking one of us."

Simon's lips twitched to a smirk. "Are you sure that will work on me?"

"The Speaker said so. He—it—said you can't bring back the dead, you can only save the dying. That's why you kept following me, right? You tailed me all week."

Simon's smirk wavered.

"At the docks, at Deirdre's place, even by the car park, by Captain Wallace's pier. Everywhere. Because you had to be there, just in case, to keep your plan going. You can't bring back the dead, and if I pull this trigger, we'll all be dead. You, me, her…all of us."

"Paul?" Mali said.

Simon's nostrils flared, a tic flexed his cheek. A storm darkened the sea of his eyes.

Around them, oxygen hissed.

"Do not test me," Paul snarled.

"Paul," Mali repeated, this time not a question.

"I'm on it," Simon said, raising his hands in surrender.

"Hurry."

Pauly, the Speaker said, its voice resonating basso through the floor and up the bones of his legs. *I'm impressed. look at the pair of brass ones you just dug up. you're a man after my own heart. or you would be, if I had one.*

Simon crossed the room to Deirdre and bent over her, licking his lips as he placed his hand against her ruined shoulder.

"Would you really do it?" Mali asked, stepping between the barrel and Simon's body. "You'd kill us all? Me?"

"To save her? I…" he hesitated, his eyes meeting Mali's. Her gaze doused the heat in him. "I don't know. I screwed up so much else…"

"He would've," Simon panted, sweat pouring from his face as he worked magic on Deirdre's wounds. "Most people are willing to go much further than they think when the chips are down." Purple-black glow flickered, and Deirdre's shoulder began stitching itself together. "Though he didn't need to. There was already a deal in place."

An angry sneer wormed across Paul's face. "So what the hell was this then?"

Simon withdrew his hand, Deirdre's shoulder healed into scabrous tissue, stitched flesh, and wiped sweat from his brow. "Call it a test, if you want."

"A test of what?"

"Not loyalty or anything, if that's what you're asking." Simon lowered his hand to Deirdre's abdomen next, to the crimson stained fabric over her left hip. "The Speaker doesn't care about loyalty. I don't know how much it cares about disloyalty either, though I try not to push that particular envelope."

Paul lowered the gun, uncomfortable with Mali's closeness to the business end. "So what then?"

"The Speaker knows what you're willing to do, how far you're willing to go to get what you want. You know it now too. Everyone does."

Paul glanced at Mali, met her eyes, and looked away.

Mali said nothing, but stepped closer to Simon.

Deirdre sucked in a ragged breath, fluttered her eyes, and fell unconscious again. Simon mopped more sweat from his brow and kept working.

Simon nodded to Deirdre's claret-wet body, panted as he spoke. "This one, for all her talk, was willing to die for her cause. To finish what she started. She would've sooner killed herself than let Randall take her. She'd have given anything to see Butler's plan ruined. You don't meet many people with that kind of dedication." He swallowed hard, sagged, and groaned with exertion. His sweat had soaked through his Kevlar and moistened his suit. "You, apparently, are willing to kill us all for a chance at saving her. You're even willing to kill one of the people she was dying to help."

Mali shifted in Paul's periphery—he kept her there.

"What do you make of that?" Simon asked.

Paul shrugged the rifle over his shoulder and stooped down to collect Deirdre's revolver.

Deirdre drowsed as the wound in her gut closed into scab and scar. She rose onto on her elbows and mumbled something only half-comprehensible.

Simon heaved, choked, and swallowed a mouthful of vomit. He coughed, ran a hand through sweat-flopped hair, and sat down. "How do you feel, Deirdre?"

"Better than you will after I knock your teeth out."

Despite the threat, she only seemed half-conscious, her body somnambulant-loose, eyes half-lidded.

"Let me rest a bit. I'll do a little more work," Simon said, "but once you're back on your feet, I need you and Paul to leave. On foot."

"What?" Paul and Deirdre asked simultaneously.

"Every single cultist in this building has been beaten, concussed, or murdered. Most of them were in their teens and twenties. There are going to be questions. A lot of them. I.A. will be up my ass for months. There'll be an official investigation, a lot of parents with questions to ask."

Paul's mouth gaped with realization.

"I have a narrative to finish building, and you two won't want to be part of it."

"No, we don't," Paul said.

Deirdre glared at Simon as if to argue, but nodded instead.

"Good. Then consider yourselves innocent."

Paul pursed his lips, avoided Mali's gaze, and tried not to wonder how many ghosts would shake themselves loose of the night's work.

Consider yourselves innocent.

Easier said than done.

CHAPTER THIRTY-NINE

Ten Days Later...
(in the afterimage of seeing too much)

"Our guys in the Québécois say the big bosses didn't know." Virgil sipped coffee in Paul's kitchen, winced at the flavor. "This fresh? Anyway, I can't say for sure if they're lying or not, but it scans with what we dug up. Some mid-level players in the mob were jockeying for power, dealing with the Aryans under the table."

"So that's it?"

"Hell, we got fifteen arrests out of this, and Luc Grenier's testifying against some of his own men. That's plenty."

"You're not going after Grenier?"

Virgil snorted. "Him and his accountant are trading testimony for amnesty. It'll be smack-on-the-wrist charges for them."

"So they get away with it?"

"Grenier's untouchable. Unless someone in his inner circle squawked, or unless we could tie him directly to the crimes, he's free and clear. But fifteen arrests isn't small potatoes. We can track the money into one of their motels, maybe even a B&B. This is the second biggest bust in town history. We even made TV. *National* TV. We got folks from Bar Harbor calling us, scared the press coverage is going to ruin the rest of tourist season for 'em. I told 'em they could always rent rooms to the reporters."

Paul sipped his own coffee, two days old, and slumped in his seat. "What about the...the cult?"

"Well, that's something else."

"It's tied up with all this other crap, isn't it?"

"Sort of. Just that, well, it's a more complicated investigation, on account of the shoot-out and the fire and such."

"Right."

The shoot-out. The fire. Simon's narrative.

"We got IDs on some of the bodies, the ones that weren't burnt too bad. The survivors are awaiting trial, but they'll all plead insanity. It's the strangest thing, though…" Virgil swirled his coffee.

"What?"

"You'd think, I don't know…you want to believe people like this, that they'd come from away. But almost all of these kids came from Oceanrest. Half of 'em from Denton, of all places. I know some of the parents. Two of 'em were trying to get hired on the force." Virgil turned away, staring out the kitchen window at the slouched docks and the summer rainclouds gathe= ring overhead.

For a long time, neither of them said anything.

Virgil reached up with one hand to wipe at his lips, to rub his chin.

Paul cleared his throat. "You okay?"

Virgil turned around as if snapped from a trance. "I'm fine," he said, hollow-voiced. "Just remembering something." He coughed, drank more coffee. "Anyway, the kids going to trial, they're all babbling nonsense. They'll get insanity."

"Too bad."

Virgil's gaze drifted back to the window. "Do you suppose people can change, Paul? Not like you or me, but…all of us?"

"As a species?"

"A'yeah, I suppose."

"I don't know."

"Seems to me sometimes that it's the things you want to change that never do, the things you want to keep that always change."

Paul gulped cold bitterness from his mug and considered the man in his kitchen. Virgil LeDuff, nearly sixty, had been a cop most of his professional life, as had his father before him. His father, who had beaten a kidnapper to death, and intervened for the man who would have been charged for it.

Paul found himself opening his mouth to ask a question, the words poised on the tip of his tongue. He didn't ask. Changed the subject instead. "You didn't get any of the messages? The night of the fog?"

"No. That fog plays havoc with all kinds of machinery. Radios weren't working either. Nothing was."

Paul nodded, adding nothing.

"You didn't happen to find anything, did you?" Virgil asked. "I know you had a run-in with Randall Hill, and Simon looped you into his investigation."

"No, I didn't find anything. I'd seen Randall's truck driving up to Route One so I knew he was somewhere up in that area, but I never got through to you."

"Goddamned fog," Virgil muttered. "Cost us everything."

He was referring to the police officers who died in the shootout with Randall's cultists, Paul knew. The ones who'd gotten into Simon's car to follow a lead. The ones who allegedly radioed for help once the gunfire started, but whose communications were lost in the sea of static the fog brought down on the radio-waves. The ones who'd died in the parking lot and in Howland Butler's cathedral.

(blood in the grass by an abandoned car)

(the door hanging open)

(drag marks where the bodies had been pulled into the woods)

"I'm sorry," Paul said. "I know they were your guys."

"Yeah, well. The whole thing's fucked up anyway. A bunch of teenagers and twenty-somethings kidnapping girls, shooting cops, all manner of shit." He sighed. "Kids, for Chrissakes. There was even an eighteen year old we ID'd. Eighteen goddamned years old. How does someone so young get to be like that?"

"At least it's over."

Virgil snorted. "It's far from over. We've got a bunch of suspects screaming like madmen, all liable to get judged incompetent to stand, all liable to get insanity, and fifteen Québécois mobsters waiting for prosecution. Over? It's just begun."

Paul considered his coffee. "And Frank?"

"Who?"

"The squatter."

"Oh, right. Nobody's seen him."

Of course they hadn't. Nor would they ever again. Deirdre and Simon had agreed on that point.

"Think you'll keep looking? He was attached to Randall, after all."

Virgil shook his head. "More than likely the guy just picked up stakes and left town. With everything else that happened that night…well, whether he was connected to Randall or not, nobody wants to spend a bunch of time and money looking for a hop-headed squatter. It's not like he'd make a reliable witness."

"Guess not," Paul said.

They'd been counting on it, in fact.

"Well, the precinct thanks you for your testimony. So does Simon Perdue. I just figured I'd let you know how things played out, given your, ah, involvement."

"Thanks."

"Suppose I'll see you around," Virgil said, putting his mug on the kitchen counter. "Hopefully not in an investigative capacity next time."

"I'm pretty sure my days as a PI are behind me. Besides, I've got a lesson plan to write."

Virgil paused at the exit, squinting at the new carvings etched into the doorjamb. "What's all this?"

"A friend of mine is kind of a spiritualist. Those are, um, traditional protective markings."

Virgil chuckled. "Never pegged you as the superstitious type."

"I guess Oceanrest is rubbing off on me."

"Guess so. Well, be careful what kind of poppycock you buy into. Some of these weirdos are crazy."

"Oh, I know. Believe me, I know."

"And, Paul? Get some better coffee. This garbage tastes like mashed-up cigarettes."

CHAPTER FORTY

Three Days After That...
(as life shambles forward again)

Deirdre carved runes into the doorframe, a splay of papers surrounding her seated form in a half-circle.

She wiped sweat from her forehead. "I'm a goddamned apothecary."

Paul smirked. "You're the only one I know who could make heads or tails from the instructions." He sipped iced tea from a Collins glass. "Want another drink?"

"Yeah," she said. "Shit ain't easy."

The laptop on his desk streamed a news report, the anchor re-revisiting a story everyone in New England already knew, about the ultra-right-wing militia-cult holed up in the abandoned church north of Oceanrest; the sex trafficking Aryan and his Québécois allies; the final, bloody shoot-out; the heroics of three Oceanrest PD officers and one FBI agent.

"_...flags remain at half-mast to honor..._"

The three officers hadn't made it. They'd died, allegedly, in the stand-off between law enforcement and the militia.

Paul knew that wasn't the case. Simon had killed them. The evidence would never reach that conclusion, however. The damage to the bodies had been too severe. There'd been an explosion at the church that night. According to the standing narrative, Reverend Howland Butler had found himself caught out. In a desperate last stand, the good reverend had filled his room with oxygen and struck a Zippo. There'd been little to salvage from the scene once the fire department got things under control.

The women the emergency workers had pulled out of the basement, the White Room, were being ministered to by a host of doctors and psychiatrists.

Many of them had been captive for years. Their memories fragmented, perforated by drugs and trauma; most of them suffered from weeks or even months of "missing time." Black holes in their own minds. But they'd cobbled together enough details to warrant a handful of arrests, and police were hoping to find a client list from one of the Québécois or Aryans during plea bargaining.

Someday soon, the women would be expected to re-integrate themselves with society. They would be expected to get jobs and make friends and resurrect themselves out of the ashes of their histories.

Paul had a nagging suspicion that many of them wouldn't make it.

It was funny how little justice seemed to come in the wake of justice being done. It was funny how often the word "funny" described horrors that couldn't be screamed away.

"Six women were rescued from the compound," the anchor said, "though no names have been released." Which was almost the right number. Almost.

Minus one unaccounted for.

Mali had stayed with Simon after he and Deirdre had left.

Where was she now?

"So," Paul said, interrupting his own thoughts, "how'd the thing with Shoshanna turn out?"

Deirdre set down the carving knife, wiped more sweat from her brow, and sighed. "I have no idea. She wrangled things with her brother to keep me out of trouble, at least for *now*. I get this feeling that she's trying to rope me into something, but I couldn't say what. I don't know. I guess she came through for me."

"What about everything else?"

"Who knows? Half of Squatter City is scared shitless of me now. There's a rumor that I'm the person responsible for Frank's disappearance."

"Is that something we'd call a 'rumor?'"

"He hurt Razz," she said. "He—"

"You didn't do anything wrong."

Deirdre glared.

"I, uh…I'm sorry too, about my part in things. I was so caught up in my own bullshit, I—"

"We don't need to talk about this now," Deirdre cut in.

He sipped iced tea, glancing back at the summer sun drying rain-wet docks. Gulls circled overhead, boats floated on Atlantic waves. Cassandra stood on the docks, translucent blur shimmering pierside. A joint of psychic downers perched on the windowsill. Paul drank more iced tea. Cassandra stared at him, but he couldn't make out her expression through the single toke he'd taken earlier.

A silence fell between them. Deirdre turned back to the doorframe, scratching symbols into it with the knife.

Paul caught movement on the dock—not the shimmer of a lost spirit, but something material. He tilted his face to the window just enough to get a better look. It was Nora, the teenage recluse archivist, a black Dead Kennedys hoodie wrapped tent-like around her body with the sleeves rolled back to her elbows. Oversized Manchester boots carried the girl across the pier in a long, straight line toward his door.

"Nora's here," Paul said.

Deirdre swept up all the papers and slipped them into a manila folder. "I'm not done."

Paul pushed away from the kitchen and went to the front door. "Somehow I don't think she's here to take those back."

"More questions?" Deirdre asked.

"I hope not."

He got to the door just as the first staccato knocks broke the air. *Tap-tap-tap.* He swung the door open. The first thing he saw was the bleach-blonde hair nested atop Nora's shaved scalp. The second thing he saw were the pinched white scars puckered along both of her arms. Some of them looked like symbols, he realized, and some like names scratched into her skin, but most were just short, straight lines.

She pulled down her sleeves and Paul realized he'd been staring.

"Um…" he cleared his throat, dodging eye contact with the girl, "can I help you?"

Nora folded her arms around her body. "Is Deirdre here?"

"Uh, yeah." Paul moved out of the doorway. "Yeah."

Nora crossed the threshold in front of him, and he saw that she'd bundled her hands up inside her sleeves, leaving nothing to show.

■■■

Nora came through the door fast, and froze.

"Yes?" Deidre asked.

Nora narrowed her eyes at the laptop. "Can we put something else on?"

"Help yourself."

Nora scanned the area. After a few seconds, she crossed the room to the computer, leaning in and letting one hand slip from a bundled hoodie sleeve. She paused the news report and found Paul's music player. The speakers growled out a punk rock dirge, something Deirdre didn't recognize with rumbling, choppy guitars, and female vocals. Something she wouldn't have guessed Paul would listen to.

"Sorry," Nora said. "I just can't focus with…" she gestured at the pause-frozen visage of the news anchor.

"Sure," Deirdre replied. "So, what's up?"

"Olly's staying at my place," Nora said, not really answering the question posed to her. "She's been anxious lately. I think, uh, I think maybe she's still *scared* about the *monster*? I gave her the room next to the library. I gave her the room next to mine first, but then I usually fall asleep in the library, and Olly's been having nightmares, so I wanted to make sure she didn't feel alone."

"Uh-huh. What did you want to talk to me about?"

"Well, Olly and me, uh, Olly and I, we were thinking…we want to have a memorial service for Razz. I know it's not much, but it's something we can do and, um, well, we want you to be there. We need you to be there."

Deirdre stood, made distance between herself and everyone else in the houseboat. The thought of it made her itch. After the mess at the Church, all the blood and carnage and magic…to go back to the Lafayette crowd, to Olly and whoever else she knew now that Frank was taken care of; to go back and pretend to understand them, or pretend that they could understand her, to pretend that they'd always been friends; to pretend that Razz wasn't dead because some old, egotistical junkie couldn't keep his shit together; to see them leading their lives and try not to imagine some version of Razz leading some version of his, just any number of days older than the day he—

Nora cleared her throat. "I just don't think anyone else could give the eulogy. You know? Because he and Olly were *together* or whatever, but it was kind of a new thing, and even Olly thinks it should be you. She says you're the only person she could think of."

"I, uh…I don't know if I'm ready for something like that."

"I get it. I never did anything for Ambrose. Every time I'd think about it, I'd kinda get…" she trailed off. "It's hard, you know? Because you get to believe that someone's like a part of you, and then when they're gone, they take that part with them, and it's gone too, and you sort of, I don't know, you just never feel quite whole anymore."

(his blood slicking her fingers)
(his futures falling apart one by one)
Deirdre choked.

"Nora," Paul stepped away from the counter, "I think maybe we should talk about this later, yeah?"

"But you were Razz's family, you're all the family he was going to have," Nora seemed manic now, louder, her birdlike frame threatening to unravel with all the stuff inside of it. "He was a runaway, and whatever family he left behind, they weren't his real family, you were. And you're a runaway too. So is Paul."

"Nora—" Paul started.

"You are! You're just older than most runaways so nobody wants to call you a runaway, but you are. You *ran away*, didn't you? That's okay. People do. People run away for a lot of reasons. Olly ran away, I ran away. And when you run away, you lose everything, and you have to build everything up again. You have to find a new family. Ambrose..." she stopped, sucked air, seemed to vibrate. She stared at Deirdre, eyes glowing opalescent, burning. "You were Razz's family. So was Olly."

"So was Frank," Deirdre said, her throat threatening to close, tears rimming her vision.

"We can't do this without you." Nora spoke quieter now, but the manic quality, the threat that she might splinter before their eyes, remained. "Ambrose was my family and he's gone, he's just gone, and I never—I never..." she sucked more air. "But he left me all this *stuff*, this whole mansion, *everything*, and I don't know what to do with it, but I know none of it means anything if I don't do *something*. And I can do this thing to make sure Razz gets the honor he deserves, that he gets a real memorial, but I can't do it without you because you're *it*. You were Razz's person, the only one he could count on."

Deirdre wiped the lone tear from below her eye, trying to restrain the rest of them, throat and face tight and tightening with the effort. "Sure," she squeaked out. "I'll do it. I'm in."

Nora's smile seemed to stitch her back together. "Thank you."

Deirdre nodded, body shaking from everything held inside, as if Nora's threatening collapse had transferred to her. "Excuse me," she coughed. "I'll be right back."

She went for the restroom and barely made it.

■■■

After Deirdre locked the bathroom door, Nora left. Deidre stayed in the restroom for almost fifteen minutes. She made no noise.

Or almost no noise. She made enough noise for Paul to know what she was failing to hide.

Paul mixed her a strong drink and had it waiting on the desk for her when she came back out.

"Thanks," she said.

Deirdre took a sip of her drink. Her face puckered involuntarily against the strength of it.

"I could…I could go up to the house," Paul offered, "if you wanted."

"It wouldn't change anything."

"I guess not. But I could. I would."

"I'll let you know." She unsheathed the hunting knife and spread the ward instructions across the floor.

"You don't have to finish it all tonight."

"I'd like to."

She sat down on the floor cross-legged and went back to work. Paul sipped iced tea and tried not to look out the window at the shimmering after-image of his lost daughter. Wind whistled around them. Gulls cawed. Men yelled at each other on the docks. Oceanrest settled into their background. Music played through the laptop speakers.

"I'm glad you agreed to do it," Paul said. "It's weird, but I think we all need it. Nora, too."

Deirdre nodded. Carved. "She was right, you know."

"About which part?"

"All of it." She lowered the knife. "My dad was…he had problems. Hallucinations, delusions, and sometimes he'd get to thinking something and you couldn't convince him out of it, even if it was absolutely insane. They had him on drugs but he forgot to take them all the time, or refused to take them because he was sure they were poison, that my mom was trying to poison him with fake pills."

"I'm sorry."

"No, no, this is so long ago…and I ran away. It wasn't his fault, he didn't do it on purpose. But I ran. And Nora's right, I lost everything, I gave everything up. I even gave myself a new name. I guess…I guess I did kind of build myself a new family. Razz, Olly, you, Shoshanna…"

"Your cat," Paul added.

Deirdre chuckled. "Yes, my cat, the half-blind little shit. And even my cat's a stray. But that's the thing, maybe. We're all strays in one way or another, we're all stranded here on the edge of the country, we're all fucked up, and we're all that we have. We're all we're going to have."

Paul sipped his drink, considering. "Could be worse."

"Sometimes…I don't know if it could really be better."

"What a depressing thought."

Deirdre smirked weakly and went back to carving.

For a long time, the only sound was the music coming from Paul's laptop speakers. Otis Redding's "Change Gonna Come."

Paul gestured to the doorframe with his drink. "This will keep things out?"

"If I'm doing it right, yeah." Deirdre set the knife aside and looked up at him. "I'm not well versed in this kind of magic, but from what I understand, this should keep out all the spirits and everything."

"Everything?"

"Unless you invite something in."

A cool shiver rived up his spine. He glanced at the joint perched on the windowsill, but lowered himself to the floor instead.

(unless you invite something in)

The laptop speakers crackled. Otis Redding sang, anguished, about his uncertainty about the things waiting beyond the clouds.

Beyond the sky.

(hard living but afraid to die)

The speakers crackled and the song skipped. The track changed. The opening notes of The Doors' "The End" played into the room. Paul shivered, closed the laptop before Jim Morrison started singing. He stared at the computer for a while, bracing himself. Turned toward Deirdre. "We can't not talk about it."

"We can," she said.

"What I did…what I didn't do…"

She set the knife at her side, still gripping the hilt. "I will tell you when we're ready to have this conversation."

"Deirdre…"

"Don't push this. Because that conversation, however it goes? I don't forgive you at the end of it. Not now. Maybe not ever."

"Nothing like that will ever happen again."

"No, it won't. We're both out of people for it to happen to." When she brought her gaze to him, he saw it as broken glass veined in ruby.

"I'm not," he said.

Deirdre watched him for a while. Swallowed. "Yeah," she half-whispered. "I noticed that."

He lowered himself to the floor next to her. "I know I don't deserve forgiveness. I can't ask for that. But…" She looked away, back toward the borrowed warding notes. He sighed, searching for words. "Where do we go from here?"

She paused, stopped pretending to read the thing she wasn't reading. A joyless smirk slanted across her face. "I guess forward's the only way."

For a while, gulls cawed, waves lapped the sides of the boat, distant voices laughed at unheard jokes.

They remained still, poised on some unknown fulcrum.

"Do you think we make it out of this?" he asked.

"I hope so."

He reached out and found one of her hands, touched tentatively, fingertips only. Her palm opened. Their fingers wound together. "I think," he said, pausing, pursing his lips, unpursing them. "I think the Vegas odds look good, then."

"Vegas odds?"

"If anyone's gambling, my bet will always be on you."

She snorted, some light returning to the vast stretches of her eyes. "And you wait until now to reveal a new, cornier Paul Somers?"

He answered the glimmer of her gaze with a smile. "Seems like the right time. We almost had a moment."

She withdrew her hand, turning back to the notes. "Almost."

She carved the sigils and muttered the spells. He brought her another iced tea. Somewhere in the long sag of the sun westward, they met eyes and saw each other. Paul started making dinner, and Deirdre took a break from her work to eat. When the maw of night consumed the sky, Paul made up the loveseat to use as a bed, indicating Deirdre use the larger mattress. Deirdre did not trek back to her home beneath the clouded, lightless sky. Monsters were real, they knew.

But so was magic.

ACKNOWLEDGMENTS

You hold in your hand five years of rage and self-loathing and false starts. Cool, right?

These years would be for naught without the great folks at Permuted Press. I would particularly like to thank Heather King for taking the reins as managing editor, keeping me on time, in line, and active; and John Bogdal for help with publicity, a subject I know literally nothing about.

I would also like to take this time to thank David Vigliano and Nicholas Ciani for representing the work; as well as Nikki Sinning for noticing it.

It would be remiss of me not to thank my exquisite collection of friends, family, and loved ones who helped make this possible. Susan and David Hughes-Sharp, John Hughes and Brigitte Kana Hughes, Meghan Hughes— thank you for your continued support despite numerous false starts. Thank you, too, to Janet Knapman, for your continued kindness, and to Roland Knapman for who he was and what he left behind. Matt Mingle, Jamie Walsh, James Edward Becton III, MJ Henkels, Christina Roman, John Benjamin, and especially Pam Benjamin: thank you for your bolstering, notes, ideas, support, and other variety of moral, literary, and physical aid.

Thank you also to anyone who had to suffer through my occasional rants, raves, and impromptu diatribes, especially those engaged in while less-than-sober.

As no creation births itself, I would like to take some time and page space to thank the creatives who contributed to the world sludging around in my skull. The sheer lingual brilliance of Cassandra Khaw, Caitlin Kiernan, and Brooke Bolander served as an inspiration to every sentence. The storytelling power of Victor LaValle, Edgar Cantero, and William Gibson drove me to examine each paragraph as an articulated bone. Everything I know about writing, I learned by reading. Oh, except for all that stuff that Dr. Juliana Gray taught me. Shout out @Dr. Gray.

As an expansion on the previous paragraph…if you, dear reader, ever have an opportunity to read one of the following, I recommend you take it: *Hammers on Bone*, Khaw; *A Song for Quiet*, Khaw; *Rupert Wong, Cannibal Chef*, Khaw; *Black Helicopters*, Kiernan; *Agents of Dreamland*, Kiernan; *The Only Harmless Great Thing*, Bolander; *The Changeling*, LaValle; *Destroyer*, LaValle; *The Devil in Silver*, LaValle; *The Supernatural Enhancements*, Cantero; *Meddling Kids*, Cantero; *The Peripheral*, Gibson; and *Neuromancer*, Gibson.

Other influences come from more visual media; including video games *The Vanishing of Ethan Carter, Resident Evil 7, Life is Strange,* and *The Secret World*. In terms of movies, *The Green Room* and *Get Out*; with special thanks to Sergio Leone and Cormac McCarthy for godfathering the multi-media genre language that possessed my third act. TV-wise, the first season of *True Detective*, the limited series *Residue*, and *Hap and Leonard*.

This book is littered with stowaway references.

It would feel relentlessly cruel and manipulative of me to write on these subjects without providing real world direction, and so I recommend:

The Southern Poverty Law Center
https://www.splcenter.org/

Planned Parenthood
https://www.plannedparenthood.org/

Black Lives Matter
https://blacklivesmatter.com/

TGI Justice
http://www.tgijp.org/

RAINN
https://www.rainn.org/

Project NIA
http://www.project-nia.org/

National Sex Assault
Hotline (Free): 800.656.4673
NAACP
https://www.naacp.org/

Anti-Slavery International
https://www.antislavery.org/

Free the Girls
https://freethegirls.org/

And lastly, thank you for reading. Thank you so much.